FIVE WAYS TO
KILL A MAN

FIVE WAYS TO KILL A MAN

Alex Gray

sphere

SPHERE

First published in Great Britain in 2010 by Sphere

Copyright © Alex Gray 2010

The moral right of the author has been asserted.

Grateful thanks to Enitharmon Press. Edwin Brock's 'Five Ways to Kill a Man'
is reproduced from *Five Ways to Kill a Man: New and Selected Poems*
(Enitharmon Press 1990).

Grateful thanks to Hodder and Stoughton Limited. *A Calendar of Love
and Other Short Stories* by George Mackay Brown. © George Mackay Brown 1967.
Reproduced by permission of Hodder and Stoughton Limited.

A CIP catalogue record for this book
is available from the British Library.

HB ISBN 978-1-84744-196-6
C ISBN 978-1-84744-197-3

Typeset in Caslon by M Rules
Printed and bound in Great Britain by
Clays Ltd, St Ives plc

Papers used by Sphere are natural, renewable and
recyclable products sourced from well-managed forests and certified
in accordance with the rules of the Forest Stewardship Council.

Mixed Sources
Product group from well-managed
forests and other controlled sources
www.fsc.org Cert no. SGS-COC-004081
© 1996 Forest Stewardship Council
FSC

Sphere
An imprint of
Little, Brown Book Group
100 Victoria Embankment
London EC4Y 0DY

An Hachette UK Company
www.hachette.co.uk

www.littlebrown.co.uk

To Renée and Winnie,
remembering you both with love

'Five Ways to Kill a Man'

There are many cumbersome ways to kill a man:
you can make him carry a plank of wood
to the top of a hill and nail him to it. To do this
properly you require a crowd of people
wearing sandals, a cock that crows, a cloak
to dissect, a sponge, some vinegar and one
man to hammer the nails home.

Or you can take a length of steel
shaped and chased in a traditional way,
and attempt to pierce the metal cage he wears.
But for this you need white horses,
English trees, men with bows and arrows,
at least two flags, a prince and a
castle to hold your banquet in.

Dispensing with nobility, you may, if the wind
allows, blow gas at him. But then you need
a mile of mud sliced through with ditches,
not to mention black boots, bomb craters,
more mud, a plague of rats, a dozen songs
and some round hats made of steel.

In an age of aeroplanes, you may fly
miles above your victim and dispose of him by
pressing one small switch. All you then
require is an ocean to separate you, two
systems of government, a nations' scientists,
several factories, a psychopath and
land that no one needs for several years.

These are, as I began, cumbersome ways
to kill a man. Simpler, direct and much more neat
is to see that he is living somewhere in the middle
of the twentieth century, and leave him there.

Edwin Brock

CHAPTER 1

The First Way

Mary listened to the noise of something rattling in the lane outside. The wind had strengthened as the evening progressed and she really should have made tracks for bed by now, but there was still a chance that he would drop in. How she had enjoyed her day with them yesterday! Christmas with the family meant so much. Sarah had picked her up just before midday, taken her to that fancy restaurant where they'd pulled crackers and enjoyed the same meal as fifty other strangers sitting at adjacent tables.

It wasn't like the old days, Mary told herself. Then she'd have had a turkey in the oven by seven o'clock in the morning, all the trimmings prepared the day before, vegetables peeled ready in pots of cold water with just a wee dash of milk to keep the starch from leaching out. Her Christmas pudding would have been made months ago, like the rich fruit cake that she baked from a recipe that had been her mother's. No shop bought fare for *her* family, Mary thought indignantly. Oh no, it had all been the best of stuff.

She'd thanked them all nicely afterwards, though, aware of the size of the bill that Malcolm was having to pay, but in truth the thin slices of turkey meat swimming in tepid gravy had given her a bout of indigestion afterwards. It was either that or these under-cooked sprouts. Frozen probably, she decided, for who would spend their Christmas morning in a hotel kitchen peeling masses of vegetables when they could open a catering pack?

Danny had slipped away just as the meal was finishing, a wee pat on her shoulder and a half-promise to come round to see her tomorrow. Well, Boxing Day was almost past and not a soul had appeared at Mary's door. Not that she blamed the boy, of course. Her grandchildren were all nice kids, well brought up, but they led such different sorts of lives from the one she had known as a teenager.

'Och, well,' Mary said aloud. 'He'll be with his pals having fun. Who needs to see an old crone like me anyway?' She smiled at that. There was no self-pity in her tone, even though the hours had hung heavily between bouts of watching TV. Danny was her favourite out of them all and he'd come round and see her some time, just as he always did. His visits were all the more special for being unexpected and Mary was bound to be in to greet him since she never went out much these days, what with her bad hip and the arthritis that made walking so difficult.

When Mary heard the back door being knocked, a smile lit up her wizened features: it was him! Danny hadn't let her down after all, she thought. Shuffling through the hall, the old lady placed one hand on the papered walls for support, breathing hard at the effort. She switched on the kitchen light, an expression of delighted anticipation on her face at the shadow beyond the half-glazed door. The tea tray was still prepared for them; Danny's favourite biscuits on a plate beneath the embroidered cloth, two china cups and saucers all ready beside them. Mary smoothed down her skirt and patted her tightly permed white curls, just as if she were about to welcome a young suitor to her parlour.

Eager fingers turned the key and then the cold air rushed in, sweeping Mary's skirt above her knees, making her tremble at the empty darkness. Where was he? The trees outside swayed in the gathering storm. Had she really seen his shadow there on her doorstep? Or was it a trick of the light?

'Danny? Danny! Are you out there? Come in, lad, it's too cold for me to leave the door open.' Mary's smile faded as she heard the branches of the old apple tree creak in the wind. Had she imagined the door being knocked? Had her heightened anticipation tricked her into imagining that familiar sound? Was it the wind?

Disappointed, Mary was about to shut the door once again when she heard it: a pitiful cry just out there in the garden, some small animal in distress. Was it a cat? She'd had cats for years, but after Tiggle had been put down Malcolm had persuaded her not to have another one. *It's too much for you, Mother*, he'd scolded. But Mary still missed the companionable creature and on a night like this a furry body curled on her lap would have been very welcome. So, was it a stray cat, perhaps?

Peering into the darkness, Mary heard it again, a bit closer this time.

'Puss?' she queried. 'Here, pussy,' she said, her words drawn away by a gust of wind. Venturing forwards, Mary took one step down, her fingers gripping the rail that the nice man from social services had put in for her, and called again. 'Puss, puss . . .'

The figure seemed to come from nowhere, the hood concealing his face.

'Danny?' Mary stood still, wondering, doubting as he mounted the steps towards her.

But in that moment of hesitation she felt her fingers being prised from the railing, then the figure was suddenly behind her.

One blow to her spine and she was falling down and down, a thin wail of pain coming from her mouth as the sharp edges of the stone steps grazed her face, cut into her flailing arms.

Mary closed her eyes before the final thud, her skull smashing against the concrete slab below.

'Meow!' the hooded figure cried, then laughed softly at the inert body splayed at the foot of the steps. Bending down, it lifted one of the woman's thin wrists, feeling for a pulse. A moment passed then the hood nodded its satisfaction, letting the dead woman's arm fall back on to the cold, hard ground.

They had all gone away, whooping and screeching as the yellow sparks flew upwards but I remained, standing still and silent, watching the skeleton of the car emerge from the flames, its white paintwork already melting in the heat.

It had been our best Hallowe'en night ever: the others had been eager at my suggestion, so casually slipped into the conversation that afterwards nobody could remember just whose idea it had been in the first place. The Beamer had been left by the kerbside and it was pretty obvious no one was at home that night, probably out partying, we told one another, sniggering that they were too goody-goody to drink and drive. Didn't bother us, did it? We laughed at that, as the stolen car careered over the hilly track and down into the shelter of the woods, bright and alive with the rush of booze and adrenaline in our young veins.

Setting fire to it afterwards had been my idea too, though everyone had a hand in starting the flames licking at the cloth upholstery. We'd sneered at these owners; it was just a basic model, not like the better cars belonging to our own fathers. (Mine had smooth biscuit-coloured leather to match its classy exterior and it was not the sort of car that anyone would leave carelessly outside our home.)

When the engine caught fire and the petrol tank exploded we all dived for cover, screaming and laughing as though it was bonfire night come early and we were little kids again. But after that the rest of them became bored with the fire and wanted to go back up the road, bent on other mischief.

They thought I wanted to watch the car until the flames died down, but I had quite a different reason for staying behind. The tree right beside the wreck of the BMW had caught fire when the petrol tank blew up, a river of flame leaping up and scorching its branches. Now it was quivering as the fire burned away the bark, each limb blackened and shrivelling as the tree began to die. The trunk that had been smooth and grey in the firelight was now covered in patches of glowing red embers as if the wood was bleeding from within. I stood there, watching and waiting, one ear tuned for the possibility of a fire engine that might roar up from the coast, tensing myself to slip through the fence that bordered the wood.

I had never seen a living thing die before and it was with detached curiosity that I stood there seeing the tree shudder, imagining the noise in its crackling branches to be a groan of anguish. A small wind sprang up and I had to shield my eyes from the cinders coming directly towards me, so it was a little while before I noticed the adjacent pine trees begin to sway. They seemed to be trying to put a distance between the dying tree and themselves, bending to one side away from the conflagration. I grinned at that: as if trees had any sense! It was just a trick of the imagination and the direction of the wind. Only stupid girls in my class at school who raved on about Tolkien would think the trees were living creatures. I'd hated Lord of the Rings, *though more recently I'd made myself watch the whole damned trilogy so nobody could catch me out.*

But then, alone with the sound of crackling wood and that moaning voice, it was easy to think I was seeing a living thing in its death throes.

And I liked what I saw.

CHAPTER 2

'All for Rosie's wedding!' Maggie sang the words out loud as she let herself be twirled about in the 'Gay Gordons', the band playing the familiar tune of 'Mairi's Wedding'. She felt skittish with the dancing and the champagne; its bubbles had tickled her nose as she raised a glass to the happy couple.

'What a night!' she laughed as Lorimer drew her into his embrace. She could feel the rough texture of his kilt against her thighs, the silk dress a mere slither of fabric covering her body, and it made her tremble suddenly, desire for her husband flaring up inside her. His kiss on her earlobe was a promise of things to come, but not yet, not while there were still hours of dancing and celebration for Solly and Rosie.

The band had started up a 'Pride of Erin' waltz, but Lorimer was leading her by the hand back to the table, where they'd been joined by friends and colleagues from work. Alistair Wilson dropped them a wink as he escorted his wife, Betty, towards the dance floor, leaving them with Niall Cameron, Lorimer's other Detective Sergeant from the Division. Doctor Solomon Brightman had a colourful gathering for his wedding to Rosie, Maggie thought, noticing a couple dance past, their dark looks so like the psychologist that they had to be near-relations. The whole Brightman clan seemed to have arrived in Glasgow to see their boy wed to the forensic pathologist.

'What'll you have, Niall?' Lorimer lifted a bottle of white wine, dripping from its ice bucket.

'Oh, I'm on the orange juice tonight, sir.' Niall Cameron smiled, his Lewis accent reminding them that the young man was teetotal by choice. Too many folk end up ruining themselves with the drink, he'd once told Lorimer. And he'd been referring to what he'd seen on the islands just as much as some people here in this city whose wasted lives in drunkenness had often led to violence.

'Cheers! And here's to our new Detective Superintendent!' Niall nodded across the table, his eyes soft with the glow from the candlelight between them.

'Och, it'll just be acting Super for a while,' Lorimer laughed, then turned towards his wife, seeing her pleasure at the mention of his temporary role. Detective Superintendent Mark Mitchison had been seconded to the Met in London to the Anti-Terrorist Squad, and so Lorimer would take over his duties from January first. Maggie returned the smile and lifted her empty glass, shaking her head at the offer of more wine. They might well be a bit giddy with drink by the time the night was over but the dancing fairly gave her a thirst for the bottles of still water that were arrayed on the white tablecloth.

The tall creamy candles were half-burned down now but the flowers were still as bright as ever, the delicate white petals of stephanotis in deliberate contrast to the scarlet roses. Rosie had chosen red and white as her wedding colours; blood-red roses for her name, she'd laughed, not her profession.

She was coming towards them now across the dance floor, a diminutive blonde, her normally pale skin specially tanned a light golden colour to offset the ivory fairytale dress that twinkled as she walked, its hundreds of tiny seed pearls catching the light. Maggie had gasped when her friend had entered the marriage room at the Registry Office earlier that day. Rosie Fergusson's appearance was so at odds with the woman who spent half her life in scrubs or white scene-of-crime boiler suits: her hair had been caught up by a slim gem-studded tiara and those small hands with their pearly manicure were surely not the same ones that had delved into so many human cadavers. Even Lorimer had raised one dark eyebrow, his eyes crinkling in a smile of surprise and admiration.

'Enjoying yourselves?' Rosie stood beside them, both hands holding the back of one of the gilded chairs as if for support. Her face was flushed and radiant, her small breasts rising and falling under the constraints of her bodice.

'Best night of the year!' Lorimer exclaimed.

Maggie reached out and lifted the bride's left hand. 'Lovely,' she said, fingering the wedding band that sat snugly next to the diamond Solly had given her just one year before, on Christmas Day.

'Yes,' Rosie replied, 'who'd have thought . . .' She gave an insouciant shrug, leaving the words unsaid. Yes, thought Maggie Lorimer, they were an unlikely pair: the shy Jewish psychologist with his exotic dark beard and huge brown eyes and Rosie, the consultant pathologist whose work demanded a strong stomach and steady hand. But she may have meant more than that, Maggie told herself. The accident that had almost taken her from them . . . the very idea of Solly and Rosie's lives being torn apart by that event was more than anyone could bear. So, yes, uttering such words would be wrong on this the happiest of days for them both.

'Aye,' Lorimer replied, 'he's one lucky man.'

'And don't I know it.' Solly Brightman was suddenly there beside them, his arm encircling Rosie's tiny waist. 'Time to cut the cake, I believe, *Mrs Brightman*.' His grin was suddenly so boyish that Maggie found herself clapping her hands and laughing aloud for sheer pleasure.

'Got your scalpel, Rosie?' someone called out as the bridal couple approached the three tiered wedding cake. A ripple of laughter broke out as Rosie lifted the knife, pretending to examine it from every angle, then Solly's hand was over hers and they directed the blade through the white icing to another resounding cheer.

Wiping away a stray tear, Maggie felt her husband's hand on her arm and, looking up, she grinned at his expression. Was he, too, remembering their own wedding day?

'C'mon, let's get a wee bit of fresh air,' Lorimer said, leading Maggie away from the crowded room and into a spacious hallway where huge floor-to-ceiling windows were draped in sage green damasked curtains held back on gilded hooks, the darkened balconies beyond almost invisible in the massed brightness of the crystal chandeliers.

Maggie shivered as her husband opened the French windows, the cool night air chilling her skin.

'Here,' he said, taking off his jacket and draping it around her shoulders. 'I'm fine,' he added as she looked pointedly at his shirt sleeves stirring in the wind.

Then he was holding her close and Maggie felt herself relax against the warmth of his body.

'Look at that,' Lorimer said. 'All these people. Wonder what they're doing tonight . . .'

Below them the city was stirring; sounds of Boxing Night revelry coming from the streets, Christmas snowflake lights swaying as the wind increased. And beyond the shapes of buildings the cityscape twinkled into the distance, reminding them of a great mass of humanity all living out their disparate lives. Some, like themselves, would be celebrating, but for others this would be a bleak and lonesome time of year. Maggie glanced at her husband's face, half hidden in the shadows, that fine profile she loved so much, his blue eyes seeing something that she could only imagine. His thoughts might not be very far from the troubles that the festive season might produce; and didn't she know only too well the very different take policemen had on Christmastime? And this coming New Year would bring some changes for him. Was he looking forward to this temporary promotion? Or was he wishing for the days when he had been out on the hunt like his younger officers?

'Let's go back inside,' she suggested, sensing the quietness of his mood turning to something too sombre for this wedding night.

'In a minute,' Lorimer replied. 'Look up. Can you see anything?'

Maggie shook her head. The sky was a black mass with faint patches of cloud scudding across.

'Wait. Look,' he urged her, pointing at a patch of cloud beginning to shine at the edges. Then for a brief moment she could see the full moon emerge from the scraps and rags of vapour, only to disappear again behind another storm cloud.

'Good omen?' Maggie offered.

Lorimer grinned down at her. 'Don't think that pair need any omens. They're well blessed already.'

And as they left the darkness of the balcony behind, Maggie was nodding her head in agreement. Rosie and Solly would be fine. Here, inside the brightness of this hotel, it felt as if nothing bad could ever touch them again.

CHAPTER 3

'Mary MacKintyre. Eighty-seven years old,' the policeman said, tapping the information into his PDA. 'Suffered from . . .?'

'Arthritis,' Malcolm replied, swallowing hard as he tried to answer the officer's questions. Sarah had left the room, holding her hand to her mouth as though to stifle another bout of weeping, leaving Malcolm to deal with the aftermath of his mother's terrible accident. 'She should have had a hip replacement, but the doctor reckoned her heart wouldn't stand another operation,' he added.

'Doctor Bennie?'

'Yes.' Malcolm swallowed again. His mother's GP had been very good, his matter-of-fact manner as much of a comfort as that kindly pat on the arm as he'd left. Cause of death had been obvious, though. The doctor hadn't needed to stay too long to see how she had died. Malcolm fidgeted, desperate for this policeman to finish his questions and let him get on with cleaning up the mess. He itched to hose down that bloody patch on Mum's patio, the pink and grey slabs that he'd laid himself. To make it easier maintenance, Mum, he'd told her, never once imagining . . .

'Was she in the habit of going out of doors at night?' the policeman was asking Malcolm.

'No, she wouldn't have gone out in the dark. I can't imagine why she was out at all,' Malcolm gritted his teeth, sudden anger at his mother flaming inside him. 'Why would she?' he asked, as much to himself as to the young man sitting in his mother's armchair.

'Needed a breath of air, perhaps?' the officer suggested.

Malcolm shook his head. 'Well, we'll never know now, will we?' he added bitterly.

I decided not to go to her funeral. Seeing the death notice was enough. Mary MacKintyre her name was. I'd seen the tartan nameplate on the front door, knew it was the same old lady I'd decided to kill.

In some ways it was a disappointment, being so dark, but then perhaps I'd needed the cover of night to commit this first one. Plus it was all over far too quickly. Still, I did have to begin with something easy, didn't I? Seeing her fall through the air had been fun though and there was that extra tingle of anticipation when I could have mucked up, not done her in at all but merely injured her.

Feeling that little piece of skin had been the best bit. No pulse. No life. I'd snuffed it out in seconds. And afterwards I could congratulate myself on a job well done. It had been my apprenticeship, after all.

Now that I knew I could kill, the next one would give me much more satisfaction than this helpless old lady.

CHAPTER 4

The Second Way

Y ou could depend on him to be there.

The flattened earth made a shallow pit for his curled form, the unfolded newspapers coloured yellow as if something putrid had leached out of his body through layers of stained and tattered rags. Regular as clockwork, the tramp could be found near the banks of the Clyde, his makeshift den consisting of one strut of the concrete bridge that soared skywards into an uncertain blue and three sides of not-so-fresh air. Only after the cold light of dawn glittered against the water did he make his shambling way from this untidy nest, picking up anything that might keep body and soul together for another twenty-four hours.

The metal mesh bin at the top of the narrow path was his first stop of the morning. Stooping low so that his arm could reach right down into the base, he would forage among the bits of rubbish left from the night before, ever hopeful of a discarded bit of food that the urban foxes had failed to recover. Sometimes he had to stand aside as early morning cyclists or joggers dodged past and he would utter an oath, shaking one gnarled fist at their retreating backs, swaying like a demented scarecrow.

This morning was no different, except for one thing. As the tramp lifted his eyes from the bin he saw the figure speed towards him, one arm flung out as if to push him out of the way, and just in time he leapt back, a cry issuing from his cracked lips. In seconds his fury had dissolved into anticipation. Forgetting his sudden panic, he came back to the mesh basket, eager to see whatever it was the cyclist had dropped. He was salivating as he fished it out, recognising the Subway wrapper.

'Miracles!' he murmured to himself, fingers trembling in excitement, hardly daring to believe that so much of the baguette was still intact. Turning around his mouth curled into a sneer. 'Nae idea, nae idea at all. A couple o' bites and ye think ye're finished. Eh? Eh?'

But there was nobody there to upbraid; there was no swish of cycle tyres to be heard along the path, only the comforting rumble of traffic overhead. Left alone to enjoy his unexpected breakfast in peace, the man shuffled back to his place by the bridge, easing his aching bones on to the patch of hollow ground. Greedily he bit into the sandwich, feeling the shreds of salad escape from his mouth, tasting the tuna fish as he slavered and swallowed, the hard crusts biting into his bleeding gums.

The unexpected fire of chilli made the tramp shrug and for one second he took this as the reason why his benefactor had chucked the food away. His shoulders were still raised in an indifferent shrug when his whole body tensed. Before he knew what was happening, the fire inside his belly roared up.

He tried to scream. But all that issued from his lips was a faint bloodied line of froth. Eyes bulged in their sockets as he glared at the empty path and the bank of withered grass. Then the first convulsion whipped him in two and the fire engulfed him in such pain as only the damned would ever know.

It was not over quickly. Tears streamed down his filthy cheeks, his gaunt face a parody of some ancient gargoyle, jaws strained in an effort to spew up the monster within. Torn by the convulsions, his head cracked against the concrete behind him and then the spasms ceased as oblivion claimed him. Slipping sideways, the weight of his body took him towards the steep side of the river where it lay like some discarded heap of rags.

Up above him, the cyclist leaned against the handlebars, watching and waiting. At last, satisfied that it was all over, one foot pushed against the pedal, making the wheels turn and swish along the empty street.

CHAPTER 5

The Third Way

'His name's Connor Duffy,' Jenny said, looking up from her screen. 'Mum's got twin girls of eighteen months,' she added, raising her eyes to heaven.

'Poor bitch!' Jackie replied. 'Is Charlie away to take their photo, then?'

'Aye,' Jenny replied shortly. 'Boss wants the copy in by close of today, so I best get cracking.'

The young journalist pursed her lips as she glanced at the scraps of notes lying next to her computer. Connor Duffy, aged five, had wandered away from his home in Upper Port Glasgow and been discovered drowned in the waters of the local quarry before his mother had even known he was missing. It was tempting to put that little snippet in, but Jenny found she simply hadn't the heart. The poor woman was beside herself with anguish; why rub it in? With twin toddlers to run after it was hardly surprising that she'd taken her eyes off the wee boy for a while. No, she'd milk the grieving mother bit instead; readers loved that.

Jenny shifted her shoulders as though something inside was itching, but in truth it was nothing more than an overburdened conscience.

Connor Duffy, aged five, she began to type, immediately deleting the words as she sought a better beginning. Jenny shook her head at the waste of such a young life, refusing to let her thoughts dwell on how awful it must be for the parents.

Angela Duffy stared at the ceiling, her head throbbing. Was she ill? Was that why she was in this room with the blinds drawn against the daylight outside? She tried to swallow, feeling her throat thick with mucus. There was a metallic taste in her mouth that was unfamiliar. Had she been given drugs of some sort?

Gradually the reason for her presence in this hospital bed came back to her and with it the awful realisation that she would never see Connor again.

The mewing sound that came from her throat rose to a crescendo like an animal being tortured.

Angela was oblivious to the door being pushed open, the nurses scuttling to her bedside or the needle being inserted into her arm. All she could feel was the searing pain of guilt and rage and loss.

NEWS: In Brief

A young boy who died on Wednesday after falling into water at Whitemoss Quarry in Inverclyde has been named as Connor Duffy. Emergency services were called out after a passing cyclist found the body. A report has been sent to the Procurator Fiscal.

So now he had a name. I shrugged. It wasn't as if I was keeping a diary of my exploits, but it was reassuring to see it written there in inky newsprint: Connor Duffy. I even had a modest walk-on part in the drama: the passing cyclist who calls out the police to tell them what has happened. Except I didn't, of course. I would never tell them how I had swung the child's hand up and down as we'd sung songs strolling over the rough stones. Swinging his hands had given me the idea. He'd giggled then chuckled as I'd picked him up, grasping one hand and one foot, swinging his arms and legs round and round. It was a good game, that, I could tell. Someone else had swung him like that before, up and down as if he were a small flying bat, his shirt tails billowing in the breeze.

The look of surprise on his face when I let him go was almost comical. It was as if he didn't know how to change that stupid grin into something more appropriate. Perhaps when he hit the water his mouth had contorted into an expression of fear. I don't know, because he was turned away from me. But I did see his wee face bobbing up and down, gasping fish-like for air, his eyes goggled with terror. And that did reward me with some satisfaction. I could stand there watching his final moments, seeing him slip under the surface until the bubbles finally ceased and I knew for certain that he was dead.

The first two had been easy, though I'd had to plan meticulously, of course. Leaving things to chance was never my forte. The old woman hadn't understood what was happening and the itinerant was so greedy he was gagging for breath almost as soon as he'd taken that first bite.

Deciding to kill a child had been something of a challenge. It would test my powers of resolve, diminish any residual sentimentality and provide me with an opportunity to be at the scene when the police arrived; the innocent bystander doing the right thing. But I'd wanted to see the kid's face when they pulled him from the water, make sure that he was as dead as I'd supposed. Those huge blue eyes gazing into mine, the trustful little hand letting me lead him over the hill and down to the quarry; he'd never look into anyone's eyes again. If he even reached the pathologist's table, all that would remain would be twin orbs of viscous jelly.

I'd passed my own test then, I decided. I was capable of killing anyone I wanted. And that little thought led me to ask the question: of all the people in my world, whom exactly did I want to kill?

CHAPTER 6

Mike Reynolds gave a deep sigh. It had been a long day. The flight up from Heathrow had been delayed and the interminable wait for another aircraft had made the jet lag kick in worse than usual. He was accustomed to the transatlantic crossing and normally managed to be home by early evening, but occasionally something like this happened and he ended up in the back of a taxi, limp with fatigue. It was the deep darkness of midwinter, only the headlights from the Skoda showing the ribbon of road as it snaked through the countryside above Port Glasgow. Another few minutes and they'd be around the last bend and seeing the lights of Kilmacolm. God, how he longed to be home and into his own bed!

Suddenly the car swerved then came to a bone-juddering stop as Mike felt his shoulder hit the hard glass of the window.

He had an impression of a dark figure speeding into the night, two wheels disappearing behind them.

'Jeez! What a wally! Idiot could have got himself killed. No bloody lights! What does he think he's playing at?' The taxi driver added more imprecations under his breath as he drove the Skoda back on to the road.

Mike nodded his agreement, too shocked to speak. What

if . . .? No, that didn't bear thinking of. The cyclist hadn't come to any grief or the chap wouldn't have been so quick off the mark. He found his hand grasping the handle above his head, steadying himself as if there could be another hazard round the next corner.

But Mike Reynolds was driven safely home to Lochwinnoch Road at the other end of the village, the incident quickly forgotten.

It would be weeks before it came to his mind again, the tragic events of that same night overshadowing their near miss with the crazy cyclist who been riding along without any lights.

'I'm glad your name's not on this one,' Maggie told Lorimer as she glanced up from the early evening news. 'What a horrible thing to happen!'

Detective Superintendent Lorimer nodded his head. He'd already heard about the case from a colleague in K Division. There was some speculation that the house fire out in Kilmacolm had been deliberately started. And the two charred bodies within might well have been the victims of someone with a warped sense of retribution. That was the current internal gossip, anyhow. Lorimer watched as the camera panned around the scene, sitting up suddenly as he recognised a familiar white-suited figure. So, Rosie Fergusson was involved, was she? Rosie *Brightman*, he corrected himself, though in truth he knew that the pathologist was retaining her maiden name for work. It must be her first major case since arriving back from honeymoon in New Zealand, Lorimer thought, stroking his chin. And the first since she'd been off on sick leave last year. Well, what a baptism of fire, he told himself, then groaned slightly as he realised the irony of his own unspoken thought.

'You okay?' Maggie asked.

'Look, it's Rosie . . . oh, you missed her,' Lorimer said as the news reporter came into the full frame of the TV screen.

'Rosie? Oh!' Maggie seemed deflated as she realised that she had failed to see their friend.

They listened as the TV presenter turned to a woman at his side. Lorimer made a face: what had he said? Was she a neighbour? A friend? The clipped English accent made him wonder. Kilmacolm was so like a small English village that it attracted lots of affluent incomers from South of the Border, but the victims had certainly been Scottish. *Sir Ian*, the woman was saying, in the hushed deferential tones reserved for the newly dead. But it was rather more than that, Lorimer thought: she was speaking about him now as if he had been someone rather special. And certainly Sir Ian Jackson had made a considerable name for himself during his lifetime. The financier was numbered among Scotland's top ten in the Rich List after many successful years as a merchant banker. The woman's voice tailed off as the newscaster addressed the viewers once more, one hand waving behind him at the scene of the tragedy.

Lorimer gave a little shudder as the camera panned across the ruins of the once stately house, the outlines of twin turrets still visible above the skeleton of roof beams, smoke still issuing from somewhere inside. What a hellish way to die! Then Lorimer found himself echoing Maggie's opinion.

'You're right, I don't fancy this one. It'll probably be Colin Ray who'll be SIO.'

'Is he still in charge at Greenock?' Maggie enquired. 'I thought his wife was in a hospice now?'

Lorimer nodded. 'Someone told me she'd been admitted to St Vincent's. Must be only a matter of time, poor woman.' He thought of Colin Ray, a man more than ten years his senior who had a reputation as one of the old school of hard-nosed cops. Juggling time with his terminally ill wife and being in charge of serious crimes: what kind of a strain must that put on a man? Lorimer found himself hoping that the arsonist would be caught quickly.

But in the meantime he might have a word with Rosie Fergusson, just to see how the pathologist was coping. Lorimer grinned. That was what his excuse would be, anyway, though he recognised his policeman's natural inquisitiveness asserting itself in this high profile case.

Rosie hummed to herself as she flicked through the glossy brochures. She'd driven BMWs for years now but maybe it was time for a change and after the accident perhaps a different car was a good idea. Audis had always appealed to her and this model with its soft top looked just the ticket. She could imagine herself driving Solly out into the countryside for a picnic in one of these. The pathologist smiled at her whimsy as she heard the rain battering down against the mortuary windows; it would be a good few weeks before they could think about picnics never mind open-topped cars. Her husband had never learned to drive and was quite oblivious to the allure of classic marques, but Dr Rosie Fergusson delighted in cars, despite the horrendous accident that had almost proved fatal. She was a huge fan of TV's *Top Gear* but Solly simply couldn't understand the pleasure it gave her to watch all these beautiful, sleek motor cars being road tested. Her own BMW had been a total write-off; now it was time to stop taking black cabs all over the city and find something she really wanted to drive.

With a sigh that was not wholly unsatisfied, Rosie put the

brochures to one side of her desk and picked up her mug of coffee, draining what was left of it.

'Time to get on with the job,' she muttered to herself, pushing back her chair and giving one final wistful glance at the picture of a low-slung Jaguar that she knew was way above her budget. There were cases waiting for her examination, two corpses blackened by fire. A short while ago these had been living, breathing human beings, a middle-aged man and his wife; any evidence she could find that helped the Crown Office to find how and why they had died would also render some kind of service to the deceased.

The woman had been alive during the fire, most probably conscious and aware of the full horror of her fate. Her arms had been raised in a familiar pugilistic stance, now fixed rigidly in death, and it seemed to Rosie that she had been trying to ward off the poisonous smoke and flames. Some people thought of death as an instantaneous event, like a light being extinguished; but death wasn't really like that. It was a process: more like the sun slipping behind the horizon than the flick of a switch. But this hadn't been a pleasant death at all. Rosie looked at the remains of the woman's face, now a charred skull whose gaping mouth told of one final desperate scream. It would have given the scene of crime photographer an easier shot for the forensic odontologist, Rosie told herself, trying shake off an unfamiliar feeling of queasiness that had grabbed her stomach.

'Too long away from the job,' she muttered into her mask. But it wasn't that: Rosie had never enjoyed the post-mortem examinations of fire victims. Often there was so little left by a giant conflagration that one person's remains could fit into a shoebox. Other times the yellow, leathery skin gave such an unnatural appearance to a cadaver that it was like examining some alien species.

Pauline Jackson's corpse was better than some she had seen but it was still just a skeleton when all was said and done. What identifying marks she might have had in life such as hair, eyes and skin were reduced to the formation of her bones; especially the teeth, still comparatively white in that soot-stained jaw. Rosie was taking pains to scrape out all the deposits from the tips of the finger bones, just in case anything other than carbon was there. The spine had been shattered in two places and much care had been required to set the entire skeleton carefully into place on the examination table. There was still masses of forensic detail to come in but the scene of crime manager's preliminary report had given her enough to go on for now.

The Jacksons had been in bed when the fire had broken out in the kitchen below, the location of what was being considered as the primary seat of the fire. Last night's TV pundit had suggested that a burning chip pan had been the likeliest cause, but that was only partial speculation until an exact source of the fire had been officially confirmed. Parts of the first floor of the house had crashed through into the kitchen and other downstairs areas, taking with it the couple's bed and other furnishings, now swallowed up in the flames. The television voice claimed that only the metal headboard and base from the king-size bed had remained intact, the twin corpses eventually found, curled towards one another, beneath masses of other fallen debris.

Rosie blinked, concentrating on each single fingertip. A tragic accident, the newscaster had called it. And yet a small voice inside the pathologist's head persisted in asking: why on earth would anyone start to make chips then wander off to bed? And though the public might think of this as a terrible accident, she knew perfectly well that Strathclyde police were treating it as a possible case of wilful fire-raising.

'Sir Ian was one of Scotland's most generous benefactors,' Chief Constable David Isherwood declared, the crystal glass in his hand tipped slightly to one side, its amber contents threatening to spill on to the thick carpet in his spacious office. 'Don't forget that Jackson Tannock Technology Systems is one of Scotland's great successes,' he added. The man he was addressing simply nodded. Everyone knew these names nowadays, he thought, listening to the story of two men whose ideas had burgeoned into a multi-million pound firm. Originally set up by Hugh Tannock's expertise and backed by Ian Jackson's money, the business had provided welcome employment for hundreds of technical and support staff. This, coupled with Ian Jackson's penchant for supporting local causes, had earned the financier his knighthood.

The man opposite the Chief Constable stood, legs apart, considering his senior officer's words. Once upon a time Jackson had been referred to as an entrepreneur if one was being kind, and a wheeler-dealer if envy coloured one's vision of the man. DCI Colin Ray listened as the most senior officer in the Force continued to list the late financier's public merits.

Another ten minutes and he was out of here. Ray had even primed one of his DIs to call his mobile just to get him away. Every second spent here was a second more ticking away on what little time Grace had left. And he was not going to let even David Isherwood, the Chief Constable of Strathclyde Police, waste these precious minutes.

At last the Chief Constable was laying down his glass and giving Ray a pat on the shoulder. Then the DCI was out of Pitt Street and into a police BMW, speeding down towards the

Kingston Bridge, his driver ready to put on blues and twos if he was asked. But the motorway was relatively clear and it would only take fifteen minutes to drive up to Johnstone and the hospice.

Colin Ray's head was full of the Chief Constable's admonitions. Look among the lowlife of Port Glasgow and Greenock, he'd been told. See if there have been any other fire incidents. But above all, Ray thought to himself, don't look among Sir Ian's crowd for a possible enemy because, according to the Chief Constable, he simply didn't have any. He was being warned off, Ray thought. In any other circumstances he'd be the first to dig into the victim's background for a possible motive. But it suited him to play this one to the Chief Constable's tune.

A vision of Grace's wasted face smiling came to him then: some things were far more important.

'Sir Ian and Lady Jackson's children are here to talk to you,' Emma whispered to Rosie as she emerged from the shower.

'Ask them to wait in the lounge, will you? And see if they want tea. Thanks, Em.' Rosie nodded. She sighed heavily. This was one of the most horrible bits of her job. Performing post-mortems was a doddle compared to having to deal with the bereaved. Still, it had to be done and she'd have to find something to tell these kids.

Two faces looked up at the consultant pathologist as she entered the room reserved for relatives of the deceased. Rosie was surprised; the man and woman who sat there regarding her solemnly were not as young as she had expected them to be. The chap might be in his late twenties, the sister a little younger, though it was hard to tell through the huge dark glasses the woman was wearing.

'Doctor Fergusson.' Rosie extended her hand, bending down only a little towards the girl. The man was on his feet at once, good manners overriding any semblance of grief.

'Daniel Jackson,' he replied, taking Rosie's hand in a firm grip, then letting it go. 'My sister, Serena,' he added, glancing to the woman who sat very still on the couch, her head averted from them as if she was trying to hide her emotions.

Rosie breathed in hard. Daniel Jackson should have been introduced to her under some other circumstances, just so she could feast her eyes on this specimen of perfect manhood. A little under six feet, she thought, and standing so straight that he might have been an off-duty guardsman. Her first impression was of brown: soft reddish-brown hair, eyes the colour of caramels; and that expensive looking alpaca coat and these narrow brogues (hand-made?) shining like polished conkers. Soft, brown, understated, but *class*, Rosie thought, searching for an adequate word to describe Daniel Jackson. Handsome didn't do justice to that oval face, its lightly tanned complexion suggesting he'd come straight off the ski slopes. Tom Cruise without the twinkle in his eyes, Rosie decided. Taller and less rugged than the American actor; this one was smooth and calm, even under the present circumstances.

'My parents . . . *our* parents . . .' Daniel immediately corrected himself as his sister looked up sharply at him. 'May we see them?'

Rosie hesitated. It was such a normal reaction for the bereaved to want to see the last mortal remains of their loved ones, but surely they both knew what was in store for them? And did the girl really want to go through with this? Again her head was bowed, the long blonde hair covering a pale profile. So, Rosie thought, not out with your brother skiing in Klosters?

'The bodies aren't a very happy sight, Mr Jackson,' Rosie told him. 'The fire damage was considerable and there are only skeletal remains.'

A thin wail from the girl confirmed to Rosie that this was one occasion when relatives should leave well alone.

'I'd strongly advise you not to view your parents,' Rosie said firmly. 'Remember them as they were in life. Seeing what I have seen today is not how I think you would choose to bring them to mind.'

Daniel Jackson seemed to consider Rosie's words, then, hunkering down to his sister's side he asked, 'What do you think? Shall we leave them be?'

Serena Jackson was shaking her head and Rosie felt a moment of relief. It would be okay. The girl was saying she didn't want to go through with this after all.

But Rosie was wrong.

'I want to see them,' the girl told her in a voice that was surprisingly strong for one who only moments ago had shown signs of losing control. 'I have to . . .'

Rosie nodded and shrugged. It was a relative's prerogative after all and Solly had told her often enough how the bereaved could find closure by actually seeing the dead. And the family liaison officer from the police would have given them the standard information pack that did suggest viewing a body as a way of beginning to cope with grief.

'The viewing room is through here,' Rosie said and at once Serena Jackson was on her feet. Rosie took a step back, letting the pair out of the room. The girl was not much shorter than her brother, five-foot-ten, maybe, in those flat-heeled leather boots. A model girl's height, Rosie thought, watching the pair walk by her side along the corridor of the mortuary. And she had the same sort of graceful gait as a model . . . that was the word she'd been looking for. Daniel Jackson had a natural sort of *grace* about him.

The viewing room was small with subdued shades of musky pink and green, deliberately chosen for their calming qualities. Beyond the glass window the Jacksons would be able to see these twin skeletons; all that remained of their mother and father, once Rosie had pulled aside the drapes.

'Are you sure about this?' she asked again, trying to sound brisk and authoritative. 'It could be anyone, you know. They are so badly burned that there are no obvious identifying marks.'

Serena Jackson turned towards the consultant pathologist and drew off the dark glasses. A pair of amber-coloured eyes stared steadily at her and Rosie felt an uncomfortable sense of being weighed up under the woman's intense scrutiny. The gaze was so unblinking that for a moment Rosie wondered if this girl had some sort of learning difficulty. More likely the poor soul's spaced out on medication, she decided. Then Serena Jackson gave a small nod.

'It's good of you, but we'll see them, if you don't mind.' She turned her head slightly as if to deflect any opposition from her brother, but Daniel Jackson stood impassively, staring straight ahead.

It was over in a couple of minutes, that silent trio staring at the blackened skeletons laid out on the steel tables. But in that short time, Rosie couldn't help but wonder how much grief was being bottled up inside the young man and woman who stood gazing at the couple who had given life to them both.

'They were conscious when they died?' One perfect bow of an eyebrow rose as the woman spoke, her voice quiet and calm now that they were back in the lounge reserved for relatives of the bereaved.

'It's possible,' admitted Rosie. 'The smoke inhalation may have rendered them unconscious, though.'

'You can't tell?' Serena Jackson shook her head as if the consultant pathologist was somehow at fault.

Rosie stiffened. She mustn't let this young woman with the cut-glass accent get to her. 'We don't usually deal in definitive answers,' she replied, choosing her words with care. 'Whenever I'm asked to appear as an expert witness for the Crown I can only say to what *extent* I deem something possible.'

Serena Jackson's strange golden-yellow eyes were watching her intently as if she needed more from Rosie.

'They probably lost consciousness,' she said at last, hoping that was what the woman wanted to hear.

'They wouldn't have suffered at all, then?' Daniel Jackson asked, half-turning towards Rosie. The expression of hope in his voice matched the plea in his soft, brown eyes.

Rosie shook her head, a gesture that could have meant anything at all. But if Daniel Jackson wanted to think his parents hadn't suffered during their horrendous deaths, then let him, she thought, opening the door and walking them out into the corridor.

Her goodbyes to the brother and sister were murmured and then Rosie fled back into the sanctuary of her office. 'Thank God that's over,' she whispered under her breath. She heard the main door creak shut then the footsteps outside her window told her they were gone at last. Suddenly the pathologist shivered. That poor man! She tried to conjure up his handsome face again, but all that came to mind were his sister's amber eyes searching Rosie's expression for something she couldn't have. Closure? That word psychologists used so much. Maybe. Grief manifested itself in so many ways. Rosie shook her head as she turned her attention to the computer screen: forget it, she told herself. You'd go mad if you dwelt on every person who came in to see their dead loved ones. But even as she scolded herself, something told Rosie that these two people deserved her pity more than most.

CHAPTER 7

The pain shot through the top of his skull, making the DCI groan aloud. Opening his eyes, Colin Ray felt the daylight batter against his brain and he rolled over before the nausea took control.

Minutes later Ray was leaning over, clutching the cistern for support, the contents of his stomach swirling away in the toilet pan. Muttering an oath under his fetid breath, the DCI staggered to the sink, cupping cold water over his face. He let the droplets course down his body, unheeding of the damp patch forming at his waistline.

'God love us,' he whispered to the reflection in the bathroom mirror, seeing the haggard expression on his face. Then his thoughts turned to his wife: Grace would hate seeing him like this. For a moment he hesitated. Would he just call in sick, tell DI Rhoda Martin to take his calls? They all knew he wanted to spend time up at St Vincent's. Ray bit his lip, torn between his duty as a policeman and a husband. Christ! Why was he even considering it? There was no way K Division would see him today. He'd take a long shower, slather on plenty of aftershave and find some fresh clothes to wear. Then it was back to the hospice.

The bathroom still smelled of fresh vomit despite his attempts to mask it. He closed the door behind him, hoping the window left slightly ajar would be enough to take away the stink before he returned. Passing the lounge on his way back to the bedroom, Colin Ray hesitated. The place was a shambles: beer bottles were standing on the side table and the foil containers from last night's curry were poking out of the white polythene bag next to his armchair. But it wasn't just that: the whole room looked as if it hadn't been touched for weeks. Well, it bloody well hadn't been. Without Grace to do the needful, things had been completely neglected, but that was hardly his fault, was it? a little voice whined in his head. He'd either been up at the bloody hospital (and now the hospice) or trying to do his job as a senior police officer. Who could blame him if the place had become a tip? But despite this attempt at justification, Colin Ray felt a sense of guilt. He was letting Grace down. Bugger it! He'd take more time off and tidy the place up properly, or get in a cleaner. Just till . . .

The man stepped into the lounge then, his hand on the back of Grace's favourite armchair. There was no *until*, was there? She wasn't going to be coming back. Ever. This was how things were going to be from now on, just him on his own trying to cope with a job that threatened to overwhelm him and the day-to-day caring for a home that had always been Grace's part of the ship.

Colin Ray felt his lip tremble as the tears filled his eyes. And he let them fall, clasping the back of that chair, sobbing for the woman who would never sit there again.

St Vincent's Hospice was an unassuming single-storey building overlooking farmland, the hills of West Renfrewshire a hazy outline beyond. Ray parked the car in his usual spot, facing the drive so he could make a hasty exit. He was always in a hurry, he thought, cursing himself for the time he'd failed to spend up here.

Drawing in a deep breath, Ray smelled something fresh and earthy: the air was soft with the threat of rain to come above the empty flowerbeds waiting for a spring that the patients would never see. Spring was Grace's favourite season; she loved lambing time and always waxed lyrical about the hedges greening and how pretty all these cherry blossoms were, lining their street. He could almost hear her voice, her *old* voice, not that hoarse croak he hated so much. People had told him that was something that lingered afterwards – the sound of their voices in your brain. Ray hesitated outside the main entrance. He could slip away now, drive back down the road. He had plenty on his plate with this new case and nobody would blame him for doing his job, would they?

Taking a deep breath, he pushed open the door and pasted a smile on his face for Linda, the nice girl at reception. She smiled back, eyes full of a sort of understanding that he hated. That unspoken pity always made him cringe, but once past Linda's desk he was fine. There were always patients in the dayroom or the corridor leading to Grace's own room, reminding him that he wasn't alone in his grief. Seeing those others calmly waiting their turn for death to take them made things seem much more normal somehow, so that by the time he slipped into his wife's room the bitter lines around Colin Ray's mouth had vanished.

Grace was asleep, head to one side. He skirted carefully around the oxygen cylinder by her bedside, squeezing himself into his customary place by the window. Sitting back in the comfortable chair, he relaxed for the first time that day. Waiting for her to wake up was one of the best things Ray could do right now; his would be the face she saw when her tired eyes opened at last. It gave him time to rehearse all the things he wanted to tell her, leaving out everything to do with work. It was the little everyday stuff she liked to hear: what the neighbours were doing, how the garden was looking, what he'd eaten for his dinner last night . . . Ray pictured the untidy tip at home and began to fashion a different place altogether in his imagination, one that was neat and clean with home-cooked meals that he could describe with pretend relish. His lies maybe fooled her, he didn't know, but she would smile at him anyway, that look of fondness in her eyes telling him that it didn't really matter. He was there, holding her hand and that was all she needed.

Tales of malice and burned bodies could be forgotten for a while at least.

CHAPTER 8

M aggie's face lit up as she looked out of the kitchen window. The first of her miniature daffodils! Now she could almost believe that winter was over and begin to anticipate the warming days to come. A couple of weeks and the garden would be a riot of colour: grape hyacinths spreading their blue amongst the wilderness that was supposed to be her rose bed, primulas and daffies springing up all over the place. As yet the trees were leafless but other signs that the long winter months were drawing to a close could be seen in the activity of the small birds that came into their garden. Maggie watched as a greenfinch chased a smaller, brightly coloured bird from their thistle seed-feeder. It had been a particularly good year for goldfinches, she knew, remembering the results of the RSPB's annual birdwatch. Despite their cat, Chancer, pacing his territory, the birds seemed to thrive here. Maybe it was the wildness of their overgrown place; there was never enough time to cut stuff back, though she was always resolving to tackle all the jobs out there that needed doing.

Turning back into the kitchen, Maggie Lorimer looked at the bags of groceries lying on the work surface, ready to be unpacked. She might well be eating alone tonight, she thought ruefully, if her husband's telephone call meant anything.

'A pot of soup,' she told herself briskly, already thinking what ingredients she would use. 'That'll be fine no matter what time he comes home.' Then, smiling to herself, Maggie began to pack away the groceries, leaving the vegetables she needed to one side.

'Hi, sorry I'm late,' Lorimer called out into the darkened hallway. Shuffling off his coat, he looked upstairs for a light from their bedroom but that too was in darkness.

'Mags?'

'In here,' a sleepy voice replied.

He found her curled up in the recliner, a pile of jotters discarded on the floor.

'Hey,' Lorimer hunkered down by Maggie's side, 'what's all this? Falling asleep on the job?' he teased.

'Mm . . . Sixth year creative writing folios. Must've dropped off.'

'Riveting stuff then,' he remarked, giving the jotters a cursory glance.

'Less of the sarcasm, pal.' Maggie's mouth curved into a smile in the darkness. 'Some of them are not bad at all.'

'Just a wee tad soporific,' he suggested, the laugh in his voice making her try to pull herself into a sitting position.

'That word always reminds me of Peter Rabbit,' Maggie mumbled, rubbing her eyes. 'You know, when the Flopsy Bunnies all fell asleep . . . soporific effect of too many lettuces . . .'

'Come on, bed for you.' Lorimer leaned over, one arm around Maggie's shoulders as she gave an enormous yawn.

As they shuffled upstairs, Maggie lifted her head from his shoulder, stopping suddenly. 'Oh, how did today go?' She paused, waiting for a reply that was not immediately forthcoming. 'Grim, was it?'

'Yeah,' Lorimer replied shortly, nudging her up towards the top of the stairs. 'Come on, you're bushed.'

Maggie Lorimer nodded to herself. Okay, if he didn't want to discuss it, then that was fine with her. She'd learned a long time ago to let her husband begin any conversation about his work, whether it was about a case of serious crime or the day-to-day annoyances of administration. But this was a bit different. Acting Detective Superintendent William Lorimer had been appointed to another division to review a case that was going nowhere, the type of job that no self-respecting senior officer relished one little bit. There was always a degree of scepticism when a review took place and Lorimer knew well that it was the last thing he'd want on his own turf.

Listening to the sounds coming from the bathroom, Lorimer curled under the duvet. It had been grim down in K Division. *Failte Gu Grianaig* the sign had proclaimed as he'd entered the town. Welcome to Greenock. But his welcome, if it could be called that, had been pretty frosty. But that was to be expected. Nobody enjoyed being told that their own DCI was incompetent, especially under the circumstances. Colin Ray had messed up, that was obvious, but his wife had been dying of cancer! What more did they want from the guy? Lorimer's sympathies had been for his fellow officer who had made zero progress in the case of wilful fire-raising in Kilmacolm. But how he had come to be put in as a review Senior Investigating Officer was still something of a mystery. Okay, the request had come from the usual admin channels, but he still felt uneasy about it. Someone in K Division had reported Ray as being less than satisfactory on this job. That was the rumour anyhow. And if he was a betting man, William Lorimer would have put his money on the female DI who had set out to give him such a hard time today.

It was as if Rhoda Martin was on a guilt trip, he thought, remembering the way she'd glowered furiously at him. That was more than resentment on behalf of her old boss who had taken sudden early retirement. And she'd agreed too readily that the case needed to be reviewed, receiving some raised eyebrows from those among her fellow officers who'd been present in the Greenock division. So why did he have the feeling that there was more to her attitude than met the eye?

As Maggie slipped in beside him, Lorimer turned on his side towards her. Folding her into his arms and letting her rub her cold feet against his own warm legs made any thought about Rhoda Martin vanish. That could wait till tomorrow. Right now there was only room for one woman in his bed.

CHAPTER 9

It was nice being wheeled along the pale laminate floors, the porter skilfully manoeuvring each doorway with not so much as a single bump. There was a nurse with her too, but none of them spoke as the walls slid past. She'd been glad to sink against the cushioned back of the chair, her feet supported by the metal rests. It was surprisingly comfortable; but then, weren't there experts designing things like that, always bent on improving the . . . what was that word? The girl at the library. Her husband worked in that field. What was the word . . .? She frowned. It had been like this ever since that silly young doctor had asked her questions about who the prime minister was. Really! As if she didn't know a simple thing like that. But some other things had eluded her; words that she knew she should remember, just hovering out of reach. 'On the tip of my tongue,' she wanted to say, but that particular organ had taken sides against her, too, refusing to let the words come out as they normally did.

She was guilty of talking too much, she knew that. Sometimes Maggie cut off their conversation with a reminder of work to do in the evenings (she always had such a pile of marking, poor lamb) and she'd put the telephone down with the sense that she'd been rattling on good style, hardly letting her daughter put in a word at all. Now, ironically, that renegade voice of hers was refusing to cooperate. Maybe she was just tired. It had happened before: after her operation. She'd hardly been able to string two words together, feeling the edges of speech slip away into a void.

Maybe that was why they weren't engaging her in conversation right now. They knew she was too weary, wanted to spare her voice, perhaps. But, as Mrs Finlay listened to the chatter above the desk at the nurses' station she felt . . . *diminished*.

Everything was different down here. She knew there was a nurse just behind her – aware of a flap of striped, grey skirt and beige stocking-ed legs – a tall girl anyway, but from this disadvantaged point the girl seemed to have taken on Amazonian proportions. Mrs Finlay felt as though she had fallen into a strange Swiftian world. It was true, that cliché about people in wheelchairs being ignored. She might have been part of the mechanism itself for all the notice that anyone took.

Mrs Finlay had seen it first when the tall, good-looking man at the end of the corridor had paused. A consultant, she'd decided, noticing his well-cut suit and colourful silk tie; he'd hesitated before an open door several yards in front of her then raised his hand in a salute. Was it someone who had recognised her? She'd seen so many already. Or was he simply being polite? She'd attempted to lift her own hand in reply, the smile automatic, eyes bright. But then as the chair rolled nearer, she realised that he was looking over her, at someone else entirely, and in that moment she knew just how invisible she had become. Nobody up there within the able bodied of the population towering over her really took any notice of a woman in a wheelchair, except to acknowledge that there was one. *A woman-in-a-wheelchair*.

Strangely she didn't resent it. The experience was still too new, untested and, besides, it was only a temporary change until she was better. It wouldn't be long – surely – until they fixed whatever had happened to this stupid side of her; this frozen space that had somehow closed down in that spasm of pain. It had been like a jolt of electric current surging through her, then snapping off one of her terminals. Now all they needed was the right sort of engineer to fix it. Just like the nice young boy who had come to sort her TV when everything had changed to digital.

Mrs Finlay smiled to herself, unable to see the crooked lift of her lips. Yes. Someone would fix it.

Now they were off again, rolling along another long corridor, and she had no idea what was happening, where she was being taken. At the turn of a corner she saw a patient being wheeled along, travelling towards them. It was a woman. And as they passed, their eyes met for an instant and Mrs Finlay saw an expression of pity in the other woman's face followed by the merest nod of fellow feeling.

In that moment she felt a sudden shock of understanding. She tried to twist away, to raise her hand to make them stop the relentless progress of the chair. But only a low moan issued from her mouth, unheard against the roll of wheels.

And where was Maggie? Why wasn't she . . . here. To make them. Stop. Explain what was . . . going *wrong*?

'Detective Superintendent Lorimer.'

'It's Mum.' Maggie sounded out of breath as if she had been running. 'She's in hospital. They say it's a stroke . . .'

Lorimer heard the catch in her voice just as he caught the glance of the woman across the desk, one eyebrow arched in the faintest hint of curiosity.

'D'you want me there?' He hadn't intended to sound so terse, but with DI Martin listening intently to his side of the conversation, Lorimer wanted nothing more than to be alone with his wife, consoling her wherever she was, unhampered by this review case. The pause from the other end told him more than any words could have: Maggie realised he was busy and was about to tell him not to bother.

'I can be with you in less than an hour,' he continued, giving his watch a quick glance. The layout of this unfamiliar office didn't seem to include a wall clock.

'It's okay. I can call you later once I know what they're going to do.'

'How bad is she?' Lorimer asked, turning his head aside from Rhoda Martin's direct stare.

'We won't know until they have all the test results but she's paralysed down one side and can't talk too well. She knows me, though. Don't worry about that!'

He smiled, hearing the relief in her voice laced with a hint of humour. It was bad but not too bad, she seemed to be saying.

'Keep in touch. Let me know what's happening and I'll see if I can catch up with you there. All right?'

'Thanks. Love you,' Maggie said.

'Yeah. Hang in there. Okay?' Lorimer told her.

As he put down the handset, DI Martin leaned across the desk, eyes hungrily eating the Detective Super's expression.

'Bad news?' Her eagerness was almost palpable and in that instant Lorimer knew he was going to have an uphill struggle even to be civil to this woman.

'Nothing to do with the case. Now if you can let me know where all the logs relating to the inquiry have been stored for the period in question we can begin to look at what actually happened from the team's perspective,' he replied smoothly, ignoring the look of disappointment on her face.

As they discussed the initial stages of the inquiry, Lorimer's mind was racing. What on earth had happened to his mother-in-law? And how was Maggie coping on her own at the hospital? But, lodged between these two thoughts was another more insidious notion: how had this DI reacted to her old boss's predicament? Had she fed off Colin Ray's increasing absences, using them to bolster up her own involvement and hoping for subsequent kudos? There had been something malicious in her expression, as if she suddenly welcomed the prospect of this new SIO having domestic problems of his own. And that would suit them just fine, wouldn't it? Lorimer swallowed down the guilt he felt at leaving Maggie to sort this one out. He'd make it up to her. Later.

Once Rhoda Martin was gone, Lorimer reached for his mobile phone then, just as suddenly, drew back his hand. The irony of his situation wasn't lost on him. Colin Ray's dying wife had taken priority in his life over the high-profile wilful fire-raising case, resulting in Lorimer's present appointment. For something similar to repeat itself was simply not on. Frowning, he wondered for a moment what his mother-in-law would be experiencing over in the Southern General hospital. She was a feisty old bird, though, and he held her in an affection that he knew was mutual. If anyone could recover from the damage of a stroke, it would be Maggie's mum.

But suddenly DI Martin's sharp features replaced thoughts of the older woman in his mind. Office politics had been at work, to the previous SIO's detriment, Lorimer guessed, though he'd be lucky to prove that. And, besides, that was not within his present remit. What was his main concern was how the case of wilful fire-raising resulting in two horrific deaths had been handled here in K Division. That, and how he was to proceed with the review.

It would mean loads of sifting through all the paperwork for a start and setting up a small team from the existing officers here to read over and reassess the key documents – like witness statements – to ensure that every piece of evidence divulged to the police initially had been acted upon fully, without question. The old cliché of 'leaving no stone unturned' had never been more appropriate. It would be hard work and he hoped that the team he eventually chose would be less acerbic than DI Martin, but for some reason he felt he needed to keep her close, if only as a means of watching his own back.

He missed the familiar faces of his own team back in Glasgow. Here he was very much on his own and the sooner he elicited help from Ray's own CID department, the better. It was not only dredging through the paperwork that was required, though that tedious stuff had to be done; he had to decide what had gone wrong at each and every stage of the investigation and to do that effectively, he wanted to have the fullest cooperation from the folk down here in Greenock.

A knock on the door made him turn from his thoughts and as the door opened he was heartened to see a solid-looking woman in her early thirties smiling at him, a mug of something hot in one hand.

He knew that face, didn't he? It was . . .?

'Kate Doherty.' She smiled at him. 'I was one of your trainees. Don't know if you remember me.'

'Kate!' Lorimer exclaimed, his brain whirling as he struggled to place her. 'You went to Kilmarnock as a DC, didn't you?'

'Well done,' she said, coming closer and proferring the mug. 'Tea. No sugar. Okay for you?'

'Aye, fine,' Lorimer replied. 'In fact,' he added, thinking swiftly, 'even better if you were to join me.'

'Ah, fraternising with the new SIO. Bit risky, don't you think?' Kate's voice was as full of good humour as Lorimer remembered.

'I didn't know you were one of Colin's team,' he began, sipping the strong brew gratefully.

'Well, you wouldn't recognise the name. It's Clark, not Doherty now.' She grinned, wiggling her wedding ring finger. 'And I wasn't at your meeting yesterday. Midwife's appointment.' She grimaced then, pointing to the burgeoning swell beneath her shirt. 'This wee rascal's fairly making his presence felt. They think it might be a breech birth.'

'Ah.' Lorimer nodded. Yes, he'd seen all their names on the ACPOS – the management policy file – but apart from DI Martin, and now Kate, he hadn't yet put names to all of their faces.

'Maybe I should just wait and meet you officially this after-noon?' Kate suggested, the faintest hint of warning in her voice.

Lorimer looked up at her. Would she be singled out as the new chap's favourite, a friend from the past, and thus given a hard time by anyone who resented Lorimer's presence here in K Division? There was always that possibility. And he couldn't afford to alien-ate the one person who might be able to fill him in on the background to this case without a sense of prejudice.

'Take your point, Kate. But I'd love to have a chance to catch up with you properly some other time.' Lorimer gave her what he hoped was his best smile, blue eyes widening. 'Anyway, thanks for the tea. Just what I needed right now.'

'No bother, boss,' she said, striding out of the room with a grin. 'See you later.'

Lorimer drank his tea, heaving a sigh of relief. For a moment he had experienced a feeling quite unfamiliar to him: loneliness. But seeing Kate Doherty's – no, Kate Clark's – friendly face had turned his mood around. Perhaps the afternoon's meeting that he had been dreading would not be so bad after all.

CHAPTER 10

The Southern General hospital lay sandwiched between the approach road to the Clyde tunnel and a Govan housing scheme, its sombre facade dominated by the clock tower that seemed to remind one of how fragile life really was and that one day everyone's time would be up. Its reputation as one of the city's best teaching hospitals was undeniable, however, and it had the country's finest spinal injuries unit, one that Lorimer had visited during a previous case. These were thoughts uppermost in his mind as he raced up the back stairs towards the ward where Mrs Finlay had been taken. She would be in expert hands, he told himself. They'd be doing everything that they could.

Lorimer gave a quick glance at the wall to see the signs for the various wards then, stopping to give his hands a rub from the fluid dispenser outside the swing doors, he looked along the corridor leading to where he hoped to find his mother-in-law.

She was in a room of her own and sitting up in bed, propped by a bank of snowy white pillows, her eyes bright and shining as she recognised him. Lorimer tried hard to conceal the dismay he felt at the down-turned side of her mouth as she attempted a smile. And the traces of a bruise could be seen from under that dressing on her forehead.

'Mum's not up to talking tonight.' Maggie turned towards him from her place beside her mother's bed, a clear warning in her eyes. 'So we're expecting lots of stories about your day.'

Drawing a chair up, Lorimer affected a grin. 'Don't know how much I can tell you. Confidential stuff, you know.' He tapped the side of his nose. 'But I did run into an old friend.'

It was amazing how much of a one-sided conversation could be drawn out of his meeting with Kate Doherty (now Clark) and his attempt to brighten up the atmosphere by giving a little description of each member of the Greenock investigation team. He balked when it came to a thumbnail sketch of Rhoda Martin; instead he simply mentioned that a female DI had greeted him on arrival. All through his watered-down account of his first day at K Division, Lorimer was aware of Maggie relaxing by his side. She must have had a hell of a day, being called away from school and seeing her mum like this.

The bell to signal the end of visiting time came and with it a sense of relief that he didn't have to continue to fill up the empty space between the two women any more. He planted a swift kiss on Mrs Finlay's papery cheek. 'Take care now, you. Remember guid folk are precious,' he told her with a wink.

Maggie's fingers found his and held them tight as they walked together down the corridor.

'How is she, really?' he asked at last.

Maggie looked up at him, her eyes brimming over with unshed tears. 'Oh, I don't know. They've still to do more tests. But it seems to have been quite a bad one. Her whole side is paralysed and she can't talk at the moment. She was talking before . . .' Maggie broke off and Lorimer put his arm around her shoulders, drawing her against him. They were halfway down the stairs and had other visitors at their back, so he had to

54

make do with holding her close by his side as they headed for the exit.

'So she was better when you first came in?'

Maggie bit her lip to stop the trembling before she answered him. 'Well, she wasn't exactly lucid but she was able to make me understand her if I listened really carefully. Now, though – oh it's horrible to see her like this! But she's so tired. Maybe it'll come back. There'll be a speech therapist in to see her tomorrow, they said. So that's surely a good sign. And they're going to do more ECGs and stuff to check on her heart.'

'Any idea what set it off?'

Maggie shook her head. 'No. She thought she had a fall. They did tell me that she'd managed to crawl to the phone and call an ambulance, bless her. But she's still a bit hazy on the details.'

'Here, you're shivering,' Lorimer said as they left the building. 'Have you had anything to eat?'

'No. Wasn't hungry,' she mumbled into his jacket. 'But I'm starving now.'

'What d'you say to us murdering a fish supper, eh?'

'Ah!' Maggie breathed, making a white mist against the dark shadows in front of the hospital steps. 'With pickles?'

As they finally drew up outside the house, Lorimer heard Maggie give a sigh. 'Oh, I needed that,' she told him. 'Nothing like fish 'n' chips, is there?'

'Standard comfort food and mandatory fare for surveillance teams,' he told her, trying to inject some levity into his tone.

It had been a difficult evening, not just the visit to the Southern General but taking Maggie over to her mum's house to fetch all the things she'd require for a longer stay in the hospital. Being inside Mrs Finlay's home had depressed them both; the curtains open to reveal the dark night outside, the kitchen work-top full of neatly stacked dishes that were still to be tidied away as if the dishwasher had just been emptied. Looking at it with his detective's eye, Lorimer wondered if the old lady had been about to do just that when the stroke had made her fall on to the kitchen floor. The cutlery basket was still beside the sink, its contents gleaming in the artificial light.

Now they were inside their own home, its lamps reflecting the polished wood of the study desk as he tossed down the car keys and heaved off his jacket.

'Cuppa?' Maggie asked and he nodded, watching her as she bent down to stroke Chancer, their ginger cat giving his customary meow of welcome. It was late, but he'd try to help her unwind as best he could before bedtime.

Maybe, he thought with a sudden smile, bed could provide the best sort of balm to soothe both their jangled nerves.

'Okay then, Alice, darling?' The auxiliary smiled warmly at Mrs Finlay, giving a final tug at the side rail that tucked the patient in and prevented her from falling out of bed.

Alice Finlay wanted to draw the auxiliary a look, but couldn't. *Alice*, indeed! The cheek of the woman, and her just a slip of a thing! They'd all been at it. Alice this and Alice that. Are you fine, Alice, pet? No attempt to give her a choice in the matter, either. The name above her bed scrawled in untidy blue letter-ing was ALICE FINLAY. Not Mrs Finlay as she'd have liked. And with the loss of her status had come the sort of ingratiating smiles that one gave to a small child or someone not quite in their right mind. She'd had a stroke, she knew that, and it had impaired some of her faculties but there was no need to make out that she was some sort of moron. Alice darling! If she had her speech back she'd be the first to give them all a piece of her mind!

Feeling her heart throb with the sudden rage, Mrs Finlay experienced a tremor of fear. She shouldn't be getting herself all worked up like this. It would only put her blood pressure up again. Maybe even precipitate another stroke. She smiled a triumphant, if lopsided, smile. Precipitate! See, she knew big words like that. She'd even remembered what the girl at the library's husband did. He was involved in ergonomics, making things like special wheelchairs that fitted patients' needs exactly.

Suddenly she was so tired and glad to have the quietness of this room to herself. Tomorrow they'd be moving her to a main ward, one of them had told her, with other stroke patients like herself. With a small sigh, Alice Finlay turned her head to the pillow and closed her eyes. Tomorrow would bring so many unfamiliar things but at least it would also bring her Maggie.

It was an odd feeling to cycle past the gates of the house. No lights were shining along the driveway any longer; the fire had destroyed all of the electric cables that had fed the twin rows of lamps along the curving path to the mass of rubble. Nodding to myself, I took in the shapes that remained: parts of turrets etched from the backdrop of clouds scudding across the moon; the humps of rhododendron bushes encircling the lawns.

A sudden movement drew my eye and there, in the moonlight, was the small rounded shape of a rabbit, nibbling at the turf, oblivious to the destruction of the house beyond. For a moment I watched it, wondering at the warm heart beating inside its tawny fur.

And, as I watched, I felt my fingers twitch with the desire to extinguish that spark of life.

CHAPTER 11

The journey down by the river was going to be one of the best things about this secondment, thought Lorimer as he allowed his glance to drift towards the estuary. He'd left the city behind in darkness but now the water gleamed like pale grey silk in this early dawn light. From the moment the road opened out to show the Clyde and the hills of the west, Lorimer felt his spirits lift. Now, with the village of Langbank to his left, he was parallel with the widening river and the mudflats that were home to so many wading birds. A quick glance gave him the sight of a flock of redshank and a couple of easily recognised oyster catchers. It would be good to come down here sometime with his binoculars and see what else the place had to offer. All too soon, the growing traffic made Lorimer wrench his eyes back to the dual carriageway and concentrate on the journey.

There was Finlaystone Estate to his left, tall fronds of pine trees outlined against a milk-white sky. He'd been there a few times with Maggie, but not for ages; spotting fallow deer within the depths of the woods had been a golden moment. Now he slowed down as the roundabout approached. He would have to take a left hand turn here if he was going to head for the scene of the crime at Kilmacolm. But that would have to wait. His primary duty lay in K Division, further along this road, past Port Glasgow and into the heart of Greenock itself.

The town was a ferry terminal not just for the MacBrayne's boats that skimmed from the Inverclyde shore to Dunoon and beyond but it was also the terminal for the massive cruise ships that docked on a regular basis, their white hulks dwarfing every other craft in these waters. But it was the ships with their billowing sails flocking like white birds floating on the water's surface that he loved best. It had been years since the last Tall Ships race had made the old town their destination, some time back in the nineties, if his memory was correct. And it wouldn't be long till the next one, he thought to himself, seeing a hoarding proclaim 2011 as the date for the Tall Ships to grace Greenock's harbour once again.

They'd taken Maggie's mum and dad down for a glorious day, he recalled. The whole weekend had been blessed with the sort of warm summer sunshine not often enjoyed by west coasters. That, and the array of ships from all parts of the world, had given their day a holiday atmosphere. The Finlays had been persuaded to have a fish supper and stay on for the firework display later on; thank goodness we listened to you, his mother-in-law had told him later after the stunning display that had been set to classical music. They'd walked back to the car park in silence, the sounds of the crowds buzzing in their ears, too full of the sights of these cascades of gold, silver and ruby that had burst against the night sky.

Now Pop Finlay was gone and Alice was lying in a hospital bed. But, on this chilly February morning, the memories of that day still lingered like warm reminders of summer.

Detective Superintendent Lorimer arrived well before any of the other members of his select review team. It was up to him to set the standards and being first to arrive was one way of showing them that he meant business. There was, in any case, so much still to do. He'd have to establish if there had been issues in the identification of any suspects, something about which DI Martin had been worryingly hazy. Also he needed to find out the where-abouts of key witnesses to the fire; they could disappear all too quickly once an investigation appeared to have run its course. He'd have to talk to Colin Ray at some point as well, he knew. The former SIO's views about this case were of tantamount importance and he hoped he'd be able to see Ray on his own without Martin hovering over their shoulders. One aspect that he did relish was being in communication with Dr Rosie Fergusson, who had carried out the post-mortem examination on the victims. She had also seen the next-of-kin and that was something he wanted to talk to her about before he made personal contact with the brother and sister. He'd need to speak to the family liaison officer as well, but if he could do some groundwork of his own it might make things a bit easier for all concerned.

Lifting the phone, Lorimer decided that his first priority was DCI Colin Ray. He'd be in a rotten enough situation right now with Grace's death and the loss of his job without the feeling that he was being sidelined.

'Colin? Bill Lorimer here. How are you?'

There was a lengthy pause as Lorimer waited for a response. Had his question been too trite? Over-hearty? *How was he?* Bloody awful, probably, but he'd not want to admit that, would he? They were west coast males, used to hiding their feelings beneath a veneer of macho gruffness; and being police officers meant that they were used to bottling up their emotions.

'Lorimer. Aye. How's it going down there?' Colin Ray spoke at last, choosing to sidestep the actual question.

'Just started yesterday. Hoped we could have a bit of a chat about the case before I began delving into the paperwork.'

'Aye. Well, there'll be plenty of that, I suppose.'

There was another pause that became too long for comfort. He'd have to say something, now, wouldn't he?

'Maggie and I were really sorry about Grace,' Lorimer said, lowering his voice to a tone of quiet sincerity.

'Thanks,' Ray replied. Another pause followed but this time Lorimer could hear the former police officer blowing his nose and he guessed at the sort of trial this must be for Ray. All the more reason why he needed to meet up and talk about other things, Lorimer told himself.

'Any chance of seeing you today? I could come over to your place if you'd rather not come down here,' he suggested.

There was a snort of derisive laughter from the other end of the line. 'Naw, the place is a tip. And I'd rather not have you over, if you don't mind. How about somewhere down the coast? Say Cardwell Bay Garden Centre. D'you know where that is?'

'Sure. I can be there in less than twenty minutes. What time suits you?'

Again the pause as Colin Ray considered the proposal. Lorimer wondered what state the man was in, whether he was even up and dressed properly at this time in the morning.

'Make it another hour, eh? Would nine-thirty be okay? Meet you in the tea room.'

'Fine. See you there.'

'Aye, an' you're paying.'

Lorimer could just discern the faintest trace of humour in the retired DCI's tone as he put the phone down.

*

Leaving a message for the staff, Lorimer grabbed his coat and headed down to the car park. Swinging the dark blue Lexus out into the dual carriageway, he felt a slight sense of playing hookey as he left the divisional headquarters behind. But, he reasoned, the other officers would surely appreciate him giving Colin Ray his place? At least, those whose loyalty to their old boss was not in question.

Cardwell Bay lay on the outskirts of the seaside town of Gourock, on the road towards Inverkip and the Ayrshire coast. It was the main route to Wemyss Bay, the small village where ferries arrived from the Island of Bute a mere half hour's sail away. Rothesay, across the stretch of water from the mainland, had been a popular holiday destination during much of the twentieth century, particularly after the rail link had been established between Glasgow and the coastal towns. He and Maggie had spent some relaxing weekends there during their courting days. Now, as he drove past the old open-air swimming pool in Gourock, Lorimer felt a certain nostalgia for those times.

Being in the city had given him a different perspective on things. Like crime and criminals. Perhaps it was time to see life from a more rural point of view. Maybe the fire-raiser's attack on the house in Kilmacolm should be seen as a stupid prank that simply went wrong? Not as a vicious, deliberate killing. But, thought Lorimer as he looked out over the blue waters of the Clyde, their white caps tossed by a sudden squally wind, somewhere along the line a finger had been pointed at the anonymous low-lives in the district. Thugs from Port Glasgow was one suggestion he'd read on the initial report. The fire service was always being called out to random fires down there. But with no corroboration, that was all speculation. And speculation wasn't hard evidence.

As he turned into the huge open gateway at the garden centre, Lorimer watched other drivers parking as near to the entrance as they could. They'd be returning in an hour or so with trolleys full of stuff for their gardens. It was almost mid-February and the planters by the automatic doors were full of winter pansies and snowdrops. Too late for planting bulbs and too early for bedding plants, these keen gardeners might well be paying attention to stuff like feeding their winter grass or mending some storm-wrecked fencing. Or did they simply want a quick getaway after their morning coffee? The rain was never far away here on the west coast. It might be bright and blue now but give it another wee while and dark clouds could obliterate that sunshine.

Colin Ray was sitting with his back to Lorimer as he entered the capacious tea room. He remembered Ray as a big man but seeing him sat there hunched over the table, Lorimer felt that he'd been diminished by his wife's death.

'Colin?' The man stood up and for a moment each looked into the eyes of the other, hands clasped in a warm grasp that betokened nothing more than one man's feeling for the other. That was all it took, just that one handshake and a look that said how sorry Lorimer was, how grateful it hadn't been his Maggie and how he wanted to make things easier for the man who'd lost the love of his life.

'Aye,' Colin Ray said at last, the word drawn out like a sigh. 'Well, here you are, then,' he added, nodding his head as though he were acknowledging his fate.

'Tea or coffee? And something to eat?'

'Coffee. Just something with milk. Oh, and see if they've got any Danish pastries, will you?'

Lorimer grinned as he turned away. He'd order a plateful of

them, reasoning that Ray probably hadn't had breakfast; besides, he'd a weakness for Danish pastries, himself, a fact that was well known back in his own canteen.

'I didn't get down to see her often enough,' Ray began, looking down at the mug of coffee, one finger hovering over the selection of cakes. 'Too busy.'

Lorimer nodded but said nothing. It was a perennial problem with senior officers: the job taking precedence over home and family life, sometimes to the detriment of a marriage. They were always too busy. Crime didn't take a holiday, did it?

'Tried to see her when I could and then . . .' Ray broke off with a shrug that expressed more than mere words could achieve. 'Well, the job suddenly wasn't important any more, was it? Grace was running out of time, you see. I just couldn't be arsed, if you want to know the truth.'

'Don't think I'll quote that in my report.' Lorimer smiled at him gently.

'Och, I'm past bothering what you write, frankly. Retired, pensioned off. Who gives a monkey's what I say now?'

'Actually I do,' Lorimer told him.

'How's that?' Ray's head came up suddenly, frowning as he looked his former fellow officer in the eyes. 'Stickler for the details, is that it? Didn't have you down as a pen pusher, Lorimer. Thought that was more Mitchison's style.'

'Stickler for the facts, maybe,' he replied. 'Look, Colin, I don't like doing this review any more than your former officers like having me hanging round their necks, but there are things I really want to know about that fire. Call me a nosy beggar, if you like, but there were rumours at the time that not everything was being done by the book.'

Colin Ray held Lorimer's blue gaze as long as he was able, his own eyes fierce with a sudden anger. Then he looked away again, taking a sip of his coffee as if to delay his answer.

'What are you saying, Lorimer?'

'I'm asking you, Colin. About the case. It wasn't just that you spent time with Grace. And God knows no one in their right minds would blame you for that. No. It's the way the finger was pointed at local villains. But not at anyone in particular. Get what I mean?'

'You think that smells funny?'

'Aye, I do. Strikes me that not a lot was done to investigate the victims' own background.'

Colin Ray shook his head. 'Och, well, I suppose it'll all come out somehow and better you hear it from me than one of the others.'

Lorimer stopped his cup halfway to his mouth and put it back on to the table.

'Was hauled in to Pitt Street for a wee chat with our Chief Constable. David Isherwood. Did you know that he lives up in Kilmacolm? No? Well, anyway, he wanted to warn me off any sniffing around Jackson's business affairs.'

'And ordinarily you might have ignored that and just got on with the job?'

'Aye, I'm as ornery a bastard as you are, Lorimer.' Ray smiled properly for the first time that morning.

'But Grace . . .'

'. . . was a damn sight more important than bothering my ginger with what I was supposed *not* to do, see?'

'And now?'

Colin Ray gave another wintry smile. 'If I were in charge of a review I'd make it my business to see everything that had been missed. No stone unturned. No ignoring any wee slimy creatures that could be lurking among Jackson's affairs.'

The sky had closed in, grey and louring, by the time he left Cardwell Bay and headed back up the coast road, the first few drops of rain spotting the windscreen. A typical change in the weather, Lorimer thought to himself, turning the heater up a notch. The keen gardeners round these parts might well be spreading sharp sand on to their perfect lawns, but surely it would be a good while before the appearance of spring flowers heralded some warmth in the ground. As if in tune with his thoughts, a blast of wind from across the river shook the big car and the rain began in earnest.

He'd spent a productive hour with the retired DCI. And now Lorimer knew where he wanted to begin on the pile of paperwork that waited back at Greenock HQ.

Thinking of the man who had shaken his hand as they'd parted, Lorimer wondered what sort of life the former police officer could enjoy now. Ray hadn't mentioned any family but Lorimer thought he'd remembered Maggie saying something about a married daughter.

I'll be put out to grass one day, too, if I survive to pensionable age, Lorimer suddenly thought. And then what? a little voice asked. Something related to policing? There were no children to follow them on, so there would be no wee ones to tug his trouser legs in years to come and call him Grandpa. Lorimer shook his head as if to rid himself of such notions. That prospect was years away and, besides, he had plenty to occupy his thoughts right now without worrying about the distant future.

But what about Maggie's mum? How was she coping and, if she was able to come home from hospital, would she be fit to stay in her own little house again? That was something they'd need to discuss. But not until the subject arose, he told himself firmly. Meantime he'd concentrate on the case in hand. And, now that he'd spoken to Colin Ray, it offered the prospect of being a more interesting investigation than he'd at first assumed.

CHAPTER 12

Dr Solomon Brightman smiled and hummed a little tune to himself. Outside the windowless lecture theatre the rain might be sweeping down in sheets; here it was warm and dry and the babble of student voices told him that there were lots of young minds eagerly awaiting his thoughts on behavioural psychology. The spring term, so-called, lasted right up until Easter when the students would suddenly be seized with panic at the thought of final exams on the horizon; but now, with Valentine's day imminent, there was a more genial atmosphere in his classes.

'Love,' he began and, at the sound of his voice, all heads turned towards the bearded man with eyes twinkling brightly behind his horn-rimmed spectacles, the chatter suddenly silenced.

'Love is in the air,' he continued, beaming at them and evoking a ripple of laughter. 'Saint Valentine, the patron saint of love; romantic stories fuelling our desire for a vicarious experience of love; songs from the time of troubadours to present-day rap enjoining us to celebrate the coupling of men and women . . .' Solly continued to beam at them, wiggling the fingers of his left hand to show off his new wedding ring. The clapping began at the back of the lecture theatre and soon there were whistles and whoops as the entire student audience applauded their favourite lecturer.

'You see, even I am not immune from the shafts of Cupid's arrows.' Solly grinned at them as the noise died away.

'Love, however, is sometimes seen as a force of darkness rather than light. It may destroy as well as uplift a human being. In all its vagaries, there is possibly no other emotion that has the power to change the way we behave.'

Solly let his smile disappear. The lecture was sometimes regarded as harsh by those who had never heard it before; a comedown from the heights of erotic passion to the more sinister aspects of jealousy and revenge. What people in the past had done in the name of love was sometimes hard to fathom, but Dr Brightman owed it to his students to delineate such examples and use them to back up his premises about emotional behaviour.

It was a quieter and more sober group that left the lecture theatre, most of them nodding in Solly's direction, pleased with what they had heard, for it had given them plenty to think about in this basic course of behavioural psychology. Some of them would use the class as a stepping stone to a general arts degree, a few would return to junior honours and some might even apply for a post-graduate degree, inspired by people like Dr Brightman. His work was well known in academic circles within the UK now and the psychologist had begun to gain a reputation as a forensic psychologist who regularly helped police with investigations, particularly into cases of serial rapes and murders.

Solly Brightman, the married man, counted himself as one of the most fortunate people in the world. Not only did he have a job that he loved (that word again!) but now he was dizzy with joy at having pledged himself for life to his darling Rosie. They had spent a magical time in New Zealand, doing things he'd never dreamt of attempting, like white-water rafting. Rosie's outgoing nature impelled him to tackle such challenges and, to his delight, Solly found that they had evoked something inside him, a spirit of recklessness that had long lain dormant. From the behavioural point of view it had been interesting to see how far he could push himself simply to keep up with Rosie and then experience the same thrill that she was experiencing. It just proved what he had always believed: there are untapped depths in human nature. All it might take was a set of circumstances to release these hidden qualities. And now, back in Glasgow, Solly felt that his life had been changed by these honeymoon experiences. In some strange way he was no longer alone in the world, but linked to another human being whose aim in life was to care for him. He, too, had taken a vow to love, honour and cherish his beloved. And wasn't Rosie all the more precious to him since she had survived that near-fatal car crash?

Life, he mused as he closed the door of his office, had dealt him rather a fine hand. He pulled out the drawer at the front of his desk, taking out what he hoped was a tasteful Valentine's card. If Rosie sent one it would probably be a jokey sort of card, maybe even a bit rude. But this one was all hearts and flowers with a few rather nice lines to his darling wife. *All my love, Solly*, he wrote, then added a single kiss and sealed the card inside its envelope. Had he destroyed the students' attitude to romantic love by that lecture? He hoped not. Love, as Desiderata said, was after all as perennial as the grass.

Closing the drawer again, Solly turned to his laptop and opened a file. He was currently writing on the subject of female psychotic behaviour, much of it based on case studies of women in high security mental institutions. The nub of his work was to demonstrate what was behind the sort of violence that had been a part of these patients' behaviour. It had struck Solly quite forcefully that although these case studies revealed a lesser degree of violent behaviour than had been seen in their male counterparts, many of them had notched up a sizeable tally of deaths. The idea of women as killers was not something readily acknowledged by the public; perhaps it was time to redress the balance in people's perceptions of violent crime.

'If there is anything you can remember that wasn't done at the time, then now is your chance to put that right,' Lorimer told the assembled officers. 'You aren't doing this to please me or indeed the people who ordered me to undertake this review,' he continued, his tone slightly sardonic. 'And don't think that by coming forward you are letting Colin Ray down. I've spoken to DCI Ray already this morning and he's very much in favour of this review being done as thoroughly as possible.'

There was the slightest murmur of what sounded like approval, and Lorimer allowed himself a mental pat on the back. He'd already looked at staffing levels on the initial case, and in this HQ in general, and found that it was the old story of too few bodies spread too thinly over too many ongoing cases. And Kate Clark's maternity leave would bring that figure down to unacceptable, in his opinion. She had been the admin person in Colin's team and Lorimer knew it would be wise to continue her in that role.

The tannoy system burst into life from the front bar calling for someone and Lorimer stopped speaking, wondering for a moment if this was a good place to take a break. He'd made DI Martin his allocator so she was going to be kept fairly busy writing out the various actions and handing them to the other officers. It hadn't been her remit under Colin Ray and Lorimer found himself wondering why. She was clearly an able officer but such tasks meant liaising closely with the SIO; had Colin been less than friendly with the woman? And was this a reason for her aggressive attitude?

'Right, I'll be here when you have anything relevant to report,' Lorimer told them, standing up so that they knew it was time to leave.

As they trooped out, Lorimer found himself wishing for his own room back in Glasgow, not this square box of an office that was doubling as an incident room. Okay, so the view beyond the blue Venetian blinds was guaranteed to take one's mind off work, with its expanse of water and hills, but that was poor compensation for the inconvenience of having folk dropping in and out all the time.

Lorimer was happy with how things had progressed so far: it had been a fruitful morning spent with the members of his new review team. They had not been the belligerent group that he had feared they might be and he wondered if Kate Clark's influence had tempered their initial manner towards him. Perhaps his own attitude of *Well I'm here and this is a job that we must get through together* had struck a chord with them. Whatever, he was now in a far better mood to begin tackling the masses of paperwork lying on his desk. DI Martin would delegate some of the more routine stuff to members of the team, hopefully urging them to pick it over with a fresh eye even when boredom threatened. But he'd kept some things for himself; there were several witness statements that he wanted to examine.

A knock at his door made him look up.

'Come in,' he called and saw a young uniformed officer who had been among the officers earlier.

The surprise must have shown on his face for the constable immediately blurted out, 'Constable Dodgson, sir. I was one of the first officers at the scene of the crime.'

'Ah, right.' Lorimer smiled encouragingly. 'Take a seat, constable. What can I do for you?'

The young man seemed ill at ease, sitting right on the edge of his chair and biting his lower lip. 'Well,' he began, 'it might be a bit silly. In fact I didn't know what to do at the time. I mean we'd been told about it at the course. But I suppose I didn't want to seem pushy . . .'

'Woah!' exclaimed Lorimer. 'Facts, please. Just tell me what you did, constable and we'll take it from there, okay?'

The young man nodded then took a deep breath. 'I get thirsty a lot. I find the patrol cars awfully hot so I carry bottled water with me,' he began. 'So when we arrived at the fire I thought I'd do what they'd shown us on the course.'

'Go on,' Lorimer said.

'Well, we'd been told that vapours from a fire might be lost into the atmosphere quite quickly so I threw the contents of my water bottle into the fire and I also had one of these.' He fished in his tunic pocket and brought out a tiny glass bottle, a bijou bottle, used by police officers for taking samples of drink from neds on street corners.

'I let the vapours fill the one I was carrying,' he said.

'And what happened to that bottle?' Lorimer asked, thinking that he knew exactly how the officer was going to respond.

'It's still in my locker, sir,' Dodgson replied, his voice high with anxiety.

Lorimer sat still for a moment. Then he asked, 'Why? Didn't you think this might be evidence that could be crucial to the investigation?'

Dodgson immediately coloured up and Lorimer saw for the first time how young he really was.

'Thought they'd laugh at me, sir,' he muttered at last, hanging his head so he didn't have to look the SIO in the eye.

Lorimer chewed his lip thoughtfully. Dodgson had shown enough initiative to ask his supervisor to let him be seconded to CID. But not enough to bring out this wee bottle from his locker. What would Lorimer have done in this youngster's place? Would he have been too shy to have come forward with such evidence at the original inquiry? Fearing the derision of his more senior officers, perhaps? *And which officers in particular?* a little voice nudged his thoughts. Was it worth digging into that can of worms as well? Whatever else it might provide, this might well be some tangible evidence in an investigation that had been sadly lacking in such things.

'Thank you, constable. If you would like to put it into an evidence bag it can be sent to forensics. Make sure it goes to the senior forensic officer. And don't forget to put a date on it, will you?' Lorimer neither smiled nor showed any sort of annoyance that this particular piece of evidence had been sidelined. Lorimer's matter-of-fact manner took the young man by surprise as he stood and mumbled his thanks.

'Don't mention it, Dodgson. Perhaps I'll be thanking you before the week is out,' Lorimer told him, eliciting a grin of relief on the constable's boyish face.

Alone once more, Lorimer pondered that little scene. He must have gained this lad's confidence and that was hugely heartening at this stage of the proceedings. But was it also indicative of some wariness on the part of youngsters like Dodgson in their relations with more senior officers? To be afraid to come forward with evidence like that from a scene of a crime showed either the lad's own inadequacy or a reluctance on the part of some of the others in the team to listen to their younger colleagues. Fresh out of college they might be, but such officers were often more clued up in the latest techniques and were eager to tick all the relevant boxes. It was the same with young doctors, Lorimer thought. They soaked up all the information necessary during their medical studies, much of it cutting-edge stuff that older practitioners might have no time to read up on.

Thinking of this, his mind turned for a moment to his mother-in-law. What had her second day in the Southern General brought for her?

Mrs Finlay felt the chill from an open doorway as she was wheeled along, a single cellular blanket over her thin nightdress. She couldn't see the orderly who was pushing her bed along and so it seemed as if she were being propelled like some sort of strange shuttle through the brightly lit hospital corridor. They stopped by a lift and she waited, knowing that there was a figure behind her, scanning the lights to see when the doors would sigh open, but he didn't seem to want to communicate with her and she was too afraid of what would come out if she attempted to speak. She was just another job to the orderly, that was all; another live body to be shunted into its rightful place. The lift gave a twang as it opened and she felt the bed being rolled into the square space. In a matter of minutes they were out again and moving forward towards another corridor.

Just as she had expected, they stopped at the nurses' station and the man came forward to hand over her bags to the staff nurse behind the desk.

'Ward fifty-six, Jim,' the nurse told the orderly. 'Right, Mrs Finlay, we'll have you tucked up again in no time,' she added, turning a smile on to the patient. She was a small plump girl, thought Alice Finlay, the sort you'd pass in the supermarket and never give another glance. But here, in her own world, the nurse had something about her that made Alice ponder. Was it that quality of caring in her tone? Or the way she gently touched the back of Alice's hand? It was not a gesture that was over-familiar, more a small caress to reassure the older woman.

The noise hit Alice as soon as they passed through the swing doors: the sound of a television set blaring out above a babble of voices. Passing one patient after another, their aged faces turned towards her with a semblance of curiosity, Alice could see that she had been taken into what was surely a geriatric ward. One old lady whose back was bent from some spinal disorder, her mouth hanging open slackly, stared at Alice as though there was nothing much going on behind her eyes.

Dear God, she breathed silently, listening to the racket within the ward. What have I come to?

For a few minutes she had the privacy of curtains around her bed, screening her off from prying eyes as the same kind nurse took her temperature and blood pressure, then busied herself putting things into a bedside locker. But once these matters were attended to, the curtains were whisked back and Alice found herself looking out into a room full of women whose faces were turned to see this newcomer in their midst.

She did the only thing that she could think of to separate herself from these old women: she closed her eyes, tightly, feigning a sleep that she suddenly and fervently desired.

Maggie closed the book on her desk as soon as the final bell rang then marched swiftly to the door to let out her Second years. One or two of them dawdled as they left, grinning at her in such a friendly manner that she didn't have the heart to shoo them out into the corridor. But if she were to make it to the hospital tonight, she would have to hurry. The parking was murder and she had to figure out how long it was going to take so she would be there in time for the ward door opening. The phone call at the end of lunchtime had at least let her know what ward Mum was in now, she told herself, speeding down the stairs towards the main door. *Comfortable*, the voice on the other end had told her when she'd asked how her mum was feeling today. Maggie had bit her lip at that. It was like the kids saying *Fine* to their parents at home whenever they were asked how school had been that day: the sort of response that really told her nothing at all. She wanted to know more, much much more. Like what was going to happen to her mum. Would she recover from the stroke? What sort of remedial help would she have and, if they were honest, would she be able to cope on her own once discharged from hospital? Settling herself into the driver's seat, Maggie turned on the ignition and headed for home, pondering what the future might hold for her. Would she have to give up her job to look after her mum? Or would the social services provide a carer of some sort? Suddenly Maggie realised how hazy she was on such details despite the topic of conversation coming up from time to time among her colleagues in the staffroom.

Maggie's mum had always been the sort of strong, dependable person who'd laughed off illness and the knocks she'd had throughout her own life. Losing Maggie's dad so soon after his retirement had been a blow but she'd soldiered on, shrugging off the state of widowhood since it was something that happened to so many older women, after all. But this was different. Seeing her so helpless in that hospital room had made Maggie realise for the first time just how vulnerable her mother was.

Almost seventy, Mrs Finlay was admittedly a bit overweight but she'd never smoked and only took a wee glass of sherry before dinner sometimes. And it wasn't an illness that had any sort of history in their family as far as Maggie knew.

A car horn right behind her made Maggie see that she had almost overshot a red light. She braked swiftly, cursing herself for paying so little attention to the road ahead; wouldn't be much use to her mum if she had an accident. Maggie Lorimer handled the rest of the journey with care, trying hard to keep her mind off what lay ahead at the seven o'clock visiting time. By five-fifteen, just as the traffic was building up to its usual stream of madness, she was able to cut off the motorway on to a slip road and head towards the supermarket. There was a list of things she needed to buy if they were to eat anything this week and she wanted some nice stuff to take into her mum, maybe one of these chocolate éclairs that she liked so much. Or was that such a good idea? Would the nurses have her on a diet now to help her lose weight? Maybe a bunch of grapes would be better after all.

'It was horrible,' Maggie told Lorimer some hours later. 'The place is like a noisy zoo. And she looked so wee and frail under the bedclothes, not like herself at all. Not even as good as I thought she was yesterday.'

'Can't you ask someone to let her have a room to herself?' Lorimer asked.

'I suppose I should have thought about it. After all, you know what Mum's always fond of saying: *If you don't ask, you don't get.* I'll go earlier tomorrow and see if I can speak to the sister in charge of that ward. But, really, all I want is to get her out of that place.'

'Is it really so bad? I mean, do you think there are any grounds for a complaint?'

Maggie shook her head. She was clasping a hot toddy that her husband had put into her hand, insisting that she needed to drink it after coming in shivering with cold and anxiety. 'No, they're all nice nurses. Treat the patients kindly and I'm sure

79

Mum's receiving adequate medical attention. But it's that telly blaring out and the old women wandering around the ward like wee lost souls. It's no place for a sick person to rest and recover,' Maggie insisted.

'Can't promise anything, but I will do my best to come with you tomorrow,' Lorimer told her, putting an arm around her shoulders and giving her the cuddle she needed.

'How was your day today?' Maggie asked, suddenly guilty that she hadn't yet enquired.

'Fine,' Lorimer said, not seeing his wife's rueful grin at the reply.

But, had he known it, this was the last word he would have applied to the days to come.

CHAPTER 13

*S*o, *Detective Superintendent Lorimer was reopening the case. Just how good was he? And what would happen to the derelict site that had once been the handsome and much-envied home of Sir Ian and Lady Jackson of Kilmacolm?*

Promises had been made. Promises to leave well alone and let the dead rest in peace, that well-worn phrase that was a catch-all for doing damn all about a cold case. Not that this one was more than slightly lukewarm. There were certainly no embers smouldering on the blackened ground around the wrecked house.

Overtures had been made to allow for a funeral to take place. But that hadn't happened and the sense of things being in limbo had been overtaken now by this new turn of events. I'd made it my business to know about such things, not just from a sense of curiosity but from a sense of self-preservation.

It would be worth my while to find out a bit about this police officer from Glasgow. To see what he was capable of doing. And to see if he posed any particular threat to my own well-being, I thought as I pushed the pedal hard and cycled down the path, away from the fluttering rags of police tape.

CHAPTER 14

Rhoda Martin slammed her locker shut. Things weren't the same now that this Detective Superintendent had invaded their territory. By rights she should have been called up for promotion by now, particularly since Colin Ray's abrupt retirement from the Force. And Katie Clark's link with the tall officer who'd given *her* that gimlet stare was even more annoying. She'd hoped to have Lorimer more to herself, to be able to talk to him about the shambles of the case and how the way forward could be, as she saw it. Damn it, she'd spent hours of her own time making notes about how a review might be organised. But did he want her opinion? Did he hell! She was stuck with being allocator and working with all the actions from other folks' statements and the forensic reports, such as they were. And hadn't she tried her best to make sure this case was closed? Couldn't they all just leave it alone? She'd known the Jacksons, she'd told Lorimer eventually. Serena and Daniel were people she'd grown up with. Okay, so she hadn't mentioned any of that to DCI Ray. So what? Serena was her *friend*, she told herself. Rhoda didn't want to upset her, did she? But had giving him that snippet of information made any difference to this cop from Glasgow?

The DI smoothed down an invisible crease on her dark skirt,

shrugged on her jacket and turned to examine herself in the mirror. What she saw must have pleased her because a sudden smile appeared, transforming the discontented expression into a very attractive face. Her blonde hair was newly washed and straightened and she took it up in two handfuls, experimenting whether or not to pile it into a clip at the back of her head. Serena had looked good like that in magazine pictures. Rhoda let it go instead, watching as it tumbled around her shoulders. She had put on makeup before leaving home, carefully applying foundation and blusher to bring out her slanting cheekbones. Her green eyes were enhanced by smoky shadow and layers of waterproof mascara and now she rummaged in her bag for the little pot of lip gloss that always seemed to lose itself in the deepest corners.

Satisfied, Rhoda snapped the bag shut and gave her reflection a grin. Maybe it was time to let Detective Superintendent Lorimer know who really counted around here. They hadn't really got off on the right foot, had they? He seemed to be one cool guy, but she hadn't yet met any officer who was totally immune to her charms, should she choose to turn them on.

'Jackson Tannock Technology Systems. What do we know about them?' Lorimer asked. The faces of his team regarded him with some interest as he looked at them one by one. Young Dodgson seemed more at ease now and the older DS, Robert Wainwright, had put a hand to his chin as if seriously considering an answer to this question. But it was DI Martin who gave the first response.

'One of the biggest employers in the area,' she began, a smile on her face that made Lorimer look at her a second time. Had she changed her appearance today? Something was different, but he was at a loss to see just what that was. Or was it that softer quality

84

in her voice? Narrowing his eyes, Lorimer gave the woman a little nod of encouragement.

'Hugh Tannock is the whiz-kid of the outfit,' Martin went on. 'Jackson had the money and together they founded the company about five years ago. Floated it on the stock exchange and somehow managed to weather the credit crunch. There were some redundancies but nothing too dramatic.'

'Nobody so pissed off that they'd harbour a grudge for that length of time and set fire to Jackson's home,' Wainwright added.

'And no malcontents within the firm more recently?' Lorimer asked.

His question was met by an uncomfortable silence.

'Not something that seems to have been a part of the initial investigation, then?' he added, knowing that the question was simply rhetorical. 'Well, that's an area I believe to be worth examining,' he told them, once more attempting to keep any trace of criticism from his voice.

'Absolutely, sir.' DI Martin was looking his way, her face quite serious. Her head was tilted to one side as if listening to Lorimer was the most important thing in her life. For some reason it only made him distrust her more, and he experienced a moment of annoyance at himself for this irrational thought.

'Forensics suggest that the fire was started in the kitchen area: a burning chip pan. But there were traces of accelerant closer to the main entrance outside the house and so the case was then believed to be one of wilful fire-raising. Okay so far?'

The faces concentrated on the DCI's all nodded in agreement.

'Thanks to Constable Dodgson we may have a new piece of evidence. He has kept fumes from a site close to the main source of the fire and these are now being tested. If we find a different type of accelerant from the one already identified, then perhaps this investigation will take a new and interesting turn. You all follow what I'm saying? The source of this accelerant would also suggest that whoever began the fire had some way of gaining entry into the house itself. Late at night.'

'Are you saying this was a burglary gone wrong?' Katie Clark asked, her face screwed up in puzzlement.

'Course not,' DI Martin immediately retorted. 'It was definitely a case of wilful fire-raising!' Then, perhaps realising that she'd sounded somewhat disdainful, she turned a sweet smile towards Lorimer. 'That's right, sir, isn't it?'

'Yes,' he agreed. 'There's no question in anyone's mind: that fire was started deliberately. The fire officers' and forensic boys' reports show specific patterns around the windows in both the kitchen and upper bedroom where the fire was seeking oxygen, so we have some evidence that there were two points of origin. What we have to find is not only how it was begun but why anybody would want to carry out a savage attack like that. We don't always begin with motive in an investigation, as you all know. But here we should look at anybody who had a reason to hold a grudge against Sir Ian Jackson. Or,' he added, more quietly, glancing at them all to see their reaction, 'his wife.'

He let the murmurs break out among them for a few moments at this suggestion. Investigating Lady Jackson's background was something that had never occurred to Colin Ray or any one of the original team. But Lorimer was used to looking at cases from unusual angles. And here, with a case to review, he'd turn the damn thing upside down and inside out to see what he could find.

'The business aspect is the most obvious, I'll grant you,' he continued. 'But what needs to be done is a thorough examination of every bit of the Jacksons' personal lives.' He paused for a moment. 'The file on their background is sadly lacking in content. Perhaps I could have someone volunteer to cover the initial administration of that?'

'I'll do that, sir.' Kate Clark's hand was up and he had the instant impression of a chubby schoolgirl trying to please her teacher. But she was nobody's fool and this action would probably suit the pregnant woman better than a lot of slogging around the district. And her colleagues would surely realise this as her motivation, Lorimer thought, though he did not fail to see the flash of irritation crossing DI Martin's pretty face.

'Thanks, DC Clark. And someone else to take over any out-of-office work?'

DS Wainwright raised a hand in his direction.

'Right. And we'll need someone to go over the fire service's reports again.' He saw another hand raised and nodded his acceptance.

'I'm going to see Hugh Tannock myself,' he told them. 'Apart from anything else, I think he has the right to know that the case is being reviewed.' And, he might have added, it would be interesting to see just how the death of Jackson had affected the man. He had lost the co-founder of their business, after all and nobody from the original investigation had noted the man's reaction in any of the reports.

Jackson Tannock Technologies was situated high above the town, overlooking the sweep of Greenock harbour and the rows of houses that hugged the hillside. As he drove the Lexus up the increasingly steep gradient, Lorimer saw a familiar landmark jutting out of the earth; the Free French Cross, a symbol from World War Two. He hesitated for only a fraction then swung the big car across the road into the parking area and got out.

It was a view that never failed to impress, even on this grey, murky day. Images of the celebrated landmark upon calendars and tourist guides would always show the stark white cross of Lorraine, its stem firmly rooted into an anchor, against improbably blue waters and a cloudless sky. But even today the monument towering over that grand expanse could move him. Slate-grey clouds lowered right down to the horizon's rim, obscuring the hills of Tighnabruaich and beyond, but below him Lorimer could see MacBrayne's car ferry ploughing over the waters like a wee toy boat. Few other craft had sought the sheltering arms of the harbour and from this distance the fluorescent marker buoys resembled a handful of orange confetti scattered over the surface of the water.

Up here it was quiet, almost lonely, reminding Lorimer what it might have been like to have stood on the bridge of one of these French boats sailing through banks of mist and out into the dangerous waters of the Atlantic. And it was here, at the tail of the bank, that other huge liners had turned from the river to head out to sea, their destination often the great port of New York.

He turned away from the view and examined the inscriptions on the monument. To the roadside, the words proclaimed:

'This memorial was designed and erected by the officers and men of the French naval base at Greenock with the help of subscriptions raised among the crews of the Free French naval forces.'

Many had gone out into the grey ocean never to return; their sacrifice at the Battle of the Atlantic had been remembered here ever since. But it was not just the memory of sailors lost in the battle that this cross represented. Walking back to the seaward side, Lorimer read the French inscription etched into the rock surface.

*A La memoire
du capitaine de frigate Biaison
des officeurs et de l'equipage
du sous-marin 'Surcoup'
perdu dans l'Atlantique
Fevrier*

He thought of the captain and officers of the frigate, Biaison, lost in the Atlantic that February then grimaced. What unimaginable horror had the submarine's crew endured in that claustrophobic tube as the Surcoup plummeted to the depths of the ocean?

Turning back to look out across the expanse of land that lay between hill and seashore, Lorimer noticed the winter grasses struggling for survival against swathes of rusting bracken. It was cold up here, making him rub his hands together, despite the wind having dropped. The ground seemed gripped still by the iron fist of winter. Letting his gaze wander, Lorimer spied a gorse bush clinging to the edge of the cliff, its few sulphur yellow flowers a defiant reminder that life still continued in every season. And there was life everywhere, from the flat-roofed secondary school on a plateau to his left to the rank upon rank of houses marching down towards the shore, bungalows up here giving way to grey tenements down in the heart of the town. Below him lay the curve of Battery Park, its bright red swings and roundabouts deserted.

It was time to go. Hugh Tannock was expecting him. Yet paying homage here for those few minutes made the Detective Superintendent feel a certain stirring in his blood. There had been sacrifices made by brave men. And somehow the thought of their unswerving duty gave him strength.

Jackson Tannock Technologies lay hidden from prying eyes in

a hollow of land near Lyle Hill, its buildings screened behind a plantation of pine and birch trees. If the architect had designed the offices to impress a newcomer then he had succeeded. The white curving walls were an obvious imitation of a ship, the lines to one side forming a bow. Above the main entrance were banks of glass windows evoking the impression of decks on an ocean-going liner. And if the beholder was still uncertain of the visual metaphor, a line of red tiles drew the eye upwards to the scarlet chimney masquerading as a funnel. This building, he had read somewhere, was a homage to the Art Deco buildings of a century before.

The whole thing might have appeared absurd, but it didn't. Instead it showed the sort of graceful elegance that comes with good design, and that sense of solid permanence – was that meant to evoke a subliminal notion of trustworthiness and integrity? Was it Lorimer's early training as an art historian that made him see such things so dispassionately? he wondered. Or had the years of policing turned him into a hard-bitten cynic, refusing to accept the message that this building and its creators were trying to convey?

Tannock had been expecting him but Lorimer hadn't thought the man himself would come to meet him in reception. Looking upwards at an open-plan staircase, he saw a man hurrying down, holding the ends of his jacket around him as if self-conscious of that corpulent figure.

'Hugh Tannock. Good to meet you, Superintendent.'

Lorimer felt a firm hand in his and saw that Tannock was look-ing up at him with an expression that was at once warm and curious. There was something about this short, middle-aged fellow that Lorimer immediately liked. He had no difficulty hold-ing the Detective Superintendent's gaze and the smile on that face made his eyes crinkle up at the corners, giving him the look of a benign and friendly priest. For a second Lorimer had a vision of Tannock clad in a brown habit, a simple cord tied around his rotund frame.

'Let's go upstairs, shall we?' Tannock suggested, already ushering Lorimer back to the pine and steel structure that spiralled upwards. 'I always like to show off the view from the top,' he twinkled, as if confiding some secret to the tall policeman.

The room they entered had one wall completely made of glass, from which Lorimer could see the same view that he had so recently enjoyed from the Free French Cross.

'Not the sort of thing one can fail to boast about, is it?' Tannock sighed, rubbing his chubby hands as he stood looking over the expanse of hillside and water, glancing back at Lorimer to see what effect the magnificent vista might have on the policeman.

'Must keep folk off their work,' he murmured, giving the man a small courteous smile, but hoping to remind him that he, at any rate, was here on official business.

'Or inspire them?' Tannock suggested. 'Shall we have some coffee while we talk about poor Ian, Superintendent?'

The man's sudden change of subject showed he had judged the Detective Superintendent's mood to perfection. He was no fool, whatever else he was, thought Lorimer, adding respect to that instinctive liking for the man.

Directing them to a pair of cream-coloured sofas placed so that they could look out over the river, Tannock waited a moment until his visitor was seated then pulled out a BlackBerry from his inside pocket.

'We're ready for coffee now, Mattie, thanks,' he said then turned to Lorimer, 'Unless you'd prefer tea?'

Lorimer assured him that coffee would be fine then watched as

Tannock pulled his trouser legs up a little to prevent them from creasing, before sinking back into the squashy sofa opposite. It was a gesture at once old-fashioned and effete and made Lorimer suddenly recall the men from the war years who had been tutored in those same small, decorous habits.

'You explained on the telephone that you wanted to talk to me about Ian's death, Superintendent,' Tannock began. 'Has anything new come to light?'

His enquiry was at once grave and hopeful, Lorimer thought.

'The previous Senior Investigating Officer in charge has retired, sir, and I have been asked to review the case.'

Tannock frowned. 'Review? Doesn't that suggest some degree of inefficiency on the part of this officer and his team?'

'Not necessarily, Mr Tannock,' Lorimer replied, crossing one leg over the other. But he was saved from giving any further detail by the appearance of an elderly woman bearing a tray of coffee and cakes.

'There you are, gentlemen. Shall I leave you to pour, Mr Tannock?' the woman asked, straightening up and obviously anxious to take her leave. Was she uncomfortable in the presence of the police? Lorimer wondered. It didn't have to be a sign of a guilty conscience, simply an aversion to the sort of seriousness that warranted his presence there.

'No, thank you, Mattie. That's fine,' Tannock assured her.

'So what do you make of the whole sorry business, Superintendent?' Tannock continued once the woman had left them.

'I haven't had time as yet to evaluate all that the primary reports showed, sir. But I would be grateful for anything you could tell me about the business here and Sir Ian's involvement in it.'

Tannock leaned forward to set his cup down before replying.

'Sir Ian was my business partner. We owned Jackson Tannock Technologies between us.'

'And now?'

'Ian and Pauline's shares will be passed on to his son and daughter, naturally. Between them they now hold over thirty per-cent of the share capital.' Tannock paused. 'It will be worth in excess of eight hundred million, I should think. Euros, that is. We always deal in euros nowadays for our market investors.'

Lorimer swallowed a gulp of hot coffee, trying not to splurt it out in astonishment. *Eight hundred million euros.* The figure had been spoken as if it were nothing out of the ordinary in a climate of worldwide recession. If he'd been looking for motive in any shape or form, surely he had found it here?

'What', he paused, the catch in his throat making speech impossible till he swallowed once more, 'what will they do with that kind of money?'

Tannock smiled. 'Daniel is one of our younger directors here. He's actually in charge of Human Resources, so I believe he will simply leave his money in the firm. For now at any rate,' he added, nodding in a way that reminded Lorimer of a wise elderly owl.

'He's thinking of leaving the firm?' Lorimer asked.

Tannock smiled thinly. 'Not if he realises his original ambition, Superintendent.'

'And that is?'

'To take over from Sir Ian, of course. It was something that Daniel had tried to have agreed by both his father and me. That he would inherit Sir Ian's place on the Board whenever retirement came.'

There was something in Tannock's expression. Scepticism? Was he trying to say that the younger Jackson was greedy for that sort of corporate power?

Tannock was shaking his head. 'Ian would never have retired. It wasn't a word in his vocabulary.' He grinned suddenly. 'He couldn't abide the thought of endless days of golf. No matter how much he enjoyed the odd game. Liked the cut and thrust of business too much.'

'So Daniel had no hope of becoming heir to his father's position unless he died?'

Hugh Tannock paled at the implication of Lorimer's words. 'That's not what I meant, Superintendent. There's nothing wrong with having a healthy ambition and his father respected Daniel's views. Please don't think along such lines . . .' he broke off, squirming in distaste, the idea of patricide quite repugnant to him.

'And the daughter?'

'Ah, Serena.' Tannock's smile slipped a little. 'She's taken this very hard, I'm afraid. Very hard indeed. Quiet lass at the best of times, you know, but these days she's . . .' he stopped then glanced at the Super as if he'd said too much already. 'Well, let's just say that a sudden loss like this is extremely difficult to cope with. She's not been back at work since the fire.'

'Miss Jackson works here too?'

Tannock nodded. 'Serena and Daniel were part of the firm, Chief Inspector. Rather like an extended family, I suppose. They never seemed to want to do anything else but work with their father.'

'And Mrs Jackson?'

'No. *Lady* Jackson didn't come here all that much. Lots of other commitments, you see.'

Lorimer winced at his faux pas, though Tannock's stress on the word Lady had been minimal.

'And Miss Jackson, what is her role in Jackson Tannock, might I ask?'

Tannock looked at him through narrowed eyes and Lorimer

wondered if the man thought this an impertinent question. Tough, he told himself. It was his job to ask awkward questions. And he hadn't actually answered his initial question about Serena Jackson, he suddenly noticed.

'Serena didn't have a particular role in the firm as such,' Tannock began, avoiding Lorimer's direct look. 'She was more of a sort of ambassador for us. Looked after the clients' social arrangements and that sort of thing,' he added in a way that Lorimer guessed was deliberately vague. Serena Jackson had acquired a sinecure within the firm by the sounds of it, he told himself. That was something his DI had failed to mention. Was she deliberately trying to play down her friendship with the Jacksons? It was odd, surely, when Martin could so easily have provided such background details.

The Detective Superintendent's expression remained quizzical and in the ensuing silence Tannock shifted in his seat as if uncomfortable under that distinctive blue gaze. It was something that many hardened criminals had experienced in the confinement of a police interview room; something that could and sometimes did cause them to reveal things they'd have preferred to keep hidden.

'Serena wasn't really qualified to take over anything on the technical or financial side of the firm,' Tannock said at last. 'Lovely girl, though: a real asset to us in all sorts of other ways.'

Lorimer nodded his understanding. Serena Jackson was possibly a decorative part of the outfit, kept by her father, given nominal status and probably a grossly inflated salary. If she'd been a child sheltered from the harshness of the real world it was not surprising that she'd cracked up after the double tragedy of losing her parents: a tragedy that no amount of money could change.

'Do you have family yourself, sir?' Lorimer inquired. It was not an idle question. He wondered if any Tannock offspring had been treated like the two Jackson kids.

'Three, actually.' Tannock smiled with genuine pleasure. 'One's a consultant anaesthetist in London, one's making a fortune in Texas and the other runs a publishing house.'

'You must be proud of them.'

'I am, Superintendent. And Sir Ian was just as proud of his two children,' Tannock added quietly, his shrewd glance showing that he hadn't missed the import of Lorimer's questions.

'It might sound a little melodramatic, sir, but did Sir Ian have any enemies?' Lorimer asked, changing the subject.

'I don't know, Superintendent, and that's the truth. Ian and I had known one another for many years. Our partnership had grown much closer since we formed the business, naturally. But I wasn't privy to all of his financial dealings, you must understand, just to those that affected Jackson Tannock.'

'He had other businesses?'

'Oh, yes. Ian had what you might describe as a varied portfolio. Some of his assets were in overseas companies pre-dating the launch of Jackson Tannock and demanded comparatively little of his time, but they were lucrative nonetheless.'

'And you think there may have been something in one of these companies that could have engendered enough hate to cause his death?'

Tannock sat up suddenly, alarmed at the brutality of Lorimer's question.

'I didn't say that, Superintendent. Nor did I at any time imply such a thing!'

'But it is a possibility?' Lorimer added quietly.

'How would I know?' Tannock threw his hands in the air. 'Ian didn't confide such things to me. Ever. And if there had been something troubling him I think I would have been the first to notice.'

Lorimer nodded, wanting to say Yes, Mr Tannock, I think you would. This man was a perceptive sort, he guessed, and would be good at reading the people who came into his orbit.

He sighed then shook his head. 'We have to try to understand what sort of person would deliberately begin a fire when two people were inside that house. So we naturally look for a reason.'

The two men looked at one another for a long moment, then Tannock sank back into the squashy settee.

'We thought it must have been kids from Port Glasgow. A stupid dare that went wrong,' he muttered. Then once more he caught Lorimer's gaze. 'But you wouldn't be here just now if that was what you thought. Right?'

'It looks increasingly like a case of premeditated murder,' Lorimer told him. Okay, that was perhaps stretching the truth a little, but he had a hunch that Dodgson's evidence was going to turn up trumps. He could suggest something to provoke a reaction. See what way Tannock would jump.

'I don't know, really, I don't. To kill a man who'd done so much good in his life. And an innocent woman,' he tailed off, his voice beginning to show the first signs of real emotion.

Lorimer watched as the man took a folded white handkerchief from his inside pocket and blew noisily into it. He had seen lots of people simulate grief before. But this seemed quite genuine to him. Suddenly the trappings of wealth, the glorious view from this huge window, were diminished by the bowed figure before him who had lost his business partner. And more than a business partner, Lorimer realised. From the way he looked right now it was clear that Ian Jackson had been this man's friend.

*

97

'C'n I speak tae Mr Lorimer?'

Maggie frowned for a moment then, as she recognised his voice, her face creased into a huge smile. 'Flynn!' she exclaimed. 'How are you?'

'Aye, awright. I wis wantin tae speak tae the man. Is he in?'

'Not at the moment, Flynn. Can I get him to call you back?'

'Aw, away catchin crims, is he?' the voice replied, a hint of humour making Maggie smile.

'I'm just going out myself, Flynn,' Maggie said, then paused. Mum had helped this lad when he'd been down on his luck. 'My mum's in hospital,' she told him.

'Mrs Finlay? Whit's wrang? Naethin serious I hope.'

Maggie bit her lip then took a deep breath. 'She's had a stroke, I'm afraid. We don't know how long she'll be in . . .'

'Hey, that's terrible, man!' Flynn said. 'Are ye goin therr on yer own? I'm up the town the now. Here, I can get a bus and be over and see her masel, if ye want. Whit ward's she in?'

Maggie could have hugged him. Flynn's presence was exactly what she'd like tonight. And she bet that her mum would as well. Glancing at her watch, Maggie told him the visiting times and described the ward her mum was in.

'Aye, jist in thon main block. No so very far frae where I was, right?'

Flynn's words brought it all back to Maggie, then. She'd been away in Florida, her husband all on his own here at home. There had been the murder in Glasgow Royal Concert Hall and Flynn, a young homeless lad who'd hung about the place, had been seriously injured during the ensuing investigation. After his discharge from the Southern General, Lorimer had taken him home to look after him, something that the childless school teacher had resented at first. But it had been Maggie's choice to be away from Scotland that winter and Flynn had become almost part of the family by the time she returned. Her mum, in particular, had had a soft spot for the lad and they'd kept in touch ever since. Now he worked for Glasgow Parks Department over on the south side of the city, not too far from his flat in Govanhill.

Maggie put the phone down thoughtfully. She hoped the boy wasn't in any sort of trouble. He'd been in with a bad crowd, dealing in drugs, but the accident had given Flynn some sort of sense of his own mortality, Lorimer had told her, and so he'd changed his ways, big time.

Joseph Alexander Flynn pocketed his mobile phone thoughtfully then gave a grin that could only be described as wicked. The phone in his pocket had cost him a week's wages after 'losing' the one that DCI Lorimer had given him as a Christmas gift. That had been fun, Flynn remembered, holding up the policeman's plane with a fake bomb scare at Glasgow Airport. He wouldn't get away with that sort of thing now, though, he told himself, recalling the attempted terrorist firebombing some time afterwards that had trebled security in and around the building.

Poor old Mrs Fin, he mused, recalling the bossy old lady who had done her best to fuss over him when he'd first moved into the wee flat he now called home. Maggie Lorimer's mum was a warrior and no mistake; she'd not take kindly to being stuck inside a hospital, that was for sure. Raking in his other pocket, Flynn found a few pound coins. He'd enough for his bus fare and more. Och, why not? Turning into RS McColl's, the young man searched the rows of sweeties to see what might take his old pal's fancy.

The number twenty-three bus travelled from the city centre all the way out to the countryside and the town of Erskine. It wasn't a place Flynn had ever been to but he knew it was where the famous hospital for ex-servicemen and women was located. Maybe, he thought, gazing out at the darkened streets, he'd hop on this bus one weekend and stay on till the final terminus, just to see what it was like. For now, all the views he could see were of shuttered premises each side of the street, with an occasional glimpse of the huddled masses across the river. The bus turned this way and that until it came to the road that ran parallel to the Clyde, stopping near the complex known as the Quay to disgorge a few passengers on their way to the cinema or casino. Then, trundling along past the famous Angel building – its winged figure towering loftily over the intersection of two main roads – the bus headed along through the newer flats of Govan, past the glass edifices of the BBC and Scottish Television until it snaked its way around Govan Town Hall and the old dockyards. It was too dark to see the water but Flynn could make out the light on top of the Science Centre, a red needlepoint against the cobalt sky.

When they reached the stop nearest to the Southern General, Flynn wasn't surprised to see most of his fellow passengers rise to follow him. Visiting time would bring families from all over the city, he supposed, noticing a wee lassie holding her mammy's hand and jigging beside her, singing some song that only she could understand. Maybe they were going to see a granny? Or was the wee one's daddy in the hospital? Flynn quickened his step, anxious suddenly to see old Mrs Fin for himself.

PC Dodgson had been first on the scene, so it was only natural that the new SIO should ask to be taken up to Kilmacolm with him. But, thought Rhoda Martin, the new Super wasn't giving her the place she ought to have in this review team. Why not ask her to join them? She seethed, watching as the dark blue Lexus headed out of the backyard and out of sight. Dodgson was a typical wee arse licker, just like that cow Clark. If she didn't watch out they'd both be over Lorimer like the proverbial rash. And where would that leave her? Stepping back from the window, DI Martin heard her name being called.

She had loads to do for him, hadn't she? So better make sure it was done efficiently. Not like the last time.

The road from Greenock ran steeply upwards, away from the coastline below them: Clune Brae seemed to teeter on a cliff edge before turning back inland to the gentler greener slopes of Upper Port Glasgow. Up here the morning mist had given way to a steady drizzle and, as they rounded a corner, a sharp blast of wind struck the car as if to remind them this Scottish winter was by no means spent.

'You'd been coming in from this direction, on Port Glasgow Road?'

Dodgson nodded. 'We'd been answering a call when I spotted the smoke. The trees thin out about here . . . see the gap? That's where the cemetery is. The Jacksons' house is about a quarter of a mile from the road. You can see – sorry, you *used* to be able to see the turrets through the trees in winter. Up here,' he added indicating the two white posts to their left.

Masses of rhododendrons screened everything from their view as Lorimer drove towards the scene of the crime. It was a peaceful-looking place, made all the quieter by the dark bushes and stands of larches on either side of the drive, their needles soft fringes of pale gold on the damp ground.

When they rounded a bend Lorimer slowed down and stopped. The photographs of the crime scene didn't do justice to this magnificent wreckage. He'd asked to see an original picture of the house but so far nobody had provided one. Still, he could imagine something of what it must have been like. The area in front of the mansion was a curving sweep of rabbit-nibbled lawn, the tarmac driveway running all the way around in a huge arc. What might have been a stable block or garaging for a fleet of cars lay to the right of the house, now a mere outline of walls and broken rafters. But it was the main building that drew the eye: a mass of grey rubble heaped below the remaining structure, its twin towers shattered and broken. It was, Lorimer told Maggie later, as if some petulant giant had taken a mallet and knocked the whole thing down. It looked so old already, he thought. Only a few weeks ago this had been a house, a home filled with the sound of human voices, and now all that was left was this mess of stones and blackened timbers. The enormity of the crime swept over Lorimer, suddenly making him feel a sense of outrage against whoever had decided to light that flame.

'Show me,' he told the young police constable, opening the car door at last.

The scene-of-crime tape was still in place despite a vagabond wind that threatened to take it skyward. Pushing it aside, Dodgson pointed to a heap of broken stones overflowing on to the dead grass. 'That's where the front door was,' he told Lorimer. 'When we got here the place was in flames but the upper floors were still okay. I mean, they hadn't collapsed at that stage. The door was open and I tried to go in but it was impossible.' He looked ruefully at Lorimer as if the senior officer might berate him for failing to enact a hopeless rescue.

'You're sure it was open?'

Dodgson nodded. 'Later on the men from the fire service told us it could have been the heat that made the door burst open. Anyway, that was where the smoke seemed thickest.'

'And from where you took that fume sample.'

'Aye.' Dodgson heaved a sigh. 'We couldn't do a thing so we

just called the fire crew as well as our own HQ. We were told to keep back from the house in case anything collapsed. So that's what we did.'

'Not everyone can be a hero,' Lorimer remarked mildly. 'And you may already have done more than could have been expected of you.'

'But the people!' Dodgson blurted out. 'They burned to death in there!'

Lorimer glanced briefly at the young officer; Dodgson had tears in his eyes that were nothing to do with this bitter February wind. Were they tears of remorse for being unable to do anything about the Jacksons? Or tears of rage at whoever had committed this crime? Suddenly Lorimer knew that this police constable shared his sense of outrage and was heartened by the knowledge that this was why they were both here, to push this investigation to its limits and bring someone to justice.

'Can you spare a minute, sir?'

Lorimer looked up from the management policy file opened on his desk. DI Rhoda Martin had come into the room and, without waiting for a response, picked up a chair and set it down at an angle from him. As she crossed them, the DI revealed a pair of shapely legs in a skirt that would normally have been considered too short for a senior officer.

'DI Martin, what may I do for you?' Lorimer asked and immediately regretted his turn of phrase as he saw the salacious grin spreading across the woman's face. It was then that he noticed the low-cut shirt, unbuttoned to reveal a froth of lacy bra and the hint of cleavage between her breasts.

Taking his glance as approval, Martin began to swing one leg up and down in a deliberately provocative manner.

'It's what *I* can do for *you*, Superintendent,' she said.

Lorimer blinked, not willing to believe what his eyes were telling him. DI Rhoda Martin was coming on to him? How often had she done this to other senior officers? And, he thought cynically, was she quite practised in doing this to get what she wanted?

As his eyes narrowed into a frown, Martin quickly uncrossed her legs. 'I haven't had the opportunity to talk to you about my personal knowledge of the Jackson case,' she said, wriggling in her seat and pulling aimlessly at the hem of her skirt. Her tone, he noticed, had immediately become businesslike.

Lorimer merely looked at her, his fingers tapping impatiently on the file as if to indicate that he had other important matters in hand. Let her become uncomfortable, he thought, allowing the silence between them to speak volumes; it's no more than she deserves. But he was cursing the woman inwardly for adding more problems to their working relationship, even as she rattled on to cover her embarrassment.

'I was at school with the two Jackson children,' she told him. 'I know Serena quite well and,' she hesitated, 'let's just say that we all moved in the same social circles.'

Lorimer gave a brief nod. DI Martin's background might prove relevant; then again, it might not. 'What's your point, Detective Inspector?' he asked.

'Well.' The woman seemed at a sudden loss for words and Lorimer could see her thinking fast. She'd tried to come on to him and singularly failed. Now she was dreaming up a real excuse for sailing uninvited into his room.

'I suppose I wanted to let you know that I could be of help,' she said lamely, her cheeks suddenly pink with what might have been embarrassment or even anger.

'There's no mention of this in any previous report,' Lorimer told her coldly. 'Perhaps if you had seen fit to offer *help* to your previous SIO then he might have been grateful for some inside knowledge.'

There was no mistaking the rage in the woman's expression now as she began to rise. 'Well . . .' she began, but Lorimer did not allow her to finish.

'Put the chair back where you found it, if you don't mind,' he said, in a voice devoid of any expression whatsoever then, indicating the door, he looked back at the file in front of him.

There was no sound of the door slamming behind her as she left and Lorimer gave a wry smile: at least DI Martin was capable of *some* self-control. But his smile disappeared at once as he realised that the gulf between him and this officer would only have widened. The little incident might have been fuel for a good story in the pub from any other officer. But Lorimer didn't need the sort of macho boasting that sometimes went on among his male colleagues.

He let out a sigh, relieved to remember that he was only down here in Greenock for a limited time. Any awkwardness would have to be endured. Or simply ignored.

Rhoda Martin looked at herself in the mirror, hands gripping the edge of the basin. Errant tears coursed down her cheeks and she rubbed furiously with a paper hanky, smudging the carefully-applied mascara. Her green eyes narrowed into malevolent slits.

'Damn you to hell, Lorimer,' she muttered, throwing the tissue accurately into the waste basket. 'I'll get you for this,' she whispered under her breath. 'Then you'll wish you'd never been born.'

CHAPTER 15

Rosie drew one fingernail across the envelope, a smile hovering around her mouth. It was typical of Solly to have sent her the card at work, she thought, taking it out and turning it over. Yes, red roses on a highly embossed surface, the sort of extravagantly romantic Valentine's card she'd never received from any of her former boyfriends. Inside she read the equally flowery words. She should have laughed at their message as over-the-top sentimentality, but somehow she couldn't. Hand on her cheek, Rosie smiled properly now, thinking about the man who had won her heart. They'd met in such inauspicious circumstances; the scene of a crime where a young woman had been brutally murdered. She might have despised this strange man whose weak stomach contrasted so much with her own hardened professionalism. But that hadn't happened. Somehow she'd found herself driving him home that night and hoping against hope that he would ask to see her again.

Now they were husband and wife. An odd couple, some might say, but their very differences seemed to suit them both. Rosie had left her card for Solly on the bedside table, hoping he'd find it after she'd left for work. February fourteenth or not, the consultant pathologist had to be in early at the office before her first appointment of the day. Being an expert witness for the Crown meant that Rosie often had to give evidence in high profile cases and today was one such. A son had murdered his mother in a fit of drunken rage. Photographs of the stab wounds were part of the evidence that would be presented to the jury of fifteen men and women in the High Court but Dr Rosie Fergusson's verbal testimony would also be crucial in affecting the outcome. She was used to them but Rosie still took her court appearances very seriously indeed, knowing that shades of meaning might be derived from any answers she gave.

With a sigh, she placed the Valentine's card on top of the filing cabinet where she would be sure to see it the moment she returned from court.

No Valentine's cards for me today. Not that I expected any. Once there had been a little flurry of them and that had been amusing for a time. This omission wasn't something to worry me, though. My mind was occupied with far loftier things than teenage fantasies. School kids might be biting their nails, anxiously waiting for the bell to ring so they could rush home and see what the postman had left. In my day the mail had arrived before breakfast. Now it could be delivered at any old time at all; another thing that irked me about this changing world where outside forces determined parts of my existence.

That was why I could breathe easily in the knowledge that what I was going to put into motion would never rebound upon me. I would have it planned to the last detail just as I had planned every one of the other deaths. Nothing would be left to chance.

And, besides, who was going to suspect someone like me?

Jean Wilson loved crime. It was her favourite section in the local library and the assistant always gave her the nod whenever a new title came in. Not real-life crime, though she had dipped a tentative toe into those murky waters. No, for Jean the crime stories of folk like Ian Rankin and Val McDermid were her abiding passion. She was on her way to the library now. The writers' group had focused on romance today, of course, since it was February fourteenth. She'd tried to pen a wee thing to read out, but had given up and crumpled it into her bin. Others had managed fine: lovely poems that made Jean sigh. Such talent among her friends down at the community centre! Every week she walked from her home to the writing group, nodding a greeting to the old folk who were downstairs at the elderly forum, a club where the seniors of the district could be entertained by visiting singers and other folk. *The old folk*, she called them, but most were in fact a deal younger than herself. At eighty-one, Jean was the oldest member of the writing group that met upstairs in the community education room but nobody knew that little fact since she chose to keep her age to herself.

It was a windy day today and the clouds were racing across a sky whose weak winter sun managed only a faint appearance from time to time behind a mass of leaden grey cumulus. Jean paused for a moment before she crossed the road. She needed more second-class stamps to send off the articles she had finished for those magazines. Looking left and right, she crossed over to the post office, noticing as she did so the now-familiar figure of the hooded cyclist.

Jean grinned to herself. She'd seen him every week and had woven him into a story in her imagination. Not that she'd actually written it yet but it was there, percolating away inside her head. He had managed to find his way into her diary, however. Jean always wrote a few sentences last thing at night, just to record the day's events and, given that most were fairly humdrum, she added details of anything that seemed unusual just to spice things up. So the mysterious cyclist had been given some lines already.

The rain had begun to spit and there was a rumble of thunder as Jean came back out of the post office. She struggled with her black umbrella, the wind catching it and threatening to turn it inside out. As she made her way along to the corner of the street and the library, Jean saw him again. He was standing across the road and she could swear that he was watching her from under that dark hood of his. Shivering, the old woman hauled herself up the steps, glad of the automatic doors swinging outward to welcome her. Once inside the warmth of the library, Jean left all thoughts of the cyclist behind. Overactive imagination, she told herself, her eyes already feasting on the rows of novels under the heading CRIME.

Once out in the rain again, the old lady was buffeted along by the driving wind, holding on to her bag and umbrella so hard that she was unable to see the dark figure following her from a distance. Nor did she hear the swish of bicycle tyres on the wet road as the traffic splashed puddles of rainwater towards the pavements and the thunder grew louder. A flash of lightning made her hurry along the street; it wouldn't do to be caught out with her brolly held aloft. You heard such awful things about men being struck by lightning on the golf course and places like that.

It was a relief to be home again. Jean shut the door and pulled the chain across, glad to shut out the miserable afternoon. She took off her wet coat, hanging it on the hook on the wall, deciding to change her shoes later. First she needed warmth and light. She'd switch on the lamps in the sitting room, plug in her electric fire then make a nice cup of tea before settling down with that new writer they'd recommended at the library. Jean groaned, the aches in her body a potent reminder of her eighty-one-year-old bones.

The old lady was filling her kettle when she heard the scuffling sound at her back door. Was it some animal? Jean stopped and listened. The scuffling sound continued and she set the kettle down beside the sink and headed towards the source of the noise.

The door was whipped out of her grasp as soon as she opened it and for an instant she thought it must be the wind.

Then she saw the figure standing there, an arm raised above its head.

Jean's scream was lost in the sudden crash of thunder and, as the ground came up to meet her, she knew with a certainty that she was going to die.

Acting Detective Superintendent Lorimer frowned as he pored over the witness statements. At first glance the file was fine, nothing to worry anybody. But it was the lack of detailed information missing from these pages that gave him pause for thought. Dodgson's own report had triggered off the initial visits to nearby properties (Lorimer noted the word *properties*: not neighbours or even neighbouring houses. Kilmacolm was famous for its huge mansions that, even during the years of financial uncertainty, had commanded millions on the open market.) It had been during the night that the fire had been started and the pattern of statements from those living within a mile or so of the Jacksons had been depressingly predictable. Nobody had seen anything that could have helped the police. Not until the fire service had made its noisy way along the drive had anyone even awoken to hear what was going on. Then, Lorimer read, the fire could be seen over the treetops, an open window giving the sounds of crackling mixed with the sirens screaming to a rescue that never happened. No dog walkers wandering past the drive, no night-time shift workers passing by, no sign of a car full of carousing louts fleeing the scene.

Yet that was exactly what had been suggested: the fire had been started by a bad crowd from down the hill in Port Glasgow. Okay, there had been a spate of burglaries a year or so previously and a local lad had been nabbed for them. So what? Fire-raising hadn't been in that thief's case history. It was simply the old story of guilt by association. Someone from the port had been sentenced for crimes against the good decent folk of Kilmacolm and so the finger was pointed at them (whoever *they* were, and why don't the police investigate them?) He could almost hear the indignation in the voices of the outraged neighbours. And who could blame them? After all, the tragedy must have shocked local people. But these witness statements (if he could deign to call them that) were hardly more than a collection of opinions based on nothing more than anger and fear. The local crime prevention lads had been particularly busy in the week following the fire, Lorimer knew. And he would bet that the sale of electric gates and other security devices had rocketed in the wake of the Jacksons' deaths.

And the Chief Constable had taken this line as well. Look at the low-life in Port Glasgow, he'd told Colin Ray. Lorimer's jaw hardened. There were bad elements in every town, though statistically Kilmacolm could expect its own share to be very low indeed. Especially when the head of Strathclyde's police force lived there himself. And yet, the Chief Constable, David Isherwood, had issued orders for Colin to come up to see him in Pitt Street rather than ask him to visit him at home. Why? Wouldn't he want to keep it unofficial if there was anything dodgy about his request? Lorimer mused. And if there was, Isherwood wouldn't want his own name contained within the pages of this file, would he?

There was something unsavoury about this, Lorimer thought,

tapping his front teeth with a pencil. Why tell DCI Ray not to look among Jackson's associates? Was there something Isherwood knew? And if so, was it worth him risking asking questions at that level?

He was acting Detective Superintendent, a role that would probably lead to a permanent promotion if he were to succeed in this review.

A thought suddenly came to Lorimer. Was that why he had been seconded to the job in the first place? There were surely a few other Detective Superintendents who could have been posted to Greenock's HQ to tackle this one. And of course it had to be someone higher than a DCI, Colin Ray's own rank. Lorimer bit his lower lip as this new idea took hold. Did they think that his temporary promotion would make him all the more eager to toe the line? Was he simply being used to keep the lid on things? A can of worms, Colin Ray had suggested. Aye, well, maybe it was. Giving a sigh, Lorimer knew that, despite his wife's delight at the thought of his promotion, he'd be ready to risk that to get a result in this case. Maggie Lorimer might well live to be disappointed but he wasn't going to let anyone, Chief Constable or otherwise, stand in the way of doing his job.

The tannoy sounded loudly in his ear, breaking the chain of thought. Someone was looking for DI Martin at the front desk. Lorimer frowned. This review didn't take priority over any new crimes being committed for the officers in Greenock and he could easily lose some of his personnel if something major cropped up.

There was a knock at his door and the cheery face of DC Kate Clark appeared. She tugged ineffectually at the smock top covering her swelling body as she approached Lorimer's desk.

'Been a murder, gov,' she said in her best *Taggart* voice, mimicking the phrase associated with the long-running TV police drama. Then, sitting down on a chair without being invited, Kate gave a groan. 'This wee blighter's been playing football in there all morning.'

Lorimer smiled at her. It was refreshing to have someone like Kate around: for others it might mean the nuisance of the woman being off on maternity leave fairly soon, but it gave Lorimer a sense of normality. Birth and new life was a wholesome contrast to the sort of work they did, often involving violent deaths.

'Does that mean I'm to lose all of my best officers for today?'

Kate shrugged. 'DI Martin's away to the scene just now. An old lady's been mugged at her own home; or so her neighbour seems to think.'

The woman's tone gave no indication that she felt anything for the victim. But in this job an officer had to maintain a detachment from the tragedies that occurred each day. Start feeling sore at every crime that came along and you'd end up a basket case, Lorimer remembered one of his lecturers at Tulliallan saying. And it was true. But it hadn't stopped him having feelings for the victims in his own cases. Feelings of outrage, sometimes; feelings of pity for a life cut short. And shouldn't there be some heartache for an old person too? Especially one who had been brutally attacked.

Lorimer's thoughts turned to Maggie's mum. How would they feel if it had been her?

DI Martin saw that the blood had not been completely washed away by the thunderstorm, though some of it had been watered down by the driving rain.

'Jean Wilson's her name, Ma'am,' the uniform offered. 'Her son's on his way over here from his work now.'

'Okay. Get family liaison on to it, will you,' Rhoda ordered. 'And see if the doctor wants a pathologist over here as well.'

There was a small group of people gathered at the foot of the stairs, surrounding the body. Attempts had been made to conserve the scene of the crime and treads had been placed from the entrance of the house through the hallway and kitchen out into the back garden where the victim lay on the concrete slabs. Rhoda Martin seethed inwardly. The Detective Sergeant who was usually the scene of crime manager (and responsible for keeping everything as intact as possible for forensics) was at a funeral, leaving her in charge. It was demeaning, she told herself. She should be the SIO in the case, not the crime scene manager. It was all Lorimer's fault, taking staff away from them, she decided pettishly. Still, she'd put her name on this one if nobody more senior turned up. And delegate all this stuff to the DS when he came back from the crematorium.

A neighbour had called the police. A woman putting out rubbish in her bin had caught sight of the old lady lying there on the patio. She was back inside her own home now, having tea poured into her by one of the uniforms. Rhoda would have a word with her as soon as she was free here. A large tarpaulin tent was being erected now around the body, the gusting wind threatening to blow the whole thing sideways. Further along the rows of back gardens she could see one or two figures standing, watching the process. Nosy beggars, she thought to herself, wanting to go across and shout at them to mind their own bloody business. They'd be door-stepped soon enough, their fascination with this crime scene tempered by the routine questioning from police officers. At the top of one set of back steps two white-haired women stood, huddling together, their faces turned towards the scene three houses along from them. The gardens were separated by low wooden fences, easily stepped over by neighbours seeking a short cut to visit. Or by someone hoping for a quick getaway, Rhoda thought.

'Did she fall or was she pushed?' A voice behind her made Rhoda turn to see DS Wainwright.

'The pathologist'll let us know in due course, if we're to call one out, but it looks to me as if it could just be an accident.'

'Any reason to think otherwise?'

'Och, the woman who rang us up said her neighbour had been mugged. The sight of all that blood must've made her panic.'

'Right. But you're obviously not taking any chances, are you?' Wainwright's eyes found Rhoda's own and she gave him a little smile. They all knew she'd taken too many chances when DCI Ray had been in charge and now it was time to exert a little more caution, especially with Lorimer in the background.

Gary Wilson sat slumped in the chair of his mother's sitting room. Someone had switched on the electric fire and its artificial coals were glowing in the hearth but even that couldn't stop the trembling. His hands were round a mug of hot sweet tea and he'd drunk most of it without realising. Now he held onto it as if it were the most precious thing in the whole room. A uniformed policeman had spoken to him on his arrival and later there was this older woman, talking quietly to him and giving him some of the facts of his mother's sudden death. He'd cried when he'd seen her body; face down on the patio, her legs splayed at an awkward angle, rain soaking through her skirt and tights.

The questions were still coming at him and he only nodded or shook his head, not trusting his voice to speak. It wasn't like anything he'd ever experienced before. Dad's death had been a call in the night from the hospital and a quiet bedside farewell with whispering nurses hovering around him, painless and sanitised, not like this.

For a moment the female police officer excused herself and Gary's eyes wandered over the room. Mum's coffee table with its lace cover, a new pile of library books, her laptop over there on the desk with some papers to one side. Gary set down the mug on the carpet, his fingers brushing against a hard, leather-covered book. Bending over, he saw what it was. Mum's diary. It was almost a standing joke that Mum could tell you what the weather had been like years back, since she'd kept her diary for as long as he could remember. Carefully, almost reverently, Gary Wilson lifted the little book and opened it.

There was no entry for February fourteenth. Saint Valentine's Day, Gary thought with a pang. What a day to die! Now it would be forever associated with Mum's passing. Drawing the diary towards him, Gary began reading the last entry. Then the one before that. Leaning forward, he skimmed over the pages, his eyes widening as he read his mother's words.

The family liaison officer came into the sitting room, another mug of tea in her hand. Gary Wilson looked up at her and held the diary aloft.

'I think someone better have a look at this,' he told her.

'She wasn't a frail old lady,' Gary Wilson insisted. 'Ask anyone. She was old, aye, and had rheumatism, but she got around just fine. I don't think this was an accident,' he said, his mouth closing in a firm line.

DI Martin sat beside the man, his mother's diary in her hand. She'd read the entries but she'd also seen other books lying on top of the coffee table. The old lady was into crime, it seemed. The made-up sort. And she was a member of a writers' workshop. So did these diary entries bear any resemblance to facts or were they, too, a bit of fanciful fiction?

As if reading Rhoda's thoughts, Gary Wilson turned sideways in his chair to face her. 'Mum's diaries were totally factual,' he said. 'We always knew what had happened on a day-to-day basis. You could depend on her diary.' He smiled a little, his eyes looking into the distance as if remembering. 'If you wanted to know what happened on any given day a couple of years back, Mum's diaries would tell you. She even kept a note of what we had for Christmas dinner.'

'So this cyclist . . .?'

'Was real,' Gary told her, his fist thumping the arm of the chair. 'She made stuff up for the writers' group, but it was mostly articles she wrote. And sold,' he added, the tinge of pride unmistakable in his voice. 'She wouldn't invent this man, whoever he was.'

DI Martin nodded. It did look as if the old lady had been stalked. The mentions of the cyclist and the old lady's additional observations were pretty clear. *A hooded man, riding so slowly I thought he might fall off that fancy bike of his*, Jean Wilson had written. *Back again, today*, she'd put in another entry. *Is he following me???* In all, the cyclist had been mentioned five times, too many for it to have been a mere coincidence, a fact that the victim had also been shrewd enough to set down in her final entry.

'We'll certainly follow this up, Mr Wilson,' DI Martin assured him. 'But we also have to wait for other evidence like the pathologist's report and the forensic reports.'

'They take time to come through, you see,' the family liaison officer added as gently as she could.

Gary Wilson looked from one woman to the other. Did they believe him when he'd insisted that this was no accident? Or was it just a bit convenient that Mum had been an old lady of eighty-one out on her back steps in a thunderstorm? He shook his head,

118

a cynical expression hardening around his eyes. They weren't going to bother, were they? All this talk of forensics was just to placate him. Wasn't it?

CHAPTER 16

Maggie Lorimer sank into her favourite armchair. A wee cup of coffee and a bit of caramel shortcake from the school charity's tuckshop and she'd be as right as rain. With a purr, Chancer, her orange cat, jumped lightly on to her knee. Maggie stroked his fur, noting how wet his tail was. Had he been caught out in the storm too? The walk to the staff car park had soaked her almost to the bone, the wind whipping the hailstones against her as she'd struggled to her car, opening the back door and shoving in her bags full of Higher prelim papers. With a wry smile Maggie recalled one head teacher she'd taught with years ago who had opened his car door on a windy day and let loose all the department's Fifth year exam papers to a west coast gale. Every one of her colleagues had suspected the man had done it deliberately, his wide smile showing only glee that he hadn't marked them before they'd taken off towards the Arran hills.

She'd have to find time later on to mark these, though. Once she'd seen how Mum was today. It was Valentine's Day and the First years had had a great time with versifying. (Maggie couldn't bring herself to call it poetry.) The whole school had been tingling with an atmosphere of excitement, her Fourth years gossiping and giggling behind their hands. And tomorrow would be just as bad once they'd gone home to see what their postmen had delivered. She'd neither written a card nor expected to receive one. She and Bill weren't like that, though he'd given her red roses on the occasions when he remembered their wedding anniversary.

Kicking off her damp shoes, Maggie curled up on the chair, disturbing Chancer who protested by pushing his claws into her lap. This was the time of day she valued most. A little respite from the noise of the kids and the ringing of interminable bells before she set about making an evening meal was as welcome to Maggie Lorimer as the whisky nightcap her husband often enjoyed at the end of his day. It was funny, she thought, how this secondment had given her more of his time. Away down the coast in Greenock, he seemed to be keeping regular hours instead of the endless working days that solving crimes often demanded. Lorimer hadn't said much about this job and Maggie was sensible enough not to push it, but he didn't seem altogether contented about being in this promoted post.

'Not a happy lad, is he, Chancer?' Maggie said, stroking the cat's fur. Possibly it was because of Colin Ray's bereavement. And he had hinted that nobody really enjoyed a new face from a different division telling them they'd got a case all wrong. Still, there was that nice girl, Kate something, who'd remembered him from way back. Married now and pregnant, Maggie told herself, recalling her husband's words. Lucky woman, she thought. Her own future didn't include the patter of tiny feet and she was probably destined to be one of those teachers who became more and more out of touch with the kids, simply because she had none of her own to tell her what was hip and what wasn't. God knows, it wasn't from choice, or from trying, that they had no children. Suffering several miscarriages had proved that, all right. But they were resigned to the fact that she couldn't carry a child to full term and Maggie had learned to be reasonably content with their lot.

'You're my baby, aren't you, Chancer?' she crooned, smiling at herself for being so daft. The cat purred under the motion of her fingers and Maggie sighed again. Och, it wasn't too bad. And anyway, if she'd had kids how would she have coped right now with Mum in hospital?

Maggie remembered her mother's expression on that half-frozen face, appealing and sad at the same time; she was the responsible adult now and her mum was the vulnerable one. Thank God she'd managed to get her out of that awful ward and into a nicer one. 'If you don't ask, you won't get,' she'd told her Mum. It was a mantra she seemed to be using a lot these days. And it had been working. The hospital staff really did seem to have taken her mother's care to heart. Maggie believed she could see a real improvement in her condition. That was good news, of course, but what was going to happen next? Would the hospital expect Maggie and Bill to take Mum home and care for her here? Part of her longed for the chance to show her filial duty, but another part dreaded the very idea. Perhaps they'd been on their own too long, used to one another's ways and maintaining a sort of independence within their marriage. If so, would her mother's arrival change all of that? Hating herself for the thought, Maggie finished her coffee, brushed crumbs from her jumper and swept the cat off her knee. Mum was welcome here any time, she told herself. They'd just need to make adjustments; that was all.

Kate Clark flopped on to her side. It had been a good day, the baby kicking strongly, reminding her of his imminent arrival. A wee boy, they'd seen him at the time of her scan. Not sure what to call him yet, but Gregor was at the top of her own list of favourites. Funny case today, though, she mused, remembering DI Martin's report to them all. It seemed that the old lady had slipped down a flight of steps at her back door. Killed instantly when her head struck the concrete, so the doctor reckoned. But Kate Clark wasn't so sure. It reminded her far too much of that other accident a couple of months back, just along the road in Port Glasgow. Wee woman who'd been killed on Boxing Day. At her back door. Down a flight of steps. Coincidence? Or not? Kate rolled on to her back. She remembered something that Lorimer had said way back in her training days about coincidences. He didn't believe in them. Said they were one of the first signs of a pattern, or something like that. Kate yawned. He was right enough. Just look at the HOLMES database. They were forever trawling through that to look for precedents in cases of serious crime.

What had that other old lady's name been? Kate couldn't remember. And she wasn't going to task her brain with this right now when she'd been sent upstairs by her husband for a rest. His way of celebrating Valentine's Day had been to give Kate a break from making dinner. She'd sleep on it. Tomorrow she'd look up the old case file and see if Lorimer was right. About not believing in coincidences.

'It's so nearly the same MO,' Kate insisted. 'Look at it. Almost in the same street as Mary MacKintyre as well.'

DI Martin rolled her eyes. 'It's only an MO if there's any reason to believe the women were deliberately murdered,' she told Kate.

Aye but, Lorimer ... Kate had almost said the words aloud when she bit them back. There was a feeling of tension between the DI and the review Detective Super that she had sensed. Whenever she spoke Lorimer's name in front of Rhoda Martin it was like she was walking on eggshells.

'I just think it's too much of a coincidence, that's all,' Kate said mulishly. 'And the son is so sure about his mum's death, isn't he?' she continued.

'Okay, I'll have a look at the other death. See if there had been a mysterious cyclist following that old lady.' DI Martin's voice came out as a sneer and Kate stepped back, face red.

But at least the DI was taking it kind of seriously, Kate told herself, wasn't she? For two pins she would have walked into Lorimer's room and run it past him, but a sense of loyalty to her fellow officers stopped her. Handing him the odd cuppa was one thing but seeking out his opinion on an ongoing case that had nothing to do with him was surely not on. No, if there was really any link between the deaths of these old ladies, Kate Clark might well have to dig around to find it for herself.

Mary MacKintyre's death had taken place on the night of Boxing Day last year. Eighty-seven years old and not in the best of health, she'd fallen down her back steps and been killed instantly. There had been no reason whatsoever to suspect anything malicious about the death. But now, with another elderly woman falling to her death just two streets away, Kate was beginning to have doubts. The houses were almost identical, too. They'd been built in the seventies by a housing association that had won awards for good architectural design. Rows of nice split-level terraced houses overlooking woods on one side and the older council houses of Upper Port Glasgow on the other, they'd been popular with families wishing to rent. Now most of that housing stock had been bought up and only a few residents still paid their rent to the Housing Association.

Both of these two elderly ladies had been living there from the time the first houses had been let, probably much fitter then to cope with the steep steps down to their neat patches of garden.

And they had chosen to remain in a three-bedroom house after each of their families had left the nest. Kate's mouth gave a twist. Her own granny was in a great wee sheltered place down in Greenock where a warden looked in every day to see that her charges were okay. Mind you, she remembered her mum and dad having to do a lot of sweet talking to get her in there. But now she loved it. Perhaps these old ladies had been the same: reluctant to leave their homes.

DC Clark sat back, a sudden kick in her abdomen taking her breath away. A new wee life was in there, demanding her attention. But somehow she felt strongly drawn to the notion of death; those two old ladies who had perished just yards from their own back doors seemed suddenly more real to her than her unborn son. Lorimer had suggested a friendly drink. Maybe it was time to take him up on that. It couldn't do any harm to tell him what she was thinking once they were off duty, could it?

Sir Ian Jackson and Lady Pauline were two intriguing characters, Lorimer thought, tapping his foot absently against the side of the desk. He'd been a boy from the Port, she an upper class lassie from Kilmacolm – that much he knew through the station gossip. Wonder how they met? he asked himself softly. It was one of those mysteries that would probably never come to light. Not his business. But it was his business to make sense of how they had died and sometimes it paid dividends to find out how a victim had lived. Especially if their deaths had any whiff of violence or malice. Why would anyone torch that big house and leave its occupants to burn? Sir Ian had been the poor boy who'd done good, as the ungrammatical saying went. And it was apt, wasn't it? The man had lacked his wife's polish but had made up for it with his apparent skills in making money. Lots and lots of money. The beginnings of Jackson's career were a bit hazy and that was where he'd gained his reputation as a wheeler-dealer. But the man had no police record. Good at ducking and diving, some might say. But was that cynicism and *Schadenfreude* speaking? It was an unattractive Scottish trait of envious longing that sought to bring a successful and wealthy person down to disgrace *and serve them right anyway*. And sometimes it muddied the waters when a true opinion was sought about folk way up the social scale. Like now.

Maybe Sir Ian had been as pure as the driven snow. A good man who'd worked hard to achieve his millions. Multi-millions, a wee voice corrected Lorimer. But if that had been the case, who'd have wanted him dead? Years of experience had taught the Detective Superintendent that certain victims were never completely innocent when it came to a deliberate killing. There was always a something, as his old man had been fond of saying. And right now Lorimer was keen to find out what that something was. DI Martin might supply a little background knowledge, but then, if she really knew the family well, surely she would have made some sort of contribution before now? Okay, she'd been at that private school with the children, but 'moving in the same social circles' hadn't exactly rung true. Rhoda Martin had merely been trying to impress him that she'd come from a similar wealthy background, Lorimer told himself, that was all. Had she been a real friend of Serena and Daniel she would have had to put such information into a written report.

Like many men of vast wealth, Jackson had donated generously to charity, hence his knighthood. And that had certainly gained him respect. The few personal testimonials contained within the file were all warm in their praise of the man. But, Lorimer told himself with a bitter twist to his mouth, wasn't that the norm after someone had been killed? Nobody wanted to bad-mouth a victim. It was just too much like stepping across an unseen boundary between right and wrong, tempting a primeval sense of fate. No, to find out the truth about Ian Jackson, he'd have to ask those who had known him well and who weren't afraid to give a real portrait, warts and all. And who better than his own children?

The knock and the smile as Kate Clark waddled into his room made Lorimer lose the thread of his thoughts.

'Any chance of a wee dram after work?' she asked, head to one side as if she were pretending to flirt and wanted him to share the joke. But it was a harmless sort of flirtation, friend to friend, quite unlike the DI who had made a fool of herself in this very room.

'Aye, why not,' he answered. Then bit his lip as he remembered Maggie's mum in hospital. 'Might have to be a quick one, though,' he added. Kate Clark wouldn't have come in to ask that question, couched as it was in a light-hearted tone of voice, unless . . . Unless she had something on her mind that needed to be shared with him. In private. 'And I'm sure I can afford a double lemonade,' he teased, nodding at her bump.

'Och, see when this wee yin's here, I'll be ready for a double of anything so long as it's alcoholic!' Kate sighed, rolling her eyes theatrically. 'See you down in the Harbour lounge bar at five-ish, then?'

'Okay. Mind you both leave a seat for me, won't you?' Lorimer grinned, waved a hand in the direction of her abdomen and was rewarded by Kate sticking out her tongue at him. He might be the senior officer around here but they were old pals and it did his heart good to be reminded of that right now.

The Harbour was not the usual police howff since there was a bar dedicated to officers from K Division just on their doorstep. But perhaps Kate had wanted a bit more privacy, Lorimer told himself, carrying their drinks back from the bar; she might not want to be seen to be fraternising with the enemy. That's maybe how some of the others saw him, he thought grimly.

It was happy hour here and he had to push his way through a press of bodies to get back to the table where DC Clark was sitting. She'd chosen a corner by the open fire, a secluded spot in the noisy bar where they might talk in peace and not be overheard.

'So, when's the baby due?' Lorimer asked, putting down his half-pint.

'End of March,' Kate replied. 'Six weeks and five days if he's on time,' she grumbled. 'Hope it's earlier, though. I cannae be bothered with this much longer.'

The woman shifted, obviously uncomfortable even with a padded tapestry cushion between her and the wooden seat.

'Are you going to take some maternity leave early before he arrives?'

'No chance. I'm staying put right till the last minute. My blood pressure's fine. I've no reason to go home and rest and, besides, I want as much time off afterwards as I can manage.' Kate grinned. 'Slainte,' she added, raising the tumbler of lemonade to her lips.

Lorimer nodded in reply as he lifted his glass. He'd allowed himself a half-pint of lager. He was driving and, besides, he had to watch his time if he were to reach the Southern General for visiting hour. But after the first swallow, he wished he'd made it a pint. He could do with a good drink right now – like the punters milling around the bar, their cares forgotten for this interlude between work and home.

'Well, as nice as all this is, hadn't you better tell me what's on your mind? Other than the future of the Clark dynasty?' Lorimer asked.

'Ah, you sussed me out, then,' Kate joked. 'Aye, and you're right. There is something I wanted to talk to you about. And I think it involves the case we had yesterday.'

Lorimer listened as Kate took him through her thoughts about Mary MacIntyre, Jean Wilson and their two very similar deaths.

'You always said you didn't believe in coincidences and I've just got this horrible feeling . . .' She broke off, grinning. 'Woman's intuition. And don't give me any of that stuff about a preggie bird's hormones, eh?' she warned.

Lorimer smiled. It was refreshing to have a junior officer like Kate who apparently didn't give a toss about acknowledging his rank. Perhaps her pregnancy made the woman feel that there were more important things in her world than the hierarchy of the police. Whatever, it felt good to be sitting here listening to her theories.

'Intuition should never be discounted. A friend of mine says that it can point to the subconscious working things out logically after you've obtained all the disparate facts,' Lorimer told her. 'And if you have seen similarities in two deaths then of course there's justification for digging deeper. Though whether there's enough evidence to suggest the deaths are suspicious is a matter for the Procurator Fiscal to decide. But DI Martin's said she'll look into it,' he added.

'Aye.' Kate sighed as if she wasn't quite sure that Rhoda Martin was going to do as she'd promised. 'But . . .' she tailed off, looking into the middle distance. Lorimer could tell she was struggling with something else. A lack of trust in her colleague?

'See, if I was in charge of this,' Kate began again, 'I'd want to make inquiries about that cyclist. See if anyone had seen him around the area. How would we go about that?'

Lorimer raised his eyebrows. 'Well, if it were a category A we could use *Crimewatch*. But there's not enough evidence to suggest we have a serial killer after old ladies on our patch, is there?'

'So what do we do?' Kate asked, her eyes suddenly turned to his own, a challenge flaring in them.

Lorimer put down his glass again. '*We*? As in the investigation team? Or did you have something else in mind?'

Kate squirmed uncomfortably, a movement that Lorimer instinctively knew had nothing to do with her burgeoning shape. 'I thought . . . well, that is, I wondered. Och, hell's teeth, Lorimer can we no' just sniff around and see what comes up?'

'You have something in mind DC Clark?' Lorimer asked, his face deadpan.

For a moment the woman hesitated, the use of her rank and his expression giving her pause.

'Aye,' she replied at last. 'I have. How about putting feelers out among the local snouts? I've got a couple of lads in mind. One's a taxi driver. Ex-con but a reliable sort,' she told him.

There was a silence between them as Lorimer digested this; a silence that Kate Clark must have interpreted as his disapproval, for she sighed heavily.

'Should've realised it was a bit much to ask,' she muttered, beginning to gather up her coat and bag.

'Wait on a bit,' Lorimer said, raising a hand. 'I don't think you should give up that easily. DI Martin hasn't warned you off this case, has she?' And as Kate shook her head he added, 'Well, then. Go with your gut feeling. See this informant and you never know. He might come up with something. But you know I can't interfere in something like this.'

'Okay.' Kate gave him a half smile. 'But it doesn't feel like I'm doing very much.'

'And you really believe these two old dears were murdered?'

131

'Well, Jean Wilson's son certainly believes his mum was killed. And I have a feeling he's not going to let us sweep anything under the table.'

'I have to go,' Lorimer said, suddenly, looking at his watch. 'Hospital visit. But keep me in the loop with this one, will you?'

'Sure. And thanks for the lemonade,' Kate replied, grinning at him as they stood up and he helped her on with her coat.

As Lorimer drove along the M8, thoughts of Kate Clark kept coming back to him. She'd wanted to talk to him and he felt flattered by her confidence. But it disturbed him too that she couldn't put the same trust in a senior officer like Rhoda Martin. He was an outsider, only there to tidy up a particular case, not one of their own colleagues. And yet Kate had wanted his advice. He had to be careful. Feeling gratified about the woman's faith in him could obscure the more important matter of what had gone wrong within the team under Colin Ray's command.

Two old women were dead, though. What if it had been Maggie's mum? How would he have reacted? As ever, Lorimer tried to put himself in someone else's shoes. Maybe Gary Wilson had every right to protest that his old mother had been stalked and possibly murdered. Maybe, though, he was clutching at anything that would give him an answer to why it had to be *his* mum who'd died. Maybe he couldn't accept that accidents happened. Lorimer could see why DI Martin might not want to take this case any further. But Kate Clark's sharp mind had brought the other old lady's death into the equation now and Lorimer knew that he would be happy to encourage the DC, even at the risk of making himself even more unpopular.

CHAPTER 17

ON YER BIKE. The words above the picture of two cyclists racing downhill caught Lorimer's eye as he entered the hospital foyer. It was the same poster they had pinned up at the public entrance in Greenock HQ. But for some reason he stopped now and read it properly. The race in aid of a cancer charity was to take place in just a couple of weeks and he'd already been asked to sponsor one of their own officers. It was a typical Glaswegian phrase, he thought, grinning to himself; the sort of throwaway line a lassie would give an unwelcome suitor. But somehow its slightly aggressive tone worked in this context of encouraging folk to sign up for the cycle race or at least to sponsor a willing participant. Bikes had never been one of Lorimer's hobbies, though many of his fellow officers belonged to the police cycling club.

The light-hearted feeling that the poster had engendered disappeared the moment Lorimer set foot inside his mother-in-law's ward, Maggie's look of sheer gratitude at seeing him making him hurry to her side.

'How is she?' he asked, lowering his voice. Mrs Finlay was asleep, her head turned to one side of the pillow, mouth open and snoring quietly. For a long moment he simply gazed at the woman lying there. She'd become a real pal over the years, although she had been a formidable presence to the young man courting her precious daughter. And Mrs Finlay had given Lorimer plenty of well-intended advice concerning his future. He'd dropped out of university, a move that had not endeared him to his future mum-in-law. But his rapid rise within the police force had mellowed her attitude towards him and they'd developed a special bond. She was proud of her son-in-law and fiercely protective of any criticism that came his way, as it sometimes did in a high-profile case. And she'd been such a rock for them both during the sad trail of failed pregnancies. She'd never be Granny Finlay now, he thought, biting his lip as he watched the rise and fall of her breath.

'She was asleep when I arrived,' Maggie whispered. 'I wanted to wait till you were here to speak to the duty nurse. See how she's been today. If only I could see her during the day . . .' she added wistfully; but they both knew that with Maggie's full timetable at school that wasn't going to happen except at weekends.

Letting his wife leave her mother's bedside, Lorimer shifted closer to the old lady sleeping so peacefully in her hospital bed. Suddenly his thoughts turned to the visitor she'd had the other day, Joseph Alexander Flynn. He'd have to do something for the lad. He'd wanted Lorimer to act as a referee for a job he was applying for. How had that visit gone? he wondered. Flynn was a wee character, right enough. The thought of the youngster made him smile again. Mrs Finlay had taken him under her wing, her own brand of plain talking suiting the street kid. And they'd shared a similar sense of humour, Lorimer thought.

But this was silly, he scolded himself. Why was he thinking of the old lady in the past tense as if she was already lost to them? With a pang, the senior detective realised that this was exactly how it felt. Even if she survived this stroke and its aftermath, Lorimer knew he'd miss the woman she had been. Her usual bustling manner and cheery voice were gone and in their place was this old lady, a shrunken version of the person he'd grown so fond of since he'd first met her. Old age, decay and death: hadn't he seen them all in his line of work? And shouldn't he be inured to what was, after all, inevitable?

The bell sounded to signal the end of visiting just as Maggie appeared.

'She's still asleep?' her voice was raw with disappointment. For a moment Maggie seemed to hesitate, then she bent down to drop the gentlest of kisses on her mum's cheek and drew the cover nearer to her chin, a comforting gesture that a mother might make for her child, Lorimer realised, biting his lip.

He clasped his wife's hand as they left the ward, neither of them speaking for a moment as the crowds surged towards the bank of lifts.

'Let's walk,' he suggested, heading for the stairs.

Neither of them spoke as they left the hospital and it was only as the Lexus swung out of the main gate that Maggie looked at him. There were unshed tears in her eyes. Lorimer squeezed his wife's hand in a gesture of solidarity. He understood what she was feeling. Didn't he have the same hollowness inside? That fear of losing the person who was their only remaining parent.

Later, when he was certain that Maggie was asleep, Lorimer slipped out of bed and crept downstairs to the space that doubled as dining room and study. Despite the information they'd had from the medical staff, he wanted to know a bit more and so for almost an hour the detective trawled the Internet, scrolling down the various sites on the subject of strokes and stroke victims. As he hunched over the small screen of Maggie's laptop, Lorimer's mouth tightened. It all made pretty grim reading. And if he was correct in his assessment of his mother-in-law's condition, the future looked fairly bleak. If her heart were to survive this sudden onslaught, she'd be dependent on other people for the rest of her days. It would change everything for them.

A thought of Colin Ray's haggard face came to him then. He'd been through it with Grace, hadn't he? And it was something that so many of his older colleagues had had to endure. Though, if he was honest with himself, the care of a sick or elderly relative usually fell to the woman in a partnership. How would Maggie cope? Could she contemplate giving up her teaching job? Her career was more than just a job, though, he knew. Teaching English was something that defined Maggie Lorimer and to give it up before she'd even reached her fortieth birthday would be a huge blow. Was there some kind of sabbatical she might be able to take? Lorimer sat back suddenly, rubbing a hand across his eyes. What was he thinking of? Making even mental decisions like that for his wife was just not fair. Surely they could afford to hire a professional person of some sort to come in and look after the old lady if she was to be consigned to their care?

He imagined a stranger here in his own home tending to the stroke patient in a wheelchair. They'd need to make loads of changes. Install some sort of a stairlift for a start or add an extension to the downstairs loo. His eyes searched the familiar rooms of his home, seeking practical solutions to the potential problems that could lie ahead. The garden was large and rambling; no problem in adding another room on at the kitchen side and the plumbing was maybe easier there anyway. But how were they to cope with builders about the place at the same time as a sick old lady was living with them? And he couldn't take time off, not now when he'd been appointed as a review officer to this case in Greenock.

As the practical difficulties threatened to overwhelm him, Lorimer found his fingers tapping the relevant keys to close down the screen. Nobody had told them that Mrs Finlay was being discharged. Maybe she'd be in the Southern General for a good while yet, giving them time to prepare for her coming home to them.

A yawn caught him unawares, making his eyes water. He needed to sleep. Tomorrow was going to be another demanding day at work and he would simply have to put other thoughts on hold.

As he climbed the stairs, Lorimer paused to look out of the window on the landing. Down on his street some lights were still on. Were some of his neighbours awake, worrying and wondering about their own families? He was no different from any of them, was he? Life threw such things at you and you simply had to cope as best as you could.

Neither of them had spoken about Maggie's mum before they'd left for work. Instead the radio had filled the silence between them with the morning's news bulletin and the road report. Only Chancer had miaowed for his breakfast, a familiar yowl that had made them both smile. Animals and small children were immune from the problems of the grown-up world, demanding instead attention to the basics of life. As he'd passed the cat on his way out, Lorimer had bent to stroke the orange fur, experiencing a pang of gratitude as the animal purred loudly and rubbed himself on his trouser leg.

That small incident came to mind as he stood at the entrance of the flats he'd come to visit. A large white cat was regarding him from a downstairs window, a haughty expression in its green eyes. A prized breed no doubt, he thought, noting the fluffy coat and delicate ears. But he'd rather have their Chancer with his doubtful pedigree any day.

Serena Jackson lived not all that far from the burned-out house in Kilmacolm, just a few miles further west, on Greenock's esplanade. The flats were only a few years old, their raw newness contrasting with the neighbouring rows of fine dark-red sandstone tenements looking across the water. Given the choice, Lorimer would have opted for one of the older properties himself, but these gems rarely came on to the market. Each of these modern flats had a metal balcony facing west and he supposed it must be pleasant to stand up there on a summer's evening, catching the sun's last rays.

As he glanced behind him, taking in the sweep of the esplanade and the widening waters of the Clyde, another memory came back to him. Maggie's parents had been there with them as they'd stood at the railings all those years ago among crowds watching as the flotilla of tall ships had left the harbour, folk waving and cheering as each ship had sailed past them. Lorimer gave a sigh. Next year there would only be Maggie and himself coming back down here to see the Tall Ships, unless they were accompanying a frail old lady in a wheelchair. He blinked, then the image of those crowds and that summer evening was gone. All that he saw was an expanse of choppy water, the hills on the other side partially obscured by a low cloud.

Pressing the buzzer next to the name Jackson, Lorimer turned his thoughts to the young woman who had lost her parents in that blaze. She'd not be able to stand side by side with them watching as the ships left harbour next year, would she? He felt a wave of pity mingled with rage at whoever had committed this senseless act, his resolve to find that person hardening as he heard a female voice utter a quiet hello over the intercom.

'Detective Superintendent Lorimer,' he replied, shifting from one foot to the other as he uttered the words. He still wasn't used to this new title and somehow it didn't come easily from his lips.

In a matter of minutes Lorimer was standing by a grey-painted door, listening to the rattle of a security chain being drawn back. He frowned. Serena Jackson was expecting his visit, so what was this young woman afraid of? Or was she habitually cautious? Hugh Tannock had told him how hard the daughter had taken her parents' deaths. Was she a nervy type by nature, perhaps? His first impression of the woman dispelled that notion the moment he saw her.

Lorimer found himself staring into a pair of amber-coloured eyes belonging to a tall, slender female whose light blonde hair was swept into a ponytail. She had the sort of face that one might find on the pages of some glossy magazine, he thought, a perfect face: flawless, luminescent skin with high cheekbones and a wide mouth that was only lightly touched by something cosmetic. She was tall and carried herself like a model; there was no rounded back or slumping shoulders that might indicate an individual weighed down with the burdens of life.

'Miss Jackson?' he asked and she gave a slight nod in reply then stepped back, motioning that he should enter the flat. Lorimer muttered 'Thanks', as she closed the door, then followed Serena Jackson along a white hallway into a square room that should have looked on to the river. A quick glance showed that the linen blinds were closed, obscuring any sort of view, and he found himself oddly disappointed. Yet it didn't seem as if the young woman had been unprepared for his visit or had just rolled out of bed. A quick glance showed him that the girl was fully dressed in soft beige slacks and a cream knitted sweater belted at the waist with a heavy dark brown leather belt; expensive clothes whose very simplicity showed their quality.

The woman still had not uttered a word since his arrival and she stood regarding him silently, her face devoid of any expression that he could interpret. His first instinct was to wonder if the girl was still in shock, but then she waved a hand towards a honey-coloured sofa and walked out of the room again. Instead of taking the seat she'd offered, Lorimer followed her and found himself in a kitchen that looked as though it had been lifted straight out of a stand at the Modern Homes Exhibition, all chromes and dove greys with a plethora of gadgets parked at various electrical points upon gleaming worktops. It was immaculate and rather imper-sonal, he suddenly realised, like the room next door.

'Oh!' Serena Jackson spun round, her hand grasping a kettle jug as she heard Lorimer's footfall.

'Sorry.' He smiled. 'Didn't mean to startle you. May I?' And taking the kettle out of her unresisting hand, he stepped over to the sink and began to fill the kettle with water. A glance in her direction showed him what he had begun to suspect. Her mouth was half-open in surprise, but the vacant expression gave an indi-cation that it was not shyness that left the woman nothing to say but a mental vagueness. Again he recalled Tannock's words about the youngest Jackson and that he had given Lorimer the impres-sion that her part in the business seemed to have been more decorative than anything else.

'Tea or coffee?' The question came as a surprise as it dawned upon him that these were the first words he'd heard her speak since his arrival. And even her voice had a limpid quality, soft and clear but with a politeness that spoke of good breeding rather than a genuine wish to please this new visitor from Strathclyde Police.

'Coffee, please. Black, no sugar,' he added. Lorimer watched as Serena Jackson went about the business of preparing a cafetière of coffee, spooning three generous measures of Taylor's finest Arabica into the glass jug. He wasn't going to be treated to coffee from one of the gadgets, then, he thought. Perhaps a policeman was somewhere further down the pecking order in this wealthy young woman's life, he wondered, immediately ashamed of himself for such a thought. Wasn't she making the coffee herself? Yet it was an activity that seemed to wholly engross her to the point where she appeared to be ignoring him. It was a bit odd, though, this lack of small talk and the Detective Superintendent found himself becoming disconcerted by her silence. It was far more usual for someone to prattle on through sheer nervousness during a visit from a senior police officer. And for the moment he couldn't think of anything to say that would break the tension that he felt building up between them. *Has the cat got your tongue?* his mother-in-law was used to saying. Well, maybe just at this minute, he admitted and watched the graceful curve of the woman's back and the way she lifted the kettle jug, her wrist so slim and frail. Was she usually so thin? Or had she suffered physically after the loss of both her parents? It was hardly a question he could ask her right now, was it?

Once the coffee was made, Lorimer gave an encouraging smile and carried the tray back into the lounge. He laid it down on a glass-topped table and sat back, allowing the girl to pour coffee and hand it to him. He watched, fascinated as her long white hands gripped the handle of the coffee pot, the fingernails perfect ovals of pearly pink. Again he had the impression that he was seeing some otherworldly creature, not a flesh-and-blood woman whose parents had been left to die in that dreadful fire.

'Now, Miss Jackson, I'm afraid I will be asking you quite a lot of questions relating to the death of your parents,' he told her gently, leaning forward as if to ensure that she understood him. 'Do you think you can cope with that?'

'Yes,' she told him, meeting his blue gaze. 'I can cope, Superintendent.' She sat back, her expression both cool and impenetrable. Perhaps that deliberate silence had been a ploy calculated to compose herself or to control her emotions? Lorimer had seen so many different personalities in his professional life. But he had never come across anyone quite like Serena Jackson.

Now she was looking at him over the rim of her coffee cup and he could swear that there was a flicker of intelligence expressed in these topaz-coloured eyes.

'The family liaison officer has explained to you why I am taking over this case?'

Serena Jackson set her coffee cup down carefully then looked straight at him.

'It was an accident. That's what Daniel and I believe. We don't really see the need for you to come and talk to us all over again,' she told him, her mouth closing in a firm line as if there was no more to be said on the subject.

Lorimer cleared his throat and swallowed. This was going to be more difficult than he'd expected. But then, what had he expected? A woman ready and eager to discuss her parents' murder? No.

'There is some forensic evidence that suggests the fire was started deliberately, Miss Jackson. And we are now looking into the possibility that someone had broken into the house to use an accelerant. It wasn't just the chip pan, you see.'

'Acc . . .?'

'Some sort of fluid – like petrol – that would instantly combust when set alight. Whoever did that knew perfectly well that the blaze would begin in minutes and that anyone inside didn't stand a chance of escaping.' He heard his own words sounding brutal, but there was no easy way to explain the truth. Besides, she needed to understand why he was here.

'It wasn't an accident that someone spilled it, then?' She was looking down at her hands now, clasping and unclasping them in a gesture that he recognised as anxiety. If Serena Jackson and her brother had been convincing themselves that this had been a tragic accident, then what he was telling her was like opening a horrible wound that had only just begun to heal.

'I'm really sorry,' he said quietly. 'It seems not. That's why I have to ask you questions about your late father and mother.'

She looked up at him again then, as though she were unable to meet his eyes, she turned away with a sigh.

'We have to know from those who were closest to them if there was any reason for their deaths,' he continued, hoping that she was hearing what he said.

'My parents were very ordinary people, you know,' Serena began, her eyes fixed on something in the middle distance, making him wonder if she was reliving some memory of them. 'She played golf every other day, went to the local art class every week. The sort of thing that loads of Kilmacolm ladies do. None of her friends ever said anything bad about her, as far as I know.' She tailed off.

'And you father?' Lorimer's interjection was dropped quietly into the ensuing silence, encouraging her to continue.

'Just the same, I suppose. He worked at the office, took business trips, played golf. All the same stuff as everyone else's father did around here. Well, I mean, up there.' She made a face as she realised her mistake. 'I suppose I'm still not used to being away from home.'

'You moved here very recently then?'

'Yes. I got the keys the week before . . .' She tailed off again and this time Lorimer did not press her.

It struck him as a trifle odd, though. Serena Jackson was an independent young woman in her mid-twenties and yet had only just left the parental home. Perhaps that explained why everything here looked so new and shiny; things were only just out of their boxes and with the advent of her parents' deaths she would hardly have had the energy to personalise her own space. Taking a quick glance around confirmed his thoughts; there was not even a single photograph on display – nothing to remind her of her mum and dad, only such memories as she had locked up in her head.

Something told Lorimer that he was not going to get anything else useful from the girl. She seemed to have faded into another silence that left him feeling like an outsider. And yet he couldn't let himself leave it like that.

'Are you intending to return to work?' he asked.

The rise of one shoulder signalled what? Indifference? Uncertainty?

'You don't mind living here on your own?'

The eyes Serena turned upon him were at once large and vacant as if something had taken away her innermost spirit and Lorimer wondered if she were even taking in these simple questions.

'Do you miss them?' he asked softly, leaning forward so there could be no chance of her missing his words.

For a moment she didn't move, then he saw the slight nod of her head and the way she bit her lip as if to stop herself from weeping.

'Would you excuse me?' she asked and rose suddenly, crossing the room in a couple of strides and disappearing into the hall. He heard the hollow sound of a door closing and guessed she had gone to the bathroom rather than show any sign of grief in front of a stranger.

Lorimer looked around the room, trying to see anything that would give him more of a clue about this young woman and the sort of life she was now living, but there seemed to be no personal things at all, not even a magazine in the metal rack beside the coffee table. But he did recognise something there. The turquoise cover of a square-shaped folder caught his attention. He bent down and picked it up, reading the familiar words on the front cover: *Information for Bereaved Families and Friends Following Murder or Culpable Homicide.* So, she had already been given this by Family Liaison. Why, then, was she insisting that it was an accident? A refusal to acknowledge something more dreadful, he supposed. He'd come across denial like that before, he thought, flicking open the folder until he came to the section headed *Important Contacts.* There, against the box for the name of the SIO was the name Detective Chief Inspector Colin Ray. But it had been scored out with a single line and beneath it a different hand had written Mr William Lorimer. There was no change in the postal address or telephone number of the HQ at Greenock, though. Lorimer frowned for a moment. He was not being dignified by any title other than plain Mister. Then he shrugged. Maybe there simply wasn't enough space under the original name.

Hearing the sound of a toilet being flushed, Lorimer put the folder back where he had found it and stood up ready to take his leave.

Serena Jackson didn't seem surprised to see him standing waiting for her.

'Thanks for seeing me this morning. And for the coffee,' he added.

She gave a sight nod and headed for the front door at the far end of the hall, opening it wide as if to ensure that he really was leaving. Then, before he could say goodbye, she caught his sleeve, making him turn to face her.

'Do you like being a policeman?' she asked, her tawny eyes wide, like that of a curious child.

'Not always,' he replied. 'But it's a good job most of the time.' Then, as she let go of his coat sleeve, he smiled at her. 'Take care,' he told her, nodding as she stepped back into the sanctuary of her new home. Then the door closed and he heard again that rattle of metal against wood as she secured the safety chain.

Once out in the open air, Lorimer drew a deep breath. That had been less than pleasant, but then what had he expected? Hopefully his visit to the older brother would produce a bit more in the way of information. All that he had found here was that the Jacksons' daughter was a strange creature, one that, for all his experience, he simply couldn't fathom. For a moment he felt a certain pity for the girl; she seemed incomplete despite her unde-niable beauty. But wasn't there something odd about such perfection? Then Lorimer caught himself wondering what she would look like if she had given him a smile. And for a moment he wished that she had.

'I wish you'd told me you wanted to see Serena, Superintendent. I'd have made the effort to be there with her,' Daniel Jackson told him.

They were sitting in an airy room overlooking one of the city's dear green places in a quiet corner of the West End. It was only a mile or so from the comprehensive school where Maggie taught but it might have been in a completely different world. That was one thing his friend Solly Brightman was fond of telling him: how Glasgow was full of contrasts, those who had and those who had not rubbing shoulders with apparent ease.

Daniel Jackson's home was one of the most gracious houses that Lorimer had ever visited, though he had been inside all sorts of Glasgow properties during his career. On either side of the bay windows were twin pillars made of tawny marble, half hidden by thin, gauzy draperies drawn beside them. The high ceilings still had all of their original cornicing, a feature that someone had picked out in a pale shade of gold in the elegant sitting room. Some nineteenth-century merchant with pots of money at his disposal, Lorimer thought as he took in the pleasing proportions of this room. And now another wealthy young man had taken over the care of the house, lavishing his own attention upon it. It was the sort of period home that would have been ruined by anyone trying to impose a modern style upon it and the policeman's artistic sensibilities were gratified by seeing that so many of the furnishings were in keeping with the age of the house. No doubt Daniel Jackson would have the same up-to-date quality of kitchen as his sister had in her new-build flat by the river, but here, in this sitting room, there was every sign that the owner was in sympathy with his surroundings. Though right at this moment he seemed distinctly out if sympathy with the tall policeman sitting opposite.

'It's only usual to have a family member present when interviewing a minor,' Lorimer told him, meeting the young man's gaze. Daniel Jackson gave a sigh and turned away as if to gather his thoughts. Then he looked back at Lorimer, his brown eyes soft with a sadness that made the policeman immediately warm to the man.

'I'm a bit protective of my little sister, Superintendent. She's

147

not like other young women you may have met. Don't get me wrong,' he waved his hand as though to banish any wrongheaded ideas, 'she's perfectly capable of looking after herself and all that. It's just . . .' He tailed off, as though seeking the correct words. 'Serena's always needed a bit more care than me. She had a hard time at school till they found she was dyslexic. And by that time she'd missed such a lot. Anyway, she's been really badly affected by all of this and one can only admire her for staying put in her own place.'

'What was her alternative?' Lorimer asked. After all, hadn't the family home been practically razed to the ground?

'Well, moving in with me, of course. It's plenty big enough for both of us. In fact, I keep one of the bedrooms just for Serena.'

'Ah, yes. Kind of you,' Lorimer said, thinking immediately what a trite remark that was. Daniel Jackson looked like a kind man, his handsome face full of concern as he uttered his sister's name. 'You're close, then?'

'Oh, yes. We do lots of things together. Always have. Skiing, cycling, sailing: you name it, Serena and I tend to spend a lot of our leisure time with one another.'

'And your parents? Did you spend a lot of time with them?'

For a split second Lorimer could have sworn that an expression of anger passed over the man's face but it was gone as suddenly as it had appeared.

'No. Mum and Dad were keen golfers and it wasn't a game that either of us aspired to, I'm afraid,' he replied, swinging one leg across the other. 'Dad and I saw one another at work, of course. And Serena always had Mum to see that things were okay for her at home. But we weren't a family that did a lot of stuff together as adults,' he smiled then, as if he really didn't mind sharing this little bit of his private life with this policeman.

Lorimer nodded as if accepting the man's words. 'But you all got along together amicably?'

'Oh, yes. Oh, never any question about that!' Daniel's eyebrows shot up as if slightly shocked by the very idea. 'We were a very ordinary sort of family,' he added, unconsciously echoing the sentiments expressed earlier by his sister. For a moment Lorimer wanted to lean forward and tell him earnestly that ordinary people weren't multi-millionaires burned to death deliberately in their own homes, but he remained sitting still in the comfortable wing chair, pondering the statement instead.

'Your position in the firm, sir. You are head of Human Resources, is that right?'

'*Director* of Human Resources,' Daniel Jackson's polite voice corrected him.

'Yes, of course. Sorry. But weren't you due to be promoted into a more senior role?' Lorimer gave a frown as though he was uncertain of some information he had been given. It was a ploy he used when needed; playing the thick copper sometimes paid off.

Daniel Jackson's sharp intake of breath and a tightening of his features was enough to make Lorimer see that he'd hit gold. It was just as Tannock had said; the young man had been passed over by his own father for promotion. But was that enough motivation to destroy his parents and family home by fire?

'I think you've been misinformed. Though perhaps things will be a little different now. After all,' he smiled that handsome, disarming smile, 'I'm really needed far more these days in a senior managerial capacity.'

Lorimer nodded, resisting the urge to tug an imaginary forelock. Yet, although Jackson exuded the sort of social polish that defined his class, he was also possessed of a natural charm that the detective found engaging. Still, he mustn't be deflected from his purpose: he had to dig under the social veneer presented by this man, however painful that might be.

'I must ask you the same question that I asked Miss Jackson, sir. Can you think of any reason why someone would have wanted either of your parents dead?'

Daniel Jackson blinked as though Lorimer had indeed reached across and invaded his space. His tiny shake of the head seemed to indicate that it was not a question he had been expecting.

'There appears to be some recent forensic evidence that suggests a person had broken into your parents' home to deliberately set fire to it during the night.'

Lorimer watched the effect of his words on the young man, seeing the parted lips and eyes widening in horror.

'But who . . .?' he asked at last, in a whisper.

'That's what I wanted you to tell me, sir. Who might have had reason to wish either your father or your mother, or indeed both of them, to die?'

Daniel Jackson had uncrossed his legs and was now sitting stiffly, his arms around his body as though to control a sudden fit of shivering.

'I really don't know. Dad . . . there were people in his past . . . I don't know much about it, but . . .' He bit his lip then let a huge sigh escape from his throat. 'My father was a good man, Superintendent. A well-respected man. But, like every human being on the planet, he'd made mistakes. Some of these were matters of misjudgement.'

Lorimer listened as Daniel Jackson spoke clearly and slowly as if weighing every word. He was being careful now, eyeing the policeman with a new wariness in his manner. Lorimer nodded encouragingly as if expecting more.

150

'There were men who occasionally cropped up from these days. You could always tell.' He shrugged.

'I'm afraid you have the advantage over me there, Mr Jackson. You'll have to describe them for me,' Lorimer told him, trying to keep any trace of sarcasm from his tone.

'Oh, yes, of course.' Daniel frowned, looking vague for a moment as though he had lost his own train of thought. Suddenly Lorimer could see a resemblance between this man and his sister. How would he describe it if he were being cynical; the ability to dissemble, perhaps?

'They were always from overseas. South American, I think. Tannock might be able to tell you more about them. Dad never let me join in any of their discussions but I do remember one thing.' He looked up, his face alight with the sudden memory. 'Dad was always in a real temper for days after any of these visits.'

'And when was the last time any of these visits took place?'

'Oh,' Daniel took a deep breath then exhaled, 'that's a hard one. Not in the last year to my knowledge.'

Lorimer turned in his chair so that he was facing into the room. He pointed to a glass-fronted cabinet full of lead soldiers, the sort of collectable items that might have been handed down from an older family member. But it was not what was within the cabinet that interested him but the silver-framed photographs on top.

'That's your parents?'

Daniel nodded then half-rose from his chair. 'Would you like to see them? Let me bring them over to the light.'

'Yes. Thank you,' Lorimer said. He watched as the man picked up the photographs delicately as though he were handling precious objects and brought them over, placing them on top of a small, polished rosewood table near the window.

'There,' he said, setting them down and turning the pictures so

151

that the silver frames glinted in the sunlight. A smile played around Daniel's lips as he looked at his late mother and father, and Lorimer could only imagine what emotion was going through his mind.

The photographs were seated portraits, each subject on their own but against a similar background that appeared to be a reception hallway of some sort. Lorimer could make out doors behind the posed figures. The Jacksons were dressed in elegant day-clothes as if preparing to go to a function: Sir Ian in his kilt and his wife wearing a formal suit that looked like silk. Lady Jackson was smiling into the camera lens, lips slightly parted as if she had just uttered something amusing. Lorimer saw a pretty, blonde woman of around fifty with hair styled into a sleek bob, and guessed that the photo must have been taken shortly before her death. The detective felt he would have liked this woman with her infectious smile, so like her son's, he realised.

Sir Ian's presence dominated his portrait. There was no other word for it. His whole body seemed to fill the frame. He'd been a big man, in more senses than one, thought Lorimer, seeing the large hands grasping the sides of the ornate chair, the muscular legs under the hem of the kilt, feet planted firmly together. Jackson had the look of a man who was only there on sufferance and was preparing to get up and go at any moment. But there was a direct quality in the eyes staring into the camera lens that Lorimer found fascinating. Here was a man of some considerable strength, the sort that would call a spade a spade and not mess about with any niceties. This wasn't a man who would allow himself to be intimidated, the Superintendent was sure. Lorimer thought of the moodiness Daniel had mentioned, following these visits from South Americans. Ian Jackson's reputation had been as a man who'd followed his own path fairly ruthlessly, but whose public generosity in recent years had become its own legend.

'Were these taken in your old home?' he asked.

'Yes. Mum and Dad were just off to a wedding and one of the cousins took it, I think. It was on the upstairs landing, just outside their rooms. That's their bedroom to the left of the pictures.'

Lorimer nodded, seeing the dark varnished wooden door, its brass doorknob above a keyhole, the key protruding from the lock. A vision of flames licking at the edges of the solid door came to him then, and of two people overcome by smoke inhalation, unable to rise from their bed. At least that was the conclusion he'd read in one of the forensic reports.

'Your sister didn't appear to have any photographs that I could see,' Lorimer remarked, recalling the stark emptiness of Serena Jackson's new flat, so at odds with her brother's comfortable home.

'No,' Daniel told him. 'All of Serena's personal things were at home. Destroyed by the fire; sports trophies . . . everything. It wasn't just her parents she lost, you know. It was her home, too, until very recently. And now all of her childhood memories have gone as well. Can you begin to imagine what that does to a person like Serena?' Daniel was still standing, looking down now at Lorimer, shaking his head as if bewildered that the policeman should lack an understanding of what had happened to his sister. 'Perhaps you can see now why I'm not so happy that she had to see you on her own this morning.'

'You would have preferred if I'd had her friend DI Martin with me, perhaps?'

Daniel Jackson frowned. 'Who? Sorry, should I know that name?'

Lorimer shrugged. 'It doesn't matter.' But that throwaway remark was interesting. Perhaps Rhoda Martin wasn't quite as close to this family as she would have him believe.

'We do offer counselling, though. In fact, I'm sure the family liaison officer will have brought that subject up with your sister,' he continued smoothly.

Daniel Jackson shook his head. 'It's probably exactly what she needed then and still needs now, but d'you know what, Superintendent? These are the only people who might have persuaded her to go down that route.' He tapped the silver-framed photograph. 'And they're not here to take charge of anything in her life any more.'

He had stayed for more than half an hour after that, seeking gently to prise more information about the Jackson parents from a son who had so obviously cared about them. But despite listening to childhood reminiscences and the success of Jackson Tannock, Lorimer found out little more than the dark hints he'd been given about the men from Ian Jackson's past. If the daughter was stricken with grief and still suffering from shock, then her brother had dealt with his loss in a more controlled and pragmatic way but, oddly enough, Daniel had been the one to display more emotion.

Lady Jackson had not excited anyone's imagination regarding the fire, he thought. Her high-profile husband was the more likely target of any vicious attack. Yet, why should she be so discounted? After all, crimes had been committed for reasons of passion and she had been a highly attractive woman. Lorimer shook his head. Not a single part of Colin Ray's investigation had focused on the background of the woman other than as the corporate wife. And in Lorimer's book making such basic assumptions was always a mistake.

CHAPTER 18

Lorimer was just about to turn the car from the cobbled lane into the yard when he braked hard to stop for a cyclist emerging from the police car park. It was a woman, but she wasn't wearing the familiar sulphur-yellow protective waterproofs that all officers wore on cycle duty. Instead she sported a tightly fitting red jacket over black cycle leggings. He looked up for a second as she passed him, then looked again just to be certain. Yes, right enough, it was DI Rhoda Martin pedalling away from the building. A quick glance at his digital clock showed it was in fact lunchtime and he wondered whether the DI was off on some personal business.

'That's DI Martin?' Lorimer smiled at the duty officer as he passed through the public office.

'Aye, she's off for a wee run. Has to get in practice for the race, y'know,' the burly sergeant replied, indicating the 'On Yer Bike' poster on the wall.

'Ah.' Lorimer nodded, understanding suddenly. 'Are there many officers from this division taking part?'

'Aye, a few: the ones that are usually out on duty on their bikes and some from the local cycle club. DI Martin's a member there.'

Lorimer digested this information as he mounted the stairs that would take him to his temporary office. Perhaps he should mention this to Kate Clark, if she was still keen to hunt up the cyclist that had been stalking that old lady.

As if his thought had taken substance, DC Clark emerged from her room at the very moment Lorimer turned the stairs.

'Kate, a wee word,' he said, motioning for the woman to follow him into his room.

He switched on the light against the sudden squall that had darkened this side of the building, which overlooked the river. 'Sit yourself down. Now, I just saw DI Martin riding her bike. Did you know she was a cyclist?' Lorimer began.

'Well, yes. In fact I thought she'd be able to nose around a bit if we took the stalker thing seriously. But maybe we won't have to!' There was a triumphant gleam in the DC's eye as she settled her bulk more comfortably into the chair next to Lorimer's desk.

'See, I've a nice little association with this taxi driver who keeps tabs on things for me. And I asked him to put the word out about the cyclist in case anyone had seen him following the old lady.'

'And?' Lorimer could feel a palpable excitement emanating from the woman.

'And he told me something very interesting.' Kate grinned, obviously relishing her tale.

'Aye, come on, then.'

'Well,' she leaned forward conspiratorially, 'I was just coming to let you know this minute as it happens.' She edged her chair towards him. 'The night of the Jacksons' fire one of the local taxi drivers was taking a fare back to Kilmacolm when they nearly collided with a cyclist fleeing down Port Glasgow Road. *As if all the bats of hell were after him*, was what he said, apparently. And guess what?'

156

Lorimer smiled, infected by her enthusiasm.

'The cyclist looked as if he'd just come out of the drive at the foot of the Jacksons' house.'

Lorimer's smile faded. 'Time?'

Kate nodded. 'Just a wee while before the alarm went up.'

'So this cyclist . . .?'

'Could have been leaving the scene of the crime!' Kate finished for him, her eyes shining.

Lorimer shook his head slowly, not in disbelief but at the way this had come to light. It wouldn't be his first experience of finding a piece of evidence during the investigation of a different case in the same district. It happened all the time. That was one of the advantages of having a good relationship with local informants.

'Don't suppose there was a decent description of the cyclist?'

'No chance. It was too dark to see much. The taxi driver was just glad he hadn't hit the guy.'

'And the passenger?'

'A local businessman. Here's his name and address. He has an account with the taxi firm.'

'Mike Reynolds,' Lorimer read, once Kate had passed him the piece of paper she'd been carrying.

'Want to follow this up? See if he can remember anything about the cyclist? It's a long shot, mind you,' Lorimer told her. 'The address is Kilmacolm, Lochwinnoch Road; think I might have driven along there one time,' he mused. Lochwinnoch was home to one of the RSPB's reserved and Lorimer and Maggie had been out there several times on field trips. 'Do you know it?' he asked.

'Well, sort of. It's one of the roads with these huge big houses. Like a lot of the village up there.' She grinned. 'They do say it's the place with the most expensive real estate in the whole of Scotland.'

It was a nice change to be out of the office, Kate thought, humming to herself as she drove into the village of Kilmacolm. The road wound up from Port Glasgow, twisting and turning before easing out over an expanse of moorland on either side. Few houses could be seen along this desolate part of the countryside and Kate shivered at the low clouds on the horizon threatening snow, then gave another shudder as she passed the dark gap on her left just before the cemetery gates. She'd seen enough of the scene of crime photographs to imagine what it must have looked like in the aftermath of that fire and was thankful that it was not within her remit to go up the shadowy drive.

Lochwinnoch Road led Kate through the heart of the village, past rows of shops and over an ancient railway bridge. She had telephoned the Reynolds house, not expecting any reply, and had been surprised to find from his wife that Mr Reynolds would be at home during the afternoon. Yes, she could come up and speak to him, the woman reassured her.

Later Kate would report back that she had little to tell. But she had stayed long enough to enjoy a good cup of coffee and some homemade lemon drizzle cake that Mrs Reynolds served on pretty Emma Bridgewater plates. Mike Reynolds had been nice, she thought. Frowning hard as if to remember as much as he could, but all he'd said was that he had the impression the cycle had been a silver colour and that the rider had worn black. And maybe a hood. Looked like he was out on a training run, speeding along, bent low over the handlebars. Weird, though, at that time of night, wasn't it? No lights, he'd added, his brow deeply furrowed. Strange, that, don't you think? Yes, and Kate put it in her report. Cycling without lights on and not wearing the usual fluorescent gear. It was indeed strange. But not if the cyclist had been deliberately trying to conceal his presence at that particular time and in that particular place.

The budgetary constraints on Strathclyde police, like every other public body in the country, were such that acting Detective Superintendent Lorimer could no longer justify asking his old friend, Dr Solomon Brightman, to step into a case in an advisory capacity. It would take a series of high-profile murders before that was going to happen. Besides, the role of the psychologist in cases of serious crime was beginning to lose its appeal since what was perceived as a major blunder by a criminal psychologist south of the Border had led to the conviction of an innocent man. Solly had always been ready with his words of wisdom, sometimes taking a while to prepare a profile, but in previous cases it had been well worth an investigating team listening to what he'd had to say. But lack of resources to engage Solly's services didn't stop Lorimer from consulting him as a friend.

It was an interesting scenario for the man from Glasgow University. What made a stalker of old ladies tick? And one that followed them on his bicycle, if that were indeed the case. After visiting his mother-in-law that evening, Lorimer and Maggie were meeting up with Solly and Rosie in one of their favourite West End eateries, the legendary Shish Mahal. It was Friday and Rosie wasn't officially on call, though a major emergency could drag the pathologist away from her evening out with friends. Perhaps that was why Lorimer had always felt a certain kinship with Rosie; they both understood what it was like to drop everything whenever work demanded it.

So there was an extra spring to his step when Lorimer finally left the Greenock headquarters and headed for his ancient Lexus.

The big car seemed restless and impatient as one set of traffic lights after another made it stop and start, but at last the long stretch of dual carriageway alongside the River Clyde came into view and Lorimer swung into the outside lane, accelerating with a sense of relief. Work was behind him for another day. The chaos left by Colin Ray's sudden departure was gradually coming under control and each aspect of the case was being dealt with. His final report could make the former SIO look like a total incompetent but Lorimer knew he would temper it with a lot of sympathetic detail about Grace's demise. For now it was not only his responsibility to sort out what had gone wrong with this case but to try his level best to make new progress. And he felt that he was beginning to do just that.

The Shish Mahal restaurant in Park Road was always full on a Friday night and so booking a table had been essential. Maggie smiled as a waiter took her coat and led them to their table.

'I still think of this as the new place,' she confided as they sat down opposite one another. 'How long has it been here now?'

Her husband shrugged, his mind clearly on other things. He'd not spoken about work today either before the hospital visit or on their way across town, but that didn't mean that his thoughts weren't occupied by what was going on down in Greenock.

Maggie looked around, admiring the décor. Muted beige blinds were rolled down to head-height on the huge expanse of windows to keep out the darkness; the remaining glass was scattered with lozenges of circles and stars. Above them a giant seven-legged brass disc was suspended from the ceiling. Maggie smiled. The chandelier always reminded her of a strange spaceship, something that might have escaped from the *War of the Worlds*.

In the old days the Shish had been around the corner in Gibson

Street, a haven for students like themselves. Now the building that had housed the former restaurant was demolished and only Maggie's memories of these times remained. Her reverie was disturbed by Rosie bouncing in beside her, one arm flung around her neck and a kiss firmly planted on her cheek.

'Hi, you two. Sorry we're late. Met up with a neighbour and his dog as we came over the park. Typical! We live a stone's throw from the Shish and you're here before us!' Rosie leaned across the table and blew a kiss in Lorimer's direction. 'How goes it? No, don't tell me or we'll be talking shop all night. Anyway, we've got some great news!'

Maggie looked from her friend's shining face to the bearded man sitting beside her husband. Solly Brightman seemed both shy and embarrassed at once.

'You're not . . .?'

'Preggers? No chance!' Rosie laughed, showing twin dimples in her fair cheeks. 'No, my clever man here's got himself a fabulous book deal!'

'Well! Congratulations, Solly. Think this may call for champagne. How about it?' Maggie suggested.

Lorimer nodded his agreement and smiled at his companion. Solly had written several books on the subject of behavioural psychology and Lorimer was curious to know why Rosie was making a fuss about another one. 'Something special?' he asked.

'Well,' Solly began, pausing as though the three pairs of eyes upon him were rendering him speechless. Then he grinned, his expression one of boyish glee. 'It's about female serial killers, actually. And a London publisher has offered me rather an attractive advance.'

'Seems the public can't get enough of real-life crime and Solly's been doing work on this area for ages now,' Rosie enthused.

161

'I wouldn't have thought that there were all that many women who committed crimes like that,' Maggie began. 'It's not something you hear about, is it? I mean, there are the women who are in thrall to men who are multiple killers, but I can't think of any single woman who has been on a killing spree.'

'Perhaps that's why the publisher found it so appealing,' Lorimer countered. 'What we don't know is going to become all that more interesting once we read about it. Though I suspect Solly's case studies won't be confined to the UK. Right?'

Solly nodded. 'There are a few cases in the US that will come into the book. But it isn't all contemporary crime. I do use some models from the previous two centuries.'

'But be warned,' Rosie told them, pretending to be stern, 'every unsolved case you have from now on is potentially by a female warrior!'

Maggie laughed with the rest of them, knowing that the pathologist's words were only half-true. Solly might be pretty focussed on this topic right now but in every case where he had collaborated with the police, her husband had respected his judgement concerning a possible profile.

'Have you included Aileen Wuornos in your study?' Lorimer asked and immediately the conversation turned to a TV programme that they had seen on the subject of the American serial killer.

Maggie listened for a little, nodding as they spoke. Solly's book, she realised, would make good reading.

A pretty Polish waitress glided up to their table, asking for drinks orders, and Maggie let her eyes wander across the room to where other diners were already busy over their plates of food. A dark-suited actor whose name she couldn't recall was regaling his young female companion with a story that involved a lot of hand waving and facial grimaces. Maggie took a surreptitious look at the girl to see how she was responding but saw only a fixed, polite smile on her face. Every table was full. A quick glance towards the door let her see a foursome of hopefuls enter only to be told with dignified courtesy that there would be no place for them that evening. The disappointment on their faces told its own story.

Then a smiling waiter was at her side, blocking any further chance she might have of people-watching, and Maggie joined the others in ordering their favourite dishes. To her relief, Solly's book was still being discussed and nobody seemed to mind that she did not contribute to the conversation. It was enough for Maggie that nobody had asked the all-encompassing question of her mother's welfare: for once she wanted to forget the daily visit and the problems that might lie ahead. As if something of this thought had been uttered aloud, Solly caught Maggie's eye and for a long moment he smiled at her. There was more than sympathy in the psychologist's expression: it was as if he could read her very thoughts, see into the depths of her soul. Instead of being disturbed by this sudden insight, Maggie Lorimer found it oddly comforting and she reached across the table, giving Solly a light pat on the back of his hand.

The rest of the evening passed pleasantly enough and only towards the end of the meal did Lorimer mention the subject that had been concerning him.

'A stalking cyclist?' Solly murmured. 'That sounds a little bit complicated. I don't think I've come across an example of that, but do let me check up, will you? The old ladies sound as though they have little else in common, however. One very frail and practically housebound, the other out and about on a daily basis.' He smiled his slow smile at the tall policeman sitting next to him. 'If their deaths hadn't been so similar nobody would have bothered, would they? But,' he added with a twinkle, 'you don't believe in coincidences, do you?'

It was a frosty night, the air clear and sharp, promising a day of bright skies to come. Every star and planet that had fizzled into the Universe seemed to be demanding attention – especially the moon, its one baleful eye bearing down on me. The ticking sound of the bicycle pedals ceased as soon as I stopped walking and I held my breath, waiting for the right moment to continue my preliminary study of the street. It was several blocks away from the ones that I already knew but this particular row of homes looked promising.

The back of the houses faced a sloping hillside that had once been divided into allotments but was now overgrown with winter grass and banks of bramble bushes. A path ran all the way along, behind the high fences, leading away from the estate and petering out at the entrance to an electricity substation. The edges on each side were littered with empty bottles and polystyrene containers, the detritus from the take-aways a short walk across the fields. I thought about the people who had been there, smoking dope perhaps, seeking a bit of seclusion away from prying eyes. There was a track of sorts trodden into the winter earth, showing a short cut from the houses to the back of the local shops.

As I looked across the darkened patch of grass I realised that it could provide me with an escape route.

All I needed now was another victim.

CHAPTER 19

There was no pain. And she supposed that she ought to feel grateful for that. But it was hard to reconcile herself to the absence of any feeling down one whole side of her body. Today the physiotherapist was coming to take her out of bed. To try to make her walk again, she'd told her cheerfully.

'We'll have you up and about in no time at all, Mrs Finlay,' the girl had said. Alice had attempted a lopsided smile, glad that someone was addressing her by her full title and not in that patronising tone she'd come to hate when they called her *Alice dear.* Oh, dear God, she thought, eyes welling with sudden tears. What was she thinking? Shouldn't she be grateful for what kindness they were showing her instead of worrying about wee things like that? But this ward was so full of old geriatric women, so different from any of her own lady friends back at the Seniors club. A sudden rush of self pity filled her and Alice gripped the bedclothes in both fists, momentarily overwhelmed by feelings of fear and loneliness.

So now it was all a question of waiting. Alice Finlay was becoming quite good at waiting. Waiting for a bedpan to arrive when she thought that her bladder would burst and flood the sheets beneath her; waiting for the doctor on his rounds; and waiting for visiting time to see Maggie's face again. Oh, such heaven to see Maggie! Though once, when she'd been asleep, the bell for visiting had rung and she'd only had a few minutes with her precious daughter. Haltingly, she'd made Maggie promise to wake her up if such a thing ever happened again. After that visit she'd wept tears of frustration and disappointment into her pillow.

Alice Finlay looked up at the ceiling, noting the patches of flaking paint and a dull grey corner that might have been spiders' webs. It wasn't much to look at. But the alternative was to ask to be heaved up on a bank of pillows and then risk being engaged in conversation with one of the other patients. And that was something Alice dreaded. One old dear, her white hair fluffed round a thin, slack-jowled face, had stared at her for a long minute yesterday before shuffling up the ward to wherever she was going: the day room, perhaps? Alice had been slightly unnerved by the woman. She'd seemed to look at her with a vacancy in her expression that made Alice shiver. It was as if a dead person had been looking out of those pale blue eyes.

She closed her own eyes and began to drift away in her mind, conjuring up memories. There was something Maggie had always been fond of quoting from Wordsworth's 'Daffodils'; something about being on a bed and using your imagination to remember times past. That was what she would do now. Maybe her body was beginning to let her down, but there was nothing wrong with her mind.

She conjured up the cold spring day long ago when Mother had taken her to Pettigrew and Stephens. That was the preferred department store for ladies who had wanted quality in those days and little Alice had trotted along by her mother's side as they'd made their way up Glasgow's Sauchiehall Street. They may have taken a tram, but that was one memory that eluded her for the moment. She could remember the rumble of trams on their shiny metal rails. And hadn't they all had fun a few years back at the Glasgow Garden Festival? Alice yawned, suddenly aware of the frozen side of her face. Not the Garden Festival. Think about Pettigrew's. Why had they gone there? Alice squeezed her eyes tight as if that would bring back the images she sought.

It must have been for some treat, surely. Why else had she been taken to Pettigrew's? A sudden memory came back to her. She could see a little green boat with the Owl and the Pussycat painted near the bow. *The Owl and the Pussycat went to sea in a beautiful pea-green boat.* Had she been inside it? She thought so, remembering the sensation of motion, rocking back and forward, back and forward. Had there been other children? That was something she couldn't visualise. But Mother had been there and Alice could see her now, wearing her brown full-skirted coat with the fur collar that made her look so glamorous. And the hat: a small felt hat with feathers on the side, blue and bronze feathers from some exotic bird that Alice had never seen. She rocked in the little wooden boat, feeling her soft ringlets brush against her cheeks.

Alice froze. Her hair! She'd gone there to have her lovely hair cut off! Suddenly a feeling of panic arose in the old woman's chest as the memory became more vivid. The play toys in that small ante room had been no more than a ruse to lull her into a false sense of security and once she had known what lay beyond the frosted glass doors, Alice had felt the same stomach churning sensation that had seized her whenever she'd been taken to the dentist's.

One hand crept up to her head and Alice Finlay felt the wisps

167

of hair and the skull beneath. She was an old woman now, sick in this hospital bed. Her four-year-old self vanished into the distant past, gone forever.

'Mrs Finlay?' A voice made Alice open her eyes. A young woman in a white tunic stood by her bedside, a kindly smile on her face. 'It's Hazel, your physiotherapist,' the girl told her, smoothing her pillow gently. 'I'm going to see if you can get out of bed this morning. Make a wee bit of progress, eh?' The smile reached the girl's eyes and Alice felt her own face respond. The girl seemed a friendly sort, not intimidating like the doctors could be. She was dressed quite casually as well, a short-sleeved tunic over navy slacks and big trainers. Hazel had a soft voice, not a Glasgow accent, more as if she were from one of the Gaelic-speaking islands, like that nice young man who worked in the police with her son-in-law.

'Do-do-do . . .' Alice wanted to ask her if she came from Stornoway, but the words stuck at the front of her mouth and she closed her lips in a thin line, terrified at the sound. It was like hearing some imbecile. Oh, God! What if she was like that other old woman? The one with the weak, staring eyes.

'Shush, now. No trying to talk. The speech therapist will give me what for if I let you make even a peep!' The girl gave a conspiratorial grin and Alice felt her body relax. It was all right not to speak, then.

Her voice sometimes let her down completely without any warning. Why did that happen? Alice had the sensation of her mind clearing as she considered this. Was it the rush of emotion that stifled her voice's ability to make coherent sounds? Perhaps. She swallowed hard, hoping that the errant vocal chords would appreciate some fresh saliva and begin to work properly again.

'Now, let's see what you can do.' The young girl was reaching under her pillow, easing her up into a sitting position.

Alice Finlay let herself be manoeuvred by the firm hands, aware that she was as helpless to resist now as she had been as a little child all those years ago in that department store.

It was better to go on foot for the first few days. That way much more could be observed. Cycling meant that things zipped past too quickly, and facts had to be absorbed if I were to make sense of the place and the person. So I walked across the muddy path, hood over my face against the February cold, hunched up under layers of clothing that were as much for disguise as for keeping out the chill. The corner house had been my first choice and when the woman closed her gate and headed off towards the flyover that crossed the main road to the shops, I slowed my step, following her at a distance. She was small and walked with a jerky step as if she had a pain of some sort. A recent hip replacement, maybe? It was pension day and some of the old people still trotted down to the post office every week rather than have their money paid directly into their bank accounts. Old habits died hard, I told myself. And perhaps this indicated that the old dear was a good age. I narrowed my eyes against a sudden gust of easterly wind, watching the woman stagger as it caught her. The older they were the weaker they became, I told myself; and all the more reason why they should be dispatched.

Freda hobbled down to the end of the slope. There was a huge, dirty puddle right at the bottom where the ground needed filling in by the council, but it had been there for so long now that she doubted whether it would ever be mended. She'd just have to take an extra big step across it; that was all. Her fingers trembled as she shifted the shopping bag from one arm to the other, reaching out for the metal railing. It might only be a few steps from the flyover to the entrance to the post office, but there was a broken bit of pavement to negotiate as well as these horrible self-opening doors that swung outwards at her.

Freda was aware of every potential hazard since her last fall. It had been such a simple thing, just missing her footing at the edge of the pavement then down she'd gone, breaking her leg as she'd crashed on to the hard concrete. There had been so many accidents lately involving older people. Like that one along from Jess Innes. No, Freda stopped in the middle of the street, pondering for a moment. Two had died. That was right. Two elderly ladies had fallen down their back steps not all that long ago. Terrible thing to have happened. Tommy next door had been on to the council to have rails put in at the back and front doors, but so far nothing had happened. You had to be on the social to get anything these days, Freda remembered him saying in that puffed-out exasperated way that he had, like a wee fighting cock. And it was true enough, she thought, stepping back to let the doors open fully before she entered the brightness and warmth of the grocery-shop-cum-post-office.

There was the usual queue of folk waiting for their turn at the counter and Freda turned to see if there was anyone she knew; having a wee blether with one of her friends would pass the time. But there was nobody, just a tall man stooping over the newspapers as if he couldn't decide which one he wanted, and a couple of other folk by the display of greeting cards. Freda sighed. She'd go across to the Spar and buy a few things, just enough to tide her over the weekend. And maybe a quarter pound of mince from the butcher's. A shepherd's pie would last her at least two meals, wouldn't it?

As Freda Gilmour left the post office she had no sensation of being followed. No extra sensory element within alerted her to

170

the eyes that watched her every faltering step, nor did she feel the weight of malice that had begun to bear down upon her small, slight person.

CHAPTER 20

Lorimer had not forgotten Colin Ray's words, nor was he particularly afraid of pushing this investigation into the delicate area of internal police matters. But other aspects of the case had taken up his time and it was only today, at the start of this new week, that his thoughts turned to the Chief Constable of Strathclyde. Sir Robert Caldwell, the previous Chief Constable who Lorimer had respected and liked, had retired to his holiday home in Bute and the present head of their force was someone he knew less well. David Isherwood was a man in his late forties who had come to them from the Grampian Region. Whether he missed the cold easterly winds or not, Lorimer couldn't say, but Isherwood's choice of home had been the village of Kilmacolm, a place that seemed to have its own particular climate. Every wintry spell appeared to be more biting up there than in other villages; even the annual rainfall was greater, according to the officers who knew the area.

Oddly enough, the fact that Isherwood lived in Kilmacolm was one thing about the Chief Constable that Ray had forgotten to tell Lorimer, and Lorimer felt curious about the omission. Had Ray still been reticent about his anxiety to follow the Chief Constable's advice? Or was there more to it? Perhaps, Lorimer told himself, putting pressure on Ray had been no more than a desire on the part of the recently-promoted Isherwood to keep his own name out of the newspapers. Being a resident of the same village where a major crime had taken place could have unpleasant repercussions. But Lorimer wondered if it was more than that. Colin Ray had given him the impression that he had been warned off investigating any of Sir Ian Jackson's known associates. Now, what had made Isherwood issue such a directive? Perhaps, thought Lorimer, looking at the grey skies over Greenock Harbour, today was a day to find that out. His appointment with Isherwood was at eleven o'clock. A wee trip back up the M8 to Glasgow would suit him just fine.

It was not long before the river became a haze of grey with dim shapes of cranes obscuring the horizon, the motorway eventually swinging across from south to north and into the heart of the city. Lorimer noted the massive changes that had been wrought in Glasgow's topography in recent years. Now more bridges than ever criss-crossed the dark waters in an attempt to stem the tide of traffic that flowed across the M8's Kingston Bridge. The Clyde Arc (nicknamed the 'Squinty Bridge' by locals) served the area between Govan, where the television studios had made their home among rows of designer flats, and Finnieston with the Scottish Exhibition and Conference Centre on its doorstep. A new footbridge had also been built on the site of a former chandlery between Broomielaw and the Quay, allowing a passage from the newer homes bordering the south shore to the older part of the city. But some things never changed, Lorimer thought, glancing at some familiar shapes on the skyline. Glasgow University still dominated the cityscape, its peculiar spiked tower piercing the skies, reminding

Lorimer of the path he might have taken had he remained a student of Art History.

The road swept round in a curve, taking him along Bothwell Street. He was almost home, he thought, surprised at the notion. He gave a wry grin at his reflection in the driving mirror. That was almost true. After all, hadn't he spent more time in A Division than anywhere else in his career? And he missed the place and the people there, he suddenly realised. It was unusual for a police officer to be in one Division for so long, and perhaps this secondment would take him away from his Glasgow base for good. If full promotion to Detective Superintendent were to take place, he'd have very little option but to go where he was sent. He'd miss them, though, these people who had become his friends – like Detective Sergeant Alistair Wilson and even the wee woman in the canteen, Sadie Dunlop, whose politically incorrect remarks were dished up to every officer regardless of their rank.

He parked the car on a hill and walked along to Pitt Street, pulling his coat collar up against a blustery wind that was sweeping in from the east. The red brick building dominated the corner of the block as well it might. Strathclyde Police Headquarters housed much of the expertise that was used in the detection of major crimes, as well as the most senior officers who administered the various departments. As he entered the building, the first hailstones began to fall, pattering icy bullets on the dry pavement.

Giving a nod to the commissionaire, Lorimer headed for the stairs and the office that David Isherwood presently called home.

It had been a little while since Lorimer's previous visit, when he had held a press conference down in the assembly hall. That was the area most usually recognised by the public on television during serious cases, the prominent thistle badge on the wall always reminding the viewer of the Force's duty towards them.

Lorimer's invitations to see the Chief Constable had been far less frequent than those from other colleagues in Pitt Street wanting his input into various cases of vicious crime.

David Isherwood was a man of middle height, broad-shouldered with a large, square-shaped head that had required Strathclyde's uniform department to find a way of creating an outsized hat that would fit their new Chief Constable. It lay on his desk now, its silver braid gleaming in the cold afternoon light that slanted from the window behind him. As Lorimer entered the room, Isherwood stood up, came around from behind his desk and on two swift strides was clasping his visitor's hand, a quick up and down.

'Take a seat, Lorimer.' Isherwood gestured to the pair of comfortable chairs placed to one side of the room, a small wooden coffee table between them. 'How are things progressing down at K Division?' he asked, without any preamble.

Lorimer nodded. This was one of the busiest men in the Force so there would be no messing about or wasting precious time in discussing niceties.

'I'll come straight to the point, sir. I want to know why DCI Ray was warned off investigating certain areas of Sir Ian Jackson's life.'

Isherwood's grey eyes widened and he leaned forwards, his two meaty hands grasping each kneecap. 'Warned off? By whom?' he asked in a tone at once aggressive and blustering.

'Yourself, sir,' Lorimer replied, keeping his gaze fixed on the Chief Constable's face. He would not let the man go from his penetrating stare, a technique that he was well used to employing during difficult interrogations. But an experienced officer like Isherwood surely knew all of these tricks and more besides, Lorimer thought. Nevertheless, he continued to keep his eyes focused on the man as he spoke again.

'It appears to me that there was an attempt to divert attention away from Sir Ian's home and business life.' He spoke the words slowly and quietly, watching as Isherwood's jaw hardened and a faint flush of dark red crept over his spade-shaped chin. 'And I would like to know why,' he added.

For a long moment the two men stared at one another, then Isherwood dropped his gaze and gave a short sigh.

'Do you know, Chief Inspector,' he said, examining his hands as he spoke, 'I have never come across an officer who has questioned me like this before.' His eyes flicked back to meet Lorimer's and there was a different quality in them, something akin to a slow, smouldering anger. 'My motivation in directing Ray to a particular area of inquiry was perfectly in order and you have no business coming here asking questions like that!'

'Perhaps living in Kilmacolm, so close to the scene of the crime, has something to do with it?' Lorimer suggested, his hands clasped loosely on his lap, his expression both calm and unruffled.

'Preposterous! What gives you that notion?' Isherwood thumped the arm of his chair.

'There must be some reason that you told Colin Ray to stay away from certain areas of Jackson's life, sir,' Lorimer continued, knowing that his reasonable tone was probably infuriating the Chief Constable.

'And I suppose you have begun to poke around in *these areas*, as you call them!'

'I'm sorry if this sounds offensive, sir, but I have to remind you that I was appointed by the Procurator Fiscal to undertake this review,' Lorimer told him quietly. 'And since I have been attempting to fulfil that objective I have to tell you that the inquiry has taken on some more serious dimensions. The forensic evidence now suggests that whoever began the fire may have had access to the interior of the house. A deliberate step like that was not what I would call a random act of vandalism.'

Isherwood sat back, his hand rubbing his chin. And for a long moment he seemed to consider Lorimer's words. Then, clearing his throat, he began, 'I think, Detective Superintendent, that you must do what you think best in this case. But remember, Sir Ian was a well respected member of the community and it would not be to anyone's benefit to have his name sullied in any way.'

'You mean by revealing his overseas connections?'

'Precisely. Nobody is very sure just what these involved. Tax evasion, possibly. But that was a long time ago and what the man achieved for society more than made up for any irregularities.'

'So you want me to brush anything dirty under the carpet? Is that it?'

'I want you to do what you are told to do!' Isherwood roared suddenly. 'And without casting any aspersions in the direction of this office! Find out who began that fire but don't drag the good name of Ian Jackson through the mud in the process, is that clear?'

He stood up, obviously considering the meeting at an end. This time there was no handshake. The scowl on his face as he thrust open the door might have deterred a lesser mortal, but Lorimer nodded politely and checked a small salute before turning to leave.

CHAPTER 21

'Well, what of it?' The tall, blonde policewoman looked down at DC Kate Clark, one hand on her hip.

'I thought you'd be able to help!' Kate protested. 'You have got some inside knowledge about that sort of stuff,' she raged, adding, 'Ma'am,' as Rhoda Martin's eyebrow rose menacingly. It didn't do to forget who was boss around here when Lorimer wasn't around, the DI's expression seemed to be reminding her.

'So?' Rhoda Martin countered. 'Everyone knows I'm a cyclist. I just don't see what being in the cycle club has to do with the investigation. After all, the only thing our witness can tell us is that it was a bloke riding without any lights on.'

'He thought the cycle was silver,' Kate mumbled.

'Ha! If I had a pound for every silver cycle in the district I'd be retiring next week!' Martin snorted. 'Come on, Kate. I mean, there's not a shred of evidence to go on, is there?'

The DI's derisive tone made Kate Clark seethe inwardly. *Lorimer doesn't think that*, she wanted to tell the woman but mentioning the Super's name was like a red rag to a bull these days. Kate was ready to bet that Rhoda Martin hadn't managed to charm the pants off this particular officer. Lorimer had more sense than to fall for the DI's usual tricks, she thought, remembering his keen blue eyes appraising each one of them during recent meetings.

'What about the other folk in your cycle club? Would any of them have been up there at that time of night?'

For a moment DI Martin's face became thoughtful. Kate waited, wondering what her colleague was going to say. But then the woman shook her head and gave a shrug as if to dismiss whatever idea had occurred to her.

'Is the son still bothering you?' she asked instead.

'You mean Gary Wilson? The man whose old mum died?'

Martin nodded. 'Yes. All that stuff about a stalker seems a bit like clutching at straws to me. Okay, you have to feel for the guy, but don't let yourself get too involved. It's a matter for family liaison to deal with, DC Clark. It's not your job to mop up Mr Wilson's tears. Besides, I'd have thought you had other more pressing things on your mind these days,' she smirked, her green eyes flashing with mirth as she pointed to Kate's belly.

Kate gave a half-smile in return, her hand moving instinctively to the swelling bump as she felt the baby kick. The DI was right enough, she supposed. Becoming too involved with the victim's family was a bad idea. And she didn't have all that long to go now until her maternity leave. Maybe this cyclist thing was just a bizarre coincidence. Loads of people rode bikes, after all, and maybe the bloke in Kilmacolm had simply forgotten to switch on his lights that night.

But as she walked back to her desk, something was niggling at the back of her mind. What had Rhoda Martin been thinking about just then? It was typical of the woman not to share her ideas with the rest of them. DI Martin was the type who would work on her own if she could, just to show them all what a great cop she was. Maybe that private school education had instilled the competitive spirit into her, Kate thought. Then the telephone rang, dispelling any further consideration of the incident.

Tommy Rankin stopped by his gate, puffing as he heaved the last of the bags of groceries on to the path. He was getting too old for this. But his pride wouldn't let him ask that son-in-law of theirs for help. So long as he could walk across to the shops, he'd continue to bring home all the things on Maureen's list. The old man pushed the gate, fiddling with the catch to make sure it was secure. Maureen had kept him awake half the night moaning about the gate banging in the wind. He was sure he'd closed it last night. Maybe it was Freda-next-door's? He was about to pick up the bags of groceries when his eye was caught by a bundle of rubbish left at the foot of his neighbour's steps. What on earth had Freda left out?

But as he bent to retrieve the bulging plastic bags, Tommy Rankin froze. A gust of wind had caught the edge of the heap lying on his neighbour's path, revealing the sole of a small black shoe.

For a moment Tommy's mind refused to recognise what his eyes were telling him.

Then he heard a thin cry coming from his own throat as the bundle of rags was transformed into the shape of a woman's body.

'Three? That's not a coincidence then, is it?' Detective Sergeant Wainwright asked, his eyes gleaming with expectation. 'We've got a serial killer on our patch,' he added, folding his arms and glaring around as if daring to any of his fellow officers to defy him. 'Someone's bumping off poor old ladies. And with the SOCOs having found the tyre tracks, we'll have to look again at Gary Wilson's statement, won't we?'

Rhoda Martin had the grace to keep quiet and Kate Clark noticed that the DI was deliberately avoiding her eye. It was typical, though, that all this had blown up on a day when Lorimer wasn't around. A meeting with the Chief Constable took precedence over the day-to-day business of policing, she told herself huffily, then immediately felt cross at herself for such cynicism. Most of that morning and early afternoon, officers had been busy at the locus; now that the body had been taken away to the mortuary they were back at HQ for the initial meeting with the scene of crime manager and DI Martin who had been appointed SIO.

'Ma'am, the doctor who issued the death certificate for Mrs Wilson and Mrs MacKintyre wants to come in and make a statement,' PC Dodgson piped up. 'It's a Doctor Bennie. He attended the latest death. Seems all three of them were his patients.'

'Okay.' DI Martin sighed and looked at the papers attached to her clipboard. 'That's something to go on for the time being. Right, what else have we got? Last night's workload includes the fracas down at the harbour. A couple of local gangs knocking bits out of one another.' She looked up to the area beyond the incident room as though she could envisage the prisoners. 'So that's most of the cells full. And we've already had one report of a mugging and another incident that might end up being an attempted rape.'

'Can they not at least have the decency to wait till it's dark?' Wainwright asked, receiving a few guffaws in reply.

But DI Martin refused to rise to the bait as she continued, 'So with what remains of this afternoon, ladies and gentlemen, just for some extra light entertainment,' she said, sweeping a green glare over DS Wainwright, 'we appear to have a serial killer out there. It's what you've all been *hoping* for, after all, isn't it?'

Kate Clark winced. Rhoda Martin was one hard bitch, but she'd never heard such a tone of bitterness in her voice before.

Even Wainwright looked surprised, and he'd been around long enough to take sarcasm in his stride. Something was biting the DI today and Kate was curious to know just what that was. Could it be the menace from an unknown killer who was systematically murdering old ladies? She shivered suddenly. None of them had encountered anything like this before and perhaps DI Martin's words were simply covering up her own fear of tackling a case this big.

As DI Martin was issuing the various actions to her colleagues, the man who occupied her thoughts was driving back down the M8 from Glasgow.

Lorimer wondered if his words to Isherwood at Pitt Street today had found their target. He thought so, remembering the man's turkey-red jowls and his explosive reaction. Whatever the final outcome, he knew his card was marked now and it would be highly unlikely that there would be any promotion to Superintendent in the near future for DCI William Lorimer if the Chief Constable had anything to say about it.

His hands grasped the steering wheel tightly. There were other things that might count against him as well: being out of his own office meant that he was well behind with all the staff appraisals waiting for him back in Glasgow. Their annual MOTs had to be done and he had to find time to do them but, what with the hospital visits and this review case, he felt as though things were slipping away from him. With these thoughts in mind Lorimer had taken the opportunity of being back in Glasgow to call in at his own HQ and pick up some of the paperwork, hoping he might have a chance to see to some of it over the weekend. If he could just tie up this case in Greenock then perhaps he'd be able to return to a semblance of normality.

As he turned off the dual carriageway and headed towards Port Glasgow, Lorimer smiled a bitter little smile to himself. When had his life last been normal? Surely the life of a police officer was by definition anything but normal. And that was the choice he had made for himself, a long time ago. He recalled the day that he had been summoned from his vacation job in the bank. A simple request to take part in a line up following a series of bank robberies had resulted in the young William Lorimer asking questions about the work of a police officer. And what he had learned had intrigued him enough to drop out of his course at university and join the Force.

What had made Rhoda Martin become a police officer? Lorimer wondered. She was a fast-track graduate who was obviously intent on becoming more than a mere detective inspector, he reckoned – even if she had to sleep her way into promotion, a bad little voice whispered in his ear. In the course of the review, the first thing Lorimer had done was look at all of the information about the individuals in DCI Ray's team. He'd seen DI Martin's personnel file as a matter of course, noted the private education, the glowing commendations from past teachers and tutors at university and the terse comment *'this one will go far'* from Tulliallan Police College. But, having seen her at work, he felt that there was something that didn't fit about the woman. Perhaps it was that upper-class voice or the way she moved around her female colleagues as if she believed they were her inferiors. Lorimer shook his head, irritably. He shouldn't even be thinking of the dratted woman when there were other more important matters on his mind.

He turned into the filter lane leading to the stark grey building, with its chequered stripe that proclaimed to the world that this was Greenock Police Headquarters. Maggie had stared at it when they'd passed by in the car before last Christmas, musing in that whimsical way she had. What was it she'd said? 'If that building could talk, it would say "Nae messin".' He'd laughed, then, completely unaware that in a matter of weeks he would be coming up and down from Glasgow to Greenock HQ on a daily basis.

As he pointed the key to lock the car, Lorimer's thoughts were already considering the next step in his review of the Jackson case. He wanted to talk to the sort of people who would welcome a chat about their departed friends, Ian and Pauline Jackson: people who had known them outside of Jackson Tannock.

And he thought he knew just where he might obtain such information.

The HOLMES room had been set up as an incident room, given that Lorimer had appropriated the only other available space. He stood at the doorway, arms folded, listening to the DI as she directed questions from her colleagues. Something was up, that was clear, and it didn't sound as if it had anything whatsoever to do with the Jackson case.

'Right, I want everyone back for a meeting at eighteen hundred hours. DS Wainwright's your crime scene manager so if I'm not here for any reason you make sure your reports are with him. Understood?'

Lorimer listened to the woman's voice. It was hard and clear, like brittle glass, but the way she stood there, tall and commanding, looked anything but fragile. And he could see that every eye was upon her. Not one of them had noticed his presence, lurking in the shadows. She was good; Lorimer had to grant her that. And with her sort of authoritative manner, yes, she would go far.

Before the meeting broke up, Lorimer came further into the room and stood to one side, waiting for the opportunity to speak with the DI. One or two of the officers gave him a half-smile as they passed him but there was a sense of urgency in the way they hurried out that made his eyebrows rise in curiosity.

'What's up?' he asked, stepping forward as soon as the DI had finished speaking to Robert Wainwright.

Rhoda Martin turned and for a moment her mouth fell open in surprise at seeing him there. Then the green glint was back in her eyes, the blonde head raised in a defiant manner.

'Another killing,' she began shortly. 'A third old lady. Same MO. Same district.'

'Upper Port Glasgow?'

She gave a bitter smile. 'Yes. Not down in the main drag where you might expect a few CCTVs to help us. A housing estate. There are a lot of old folk living in that part of the area now.'

'Dying too, by the looks of it,' Wainwright put in, his grin cut short by the glacial look Martin shot at him.

'Anything to go on?'

Martin seemed distracted, avoiding his eye as if she wanted to look around the room for something she had forgotten. 'Cycle tracks, if you must know. Forensics are on to it and the elderly neighbour next door claims to have seen kids hanging around on their bikes a couple of nights ago.' She shrugged then turned back to face him. 'So if you don't mind I've got a lot to do. I'm the SIO on this one. All right, sir?'

She marched past him without waiting for an answer and he caught a whiff of her expensive perfume. It was one that he recognised; Maggie wore it whenever they were going out somewhere. DS Wainwright gave him a nod as he followed the woman out of the incident room. Lorimer stood back, letting them past.

Being the Detective Superintendent on hand did not mean that by rights this case should have come to him, he reminded himself. He was only here on sufferance: just a review officer seeing to a case that had been botched. That was all. And if things carried on the way they had been, he might end up back in Glasgow as a DCI quicker than he would like. Okay, he decided. They were all intent on this new case and it was imperative that they found out as much as possible as quickly as they could to maximise their chances of apprehending this killer. He looked at the spot where Rhoda Martin had stood moments ago. He had a lot of experience in dealing with murder cases and she knew it. So why not ask him for help? Because she wants to prove she can do this one herself, a little voice told him. And if the Detective Inspector did manage to catch this killer then she'd see it as a chance for promotion, satisfying that ambitious streak he'd seen in her.

Meantime he would take a trip up the country to Kilmacolm. That trail might be colder now, but perhaps he could rake around and see what he could find. There was something missing. Many things had been lost in that fire but memories of the dead might still be fresh in people's minds. And it might help the case to bring those memories alive once more.

CHAPTER 22

Rosie Fergusson stood back from the stainless steel table, scrutinising the body. She had to admit that the perpetrator of these attacks had left no visible clues as to their identity. There were no ligature marks, no defence wounds; nothing that might help the police find whoever it was that had shoved the old woman down the flight of stairs. Had it not been for the other deaths this would have passed her by and been filed as a tragic accident. And the fact that this old lady was under her care showed that she was being considered as something special. Freda Gilmour was to have the dubious distinction of being kept in cold storage whereas the other old dears were now either in a family urn or scattered to the four winds of heaven. A report was always sent to the Procurator Fiscal following any sudden death and it had been an easy decision for someone at the Crown Office to find that Mary MacKintyre and Jean Wilson had each died from a simple accident. They all had the same GP, though, Rosie had noticed. Wonder what *he* had made of the second death? Had Dr Bennie put it down to a macabre sort of coincidence? This third death wouldn't allow that sort of conclusion, though, would it?

The pathologist's report would of necessity be brief and to the point. The injuries were consistent with a fall from a height on to concrete paving stones: the skull fracture and damage to the arm and both legs showed signs of very recent injuries. The poor old thing hadn't had much luck, Rosie thought, stepping forward and feeling the left leg. She could see another break that had been sustained not all that long ago. The pathologist shook her head, wondering. It might have looked just like bad luck: an elderly lady who had a history of falling, crashing to her death outside her own back door. One thing she wasn't looking forward to was the part of her report that dealt with the time of death. For Freda Gilmour had not been killed on impact. Her injuries had gone unseen throughout the night as she lay alone. Rosie would write down that the victim might have been unconscious after the fall, hoping that, mercifully, that had been true. Death, she reminded herself, was a process. But few people ever wanted to think of that.

Glancing up at the viewing window a few feet away, Rosie could see the face of that tall Detective Inspector from Greenock. She was gazing intently at the corpse, interested no doubt to see what Dr Fergusson was going to do. She didn't look the squeamish type, Rosie thought. And the pathologist was experienced enough to know.

For a moment her thoughts turned to Lorimer. The DI up there above the post-mortem room had not mentioned Lorimer's name at all. Would he be in touch? Was this case to come under his jurisdiction now that he had been seconded to the divisional headquarters down the river? It was a fleeting thought. Right now she had to concentrate on performing a post-mortem examination on this latest statistic of violence.

With a straightening of her shoulders, Rosie motioned to her assistant and then reached forward to pick up a scalpel.

*

'Davie! Well, well, what do you know!' DS Wainwright rubbed his hands together as a uniformed officer handed him a clipboard with the names of residents living close to the late Freda Gilmour.

'Just the sort of wee toerag we've been looking for. Pity you couldn't have found him a bit sooner.' He looked at the young police constable as if it were somehow Dodgson's fault that the old ladies had died.

The youngster flinched but said nothing in reply. From the time he had given Lorimer the bijoux bottle, Wainwright had taken to shaking his head and looking at him as if he were some sort of traitor. It wasn't fair. He'd tried his utmost to go by the book, making every effort to do exactly what he had been trained to do, but in the face of the older officer's obvious disdain, PC Dodgson had begun to wonder if he should apply for a transfer out of this division. And it wasn't only Wainwright. DI Martin had barely spoken to him since he had accompanied Lorimer to the locus in Kilmacolm. And any day now his one ally, DC Clark, would be off to have her baby. Why were they treating him like some pariah? Turning on his heel, the police constable vowed to keep his head down in future.

'David Jonathan McGroary. Previous convictions for assault to severe injury. One of them against an elderly man who needed hospitalisation!' DI Martin said, reading from the notes that the crime scene manager had given her.

There was a murmur of satisfaction from the officers assembled in the incident room.

'Does he own a bike?' Kate Clark piped up.

DI Martin looked hard at the woman, then raised her eyebrows. 'Anybody? DC Clark wants to know.'

'There was a cycle outside in the garden,' Dodgson offered.

'And we have to obtain a warrant to remove it from his premises, don't we?' Martin smiled, her eyes glinting with malice. 'Suppose you do just that, constable. Eh?'

Dodgson shuffled his feet and said nothing.

'Well, go on, get out of here and get one and don't come back without that bike!' she commanded. 'And if we find that McGroary was anywhere near Mrs Gilmour's house on the night in question, I want him in here so fast his mucky little feet won't touch the ground, understood?'

Kate noticed DS Wainwright smirking at the constable's retreating back, then catching Rhoda Martin's glance. The chemistry between that pair was interesting. With DCI Ray retired, it was plain that the tall blonde officer was making a bid to step into her former boss's shoes. And Wainwright didn't seem too bothered by that. But he wasn't ever going to make more than a detective sergeant, was he? So long as he had lads like Dodgson to bully, Robert Wainwright was happy enough. And being crime scene manager gave him as much kudos as he seemed to desire.

Kate Clark watched as the DI consulted the notes again. It was clear to them all that she hadn't had time to read them over prior to the six p.m. meeting. And Kate knew that she hadn't yet spoken to Wainwright for a rundown on the afternoon's actions. Somehow the DC couldn't imagine Lorimer coming into a meeting so ill prepared. It was a disquieting little thought that was soon banished by the DI's next words.

'The CCTV at the local shops isn't working. Surprise, surprise. So no images of bikers anywhere near the scene,' she said. 'We'll have to rely on witness statements to tell us what was going on the night of Mrs Gilmour's death and they seem to be pretty thin on the ground,' she continued, flicking over the pages on her clipboard.

'What about the next-door-neighbour?' Kate asked.

'Didn't find the body till this morning, remember,' Wainwright offered. 'And he seems to be pretty shocked by the whole thing.'

'And there's no neighbourhood watch scheme, I suppose?'

DS Wainwright snorted. 'They don't subscribe to things like that up there,' he said. 'They all just watch their own backs, depending on whatever gang's on the rampage.'

Kate Clark nodded as she listened to the crime scene manager. It was true enough. The area was riddled with factions from different parts of the town that regularly broke out in fits of violence. Knife crime had been especially bad in the last few years despite initiatives that they had tried to implement within the community. Maybe that was why this part of the country was known as the Wild West.

'We'll have the pathologist's report coming in tomorrow, hopefully,' DI Martin told them. 'There were no defence wounds, nothing under the old lady's fingernails that might have given us some DNA material. But if anything forensic does come to light, we'll be looking to make a match with someone like McGroary.'

'There's something else, ma'am'. A voice from the back of the room made Kate turn around. 'McGroary was employed as a gardener at Jackson Tannock Technologies last year. Got thrown out by Sir Ian. Just a week or so before the fire.'

'And why was that?' Martin asked.

'He was caught taking a piss behind the technology buildings. Didn't know he was being seen by a room full of Japanese visitors to the plant!'

'And when did this come to light?' DI Martin stared hard at the crime scene manager, intent on ignoring the guffaws of laughter breaking out around the room.

'McGroary told us, ma'am,' Wainwright supplied before the

other officer could add any more. 'Said he'd been looking for gardening work in the local area ever since. Seemed he'd done a leaflet drop round the houses in his own patch.'

'Better than a trouser drop,' another voice sniggered.

'Do we have a list of the addresses he visited?' DI Martin cut across the undercurrent of noise.

Wainwright smiled a slow smile as if he had kept the best till last. 'It's all there ma'am,' he said, indicating the papers in her hand. '*And* they include all the homes of the ladies who were killed,' he told her.

'Right. That's as much as we need. Get forensics on to that bicycle as soon as Dodgson comes back with it. And I want McGroary brought in for questioning. Now. And you can all forget about going home for the next few hours. I want this cleared up tonight.'

Kate closed the door of the cubicle behind her, breathing a sigh of relief. She was in and out of the loo so often these days that nobody gave it a second thought. It was, she thought, one of the few places where she could telephone him in private.

She let it ring out then, just as she began to expect the voicemail to begin its spiel, Lorimer's familiar tones echoed in her ear.

'It's me; Kate. Listen. There's been a development in the latest case. A known offender, name of Davie McGroary, lives in the same estate as the three old ladies. And,' she paused for breath, 'he worked for Jackson Tannock as a landscape gardener. Now here's the good bit. McGroary was slung out on his ear a few days before the fire. And guess who did the slinging?' She nodded, listening to his reply. 'Aye, spot on. Sir Ian himself. Now is that maybe something to consider? Maybe not enough to give you a motive but he was surely going to bear a grudge.'

When Kate heard the sound of the main toilet doors being opened she flushed the WC letting Lorimer know where she was. GOT TO GO SPK LATR, she texted, then clicked shut her phone.

Rhoda Martin barely glanced at Kate as she pushed open the door of an adjacent cubicle. The Detective Constable breathed a sigh of relief as she waddled over to the line of hand basins. Well, at least she'd contacted Lorimer to let him know. Nobody in the incident room had mentioned the review case or the Jackson fire and it was as if Lorimer had ceased to exist now that Rhoda Martin had her teeth into a murder case of her own.

Running her hands under the warm tap, Kate gave a groan. It was all very well pretending to use the loo, but Sod's Law being what it was, she really did need to go now. And for a fleeting moment she could even feel some sympathy for Davie McGroary.

The thought was quickly dismissed as she remembered the mean-faced drug dealer, that foul-mouthed girlfriend always in his wake. She'd seen them in here on previous occasions. Had he really killed those old ladies? Kate frowned suddenly, considering. *Why* would McGroary do something like that?

CHAPTER 23

The golf club in Kilmacolm was situated at the end of a winding road, high above the village, tucked tidily away from any passing traffic. Lorimer had driven up from Greenock with more hope than expectation that he might come across some background information relating to Sir Ian and Lady Jackson. His first instinct had been to revisit the burnt out mansion house and for a while he had wandered around the area, seeking something that might spark off an idea. Kate's call had come as he had just arrived back at the car and for a moment he had been tempted to turn around and head back to Greenock. If DI Martin wanted him to sit in on an interview with McGroary then surely she would be the one to call him, Lorimer told himself. And there was no way he'd want to cause Kate Clark any trouble for calling him with the news. So, as the afternoon light faded from a sky that was threatening snow, Lorimer kept to his original plan and headed towards the golf club. If this had been the place they'd come for recreation then, he reasoned, perhaps somebody here could paint personal colour and detail into what was a very sketchy outline of the famous philanthropist and his socialite wife.

The clubhouse was more like a country cottage from a bygone age, its creamy walls and low roof set against acres of neatly clipped grass. Lorimer parked the car and walked towards the entrance at the side, then pressed the bell. A call to the golf club secretary had been made, the man had apologised, he would be unable to see Detective Superintendent Lorimer this evening. Nonethless, he had decided to call in. From past experience he knew that an unexpected visit could produce more than one where answers had been carefully prepared. And surely there would be somebody here who could tell him things about the Jacksons? He stood for a moment, waiting to be admitted, then turned to look out at the buildings beyond the car park. A modern bungalow lay back from the main drive and, to its left, a collection of huts painted dark green that might belong to the resident groundsman. Trees surrounded much of the perimeter, one narrow path snaking behind them into thicker woodland.

'Hello, can I help you?' The drawling tone made Lorimer spin around to see a tall, angular-looking woman of indeterminate age dressed in matching heather-coloured Argyll-check sweater and slacks. She was, Lorimer decided, almost a caricature of the lady golfer. But there was nothing superficial about the steely gaze she had turned upon this visitor to Kilmacolm Golf Club.

'DCI Lorimer,' he said, producing his warrant card that still bore that rank. Explaining his designation as an acting Superintendent just wasn't worth the hassle.

'Monica Hutcheson,' the lady golfer offered with a nod, eyeing his card with a suspicious look. Yet she stood aside to let him enter, holding the door then closing it firmly behind him.

She did not extend her hand, Lorimer noticed. After all, he reminded himself, Isherwood was probably a member here as well. Perhaps a visit from a mere DCI was simply not enough to merit that.

'I'm investigating the death of two of your former members, Sir

Ian and Lady Pauline,' he continued, watching the woman's carefully pencilled eyebrows rise as he mentioned the Jacksons' names.

'Gracious,' the woman murmured. 'What a horrible thing that was,' she added as if it were a gross breach of manners to say more.

'I was hoping', Lorimer went on, 'to speak to some of their friends.'

'Whatever for? Haven't we all been upset enough?' The woman's outrage was palpable. But before Monica Hutcheson could continue, a door behind the main reception desk opened and a short, grey-haired woman emerged.

'Oh, Mrs H. Sorry, didn't know you had company,' the woman began in an accent that Lorimer recognised as pure Glaswegian.

'Betty.' Monica Hutcheson's mouth curved in a wide smile that failed to reach her eyes. 'Perhaps you wouldn't mind taking DCI Lorimer into the lounge. I'm sure *you* can fill him in with anything he wants to ask about the Jacksons.' And with that she sketched a tiny wave and headed towards the ladies' locker room.

Lorimer glanced around him, noting a darkened room to one side and the doors leading off this reception area. A board directly ahead of him bore the words KILMACOLM GOLF CLUB WELCOMES . . . but who or what was welcomed had been left blank. It certainly didn't feel as if it was DCI William Lorimer.

The woman called Betty stood where she was, her bird-like head to one side. 'You're Lorimer?' she asked, crinkling up her eyes as if she had seen him before somewhere. 'Like the same wan that found they wee lassies in the woods last summer?'

'I . . .' Lorimer began but before he could say another word, Betty had caught him by the arm and was leading him to the door from where she had emerged.

'Sadie Dunlop. Yer canteen lady. She's my late man's cousin. Ah get a' the talk frae Sadie,' Betty confided. 'An' I can tell ye, she thinks a lot of you, Mister Lorimer.'

'Ah, Sadie.'

'See ah'm the main cleaner in here but ah get tae do a bit of this and that. Waitressing an' other things. A'body knows wee Betty MacPherson.' She grinned and jabbed a surprisingly sharp elbow into Lorimer's arm.

'D'ye want a cup o' tea? Mikey the chef jist made some scones. They're still hoat.' Another jab from Betty's elbow came before Lorimer could dodge.

'Yes, thanks,' he replied, somewhat bemused by the little woman's flow of conversation.

'An' I tell ye,' Betty leaned towards him conspiratorially, 'there's naebody kens a' the toffs in here like I do.' She nodded as though to confirm her words. 'So jist ye ask away aboot that pair. Noo, sit doon here and ah'll fetch yer tea. Milk and sugar?'

Lorimer was relieved to see that there were few other people in the main lounge. One older man was ensconced in the *Times* and a couple of white-haired matrons were sipping tea at a table in the corner. The seat Betty MacPherson had selected was well out of earshot from anyone else in the room. Despite that, she dropped Lorimer a wink and motioned for him to follow her out of the lounge and into a smaller room next door.

'This is the family room. Naebody'll bother us in here,' she told him. 'There, ye came in jist at the right time, so ye did,' Betty exclaimed, setting down a laden tea tray on a well-polished table, beside a pair of dark leather settees. 'I wis jist gettin' ready for the off.'

Glancing at his watch, he could see that it was approaching six o'clock. It was doubtful now whether he'd manage to join Maggie in time for visiting hour. Outside the sky was darkening but there was still enough light to see the misty outline of hills, the putting greens and the starter's hut at the first tee.

As Betty poured from a silver teapot, Lorimer glanced around him. It was a pleasant little room with watercolours on the walls of what must be different vistas of the golf course. A television was set on a shelf at an angle in the corner opposite them. Had the Jacksons spent time in this room, sitting perhaps in this very spot, watching golfing events like the US Masters?

'There's yer tea. Now eat up, Mikey's scones are rare.'

'Thanks, Betty.' Lorimer smiled at the woman, suddenly grateful for her obvious attempts to make a fuss of him. 'You said you were related to our Sadie. Do you see her often?' Lorimer asked. It was always a good idea to initiate a conversation that prepared some common ground and for a minute or two he listened to an account of Betty's family and how the woman had moved away from her Glasgow home to be near her daughter after her husband's death. He had waited for that particular turn in the conversation, knowing it would arrive, and as Betty put on a suitable sorrowful face at the mention of Mr MacPherson, deceased, Lorimer interrupted the flow of her narrative.

'Sir Ian and Lady Pauline. You knew them well, Betty?'

'Oh, aye. There's not a one in here that wee Betty disnae know,' she crowed, lifting up her teacup and giving Lorimer the merest wink.

'So you would know who their friends were and what sort of family the Jacksons were?'

The older woman regarded Lorimer thoughtfully then set down her teacup with a little sigh. 'Aye, there's not much that passes me by in this place. Why d'you think Mrs Hutcheson was so ready to pass you on to the wee cleaning lady?' She smiled as though she had made some sort of joke.

'And you'll know all the gossip as well?' Lorimer grinned back, encouragingly.

'It doesnae do tae speak ill of the dead,' Betty told him sternly, her expression immediately serious.

'I'm not asking you to do that, Betty,' Lorimer said quietly. 'But if I'm ever to find out what happened that night of the fire I need to know as much as possible about the Jacksons.' He looked straight into her grey eyes, holding her in his gaze. 'What did they do? Who were their friends? Was there any earthly reason for someone to set fire to that house?'

'Och, there've been fires here afore noo. I mind a spate o' burned oot motors years back. An' then there wis that caravan. Terrible thing. See,' she nudged Lorimer with her elbow once more, 'some vandals set this caravan alight. It wis thon gas canister thing, ye know. The neighbours had tae get the family oot. An' a baby an' all. In a room right next tae where the caravan wis at the side of the driveway. I mind that yin well. Oor lassie lives roon the corner frae the hoose.'

'The Jacksons,' Lorimer reminded the woman. 'What can you tell me about them?'

The sigh that Betty MacPherson gave now seemed to come from the depths of her soul. With a shake of her head she looked away from Lorimer and out of the window as if to see something in her mind's eye. 'Och, I suppose it won't do any harm to them now to tell you. Dead is dead, after all.' She reached down for her cup and drained the last of the tea before continuing. 'Pauline wasn't as well thought of as folk make out. Nice lady and all as she was – and she was aye polite tae me – there were quite a few in here' – she jerked her thumb in the direction of

the people in the next room – 'that didnae approve of her relationship.'

Betty leaned forward, her voice dropping to a whisper. 'She wis
seein' a bit too much of thon fella frae the works. That wis what
they all said. Know whit I mean? I cannae say masel if she wis
actually . . . well, *you* know . . . but it was all the talk around the
village.'

'What fellow?'

'The wee man, Tannock. Sir Ian's partner. They were havin' an
affair, so it wis said.'

Lorimer frowned. Surely that was malicious gossip? Somehow
he couldn't imagine Hugh Tannock and his partner's wife . . .
Then a sudden memory came back to him of the man's display
of grief during Lorimer's visit. Had it been the mention of
Pauline Jackson that had sparked off the man's emotion?

'You don't believe me? Aye, well, I can see why. They were
nae whit ye wid call a braw match. Her bein' that nice looking
and him a richt wee bachle o' a man. But it's whit's in yer hert
that counts, isn't it?' Betty's bright bird-like eyes caught his
own and for a moment he sensed the woman's underlying
sympathy. 'Well, doesnae matter now, does it?' she continued,
setting down her teacup. 'And that wee man wouldn't have wanted
tae hurt Lady Pauline, I can promise ye that, Mr Lorimer,' Betty
insisted.

'Did Sir Ian know about this?'

'Well if he didn't then he must have been blind and deaf. But
then, they do say the spouse is always the last tae know, don't
they?'

'What about the Jackson children?'

'Och, they wouldnae know whit wis goin' on. Thon Serena
didnae know the time o' day never mind whit her mother got up

tae at the golf club. She wis far mair interested in goin oot tae parties an that. All dolled up. Don't get me wrang,' she turned to look at Lorimer suddenly, 'nice enough lassie. Bonnie, too. But a wee bit of a want, if you get my drift. Not quite the full shilling, as my old maw used tae say.'

'And Daniel?'

'Ah, now there's a man for you. How that pair ever produced a boy like Daniel I'll never know. First in his class at school all the time. Always top at sports an' all. Mind you, the lassie was sporty as well, come tae think on it.' Betty nodded thoughtfully. 'But such a lovely lad! Had his ain sports car, his big hoose in the toon. Aye, a real success that one. Will he take over from his faither, d'you think?'

Lorimer gave a small shrug in reply. 'So you think that Daniel Jackson had no idea that his mother and father's marriage was a bit shaky?'

'Oh, now I didnae say that. I'm sure their marriage was fine. I don't think the wee Tannock fella would've upset that. It was jist a . . .' She searched for the word.

'A fling?' Lorimer suggested.

'Aye, something like that. And I don't think that Daniel would have known anything about it. He and Mr Tannock were pals. Used to go cycling together with Serena every Sunday afternoon. See, Daniel and Serena were'nae golfers like their folks.'

Lorimer only half listened as Betty went on about the golfing fraternity in Kilmacolm's club. The Jackson children and Tannock were all cyclists. It was a hugely popular sport, after all; those familiar lines of figures in racing colours weaving in and out of weekend traffic were surely testament to that. And yet, this bit of information suddenly made his pulse beat a little faster.

*

Number 10A Greenlaw Crescent was a mid-terrace house fronted by a patch of unkempt grass, its sagging fence to one side showing years of neglect. A dirty football lay abandoned in one corner, but it was clear from the circular dark marks around the letterbox that someone had been thumping it off the once white-painted door. The curtains at the front were partially closed against the darkness, a flickering light from within showing that the television was on.

'Think our old pal will be at home, then?' PC Rab Duncan asked his neighbour.

'We'll soon see,' came the reply.

Three thumps from a meaty fist were all it took for the door to open. A thickset figure dressed in black started at the sight of the policemen but just as the man made to close the door, the police officer wedged a size eleven boot into the open space.

'David McGroary?' Duncan had shouldered his way in and was now standing in the dimly lit hallway. The pungent smell of cannabis drifted towards him.

'Aye, ye ken fine,' McGroary replied, his lip curling in a pretence at bravado.

'We'd like to invite you to accompany us—' Duncan began, but before he could continue McGroary turned as if to make off down the passageway but tripped over a discarded holdall in his haste to escape. The dark blue bag burst open, its contents scattering over the floor. Duncan grinned at the sight: he'd been around long enough in this neck of the woods to know what a cache of drugs looked like.

'Ann-Marie. Polis!' he yelled, but before he could hit the floor, Duncan grabbed him by the bottom of his nylon jacket, pulling him upright.

'Take yer haunds off of me, will ye!' Davie McGroary yelled, jerking his body sideways in an attempt to resist the strong arms of the law.

'Leave him alane ye big basturts!' A small dark figure flung itself into the fray, yanking the sleeve of the other officer who was attempting to cuff McGroary. The sound from her throat was a deep animal growl as she lunged at the policeman, sinking her teeth into the fleshy part of his wrist.

'Ann-Marie, get him aff me!' McGroary urged, swinging his body away from PC Duncan, who held him fast.

But it was over in a matter of seconds, the pair mouthing obscenities as the two officers led them out into the waiting van.

Between panting breaths, the policeman cautioned the girl who was still struggling in his grasp. 'Ann-Marie Monahan . . .'

Once in the van Duncan turned to his neighbour. 'Better get that seen to,' he said, jerking his head in the direction of the wound on the other man's wrist. 'Never know where she's been.'

Lorimer took the stairs two at a time, straining his ears to hear what was going on. Officially he knew nothing about McGroary, so he would have to feign ignorance to begin with. And he didn't have long to wait.

'Hear the latest, sir?' Young Dodgson had spotted Lorimer in the corridor and his eager face shone with the excitement of an officer who is part of a case that looks as if it is coming to a good conclusion. Lorimer knew that look. It was an adrenaline rush that made officers hyper even when the hours had made them bone-weary and cranky, wishing for a warm bed and some much needed kip.

'We brought in a suspect for the old lady's death,' Dodgson continued. 'DI Martin and DS Wainwright are interviewing him right now. Seems he thought he was being busted for dope.' Dodgson went on to describe the girlfriend's assault on one of the police officers and McGroary's panic.

Lorimer nodded. 'Great. Hope they get a result.' He paused. *Did DI Martin ask for me?* he wanted to say. But of course he couldn't bring himself to utter those words. McGroary might well be involved in the Jackson case and of course Martin would bring him into the interview situation. Wouldn't she? Lorimer hesitated then gave Dodgson a smile before stepping into his office. Sitting behind the desk, he drummed his fingers on the scored wooden surface, wondering.

It was more than an hour before the call came but, when it did, Lorimer was propelled from his chair and left the room in seconds.

Interview Room Two was the usual nondescript box of a room that would be found in any police station. The soundproof panels were one shade away from the colour of tea biscuit and the well-disinfected floor could only be described as manky brown. The room's only concession to colour was the blue chairs placed either side of the cheap fake-wooden table. There was no point in spending much on furnishings that could be thrown around by some mad bastard in a drunken fit of rage – and frequently were. Neither was there a fancy glass wall that gave access to one-way viewing. Such luxuries belonged firmly in the realm of TV cop shows, not in the real world down in Greenock Terminal.

'Superintendent Lorimer has entered the room,' DI Martin intoned, her face towards the black boxes sitting at the side of the table next to the wall.

Lorimer stood for a moment, looking at the man sitting opposite.

David McGroary was slumped into his chair, the dark tracksuit already showing patches of sweat under the armpits. His arms were folded belligerently across his chest in a typical stance of defiance against the authority that DI Martin represented. Lorimer noticed the man's medium build, the legs thrust under the table and the filthy trainers crossed at the ankle. A mulish expression around his mouth made the detective wonder if McGroary had wearied his inquisitors with a series of *No comments*. It happened so often and could frustrate even the most patient of officers. But a quick glance at Rhoda Martin showed that, despite two spots of colour on her high cheekbones, the woman looked remarkably unruffled.

'I'll be back later,' she told Lorimer. 'He's yours for now.'

'Thank you, Detective Inspector,' Lorimer replied smoothly and sat down in the chair she had vacated before switching the tape back on and announcing, 'DI Martin has left the interview room.'

DS Wainwright remained in the room, his chair slightly to one side as if to be ready to leap up and grab the prisoner if anything became violent. Lorimer smiled a wintry little smile to himself. He'd put money on Wainwright over McGroary any day, he thought, looking from the detective sergeant's prop forward physique to the layers of fat rolling over the waistband of McGroary's joggers.

'David McGroary, I'm Superintendent Lorimer from A Division in Glasgow,' he began, his tone polite and with the tiniest hint of deference.

At the word Glasgow, the man opposite unfolded his arms and sat up a little bit straighter. The big city obviously commanded a modicum of respect from the folk down here, Lorimer guessed. Either that, or his main dealer was from outside the district.

'I have been sent here to continue an inquiry into a house fire in Kilmacolm. The home of your previous employer, Sir Ian Jackson,' he said, gazing steadily at McGroary in a way that made

208

him look back. A flash of uncertainty crossed the prisoner's grey eyes and Lorimer saw the doubt in the parted lips and the worry frown appearing between his brows. *He knows he's a suspect*, Lorimer told himself. *Let's see if he'll crack enough to give us what we want.* In that nanosecond the notion of winding up this case and heading back home to Glasgow suddenly washed over Lorimer. But such thoughts were as tempting as the very devil. Nothing should influence him right now. Nothing but a need for the truth. Martin had to find whoever had killed those old ladies from Port Glasgow but it was his remit to focus on a very different case. And was this man, sitting sweating before him, a possible suspect?

'It would help us very much if you were willing to tell me about your relationship with Sir Ian,' Lorimer said.

'What relationship?' McGroary answered with a derisory snort. 'He wis ma boss, okay?'

'And he fired you, right?'

McGroary nodded.

'Mr McGroary has signalled his assent to that question,' Lorimer told the black box. 'And you decided to indulge in a little firing of your own, perhaps?' he asked, the tone so smooth that McGroary's mouth fell open. Then, as the words dawned on him, he slammed the flats of his hands on to the table, making it shudder.

'No way! Yer no goin tae stitch me up fir that. Ah wis nowhere near the place when it happened!' He was leaning forward now, breathing heavily and staring back into a pair of blue eyes that regarded him steadily.

'And where exactly were you, Mr McGroary?' Lorimer asked, not moving from his position, hands still clasped loosely in front of him.

Something about this detective's tone must have disarmed

him, for Davie McGroary began to frown and bite his lips nervously, evidently unsure of just what was going on now that the tall superintendent from Glasgow had taken over from the blonde woman.

'I wis at hame. Ask Anne Marie. She'll tell ye.' The man's eyes darted from Wainwright to Lorimer and back again and this time Lorimer saw an expression that he recognised quite easily. It was fear.

'Certainly, Mr McGroary, we'll do that. And easily enough since Miss Monahan isn't too far away at present.' Lorimer allowed the ghost of a smile to appear on his face, knowing that this would only add to the prisoner's confusion. Whatever tactics of interrogation DI Martin had employed, his own methods were certainly working.

'To get back to Sir Ian and Lady Pauline,' he said. 'You had been dismissed for a misdemeanour at your place of employment.' Lorimer smiled again, this time as if sharing a joke. 'It must have been a bit of a blow, surely?'

'Ach, he wis out of order. What wis the harm in takin a piss? Aye, I wis annoyed. Who wouldnae be? But no enough tae set fire tae his hoose and kill him. C'mon, man, that's mental!' McGroary shifted in his chair again, the arms folded once more and the eyes a shade less wary.

'But you were annoyed?'

'Ah said that already,' McGroary replied in a tone of world weariness, as if this copper was perhaps a wee bit on the simple side despite his senior rank.

'Who do you think would have set fire to that house?' Lorimer turned in his chair suddenly, addressing DS Wainwright who had been listening with growing interest to the dialogue between the tall detective and their prisoner. Kate Clark had told him about

Lorimer's interview techniques and now he was enjoying them at first hand.

'Oh, someone who didn't have much of a conscience, I suppose,' Wainwright replied, playing along.

'And someone who might just as easily knock a few old ladies down their stairs?'

'Sounds the type to me,' Wainwright agreed.

'Ah didnae do it!' McGroary roared at them, his fury igniting at being so suddenly ignored.

'Do what, Mr McGroary?' Lorimer asked him, his eyebrows rising in mock surprise as if suddenly realising there was another person in the room.

'Whit ye said ah did!' he blustered. 'Ony of it. Nae old ladies ever came tae herm frae me. An ah nivver set off ony fires!'

Lorimer turned back to Wainwright as if the uproar across the table was a mere distraction from his conversation with the DS. 'The prisoner's record shows wilful fire-raising and assault to severe injury, plus the handling and supplying of drugs. Would you say that was concomitant with a person of no conscience?' he asked, hand on his chin as though they were debating some ethical subject on *Question Time*.

'Whit's concom . . .?' McGroary's mouth was hanging open again, revealing one squint front tooth overlapping the other.

The smell of sweat was distinct now and Lorimer knew there would be damp smears on the tabletop where the man's meaty fingers were making long streaks as he swayed back and forward in a steady rhythm, as if he were bursting for the toilet. Remembering the reason for his dismissal, Lorimer smiled again. A weak bladder might just work to their advantage, putting more pressure on the man.

'What did you do when you knew the Jacksons were dead?'

Lorimer asked suddenly, turning his chair so swiftly that McGroary was taken off-guard.

'What?' The man ran a hand through a mop of already unkempt, greasy hair, making it stick up in cartoon spikes.

'I'll repeat the question,' Lorimer began again, but this time he leaned forward, grasping McGroary with his eyes every bit as effectively as if he had laid hands on the man and shaken him. 'What did you do when you knew the Jacksons were dead? Burned alive,' he added, his face so close to the prisoner's that he could smell the fear coming off him in waves.

'I nivvir done nothin. I swear. Honest to God. I nivver done nothin. Aw Jesus, ye cannae think ah did *that*!' he moaned, then, tearing his eyes away from Lorimer's steely gaze, he buried his face in his outstretched arms and began to sob noisily.

'DI Martin re-entering the room,' a voice told them.

Lorimer stood up, pulling back his chair, leaving the prisoner to add his snot and tears to the tabletop.

'A word,' Lorimer whispered quietly to Martin as she approached the table. 'Superintendent Lorimer leaving the room,' he told the black box. Signalling to the uniformed officer outside to make his way into the interview room, Lorimer closed the door behind them.

'Well?' Rhoda Martin stood before him, arms folded across her slight bosom, an expression of reluctant eagerness in her green eyes.

'Claims to have an alibi for the night of the Jackson fire,' Lorimer told her.

'So? Has to be corroborated, hasn't it? Couldn't you get him to confess?' she challenged, head tilted to one side.

'I doubt if he'll confess to something he hasn't done, Detective Inspector,' Lorimer replied. 'I take it he'll remain here overnight in custody since you've got him on the drugs charge?' he asked, already walking away from her. 'Must be off now. I'll see you in the morning,' Lorimer said, heading along the corridor and waving a hand in the air.

Lorimer didn't need to look behind him to know that DI Rhoda Martin's green eyes would now be following him with pent-up curiosity. He'd leave it to her to make a case against McGroary if there was any evidence to suggest that he had indeed stalked and murdered three old women. But some instinct told him that the man had played no part in the Jackson murder.

CHAPTER 24

'I'm telling you, it was murder!' Sarah Smith pounded a tight little fist on the table top as nine pairs of eyes stared at her in amazement. 'Jean's daughter-in-law says her lad Gary's been at the police station again. And,' she added darkly, 'they've found another body.'

There was a silent nodding from the other members of Port Glasgow Scribblers, the writers' group that Jean Wilson had enjoyed for many years before her death.

'My Andy won't let me go out on my own now,' one elderly lady confessed. 'He's picking me up after this. Any of you want a lift?'

'Aye, hen, ah'll come with you.' Sarah nodded. 'Cannae be too careful, what with a mad hoodie on the loose.'

'Think the rest of us should all walk up the road together, eh? Just in case, I mean.' A middle-aged woman by Sarah's side bit her lip, trying not to voice what was on all of their minds.

'She told us, didn't she?' someone else offered. 'About the stalker, I mean.'

'And we thought it was just her imagination running riot.'

'Great at her stories, was Jean.'

'Aye,' Sarah sniffed into a handkerchief. 'But she never expected to be the lead story in the local paper, did she?'

'Good! That's the stuff. At this rate we'll have you out of here in no time!'

Alice Finlay stretched out to grasp the zimmer again. The first few steps were the hardest, the girl had told her. Now that she had managed to stand steady enough on that rubber mat, she was ready for the next important part of her physiotherapy.

The ward gym had plenty of equipment, like these huge footballs that the therapist made her catch so that they could test Alice's balance. There were always two of them on hand, ready to grasp Alice's arms if she wobbled and looked like falling. She gripped the metal edge of the zimmer, conscious of the strain on her shoulders. Oh, how weak she still was!

Alice Finlay gritted her teeth. This stroke thing was there to be beaten. And beat it she would.

'That's it, Mrs Finlay. Great!' the girl encouraged. 'Wait till your daughter hears how well you're doing.'

Maggie waited by the lift. She recognised some of the other regular visitors standing around, looking at the red numbers flickering as they changed between floors. Her shoulders sagged as she stood there, mentally berating herself for being unable to drag her feet up those stairs. School had been particularly hard today, her five classes presenting her with differing challenges and her only non-teaching period being swallowed up by a 'please take' for an absentee teacher from their English department. Maggie was on her own for this evening's visiting hour. Bill had left her a message to say he'd be late. Again. It was par for the course, she thought wearily, and when he did come home she'd be

216

too full of her own misery over Mum's condition to have much sympathy for a tired husband.

The lift clicked into life, the doors opening with a sigh, and Maggie followed the others in. She closed her eyes, remembering the words of MacCaig's poem:

> I will not feel, I will not
> feel, until
> I have to.

Then the door opened again with a ping and the light from the corridors beckoned. Maggie blinked, the words of poetry dissolving as she entered the ward for a visiting hour of her own.

'Mum!' The sight of Alice Finlay sitting up in bed, hair brushed neatly back from her face, a proper smile reaching her mouth, made Maggie rush forwards and kiss her mother's cheek.

'Well, you look a hundred times better tonight. Can you tell me what you've been up to?'

Alice nodded and began to utter the words that were forming in her brain. Slowly she enunciated each one, pausing for breath and giving Maggie a grin at the astonished expression on her daughter's face.

'You can speak properly now!'

'Had plenty . . . of . . . practisss . . . in my . . . life,' Alice replied, giving a little nod.

Maggie heard the childlike treble in her mother's voice. Suddenly Alice Finlay had become an old, frail woman and, despite this progress, Maggie wondered if she would ever see the strong, feisty woman she had once been.

Bit by bit the story of the day's events unfolded and, by the time the bell signalled the end of visiting time, Maggie had learned that not only had her Mum begun to walk again, but that the regular speech therapy exercises had given her back that little voice.

'Mrs Lorimer? Can you spare a minute, please?' A figure in dark blue called to Maggie from the nurses' station, coming swiftly round and indicating a side room.

'Sister Kilbryde,' she introduced herself. 'Come in here, would you? I'd like a wee word about your mother.'

Maggie hardly saw the road as she drove home from the Southern General. It was good news, of course it was, but the problem of where her mother would go once discharged from hospital still remained. Maggie had fudged that particular issue with Sister Kilbryde and now her thoughts danced about between what she had been told and what was to come. Zimmers, walking sticks, a seat for the bath, a special easy chair: all the things her mother would need when she was finally ready to come home. But where home would actually be was the question uppermost in Maggie's mind. Sister Kilbryde had been full of questions about her patient's own little house. She'd shaken her head when Maggie had described the split-level design.

They could manage. Couldn't they? A mental image of her downstairs dining room swam into Maggie's mind. A bed settee would have to be purchased. They could put it against the far wall, away from any draughts, move some of the book cases upstairs. At least there was access to a loo and shower room. That bath seat would just have to wait. Maggie sent up a silent prayer of gratitude: thank goodness the previous owners of her home had built a little extension on at the rear of the building. It wasn't perfect but it would have to do until such times as Alice Finlay could cope with the stairs.

Maggie had turned into the drive before she knew it. Bill's ancient dark blue Lexus was parked to one side, facing the road as usual. A frisson of excitement (or was it fear?) coursed through Maggie's body, making her shiver, and for a moment she sat in her car, the engine idling, thinking of how to break the news that her mother would be coming here to live with them.

Sportscene was showing the highlights of the weekend's Scottish Premier Division game between St Mirren and Rangers. Lorimer knew the score already: five goals had thundered past the posts at Greenhill Road, leaving the Saints in a precarious position near the foot of the league table. But he wanted to watch the game for himself, try to take his mind off the day's events and, besides, Maggie had specially recorded the programme for him. He was dimly aware of the sound of his wife's key in the lock downstairs. Part of him wanted to heave his body out of this comfortable chair, go downstairs and offer to make a pot of tea but the lure of the game was just as strong and he sat on, torn guiltily between what he could and what he should be doing.

'It'll be all right,' Lorimer told her, smoothing her dark curls that now tumbled over his chest. 'She'll be fine. Lots of folk get over strokes. Manage to live a normal life again.' He could hear the muffled sob coming from Maggie's throat, feel the rise and fall of her chest. With every cry all the pent-up fears and worries of the last few days were being let loose. 'Anyway,' he bent to kiss her forehead, 'can you see someone like your mum giving in to this?' The sobs turned into a gurgle of laughter and Maggie sat up, wiping her face then collapsing once more against the comfort of her husband's body.

'You're all right, love. All right,' he soothed, holding her closer to his body, as though she was a little child.

Maggie needed this, he realised. It was better to open the floodgates of emotion than to continue to bottle it all up. He'd not been much of a support lately. And she hadn't complained about it, not once. Lorimer heaved a sigh. This feeling of being torn between duties, had it been like that for DCI Colin Ray? Cradling Maggie in his arms, Lorimer vowed to make it up to her. He'd telephone the social work people tomorrow, find out what steps he had to take to make their home safe for an old, infirm lady.

As her sobs subsided and he felt his wife's body relax, Lorimer began thinking about three other old ladies who had lived on their own. How would he have felt if it had been Alice? And any misgivings he had about sharing their home with his mother-in-law suddenly vanished.

'Three elderly ladies?' Dr Solomon Brightman mused. 'And they lived in the same estate? Interesting.'

'I thought Lorimer might be in on the case but that woman DI didn't as much as mention his name. Bit of a stuck up type, I thought. Good looking girl, though,' Rosie told him.

'And no defence wounds, you say,' Solly continued, his dark eyes taking on that far away look that his wife knew so well.

The firelight that glinted off his horn-rimmed spectacles was burnishing a halo around his dark curls, making the psychologist resemble some Biblical prophet. He was young still, but there were times when Rosie thought her husband had been born a wise old man. She smiled at the whimsical notion before recalling Freda Gilmour's post-mortem.

'Yes. Poor old soul. Wish there had been a better report on the first two women but there's nothing to give me a comparison. Just the technical details of time of death and suchlike.'

'Interesting.' Solly nodded into his beard again. 'It's just the sort of crime one might expect from a woman.'

'Och, Solly! You've got female serial killers on the brain just now,' Rosie protested, twisting round to admonish him. 'Come on, admit it, this book's taking over.'

Solly gave his wife an indulgent smile. 'Well, let's just say that it *is* the sort of methodology a woman might choose. As well as the type of victim.'

'Oh?' Rosie sat up a bit straighter, head to one side.

'Mm,' Solly said. 'You don't find female serial killers often. Statistically it's almost always a male. Some of the more notorious ones are paired up with a man, of course,' he added.

'Ah, like Bonnie and Clyde?'

'I was thinking more of Fred and Rosemary West, actually,' Solly murmured. 'But, yes, these two definitely come into that category.'

'But you think something like this could have happened to these old ladies?'

Solly shrugged and spread his hands in a non-committal gesture. 'Women tend to use a weapon like poison. You know the cases of nurses who have despatched their elderly patients with overdoses of insulin or potassium. They claim afterwards to have carried out mercy killings. Angels of death,' he said, raising his eyebrows dramatically. 'But here we have three killings that target vulnerable victims at their own homes *and* their killer uses minimum force. Could be a woman,' he added lightly, as though to consider the possibility once more.

'But why would anyone do that?'

'A sense that the elderly are taking up too much space on

Planet Earth? Or perhaps some sort of bitterness that each of them had a decent home to live in if the perpetrator was living in substandard accommodation? Who knows?'

Rosie's mouth gave a twist of disgust. She was well used to the atrocities that human beings performed upon one another but the idea of the wilful and capricious murder of three old ladies was a little hard to swallow.

Leaning back against her husband's knees, the pathologist wondered what Lorimer might make of Solly's suggestions.

The pathologist did not have to wait too long for that question to be answered. It was as she opened up her Internet connection next morning that she saw the email waiting for her from Lorimer. So, she thought, reading the lines, he wasn't involved in this case after all. But what was this about a possible link between the cyclist stalking that old lady and the fire in Kilmacolm? *Tenuous* was the word that immediately sprang to Rosie's mind as she felt her eyebrows rise in surprise. Unless he had some very good reason for supposing the two cases to be . . . ah! She read on, nodding to herself at the mention of the man, McGroary, who had been a worker at Jackson Tannock. Now, that did make a little more sense. The fellow's cycle had been impounded for detailed forensic examination as well. A silver racing job, Lorimer wrote. Like the one seen hurrying away from the Jackson fire that night. Rosie sat silently, letting her thoughts take her back.

It had been her first major case after the honeymoon. They had been in New Zealand for three glorious weeks, oblivious to the news back home, wrapped up in one another as only newly weds could be. It had been a holiday like no other. The memory of standing on the side of a windy hill one day towards the end of their trip came back to Rosie. 'I wish it could last forever,' she had told Solly. And she had meant it at the time. For that magical moment she had felt such a desire not to return to the world of corpses and psychopaths.

Now she read Lorimer's note and wondered what he was really thinking. Had the Jacksons died at the hand of McGroary and Monahan? And if so, why had they also targeted three elderly women? Nodding to herself, Rosie saw what the detective was up to. She would pass this on to her husband who might take more than a fleeting interest in such an aberration. And, knowing Solly, she expected he would want to offer an opinion on the two cases. Lorimer's hands must be pretty well tied down there, she realised. He couldn't just appoint Solly as part of an investigative team when he had little control over the divisional budget. But friend-ship could well make up for that sort of deficit, she grinned to herself. It didn't take a psychology degree to understand the policeman's tactic. Okay, so she was being used as a sort of go-between, but that was all right. And there were other things she could do for him. The triple murder wasn't his bag and so he couldn't risk the ire of that female DI to go poking around in the forensic reports from these crime scenes. Rosie frowned thought-fully, twin creases appearing between her eyebrows. She was owed one or two favours from certain forensic scientists at Gartcosh. Maybe it was time to call them in?

Then she remembered that day at the mortuary with Serena and Daniel Jackson. The girl had been really disturbed by the deaths of her parents, but in a way that had made her seem almost aggressive. And her brother, that breathtakingly handsome man, had been stricken not only by his own grief but by that of his sister. If Lorimer could find whoever had committed that dread-ful act against the Jacksons then those two young people might be able to pick up the threads of their lives. Pressing the reply button, Rosie decided that she could make a few inquiries of her own from among her forensic chums and pass on any relevant information to Lorimer.

'Youse'll no get onythin frae me. Ah demand tae see ma lawyurr!'

DI Martin turned on her heel, leaving the interview room where Anne-Marie Monahan had succeeded in wearing her down over the last hour and a half. Apart from a repetitive demand to see the said lawyer, there had been very little information forthcoming from the woman and Martin's reserves of patience had reached their limit. Anne-Marie had been charged with assaulting a police officer and they'd probably be able to have her for the drugs as well. But without sufficient evidence, there was no way on earth they could arrest the pair for murder. At least they hadn't had to get them to sign Voluntary Statement forms, she thought: the drugs being there had been a stroke of luck since there was now a lawful reason to detain them.

The backyard outside the police building was in darkness, a light drizzle smirring down. The DI had hardly lit up the first cigarette before her blonde hair was plastered to her head. Muttering imprecations against the relentless night sky and all creatures sent to provoke her, she leaned against the wall by the door, forcing her shoulders down. The nicotine hit was like a sigh coursing through her body, finally allowing the knotted muscles around her neck to relax. A few minutes were all she would need to regain her perspective, then she could go back in there and try another tactic with the Monahan woman.

But, as Rhoda Martin gazed at the grey mist slanting against the beam of lamplight, she knew that the cause of her disquiet was not just the prisoner upstairs. Try as she might, she couldn't forget the way Lorimer had looked at her, pityingly, as if she had no idea how to do her job. That was something she was finding hard to bear.

Still, he wasn't going to be around for much longer, she reminded herself with the ghost of a smile. Not if she had anything to do with it.

CHAPTER 25

'There isn't sufficient evidence to charge them with murder,' DI Martin told him stiffly.

'What about the tyre tracks? Any joy from the labs yet?'

Martin shrugged, deliberately avoiding the tall detective's gaze. 'They'll come in later on today or tomorrow. It's not like it's an all-out emergency.'

'But you still think they killed these old ladies, don't you?'

'Look, Lorimer, we know McGroary and Monahan. They're previous offenders. He's a vicious little bastard and if anything she's worse. Both her kids are in foster care because she neglected them so badly. Social work reports even went so far as to suggest cruelty to the younger one.'

'So you think they targeted three old ladies, then?' He spoke slowly as if he were uttering his thoughts aloud. 'Why?' Lorimer asked her, stepping directly into the DI's line of vision so she had to answer his question.

'How should I know? They're a pair of mad druggies!'

'That's not sufficient reason to target and kill these women,' Lorimer replied. 'This was a triple murder, carefully planned and carried out. Don't forget Jean Wilson's diary entries about the stalker.'

'How do you know about those?' Martin challenged him.

Now it was Lorimer's turn to give a disarming shrug. Station gossip, the gesture seemed to say. But he was not going to let on that Kate Clark was his particular source for that.

'Let's say for the moment that Monahan and McGroary are guilty. You can only charge them with possession of drugs, right? Do they present a real threat to the public if they're released from custody? That's what the Procurator Fiscal's office will say. Surely they aren't going to push any other old folk off their steps now, are they?'

DI Martin scowled at Lorimer, hating to admit that he was right. 'Well, if they didn't do it, who was it?'

Lorimer seemed to ponder the question for a moment or two. 'Look, I've got a friend at Glasgow Uni. Lecturer in behavioural psychology. He's helped me a lot in the past with cases of multiple murder.'

Martin gave a derisive snort. 'Behavioural psychologist? That wouldn't be Dr Brightman by any chance, would it? I can't see us having permission to chuck any of our budget his way!'

'Hold on,' Lorimer said. 'We might not need to pay a bean. Solly's a friend. I'm sure he would give us some insight into this if I asked him.'

She bit back a sudden retort. 'I *am* the SIO on this one, Sir.'

'I'm just trying to help,' he began, but Martin's green eyes were narrowing like an angry cat's.

For a moment Lorimer thought the woman was going to turn on her heel and stalk away from him but her fury seemed to subside as suddenly as it had appeared.

'All right then, Sir. I suppose it wouldn't do any harm if Dr Brightman came down here to have a look at the crime scenes. Give him copies of the case notes, too, if you like. But I'd rather it wasn't made official. Sir.'

For a moment their eyes met and Lorimer could have sworn that Rhoda Martin was challenging him in some way.

'Okay,' he agreed, 'I'll ask him.' *And I'm sure he'll say yes*, he wanted to add.

'Traumatic subarachnoid haemorrhage,' Rosie told him, holding the phone to her ear as she consulted the notes on her desk. 'Your DI down there has my emailed report,' she added. 'Poor old soul struck her head against the concrete and from quite a drop. Twelve stairs down. Think about the impact,' she added.

Lorimer thought about it and grimaced. The laws of physics being what they were, the woman's injuries had to be all the more severe given the distance she had fallen. He remembered something a senior officer had told him about the suicides who decided to make the Erskine Bridge their departure point from this world. Did they imagine that their bodies would splash softly into the dark waters below? From that height it was like landing on concrete. Just like these poor old ladies.

'Pity I couldn't see the other ones,' Rosie sighed.

'No, but Dr Bennie might be able to let you have a look at their medical records, surely?'

'Aye, that's true,' Rosie agreed. The women's GP had been most helpful: concerned, no doubt that he had missed the similarity in the deaths of his first two patients.

'Right, have to go. I'm still following up something from the Jackson case,' Lorimer told her.

'Report from forensics, boss.' Kate Clark waddled into his room, a sheaf of papers in her hand. 'Thought you'd like to see it, so I ran off a copy. They've analysed the different soil types around the track. Mostly just garden dirt, but there's one item that's a wee tad different. Some mulch stuff that the old lady must

229

have been using for her flower bed. A blood and bone mixture. Looked as if a cat had been digging it up,' she giggled. 'There was cat poo in amongst it as well. Who'd be a forensic chemist, eh?' She turned a page of the documents. 'Aye and it says that . . .' she read on then shrugged, obviously deciding to paraphrase the technical language in the report. 'Well, it seems that the tyre track isn't a brilliant match for McGroary's bike. They took a cast and tried to see if there were any wee bits that might have given an indication of a scar or tear on the rubber, but McGroary's bike doesn't have any and the cast does.'

'What about the make?'

'Oh, it's a similar make all right, Sir,' Kate told him, coming round to his side of the desk and pointing out the relevant paragraph.

'Racing cycle. Dead expensive make. Wonder where he nicked it from. That's his serial number from the bike frame,' she added. 'It's the same sort of tyre that loads of folk use for that kind of bike,' she sighed.

'So you're no further forward?'

'Not really. Unless we can turn up a suspect that has a bike like that with a tyre that's got a wee nick in it, we're scuppered.'

Lorimer ran his fingers through his dark hair. Was this line of inquiry simply going to lead to another dead end? They had a tenuous sort of evidence now but nothing against which to match it. A sighting of a cyclist near the scene of the fire; a cyclist that had stalked an old lady; and a tyre track that might have come from any one of hundreds.

Perhaps it was time to look at things from a different perspective. Why had these crimes against elderly women been committed? Why had someone set fire to the mansion house in Kilmacolm? Would Solly be able to figure any of this out?

'Okay, Kate. Are you all right?' he added, standing up as the police officer gave a sharp yelp of pain.

'Ooh, it's nothing, Probably just a wee elbow. Oh, son, that was a sore one,' she said, rubbing her bump with a frown.

Lorimer watched as she left the room. It wouldn't be long till Kate was off on maternity leave and he still hadn't come to any good conclusions in this review case. Losing an officer from his team would make it even harder. With a sigh of resignation, he reached for the heap of files that he'd read and re-read. Surely there must be something more significant that had been over-looked? A witness statement or a part of the forensic report following the fire investigation, perhaps? He would spend the rest of the day going through them all again then leave here at a decent time to accompany Maggie to the hospital.

It was the end of another working day and there was still some light in the evening sky above the western hills, dark and bright as only crepuscular blue can be. The rush hour traffic played its start-stop game at every set of traffic lights, each outside lane casting off like a row in some Scottish country dance. Lorimer's Lexus was ready to take off as soon as the green light blinked its signal, the drivers behind him watching the traffic lights just as impatiently. He was a careful driver, though he allowed his big car its head often enough, taking the outside lane as soon as he reached the dual carriageway. As he headed for Langbank he was unaware of a nondescript black Golf GTI that had picked him up somewhere on the road leading out of Greenock, cleverly allowing two other cars between them to mask its presence. And he was easy for the driver in the black Golf to follow: a driver who was equally used to fast cars.

It simply required patience to keep just that little bit behind, follow his lead as any driver might do, and see where the journey would end. It was almost forty minutes after picking up Lorimer's tail near the Greenock Police HQ that the Golf finally turned off the motorway and headed into the suburban jungles in Glasgow's south side. The lack of daylight was helpful, the black car being less easily spotted as it drove sedately in and out of the narrow avenues of houses.

When the Lexus finally swung into a driveway, it was simple enough for the Golf to keep going along the road, its driver taking a good look at the frontage of the house, noting its distinguishing features and continuing until the end of the street joined another, larger road again. Nobody would notice the sporty little car cruising around for a while before coming back to Lorimer's street.

Then, when enough time had passed to allay any suspicion, there would be an opportunity for its driver to make further notes about the residence of Acting Superintendent William Lorimer.

'Did you hear from Flynn yet?' Maggie asked.

'Aye, he's got an interview for that job. Is he coming up to the hospital tonight?'

Maggie nodded. 'I thought we might treat him to some supper here afterwards. I've got a pot of lentil soup made. And we haven't had him over here for ages.'

'Good idea. Well,' Lorimer stretched his arms, releasing the muscles that had stiffened up during the journey home, 'it'll be good to catch up again. See what the wee rascal's been up to.' He tossed his white shirt on to the bed and reached for a comfortable sports top. But before he could pick it up and put it on, Maggie was at his side, her arms encircling his bare torso.

His chest hairs tickled her nose and she turned her head, leaning her cheek against her husband's warm body. A great sigh seemed to flow all through her, melting her further into their single union. So long as he was there, then life was all right.

The idea of being alone, bereft, suddenly terrified her and Maggie gave an involuntary shudder.

'What was that for?' Lorimer asked, setting her away from his side.

'Nothing.' She shook the dark curls out of her eyes. 'Goose walked over my grave. Come on, time we were off to the Southern General before Flynn eats all of Mum's grapes.'

The black Golf drew up slowly once the tail lights of the Lexus had disappeared around the corner at the end of the street. They were both out. That was good. The hooded figure lifted a pair of small but powerful binoculars in order to take in every last detail of the residence of Mr and Mrs William Lorimer. The little star-shaped flowers of Winter Jasmine curled around the doorway, lit by a security lantern. The brass nameplate on the wall beside the front door bore the single name LORIMER. Behind the curtains drawn against the darkness a lamp still shone. There was no sign of any home security system, no single eye opened to watch the watcher.

The hooded figure nodded. That was even better. The next step would be so much easier to put into action.

'Och, that's awfie nice. Thanks. Lentil soup? Bet it's the same Mrs Fin used tae make fur me when ah stayed here.' Joseph Alexander Flynn grinned up at his hosts.

Maggie beamed back at him. Visiting hour had been a success. The younger man's banter had made Mrs Finlay's face twist into a lop-sided grin and she had even reached out her good hand to grasp his own as the bell rang, signalling that it was time for them all to go. A plate of homemade soup and a pot of spaghetti carbonara was scant reward for the pleasure of seeing her mother so animated tonight. Somehow Flynn's presence had made all of their own fears about her mother's discharge from hospital disappear.

Supper over, Lorimer strolled over to the drinks cabinet. 'A wee tot to finish you off, Flynn?'

'Och, no fur me, Mr Lorimer. Anyhow, I better keep ma head clear fur the morrow. Thon interview, mind?'

'Some of this, then?' Lorimer held up the orange bottle that was known as Scotland's Other National Drink.

'Where would you be working if you got the job?' Maggie asked.

Flynn turned towards her. 'Och, all over. It's a landscape business based in Erskine but they do stuff all down the coast. Contracts fur they new housing developments in Wemyss Bay, contracts fur the horse place out by Bishopton, wan fur that technology place up the back of Greenock—'

'Jackson Tannock?' Lorimer asked, interrupting Flynn as the young man counted off the businesses on his fingers.

'Aye, that's it. Couldnae mind their name. I knew a lad worked in that place. Daft eejit name of McGroary.'

'David McGroary?' Lorimer shook his head in disbelief at two coincidences landing on his lap at once.

'Aye. Huv ye come across him?' Their young friend screwed up his eyes and for a moment Lorimer recalled the scruffy lad that had been hauled off the Glasgow streets. There was still that element of the wee hard man about Flynn that hadn't been completely softened by the experience of a near-fatal accident. Had McGroary figured in Flynn's past life?

'He's been nicked. At Greenock. I'm down there doing a review of a case,' Lorimer said carefully.

234

'Ah, Davie's a bit of a space cadet. Used to be a pure nutter in the old days,' Flynn said. 'But I thought he'd got a bird and a hoose,' he added, regarding the detective thoughtfully.

'How did you come across McGroary?' Lorimer asked, screwing the top back on to the bottle of Irn Bru.

'Same course. He wis oan the . . . whatdyou call it . . . induction course wi me at Bellahouston when I started ma training. He'd been in the nick. Didnae make ony bones aboot it neither. We hung aroon wi some o' the other lads at weekends. He wis okay maist o' the time. But when he'd had some skag then he wis mental. Know whit ah mean?' Flynn pretended to blow smoke from his lips, two pointing fingers describing an arc through the air as if they were holding a joint. He grinned. 'You know *ah'm* off the stuff, though, eh?' He looked up slyly as if expecting to see a pair of disapproving faces looking at him.

Lorimer nodded, his thoughts racing. This was an unexpected source of information that could serve to enhance any background reports DI Martin might already be requesting. Tomorrow, he thought. Tomorrow he would talk to her, see if anything else Flynn could tell them tonight would be of value in their respective cases.

'See McGroary,' he began again. 'Was he the type to hold a grudge?'

Later, as he drove home again from dropping Flynn at his flat in Govanhill, Lorimer pondered the lad's words. David McGroary was a tough nut; that much he had seen for himself, but according to Flynn he'd also been eager to mend his ways. The gardening course had given him lots of big ideas, Flynn had said. McGroary had seen himself as the big businessman. Never mind that no bank in its right mind would lend someone like him the necessary capital, McGroary patently had enough self belief (or sufficient drug money stashed away) to realise his dream of making it on his own. The leaflets dropped through neighbourhood letterboxes had been testament to the man's desire to better himself. Okay, it was easy enough to label him a bad wee toerag given his past record. And he was obviously still a dealer, despite his attempts to go straight. But was he capable of cold-blooded murder? Lorimer shook his head. McGroary was a nasty character but somehow Lorimer had believed him when he had protested his innocence.

The Jackson fire wasn't the work of local vandals. Of that Lorimer was almost certain. And even though McGroary had a motive of sorts, it didn't really seem likely that he would have torched his employer's home like that. Different from setting fire to rubbish behind empty warehouses when he'd been a laddie. No, the perpetrator of this fire was someone who had wanted to kill those two people. And Lorimer needed to look more closely at their lives in order to find out why.

CHAPTER 26

Solomon Brightman smiled and sniffed the air. The damp earth bordering the swards of grass smelled rich and pungent. A few saffron-coloured crocuses were growing at the foot of a great chestnut tree, its bare branches waiting for warmer days. A scattering of snowdrops lay against a curve on the grass, a drift of white like the snow so recently melted from the park. It had been a bitter winter, snowfalls throughout the country bringing traffic and commerce to a standstill at times. But now the days were becoming lighter and the spring flowers in the Botanic Gardens would soon brighten the dull greens and browns. Solly watched as one of the gardeners drove an open truck along the pathway; boxes of primulas jigged up and down as the vehicle passed, a dazzle of pink, yellow and purple. By this afternoon the empty beds would be filled with these little plants, another sign that winter was losing its grip.

Solly thought of his conversation with Lorimer. He'd thought of apologising and saying (truthfully) that he was too busy with work to manage any extra commitments. But, listening to the man he knew so well, the psychologist had made his decision. Lorimer needed help and he could tell from the inflection in his voice that the detective was under considerable strain. Maggie's mum was never mentioned but she was there all the same, an anxiety hovering in the background.

The frown furrowing his brow made the psychologist suddenly sombre. Three elderly ladies had come to grief on their own back doorsteps. Doorsteps that began at the top of a steep flight of stairs above a concrete patio. Pushed to their death. By whom? He would visit the scenes of the crimes with a uniformed officer from Greenock, he had told Lorimer. Then he'd just have to see what came of it after that. It wasn't that he was being deliberately vague, Solly told himself, remembering the acerbic tone in his friend's voice after a lengthy pause in their conversation. But he had to have ideas of the locations in his head before he could begin to see the picture of the crimes as a whole.

There were no lectures this afternoon so he would take a train from Central Station down to Greenock, a journey he had rarely made since his arrival in Glasgow so many years before. It was a terminal for ocean-going liners and car ferries, Rosie had told him; one of the older towns strung like beads along the Clyde coast.

Terminal. It was a word that meant the end of things, wasn't it? But, perhaps in this case, it might also signify a beginning.

After the train had pulled out of Saint James's station, the urban landscape began to give way to green fields and the hint of a countryside that was emerging from its long winter's sleep. As Solly let his gaze sweep across the view from the window he saw flocks of wood pigeons, a few ducks in a stream and even caught a glimpse of a pair of hinds feeding quietly. Bishopton was the first rural village on the line, then Langbank where the view suddenly changed and the Clyde was there and Dumbarton Castle on the far side, its massive rock towering above. He could see the hills and mountains but what their names were he didn't know.

Was that Ben Lomond with snow still on its peak? Solly wasn't certain about the geography of this area and resolved to look up a map on his return home.

Maps meant a great deal to the psychologist and it was one of the integral parts of his job as occasional criminal profiler. Mapping murder had been seen as a vital part of the search for serial killers by Professor David Canter from the University of Liverpool and now every behavioural psychologist worth their salt took a serious look at the pathways and routes surrounding crime scenes. The three deaths in Port Glasgow were fairly close together but that didn't mean he would ignore the way they were grouped on a map of the area. On the contrary, Solly expected their location to give him some insight into the mindset of the killer.

If Dr Solomon Brightman was surprised to be met by a uniformed officer instead of DI Martin he didn't show it.

'PC Reid.' The man nodded towards the psychologist and led the way to a waiting police car. 'I've to take you to the houses, sir,' the officer added, opening the back door for Solly as though he were a passenger in a taxi or, worse, a felon being taken into custody.

'I'll sit up front, if that's all right, officer,' Solly murmured, wishing for a moment that he had not agreed so readily to Lorimer's request.

At last the car left the main thoroughfare and headed uphill away from the coast.

'Take a wee look down there, sir. Grand view, eh?' the officer said and Solly could hear the hint of pride in his voice.

It was indeed a grand view, the hilltop affording a vista of the widening river below and the hills beyond. He would return here one day with Rosie, once she had bought another car. In summer, perhaps, when that expanse of blue might be dotted with small boats seeking a wind to fill their sails.

Then it was gone, the road turning away from the view and curving into a street that led to a mass of houses clinging to the hillside. Upper Port Glasgow was a twentieth-century attempt to create a dormitory town in the windy spaces above the conglomerations of Gourock, Greenock and Port Glasgow, towns running together along the coastline. It seemed, to Solly, as if some giant hand had plucked the estates straight from one of the Glasgow housing schemes and thrust it down here. It was like a last urban outpost before the wilderness of field and moor staked its claim on the land.

'Here we are, sir. DI Martin asked me to take you to each of the locations in order,' Reid told him, drawing the car up in a small parking bay in a cul de sac surrounded by modest rows of terraced houses. Solly nodded, his mind already on the residents of this place. These women had lived here for decades, raising families, making lives for themselves. According to his notes, they had all lived in substantial houses, big enough for the average family. Old age and the strictures of living on pensions hadn't deterred them from wanting to keep their homes. So there was something about the area that made them want to remain. Good neighbours, perhaps? A settled feeling with all the attendant memories that meant home to them, maybe? Or had this become a little village on its own over the years? Those, and other questions, were to the forefront of Solly's mind as the police officer led him to the first house.

It was a plain pebble-dashed grey, fairly featureless to Solly's eye, with the look of a property that had been abandoned.

'She died on Boxing Day,' Reid informed him.

Solly's lips parted but no words came. How could he begin to tell this policeman that he had spent the happiest hours of his entire life on the selfsame day that an old lady had been murdered? Clenching then unclenching his fists, the psychologist followed the officer towards the high fence surrounding the terraced houses.

Solly stopped just outside the back gate. It was the end of a row of four identical homes, though he supposed that the small patches of garden and different curtains at the windows did disturb the dreary uniformity. He turned to look at the path around the house. Easy access from the main road to this end terrace and a blank gable wall from the house opposite made the psychologist nod his head as if to agree with some earlier supposition. If he was correct, then the killer had chosen the location as much as the victim herself.

Standing on the paving stones below the back door, Solly could all too easily imagine the body that had plummeted to the ground. The stairs were set at an angle to the rear entrance so that someone coming out of the house would have had to take a couple of paces forwards on to the large top step and turn around before making their descent. The metal handrail followed the line of the stairs, Solly noticed, and there was a white grab rail outside the door. A faltering pensioner might well be unsteady on their legs for a moment or two until their hand reached out, clutching. And the stairs were certainly wide enough for more than one person. Had she known her assailant, then? Whoever had pushed the old woman down that flight of stairs must have come right up to the top; and used considerable force to shake the poor old soul's hand away from her rail. Solly shook his head, wondering. The viciousness of that act alarmed him. *A woman might have done something like that*, he'd told Rosie, but standing here, the wind blowing scraps

241

of dead leaves around his feet, Solly was no longer certain of the theory he had so glibly suggested.

By the time they had reached Freda Gilmour's home, Solly had formed a few ideas about the person who had carried out these acts. All three of the houses were situated at the end of a row of terraces. The houses ran in blocks of four, separated by small lanes running between them. But the homes of the victims had not simply been on one of these corners, but at the very end of the rows. There was no street lighting right outside the main doors or back doors, nor did any of the neighbouring houses look directly into the gardens. It had been, Solly realised, the subject of careful planning on the part of someone who either knew the area very well indeed (and possibly lived in the estate) or who had carried out a detailed reconnaissance whilst under the guise of someone who would not be noticed, like a regular delivery man.

The estate itself was built into the hillside and several of the terraces were designed as split-level homes, their back gardens running steeply downwards to the ribbons of pathways. All three victims had lived in such homes, the stairs from their back doors ending in a few concrete slabs masquerading as patios.

'Do you mind if I walk around here a bit on my own? Less conspicuous, perhaps?' He smiled at the officer who merely shrugged and stepped back into the warmth of his patrol car. If this bearded, rather exotic-looking psychologist thought he was inconspicuous then he was daft, the gesture seemed to say.

Solly wanted to walk around the areas away from the victims' houses in order to see what differences there might be. He noticed that many of the terraces were on flatter ground, paths pitted by years of wear and tear, plastic bags like pale white bats clinging to the hedgerows. Some of these paths were as accessible

242

to a cyclist as the others, but with the difference that there were no steep flights of stairs descending to the gardens below.

Solly stopped abruptly. What were the chances of there being other similar locations on this estate? There was a sudden churning in his stomach. He had to know. Had to stop it happening again.

'Can you drive around all the streets, please, officer?' Solly asked, opening the car door and stepping into the patrol vehicle once more.

PC Reid stifled a sigh. His orders were to accommodate this odd chap from Glasgow University, this *beardy weirdy* as his wife would have called him, so that's what he would do, even if he thought privately that it was a bloody waste of police time.

DI Rhoda Martin had quite a different opinion of Doctor Solomon Brightman as she ushered him into the small room reserved for visitors. His quiet air of authority might have impressed the detective, but her thoughts on the psychologist had come from personal experience.

'I don't suppose you remember me,' she began, sitting down opposite Solly. 'I took your class in my first year at uni.'

Solly smiled and shook his head. 'Sorry.' He spread his hands in a gesture of apology. 'There are so many students. And my memory's awful,' he added with a twinkle that made Rhoda Martin doubt the truth of this last statement. Still, perhaps it was better not to be remembered as an average student who should have performed so much better than she had. A lower second had been okay but hadn't set the heather on fire, nor had it been something about which her parents could boast to all their friends at the golf club.

'This case,' she began, twisting her fingers together on her lap, 'do you really think you might be able to shed some light on it?'

Solly nodded, looking intently at the officer. His eyes seemed to bore straight through the blonde detective and she found herself blushing. There was a silence between them that she found a little uncomfortable; those kind brown eyes and that smile that seemed to tell her that he knew her very thoughts. Rhoda shivered. If he did . . .?

'The person who perpetrated these awful acts must be stopped, Inspector,' Solly said at last.

Rhoda frowned. 'What on earth do you mean?'

'I mean just that. Someone has killed three elderly ladies for a reason unknown to us, but from what I have seen I am afraid . . .' he tailed off, making a gesture with his hands in the air as if Rhoda should be able to finish his sentence for him, but her frown was rapidly becoming a scowl.

'You see,' he went on after another long pause, 'the method of killing was rather simple once your killer had done his homework.' It was Solly's turn to frown now. 'I say *his* advisedly, of course. It may well have been carried out by a woman. My current line of study is into acts of violence by what we call the fairer sex.' The hands spread again as if he were apologising for such a statement.

Rhoda was beginning to remember such gestures and also how much they had irritated her throughout her undergraduate year of studying psychology. But this man was giving up his time to help them so she should at least show some polite interest.

'So, any ideas?'

Solly nodded, his face becoming quite grave. 'Sadly, yes. I think you have a very dangerous type of person in your area, Inspector Martin. Very dangerous indeed. In fact,' the psychologist bit his lip as if to prevent the words coming out, 'I would go so far as to say that, unless there was something material to be gained by killing these women, this person has killed simply because he could.'

Rhoda's eyes widened. 'You're telling me there's a psychopath on the loose?'

Solly neither nodded nor shook his head but continued to gaze into the detective's eyes so that she looked away.

'I can't believe that,' she said. 'There must be something that links these three deaths,' she continued, almost to herself. 'Surely?' she added, turning to face the psychologist again.

'That's for the police to investigate, of course.' Solly nodded. 'But I believe that whoever did this had selected these homes on the basis of their accessibility as well as for the frailty of their occupants.'

'You mean he didn't even know who the women were?' Martin's response failed to hide the scornful tone in her voice.

'Oh, he would know them after a while. At least in terms of their day-to-day habits and when he might find them in alone at night.'

'So,' she spoke more carefully again, not wishing to appear discourteous, 'he stalked them for a while before deciding to push them off the steps to their deaths?'

'I imagine that will have been his procedure, yes,' Solomon answered a trifle stiffly. 'But I must warn you, Inspector, this might still be part of an ongoing pattern.'

Rhoda Martin frowned, head to one side, considering the psychologist's line of thought.

'You see, I have looked all around the area and there are still some houses that resemble those of the victims.'

'What do you mean?' Rhoda looked puzzled.

'I mean,' Solly said with the sort of sigh one might reserve for a small child who has failed to grasp something elementary, 'that the conditions the killer would be looking for still exist on that estate. And if certain houses are inhabited by vulnerable elderly folk, then . . . who knows?'

Rhoda Martin gave a wintry smile. Yes, her expression seemed to say, she'd be polite to this man, the lecturer whom she had once held in such high regard. But now *she* was the authority figure and he was simply a civilian whose theories, she was sure, would be laughed at in a court of law.

'Well, thank you for all of that, Dr Brightman. It was very good of you to take the time to come down and help us,' she said in the sweet tones she usually reserved for men that she fancied. 'Can I offer you some coffee before your journey back to Glasgow?'

Solomon Brightman was not the type of man to harbour any animosity. In fact the detective's attitude amused rather than insulted him. He'd done a favour for Lorimer and now that favour meant he could face his friend and give him his opinion on the case. That DI Martin was in charge of it was neither here nor there. Lorimer was down at Greenock and surely he could bring some influence to bear on the triple killing? Sitting on the train, watching flocks of white gulls bobbing past on the currents of the river, Solly smiled to himself. He was enough of a psychologist to understand what had happened back there. A specialist being paid a hefty fee would have attracted much more respect and probably had his views taken a lot more seriously. It was human nature, after all, to value what you had paid for. Still, he hoped the idea he had planted into that young woman's head would result in the housing estate being included in any routine police patrol.

Failure to do that might well result in one more old lady falling to her death.

246

CHAPTER 27

'I can come home!'

The four monosyllables were spoken slowly but with an obvious delight, as though Alice had been saving them up for hours.

Maggie hugged her mother, hoping the expression of alarm was well hidden as her cheek brushed the older woman's hair. It was wonderful. Of course it was. So why did she feel that sudden sense of panic?

'Oh, Mum! That's great. And just listen to you. Your speech has come on so well,' Maggie enthused. And it was true. Of course there was still that falsetto tremble and Alice Finlay's words were slow and slightly slurred, but the speech therapy had worked wonders for her.

'We've got that new sofa bed downstairs and Bill can bring over your own duvet. We know how much you like that one,' Maggie told her, aware that she was beginning to gabble from sheer nerves. 'You'll have Chancer for company every night. If you want him,' she added.

Alice smiled and gave a little nod. She loved her daughter's pet and the orange cat knew it, making a bee-line for Alice's lap every time she paid them a visit.

'Sister . . .' Alice's mouth was open but the word didn't come.

'Kilbryde,' Maggie supplied, receiving another weak nod for her pains. 'Does she want to see me?'

Alice nodded and smiled again and Maggie saw the relief on her mother's face at not having to try to utter the difficult word.

Would it be like this for ever? Having to fill in the blanks. Or would her Mum make more progress as time went on? Suddenly Maggie was anxious to speak to the senior nurse, so, patting the back of Alice's hand, she rose from the grey plastic chair beside her bed.

'I'll go and see her just now. Be back soon. Don't be dancing in the corridor while I'm away,' she joked.

As Maggie turned to leave, the realisation of all this responsibility threatened to overwhelm her. Oh, help, she was even beginning to talk to her mother as if she were a small child instead of the grown woman who had wiped her own snotty nose and scolded her for childhood misdemeanours.

The sight of the woman behind the desk at the nurse's station with that friendly smile and air of calm authority reassured her at once.

'Sister, Mum tells me she is going to be able to come home to us,' Maggie began.

'That's correct, Mrs Lorimer, but there are one or two details I'd like to explain to you before we can allow that to happen. Would you like to step into my office?'

Maggie breathed a sigh of relief. There would be health care professionals coming in every day and also in the evenings. She wasn't expected to be at home all day with her mother after all. It was a matter she had discussed with the deputy head at Muirpark, stressing how much she valued her job and how sorry she would be to have to resign, if it came to that. The sister had explained all about attendance allowance and Mrs Finlay's financial situation giving her the right to have carers in her daughter's home, paid for by the social services. In time, she had hinted, Alice Finlay might even be allowed to return to her own home, subject to various safety measures being put in place. It all depended upon her progress. A stroke was sometimes a warning of worse to come, she advised Maggie. But with a healthy diet and the correct medication Mrs Finlay might recover well and live for years. Meantime, Sister Kilbryde had told Maggie, if she wouldn't mind allowing the professionals to visit her home to check that everything was in order, Mum could be with her by the weekend. She'd be telephoned tomorrow by one of the occupational therapists to make arrangements.

As she returned to the ward, Maggie's thoughts were in a whirl. She had loads of Prelim marking to do and so a lot of midnight oil would be burning between now and Saturday. Plus she'd have to air Mum's duvet and look out fresh bedding for the sofa bed. She could go to Braehead Shopping Mall on the way home and buy one of these mattress toppers to make it more comfortable. Surely M&S would have one? There was no time for grocery shopping so she'd have to place an order online to arrive late tomorrow night. What were Mum's favourite foods? Were there any that were now on a banned list from the hospital dietician?

'Mag . . .?' Her mother looked up at her anxiously and Maggie realised that she was wearing her frowning face, as Alice was wont to call it.

'It's fine, everything's fine. Sister Kilbryde reckons you could be home by Saturday if the doctor gives you the okay,' she told her mother. A wide-mouthed smile from her daughter made Alice give a sigh and sink her head back into the pillows.

Maggie almost added *If they think our house is fit for you to stay.* But such little concerns would not be voiced. It was important that Mrs Finlay was not stressed about anything, the nurse had insisted. Quietness and rest in a familiar place would be as good as the medicines she was now receiving. Maggie could worry about the details once she was clear of the hospital. But for now, all she wanted to do was to give her mother something good to think about.

'Chancer'll be delighted to see you.' She grinned. 'Just wait till I tell him!'

'Can you do it next week?' Lorimer asked, listening to his young friend's voice on the telephone. 'Only it looks like Alice is coming home to us this weekend and we'd want her to have time to settle in.' He smiled at the reply. 'Aye I bet they're noisy. And the amount of work needing done here will probably drive the neighbours mad. Best get it over and done with during the week when most of them are out at work. Okay. Thanks. See you soon.'

Maggie looked up from her pile of marking, a question in her eyes.

'Flynn,' Lorimer supplied. 'He's going to tackle the garden next week. Clear the old winter stuff and give the grass its first cut. Says he's got a huge power mower that makes a racket.'

'Good.' Maggie nodded. 'It'll be company for Mum as well. She's always had a soft spot for Flynn.' She chewed her lip thoughtfully. 'How's he going to bring the gardening machinery all the way over here?'

'A pal's going to drop him off and pick him up later on.'

Maggie nodded again, turning her attention to a Prelim paper that was already covered in red pen marks. 'That'll please Mrs Ellis. No big white vans cluttering up the street.'

Lorimer grinned. Their neighbour was a fussy woman who found fault rather too easily with her neighbours. Still, if it hadn't been for her watchful disposition, Flynn might have suffered badly at the hands of those men who had abducted him from Lorimer's home. His smile slipped a little at the memory. It could all have gone so horribly wrong. The harrowing experiences he'd endured had made Joseph Alexander Flynn a stronger person. And, despite them all, one thing he had never lost was his infectious sense of humour. Yes, he thought, his mother-in-law would enjoy the banter with him next Monday.

There were still three days until Saturday and Maggie Lorimer was now counting them in hours. There was so much still to be done, so many little things to remember. Her kitchen calendar was disfigured with scribbles and post-it notes and she had resorted to adding items on to the magnetic shopping list that her friend, Sandie, had given her for Christmas. Once Mum was home and ensconced in their (now much tidier) dining room, it would be a lot easier. Wouldn't it? The downstairs loo was sparkling clean and decked with newly laundered fluffy towels as well as Alice's favourite *Roget et Gallet* rose perfumed soap, another of Maggie's Christmas gifts from one of her Sixth Year pupils. Their own sitting room was upstairs across the landing from the bedrooms. Originally used as a bedroom-cum-playroom by the previous owners, the Lorimers had opted to make this their main public room. The long dining room downstairs incorporated what was really Maggie's study, handy for a stroll through to the kitchen for the endless cups of coffee she required to sustain her through the hours of marking.

They would have to try to spend some time with Mum in the evenings, though it would be nice to have their own space upstairs at the end of a day. The TV would have to be kept low, so as not to disturb her. And maybe she could find a wee hand bell to let her Mum ring should she need either of them in a hurry. But it should all work out fine, Maggie's sensible self told her firmly. So why was she experiencing these little pangs of guilt? Or were they feelings of inadequacy? After all, nothing prepared you for the daunting task of caring for your own parent, did it?

'How's your mother-in-law, Sir?'

Lorimer tried to keep his expression neutral but knew from DI Martin's face that he had singularly failed to hide his surprise. 'How did you know?'

'Oh, your friend, Dr Fergusson, told me about her,' Rhoda replied, her head to one side as if she were considering her superior's situation.

'She's much better, actually,' Lorimer told her. 'Coming home at the weekend.'

'To stay with you?'

'Yes. My wife and I are having her until she's well enough to return to her own home.'

'Nice of you to do that, Sir.' Rhoda nodded approvingly. 'Thousands wouldn't bother.' And, giving him a condescending sort of smile, she walked away, leaving Lorimer feeling that she had somehow wrong-footed him.

He hadn't wanted this to be public knowledge, but then it was no use blaming Rosie since he hadn't exactly hidden his private life away. But it made him simmer inside to think that DI Rhoda Martin would now be making comparisons between his own situation and that of Colin Ray. He had to crack this case now, or be made to look totally incompetent.

*

It had been an idea gnawing away at him based on a case from way back where a man facing financial ruin had taken his own life and those of his family. The fire and the reason behind it: both had provoked this notion. Had it been the murder of two people, after all? A call to the local doctor had given Lorimer enough reason to drive back up the country road to Kilmacolm. It was a fresh day, a brisk westerly wind blowing away the last vestiges of rain clouds over the river towards Dunoon and the Cowal Hills. Inland there were signs of spring; wild primroses appearing in sheltered banks by the roadside, a lark rising from its thicket of nest to soar into the blue. Lorimer longed to pull over and watch its flight, but there were too many matters ahead of him today.

The doctors' surgery was on the main road running through the village from Port Glasgow to Bridge of Weir. Lorimer found a space in the car park and walked round the corner to the grey stone building.

'Superintendent Lorimer to see Doctor Hamilton,' he informed the receptionist in a tone that he hoped was quiet enough not to attract the attention of the other patients who were waiting behind their magazines.

'Please go right through. Doctor Hamilton is expecting you,' the woman told him, indicating the door to her left.

A quick knock was all it took, then Lorimer was in the consulting room. A pretty woman in her mid-thirties stood up immediately, came around her desk and shook his hand.

'Take a seat, Superintendent. And thanks for coming,' she added. 'I wasn't sure what to do after Sir Ian's death. It wasn't something I was prepared for, I suppose.'

'Doctor Hamilton, I told you on the telephone that I am investigating the deaths of Sir Ian and Lady Pauline.' Lorimer hesitated, then looked straight at the woman, his blue eyes holding her as he spoke again. 'Do you have any reason to think that this fire might have been started by Sir Ian himself?'

'Oh, dear.' Dr Hamilton dropped her gaze and clasped her hands together tightly. 'I should have said something at the time, shouldn't I? It was just that . . .'

'Sir Ian wanted you to keep it from his family?' Lorimer supplied.

'You guessed, then?'

'It was something to support a theory I've had,' Lorimer said.

'He had a form of prostate cancer that isn't easily treated,' the doctor told him. 'It would have killed him eventually. He knew that. But he didn't want anyone to make a fuss. No therapies, nothing. If he was going to die, then it had to be on his own terms. He was that sort of man, Superintendent,' Dr Hamilton said, shaking her head as if in despair at the vagaries of human nature. 'But do you really think he would have let his wife die in the fire? Surely that was an accident? And that beautiful house?' She shook her head again sadly.

'It's hard to surmise what was on his mind at the time, doctor. And that was one reason why I wanted to see you. As his GP you were better placed than most to know that sort of thing.'

'Well, I'm not sure,' she began. 'He was a private sort of person. A bit fierce, if you want to know the truth, but that may have been because of the pain and the fact that his sex life had been on hold for so long. Ian Jackson came to me for medical help, yes, but he was not the sort of man to ask for anything else. No hand to hold, I'm afraid.' She smiled tremulously as if she had been saddened by her patient's reticence as much as the nature of his death.

'And you would be prepared to say as much in a court of law?'

'Of course.' The woman's eyes widened. 'If it should come to that.'

Lorimer had not been surprised to find that Hugh Tannock also lived in Kilmacolm. The village was home to many captains of industry and weel kent names, as Betty MacPherson would have put it. Just a forty-minute drive from Glasgow by fast car, and half that time from the international airport, the village was perfectly situated for anyone who wanted easy access to Scotland's largest city while enjoying a rural existence.

Tannock's house was set high above Gryffe Road, minutes away from the surgery, its façade facing down the valley towards the road that led to Quarriers Village. It seemed to the detective that the windows glinting in the morning sunshine were disdainful eyes surveying the scene below. The green sward of lawns swept around the white house ending in masses of thick rhododendrons that screened the place from passing traffic. He was expected and so the tall black metal twin gates were open but, after he drove the Lexus up towards the front entrance, he saw them close silently behind him. Tannock lived alone, Lorimer reasoned, so it was sensible to have such security measures, but still he felt an uneasy sense of having been taken hostage by the man he was about to visit.

Lorimer had expected to meet at the factory but Tannock had invited him here instead. *To see how the other half lived?* Maggie had joked when he'd told her. But whatever the man's reason, Lorimer was curious. Psychologically Tannock would have the advantage of being on his home turf, playing the host. Did that mean he had some inkling about why the detective had requested another meeting? That, and many other questions, would shortly be answered.

The driveway was mossy underfoot, not through neglect but rather as if the owner preferred a rustic type of pathway. Close up he saw that the lawn was in perfect condition, more like the greens at Kilmacolm golf club, and Lorimer wondered if the same groundsman cared for it. He pressed a bell set into the side of the porch and waited.

Looking around, the detective could see the distant hills, patches of sunlight making their flanks an emerald green. That was Misty Law, surely? He'd climbed it with Maggie once after they had been to Muirshiel Country Park to see the hen harriers. For a moment Lorimer wondered what it must be like to be Hugh Tannock, living here with this fabulous view that all his millions had bought him. Then he thought of Pauline Jackson and remembered just what the man had actually lost.

'Superintendent Lorimer, do come in. Sorry I didn't come down sooner. On a call.' Tannock was suddenly there in the vast doorway, ushering Lorimer into his house.

'My housekeeper's away down to the village for some shopping,' Tannock explained. 'Do come through to the kitchen and we'll have a cup of something. Eh?'

Lorimer tried not to stare at the huge reception hall as he followed. There was a highly polished table, bigger than his dining table at home, on which stood an immense floral display. The oak-panelled walls were adorned with paintings in gilded frames and the art historian in Lorimer was provoked to wonder at their provenance. He badly wanted to examine these oils to find a signature. And that wasn't really a Rubens, hanging over on that wall, was it?

'In here,' Tannock called and the detective lengthened his stride to follow the man into a surprisingly old-fashioned kitchen from which music was playing. It looked, to Lorimer, like his idea of a perfect farm kitchen with its long, scrubbed pine table and chairs fitted with bright patchwork cushions. They were slightly faded and the stitching was a little frayed in places but for some reason Tannock had kept them. Had they been painstakingly stitched by the hand of Mrs Tannock, his ex-wife? Or were they from a more distant past? Lorimer let his eyes rove around the kitchen, enjoying what he saw. A cream-coloured Aga and a Welsh dresser full of blue and white china added to the picture. All it needed, he thought, was a cat sleeping somewhere to complete this vision of domestic bliss. As if his thought had conjured it up, a black and white moggy rose from its place on one of the chairs, stretching its back in a furry arc.

Tannock stroked its fur. 'This is Monty,' he said, then looked quizzically up at Lorimer. 'You're all right with cats? Some folk can't stand them, others are allergic.'

'Fine, fine,' Lorimer told him, strolling over to tickle the cat under its chin. 'We've got one at home.'

Tannock grinned suddenly. 'Good. Knew we had something in common. Cat people.' He stopped, listening suddenly to the classical version of 'Bohemian Rhapsody' coming from the radio in the corner. 'Freddie Mercury was a cat lover. Did you know that?' he asked, one eyebrow arching.

Lorimer nodded. The late Queen star's fondness for the animals was legendary.

'Tea or coffee?' Grosset asked, kettle in hand.

'Tea, please. Just plain old tea, nothing fancy. And milk, no sugar,' he added, stretching out his long legs under the table.

It was the first time in a long time Lorimer had felt so relaxed, sitting here in this warm, comfortable place, Monty purring between them. He had liked Hugh Tannock from their first meeting and now he found himself enjoying being here with the man

257

once more. Nice as it was, it made it harder to ask difficult questions; it would be almost unmannerly to bring up the subject that was uppermost in his mind. But, Lorimer reminded himself, he was here to do a job, not to be beguiled by this affable man and his gracious hospitality.

But when Tannock had set down the mugs and a plate of chocolate biscuits, his face took on a serious expression.

'I have the feeling you're not here on a social visit, Superintendent. I take it you bring news of an unpleasant sort,' he added gravely.

Lorimer took a sip of the tea before replying. The biscuit plate remained untouched.

'Lady Pauline,' he began and looked the man straight in the eyes.

'Ah.' Tannock sighed and gave a nod. 'I wondered how long that would take you.'

'You should have told me about your relationship with her,' Lorimer rebuked him gently.

Tannock raised his eyebrows and gave a shrug. 'But why? It wasn't in any way relevant to your inquiries.'

'I think that's a matter for me to decide, sir,' Lorimer told him.

'Well, I can't see what bearing our . . .' He stopped as if the word *affair* was too distasteful to utter aloud. 'Our friendship,' he said at last. 'How can it be important to their deaths?'

Lorimer was silent for a moment. This was the question he had been struggling with. There was one possibility that he had considered based on another high-profile house fire.

'Did Sir Ian know about you and Pauline?'

Tannock frowned. 'I honestly didn't think so. But what if he did?'

Lorimer pushed the mug of tea away. 'There was a case a few

258

years back where a house was deliberately set on fire, its occupants killed in the process. That fire was started by the owner who died alongside his wife and child.'

Tannock nodded, stunned by the memory of a tragic case that had made newspaper headlines for weeks. 'I remember the one you mean. But he'd been in a terrible financial situation, hadn't he? Jackson Tannock Technology is a thriving business and Ian had nothing like *that* to worry him.'

Lorimer let the silence between them deepen. Then the man before him groaned, his hands covering his face as the implication of his own words sank in. Had Ian Jackson taken his own life and that of his wife in a fit of jealousy? It was a question that Lorimer did not need to ask. It was there in the room, a horrible possibility that might never be proved this side of eternity. Suddenly the warmth from the Aga was stifling and the ticking clock on the wall above it seemed unnaturally loud. Monty, he noticed, had slipped off Tannock's knee and disappeared out of the room.

'The accelerant?' Tannock asked hopefully. 'Wasn't it put there by someone else?'

'Traces were found in and around the house and a chip pan had been deliberately left to burn. It was right underneath their bedroom. *If* it was done by an intruder then he had easy access to the house.' Lorimer watched the man closely, seeing the doubt in his eyes change to despair.

'It's not something that I can put in a report since it's only a theory. If forensic evidence comes to light to corroborate this idea, though . . .' Lorimer shrugged to show what might happen in that scenario. 'But there is something else I think you ought to know, Mr Tannock.' Lorimer watched the man's face carefully as he continued. 'Sir Ian was dying of cancer.'

All the colour seemed to drain from Hugh Tannock's face as he took in the detective's words. 'Are you sure?' he whispered at last.

Lorimer nodded. 'I've just spoken with his doctor. Sir Ian had insisted that his condition be kept secret from his family. But it does create a different sort of scenario now, doesn't it? A man with a reason to kill himself, and perhaps to destroy everything he loved.'

'Oh, Pauline, what have I done to you?' Tannock whispered, stumbling from the table. He groped his way towards the Belfast sink, holding on to its edge for support. Then he turned his gaze to a picture beside the windowsill. Picking it up, he held to his chest, shoulders heaving in silent sobs.

It should have been a private moment, a signal for Lorimer to leave, but something made him stop. He had seen that image before, hadn't he?

'Excuse me, sir, may I have a look at that picture?'

Tannock turned his ruddy face streaked with tears. 'It's all I've got left of her. Last photo she ever gave me.' He gulped, handing it over.

Lorimer took it carefully. It was a copy of the one that he had seen in Daniel Jackson's flat.

His heart quickened.

'Where was this taken?' he looked across at Tannock.

'On the landing. Outside their bedroom.'

'And how long before the fire was the photograph taken?'

Tannock must have caught the new note of excitement in Lorimer's voice for his eyes glittered with hope.

'Just a few days, as I recall. Why?'

Lorimer smiled suddenly. 'May I take this? I promise it will be returned to you. But I can tell you something, Mr Tannock. Looking at this photograph, I think we may have jumped to the wrong conclusion. I don't think that fire was started by Sir Ian after all.'

It was perhaps a little cruel to leave the man worried and wondering after Lorimer's earlier supposition had reduced him to tears, but it was a police matter and one that had to remain as confidential as possible. What he had seen in that photograph gave Lorimer renewed energy to tackle this case.

For, behind the seated woman smiling into the camera's lens, was a bedroom door with a key in the lock.

But it was on the outside of the room.

So some other hand must have turned that key, deliberately locking the couple in and leaving them to their fate.

CHAPTER 28

'Yes!' Lorimer gazed at the telephone on his desk as if it had conjured up some magic. Somehow the detailed information in this initial forensic report had not filtered through to Ray's investigative team. He ground his teeth, reminding himself exactly why he was here doing this review. The forensic scientist at Gartcosh had confirmed exactly what Lorimer had wanted to know. The brass door fittings had been intact after the fire had done its worst and now he knew what he had only previously suspected: the key was still in the lock, its mechanism clearly showing that it had been used to secure the bedroom door. And that photograph on the landing told him it had been turned from the outside.

This put a whole new complexion on things: now Lorimer wanted to examine the case from each and every perspective. What reason could anyone possibly have had for killing these two people? And who had easy access not only to sprinkle accelerant around the house but to ensure that the key had been put into the keyhole on the landing side? It was not, he reasoned, something that anyone would have noticed. He doubted whether either of the Jacksons would have been in the habit of locking their own bedroom door when there were only two of them at home. And he doubted very much whether Pauline Jackson had risked having her lover there. Tannock had insisted that their liaison had been discreet. But not discreet enough for the Betty MacPhersons of this world, he told himself.

No, someone had set that fire deliberately to kill Ian and Pauline Jackson.

He considered Serena and Daniel. They stood to inherit vast wealth in the form of the company shares, and money was all too often a motivator in murder. But they had struck Lorimer as already having plenty of the world's goods. And there had been nothing acrimonious between the children and parents. No, he thought, that didn't fit. He couldn't see Daniel killing anybody. The young man had enormous prospects within the firm. And, as for Serena, well, hadn't she been completely traumatised by the loss of her parents?

The offshore business had intrigued him and it was an area that he had still to investigate thoroughly. Some feelers had already been out in the UK but perhaps it was time to cast the net further afield.

'DI Martin, could I have a word, please?' Lorimer poked his head around the door where the DI and several other members of the team were sitting.

Rhoda Martin stood up, brushed invisible fluff off her dark skirt and sashayed out of the room after Lorimer.

'Take a seat, will you? This won't take long and I know you're up to your ears with the Port Glasgow case.'

Martin sat opposite the senior detective, crossed her legs and waited, hands folded neatly on her lap.

'It's the Jackson murder. We've had a real breakthrough,' Lorimer told her. 'Look.' He handed her the forensic report with his own appended notes clipped on one corner. Martin read the paper, her eyes widening.

'Bloody hell!' she said at last. 'You surely don't think that it's one of the family?'

'That's what I wanted to ask you. Daniel and Serena Jackson are your friends. Right?'

'We . . .' Martin began, 'we all went to school together. Serena and I have stayed in touch.' *Matter of fact I'm seeing her tomorrow*, she almost told him. She stopped herself, frowning. 'Daniel is a great guy. Total sporting star, clever, always had the girls following him about. If he'd gone through the US school system they'd have called him a jock. But the nicest type you could want to meet,' she insisted.

Lorimer nodded. 'I liked him too,' he said. 'And I can't think of any reason why he would want to commit such a terrible act.'

'Nor would Serena,' Martin retorted quickly. 'Okay, she was a bit daft at school. Played around with all the troublemakers, didn't work very hard at her subjects. But that was just Serena. She was high spirited in those days,' Martin added thoughtfully.

'What happened to make her change?' Lorimer asked. This description of the young woman he had met certainly did not tally with DI Martin's account of her friend.

'She's a lot quieter nowadays, I'll grant you that, Sir,' Martin admitted. 'But don't we all grow up eventually? She wanted to make her career as a model, but the lifestyle was all a bit too much for her, I guess. Nice to have the family business to fall back on, though. And she never wanted for a thing. The Jacksons were the most generous of parents. Her twenty-first birthday party was the talk of the village for months afterwards.'

'Okay, so there's no apparent motive from either of the children,' Lorimer agreed. 'And to be truthful it didn't seem likely. Did it?

No,' he continued. 'If it wasn't an insider, then perhaps it was someone known to the family who had easy access to the house.'

'You mean like staff? Cleaners and whatever? Or are we back to Davie McGroary?'

Lorimer ran a hand through his dark hair and sighed. 'I didn't think McGroary had it in him. But someone had access to that house. Someone who knew where the Jacksons' bedroom was, and who put that key on the other side of the door several days before the fire.'

'McGroary wouldn't be likely to have admission to the house, though, would he?'

Lorimer shook his head. 'No. So who else is there? Cleaners? Housekeeping staff?'

'They didn't have anyone resident. We did ask that at the time, Sir,' Martin pointed out. 'They used a firm of cleaners on a regular basis. We've got all the details on file already.'

Lorimer nodded. It had been one area that Colin Ray's original team had covered.

'Maybe we should be looking at some of these offshore businesses of Jackson's? Perhaps he wasn't as solvent as Hugh Tannock makes out.'

'It's a possibility,' Martin replied slowly, savouring the thought. 'What with the credit crunch, there might well be stuff hidden away that we know nothing about. And you said that Daniel spoke about these odd foreign types who visited.'

'Yes,' Lorimer said. 'I think we want to dig into that a bit more. So,' he clapped his hands together then gave them a rub as if to suggest immediate action, 'let's get on to this shall we?'

'You mean right now, Sir?' Martin asked, glancing at her wristwatch. 'I was hoping to be off duty in a couple of hours. Big weekend coming up.' She grinned, pulling a face.

'Oh?' Lorimer asked with a smile.

'Serena Jackson's house warming party, actually,' Martin admitted, uncrossing her legs and sitting further forward as though she were anxious to leave. 'She's decided to throw it at last. It's probably a good thing. Have friends around, and all that. Cheer her up a bit. Don't worry, I'll be there as an old chum, not a police officer.'

There was a moment's silence between them while Lorimer wondered if he should comment on the inappropriateness of his DI's social life clashing with the case. But perhaps he should keep his own counsel meantime. Plus it might sound pretty small-minded to object to this pretty girl's partying.

'Wish my weekend was going to be such fun,' Lorimer admitted, then wished he hadn't spoken the words aloud.

'Ah, the invalid comes home again? Well, good luck with that, Sir,' Martin replied, standing up. 'And maybe if we make the right sort of noises we'll have some response from overseas by Monday morning.'

'Well, let's see what we can achieve with what's left of our Friday afternoon, shall we?' Then, standing up, Lorimer walked over to the door and opened it for the DI.

'Thanks,' she told him, giving him a friendly smile as she left.

Sitting back down behind his desk, Lorimer gave a sigh of relief. The case seemed to be going somewhere at last. And his relationship with DI Martin appeared to be thawing out. She was a bit of an enigma, he told himself. All stiff and resentful one minute then trying to ingratiate herself the next. But, when it came down to work, she was all right, really. Perhaps he ought to have told her to be careful what she said to Serena Jackson and her friends. Then he shook his head. It would be fine. She was an experienced officer. Telling her something like that would only have made her bristle with annoyance. And rightly so.

'Ohh!'

'Are you okay?' Rhoda put out a hand to steady the detective constable as she bent over in pain.

'Oh,' Kate gasped again, her hands grabbing the edge of the wash basin. 'Wee blighter's probably lying on a nerve. Happens quite a lot at this stage. So everyone tells us,' she added, grimacing as she tried to straighten up again.

'Rather you than me,' Rhoda said, watching her colleague's face in the mirror, thankful to see that some colour was returning to Kate's cheeks. 'I thought you were going to pass out just now.' She gave a little shudder. 'Can't see me ever wanting to go through all of that.'

Kate grinned. 'Bet you do one day, though. Once you've found your Mr Right.'

Rhoda Martin gave a little wiggle in front of the bank of mirrors in the ladies' loo. A smirk appeared on her face, making Kate raise her eyebrows.

'Oh, aye, something we should know about then? Hot date this weekend?'

'Wait and see,' Rhoda replied, her eyes sparkling with mischief. 'Tell you what, though,' she looked down at her black skirt and jacket, 'I'll be glad to get out of this and into the new outfit I bought last week. Sonia Rykiel,' she added, tossing her hair back in the superior way that never failed to annoy Kate Clark.

'I'll just be glad to fit into something normal,' Kate muttered, watching Rhoda's slim figure as she swept out of the loo. 'Never mind anything posh.'

The sky was only beginning to darken with imminent rain clouds when Lorimer reached the car park, noting the DI getting into her black Golf, her cycle secured to the rear of the vehicle. Kate Clark gave him a wave from the passenger seat of her husband's car as Lorimer headed towards the Lexus. Kate had made a joke earlier on about having to push the seat as far back as it would go to accommodate her swelling girth.

Other officers had already arrived for the next shift, ready for whatever a Greenock Friday night had in store, but now Rhoda, Kate and Lorimer were going their separate ways, leaving the concerns of murder and mayhem behind them.

Rhoda Martin waited until the big dark blue car had left before reversing out of her parking space. Her eyes shone with a girlish light that none of her colleagues usually saw; now she could really begin to enjoy the weekend ahead of her, exchange these drab working clothes for the designer outfit that was hanging outside her wardrobe door, new high heels still in their separate cotton drawstring bags. Tomorrow morning would be spent cycling to Mar Hall for a professional manicure and facial at the Spa then back again to prepare for her night out. A night out with folk of her own sort, she thought, waiting for the lights to change, like Serena and Daniel. For, she told herself with a frisson of excitement, Serena's brother was bound to be at the party, wasn't he?

Not everybody was in a hurry to leave work for the weekend. Back in the city, Callum Uprichard was smiling to himself as he jotted down some notes. They would be typed up later on, but for now he wanted to put his thoughts into some semblance of order. 'Interesting,' he whispered under his breath. 'Not what I'd have expected at all.' The tyre pattern had been invisible to the naked eye but under the powerful forensic microscope it was amazing what could be seen. A thin line with a distinctive herringbone pattern and that one tiny V-shaped nick had told the scientist rather a lot. First of all, the tyre came from a racing cycle, but not just any ordinary sort of racing cycle. Oh, no, if what he had seen was correct, this was the Rolls Royce of racing-cycle tyres, a Clement.

Clements were totally unlike conventional tyres. Made from silk, they were super-light and only used for special events, never for long distance cycling. He imagined the cyclist whizzing along, the tyres singing under him. The possibility of puncturing one of these babies was pretty high, Callum knew, and so they'd be more likely to be found in velodromes than out in the highways and byways of Inverclyde. Still, his report would give K Division plenty to speculate about. A cyclist who could afford something like this hanging around the garden of an elderly lady in Port Glasgow was curious enough in itself. But there was more. The scientist grinned as he noted details of the tiny soil particles that had been found around the treadmark. The cycle had come to rest on a patch of ground that had been treated with blood and bone fertiliser, a type specially made up in a garden centre down the coast. The tyre may possibly have picked up some of that material, Callum wrote. It could well be found embedded in the tyre itself (see *nick*, he scribbled in the margin) or under the cantilever of the brakes. And only a dedicated cyclist, or one who was forensically aware, would clean all of that up. Still it was only one half of an equation and the police needed to find the cycle and its owner in order to make sense of this evidence.

Callum whistled through his teeth as he began to type on his keyboard. Outside, the rush hour traffic was building up to a noisy crescendo but he was happy to take his time to finish this report and send it to the SIO in Greenock. He felt sorry for those poor sods struggling away from the city, desperate to leave their work behind. This was much better fun than sitting in an endless queue of cars. He had the best job in the world, he told himself, as he considered this link in a chain between searching for and finding a serious criminal; the very best.

CHAPTER 29

The sky looked bruised this morning, flesh-coloured clouds overlaid with patches of smoky grey shapes, shifting and changing as they drifted eastwards. Somewhere the sun was struggling to brighten the horizon. Trees that, minutes before, had been stark against an alabaster sky now glowed bronze, their empty branches the colour of autumn foliage against an artist's wash of eggshell blue and violet.

Maggie turned from the window, listening to the sound of her husband's breathing. She hovered between the thought of Chancer downstairs in the kitchen waiting for his bowl to be filled and the notion of climbing quietly back into the warmth and comfort of her Saturday morning bed. Saturday mornings might not be so free and easy after today, she told herself, slipping back under the duvet and snuggling against Lorimer's bare back. He moved, still half-asleep, one arm drifting down across her thigh. He'd been restless all night, eventually waking her up at some ungodly hour with a cup of tea and an expression of apology on his face. It was the strain of these two cases; the fire in Kilmacolm and the one in Port Glasgow where a calculating and vicious killer had selected vulnerable old ladies. Maggie shuddered, remembering her husband's face as he'd told her the details. And thinking, *That could have been Mum*.

Just another half an hour and she'd get up. Everything was ready downstairs, after all; Mum's bed made up, all her new toiletries neatly arranged in the loo, their own brought up here for the duration. Maggie shivered. Duration. Where had that word come from? Was she already thinking of the time when Mum would be able to return to her own cosy wee place? She scolded herself for the thought. It would be fine. Mum was to have these health professionals in every day, after all. She'd not lack for company and they had even managed to sort out a DVD player for her to watch downstairs if she wanted to. Ever since Dad had died, Maggie had seen an independent streak in her old Mum that she really admired. Alice had never complained about being on her own. She'd just got on with the business of living, making a pattern to her week of Church, the seniors' club, shopping and pottering about her bit of garden. Yes, Alice Finlay had managed all right, Maggie told herself. And now she deserved to be cosseted and looked after. Maggie cuddled closer into her husband's back, relishing the warm fug under the duvet while telling herself that it really was time she was making a move.

Life was funny, wasn't it? Here they were, a childless couple with plenty of room for a few kids to run around, yet it was an elderly parent who would be taking up some of that space instead. For a moment she wondered what sort of lives these three old ladies from Port Glasgow had lived. Had their days been like Mum's before her stroke? And were their children stunned into disbelief by the idea that somebody had deliberately taken their lives away? Lorimer had talked to her about the case last night as they had lain together here, side by side, his hand clasping her own. Perhaps he had needed to expunge the thoughts of these old people from his mind before Mum came home to them? Somehow, Maggie thought, bringing Mum out of hospital today only served to underline the horror of these murders.

Alice Finlay was already dressed, her breakfast tray to one side waiting for the ward maid to reappear and take it away. It had not been so difficult yesterday getting her clothes on but today her fingers had seemed to be devoid of the strength she had built up again and she looked down at her cardigan, dismayed to see its buttons all awry. That was what old folk looked like, she thought, undoing the buttons slowly, her knuckle joints protesting at the effort. But I am an old person, she reminded herself; nearly at my three score years and ten.

It was odd how she had dreams of her younger self. And how on awakening she sometimes had to struggle to remember her real age. Twenty-six was the most common one. She was waiting at a bus stop, going somewhere or other, her clothes fitting neatly around the slim body she could still remember. And then she would remember Maggie, her baby, and suddenly time seemed to fast forward and Maggie was a school teacher married to that tall, dark policeman. And she was in hospital, waiting for the light to come in at those windows, grateful for another day.

Today she was going home. Not back to where she had fallen, no, not there. But to Maggie and Bill's lovely house with the ginger cat and the open plan kitchen with its aromas of coffee and home-made soup. Alice felt her shoulders relax as she contemplated the move to her daughter's home. It would be a sort of holiday: convalescence, they used to call it, after an illness that had left you so debilitated that you had to go to a rest home to build up your strength. Her great aunt had gone to one in Largs, she remembered, making the journey to Ayrshire an annual treat for years thereafter. Perhaps Maggie might take her down to the seaside one day once the weather improved. Pushing her in a wheelchair, maybe?

Alice smiled ruefully to herself. Maggie pushing her around! What a reversal of roles! It seemed only the other day that she was tucking her little girl into the navy blue Silver Cross pram and taking her for walks through the park.

'Mrs Finlay?' It was Sister Kilbryde. Alice looked up, her hands still clutching the edge of her unbuttoned cardigan.

'You look wonderful this morning! All ready to leave us?' she teased.

'Well,' Alice began, remembering to speak slowly and breathe carefully between her words, 'it's been an ex-per-i-ence,' she said, smiling as the syllables came together. 'You've been so good to me,' she added fondly. And it was true. The nursing staff had been wonderful: never too busy to help her to the toilet or give her a hand with washing and dressing herself. For a moment Alice's shoulders stiffened as she wondered what she would do without all of these health care professionals around her night and day.

'Don't you worry,' Sister Kilbryde told her, the shrewd look assessing the old woman's body language accurately. 'There will be plenty of helpers to see that everything continues just as usual. The physios and occupational health people will be in to see you on Monday. And I'm sure your daughter and son-in-law will want to have you to themselves over the next couple of days.' She paused. 'Perhaps it's no bad thing that there are no grandchildren running around, you know. What you need right now is a time of peace and quiet.'

Alice nodded, agreeing. She remembered those wee ones shouting and making a racket at visiting time last night, the parents doing absolutely nothing to quieten them down. That sort of thing would drive her mad.

'But remember, Mrs Finlay,' Sister Kilbryde added, patting Alice's hand, 'anything you feel anxious about, just give the ward a ring. There will always be someone to talk to and answer your questions. Okay?'

Alice gave a brief nod, smiling to cover the uncertainty she still felt.

'Doctor will be in later this morning to see you then we can sort out all your paperwork for going home,' the sister told her and, giving Alice another reassuring smile, the woman stepped away, nodding at the patient in the next bed as she went.

Alice breathed a long sigh. It would be all right. Of course it would. She was just being silly, her heart fluttering with the excitement of what lay ahead of her.

Rhoda Martin free-wheeled down the tree-lined drive, glad that the journey was almost over. Her cycle training hadn't been as extensive as she would have liked and the run up here had taken a bit longer than she'd expected. Still, it was a lovely spring morning now and she could smell the fresh woody smell coming from the pines to her left. As she cycled more slowly along the narrow road, a couple of rabbits stopped their nibbling to look up at her, frozen like small brown stones against the green verges. Rhoda grinned, her feet pushing against the pedals. Hopefully she'd have a different effect on Daniel Jackson tonight. But by then, she told herself, she'd have been primped and pampered, hair washed and smelling sweet, not all sweaty under her Endura jacket. She gave an involuntary shrug. Serena might sport her Assos gear when they were out for a run but it was the best she could afford right now on a police officer's salary. The Spa was in sight now, a low white building against the backdrop of the River Clyde and the Kilpatrick Hills beyond.

Rhoda slid to a stop then hefted the lightweight cycle towards the double doors of the Spa. It was only her second visit here. As a member, Serena had taken her the first time. *She* was never away from this place, Rhoda thought with a sudden pang of irritation. What money could buy for some folk! Still, it was her turn today and she was going to make the most of it. Then she'd be heading back down the road, ready to put things into action. As she entered the reception area she caught the pungent scents of Aveda candles mingling with some herbal tisane. Rhoda took a deep breath, suddenly aware of the tension across her shoulders that needed to be massaged away.

It would be fine, she told herself. Everything was going according to plan. What could possibly go wrong?

'It's always the same,' Rosie grumbled. 'Just when you're looking forward to a quiet weekend, a nutter has to end someone's life with a blade!'

'Well, you are on call,' Solly reasoned, raising his eyebrows at her.

'Okay,' she sighed. 'I know but I really wanted to come with you on that RSPB walk along from the art galleries and museum today.' Rosie made a face even as she gathered up her kit ready to head off to Glasgow's east end where a body awaited her ministrations.

'We'll go next week,' Solly promised. 'And maybe we can have a meal out tonight instead? Shish Mahal suit you?'

'Aye, well, let's see how long this takes me. I'll give you a ring when I'm through. Love you,' she added, dropping a kiss on Solly's dark curls before heading out of the flat. He watched at the window, giving her a final wave as she emerged from the front door. Rosie looked up at him grinning in girlish glee as she brandished her car keys. There her new car waited, its pale blue paint-work still gleaming in showroom condition. The pathologist had finally chosen a Saab to replace her written-off BMW, a sporty convertible with a dark navy soft top. Solly smiled indulgently, still watching from the window as his wife drove off. Despite her almost-fatal accident she was still a keen driver; it hadn't put her off wanting to buy another car.

The psychologist stood gazing over the park and the familiar Glasgow skyline. He had a day to himself now, something he hadn't planned. He could always work on the book, of course, delving deeper into the psyches of female serial killers. There were some interesting theories he wanted to propound, but they were still at the thinking stage, gestating in his brain. Perhaps he'd take a look at Lorimer's case instead.

The detective had kept him abreast of events as they had unfolded down in K Division. It seemed as though there might be a little more evidence forthcoming from overseas regarding the victim's financial affairs. Solly shook his head. It was a lot closer to home than that, he told himself. Someone who had easy access to the house and who knew the layout intimately had taken the trouble to shift that key in the lock. But who? And why? Those were questions that Solly considered even as he contemplated the nature of a fire-raiser. Careful planning had been carried out and the crime was therefore premeditated. Somebody had intended both of these victims to die. And their killer had wanted it to look like an accident. Fires often destroyed evidence that forensic scientists might otherwise find useful. And those who began a blaze would bank on that. He cast his mind back a few years to the case when he had first assisted Strathclyde Police. That was when he had met DCI William Lorimer. A fire had taken place then, too, the perpetrator hoping to destroy every trace of his crime. But even that extensive conflagration had left some traces to tell a story and now that killer was under lock and key.

Solly sat before his laptop and opened up the file on the Jackson case. He had no official remit here, he knew, but even an academic exercise might throw a little light on his friend's case. Besides, it was a case that had begun to intrigue him and Solly had asked himself whether or not it might be linked to the murder of these elderly women. A cyclist had been seen haring away from the fire at Kilmacolm and a cyclist had stalked one of the Port Glasgow victims, leaving a tyre track at the third locus. Tenuous it might be, but the psychologist had a feeling that this was a line of thought worth pursuing.

The cycle race for charity was to take place next weekend and there would be hundreds of cyclists from all over the country descending on the city. It was one of the most popular sports in Scotland and, from his place in the passenger seat of other people's cars, Solly regularly saw hordes of cyclists racing along country roads. They always looked so fit and lean, these nylon leggings and sleek, body-hugging tops making their bodies seem so androgynous. Curved backs and helmets that looked like the beak of a strange bird gave the men and women the appearance of a slightly different species altogether. He scrolled up, seeing Kate Clark's report from the gentleman in Kilmacolm. The cyclist who had sped past them from the drive of the Jackson's home had been dressed in black, possibly wearing a hood. The cycle had not been lit and there had been no reflective strips on the person's clothing. Another sign of careful preparation, Solly thought to himself. But if that taxi had struck the cyclist, then all his plan-ning would have been for nought. It had been a moment in the darkness, a fleeting sight of a cyclist racing away from the scene, but perhaps sufficient to give him an idea of the person in black.

This was a person who liked to take risks. A person who desperately wanted to rid himself of Pauline and Ian Jackson. And, if it *was* the same person who had killed these elderly women, he realised that it must be a person who had very little remorse of conscience. A psychopathic personality, in fact, Solly told himself. A killer with an endless capacity for killing. Someone, he reminded himself grimly, who had to be stopped at any cost before they were allowed to strike once more.

'Let's look at it all over again,' he murmured aloud. 'See if we can find out what makes you tick.'

Maggie switched on the kettle, turning with a smile as she heard her mother's exclamation of delight. The 'bedroom' had been made up in the dining area and she'd added a bowl of fruit and put vases of flowers where her mother could enjoy them. Bill was still taking the luggage from the car after helping Mum into their comfy recliner, showing her the lever to raise the foot rest.

'I don't think I'll want to go home,' Alice exclaimed then, as Maggie caught her mother's eye, she saw the glint of mischief and knew that she was being teased. 'Och, you know you can stay here as long as you want to, Mum,' she replied. 'Earl Grey or ordinary?' she added.

'Earl Grey please, dear,' Alice said. 'And I'll not put you and Bill out a mo-ment more than I need to. I prom-ise,' she said, her words coming out slowly but with a firmness that Maggie recognised as belonging to the Mum she had known before that awful stroke.

'Hey, Chancer, looks who's here,' Maggie told the cat as he flopped through the cat flap on the back door and strolled through the kitchen.

'Here, puss,' Alice told him, patting the rug across her lap. The ginger cat eyed her for a moment then sat back on his haunches and began to wash a front paw assiduously. He'd come when he was ready, the gesture seemed to say. Alice smiled indulgently at the cat and waited. Sure enough it was only a matter of minutes before he leapt, purring, on to her knees, a grin appearing below his whiskers as he felt the fur on his head being caressed.

Maggie felt her whole body relax as she watched the pair of them. How easily Mum had settled in and how right it felt having her here. As Lorimer entered the room with Alice's bags she met his eyes, gave a nod and smiled. She saw his blue gaze taking in the woman and the cat and he returned her grin. It was going to be all right, after all. Everything would work out just fine.

CHAPTER 30

*T*he smell hit me as soon as I opened the door. She must have thrown
up after I'd left her on that narrow bed, and the stink of vomit mingling with urine pervaded the room. I'd made sure all the windows were
tightly shut, of course, just in case she had done a Houdini and managed
to escape from her bonds. Trying not to gag, I slid against the wall, feeling the embossed paper under my gloved hands. Even with that noxious
smell filling my nostrils I found myself wrinkling my nose at the touch of
that wallpaper: horrid cheap stuff. I passed by the sleeping figure, turned
the blind rod a fraction and looked out of the window.

The room was at the back of the house, facing a row of lock-ups. Even
in the dark I could make out the shapes of their metal doors side by side,
glinting under an adjacent street lamp.

A groan from the bed made me freeze. If I stood very still, the woman
on the bed might not realise that I was there. I waited, holding my breath,
until I saw her head slump sideways again. She looked so vulnerable
lying there, hair spread out on that white pillow. My fingers twitched as
a thought prompted desire. It would take only a few seconds for me to put
a second pillow over her face and cut off that foul-smelling breath forever.

I would give her a chance of life, though, not just because her situation
amused me.

She was still under the influence of the drug. Despite the vomiting she *hadn't managed to combat its effects and it would be some time before she would awake to find what I had done to her.*

And wonder how the hell it had happened.

I suppressed a snigger. I wouldn't be here when she woke up, of course, though it would be nice to see her face when she did. What would she think, seeing her wrists stretched out, fastened to the brass bed head by these handcuffs, her ankles tied with twists of red cord? Just for fun, I'd dressed her in a red basque, an Ann Summers outfit purchased especially for the occasion. No knickers, though. That was the nice touch, that and the Vaseline I'd smeared between her legs. The riding crop lay on the floor as if carelessly discarded.

Her imagination would leap to the obvious, I hoped.

When they found her (if they found her) it would look like she'd had a steamy night in. I resisted a laugh and felt my way back to the door, taking one last look at the woman splayed on the bed. Blowing her a silent kiss, I closed the door behind me.

CHAPTER 31

Kate felt the pain first before the waters gushed out, soaking her legs and flooding the bed.

'Towels,' she moaned, digging her elbow into Dougie's side. 'Get me some towels. My waters. They've broken.' She wanted to rise from the wetness but something held her back. Was it an irrational fear or the memory of the midwife's injunction to keep everything as sterile as possible?

'Dougie!' she cried, 'Get up! The baby's coming!'

In the hours that followed Kate couldn't remember everything, just certain events, like an edited holiday video where the highlights are preserved. She never remembered her husband's calmness as he made a pad of her best bath sheets, only her irritation that he had failed to use the old ones she'd put aside just for this eventuality. The ride to the hospital was a blur of early-morning traffic, lights twinkling in the darkness before a dawn that was still hours away. And Dougie: she'd never seen him so serious yet so exhilarated. As the pains kept coming she blew her breath out, exhaling noisily as she had been shown at the antenatal classes.

Afterwards she would say that Dougie had been wonderful, letting her crush his hand as the contractions kicked in. And the

285

midwives. They'd been brilliant, she told her friends. So unruffled, so controlled. Even when she'd begun to swear like a trooper they'd never batted an eyelid. Gentle words had continued to soothe until the pain had overwhelmed her and the world threatened to tilt off its axis in one enormous rush.

Then the cry. That wonderful sound that had brought tears streaming down her flushed cheeks; their little son come safely into the world. Kate would never forget that sound, not if she lived to be a hundred.

It was the other silly things that stuck in her mind: throwing up her breakfast of toast and tea into the cardboard sick bowl; the bunch of anemones Dougie had brought in for her; her awe at seeing Gregor's little fingernails – perfect pink ovals curling into a tiny fist that struggled towards his bow-shaped mouth.

All thoughts that this was a Monday morning when she ought to be at work vanished as Kate cradled her son, Dougie's arm around them both, cocooned in the filmy wonder of new motherhood.

'Where the hell is everybody?' Detective Sergeant Wainwright banged a fist down on his desk, making the pile of papers jump sideways.

Dodgson winced. The DS was in a foul mood and the non-appearance of both female CID officers this morning was threatening to make this a bad start to the week.

'Have you tried her mobile, Sir?' he asked.

'Course I have!' Wainwright stormed. 'Not answering her landline and her mobile seems to be switched off.'

'She was supposed to be going to some party at the weekend,' Dodgson offered.

'Whereabouts?'

Dodgson shrugged. 'Don't know. But she could hardly wait to get out of here on Friday. So maybe it was out of town somewhere.'

'God almighty, this is all we need. Our SIO's gone AWOL, Kate's not come in and Lorimer's breathing down our neck,' Wainwright growled.

'Like dragon fire, perhaps?' a voice behind them asked.

Dodgson and Wainwright turned around as one, the DS blushing furiously as he realised he had been overheard.

At that moment the telephone rang, sparing the man any need to apologise.

'Ah, hello Mr . . . oh. *Oh*!' Wainwright's face broke into a broad grin as he spun round in his chair, pointing towards his belly with one hand and making a thumbs-up sign. 'Brilliant news!' he continued. 'Aye, tell her we're all chuffed to bits. Thanks for calling us.'

'Kate?' Lorimer queried, leaning against the filing cabinet in the officers' room.

'Aye, the wee fella was born this morning,' Wainwright told them. 'That was Dougie's faither on to let us know. Whew!' He took out a large handkerchief and mopped the beads of sweat that had gathered on his brow. 'At least we know where our Kate is, then. Och, that's nice for them,' he added, 'but a bit of a surprise being so early, eh?'

'My sister's first baby was three weeks early and she was fine. A good weight as well.' Dodgson nodded, his face split in a smile. The hostile atmosphere had evaporated like a passing rain cloud with the news of Kate's new baby.

'We'll have tae have a whip round,' Wainwright told them. 'One of the women can choose a wee thing for the wean.' He rose from his desk as if to go out into the other rooms and spread the news.

'I was looking for DI Martin,' Lorimer said, before Wainwright could leave. 'Do you know where she is?'

'Haven't a clue, Sir. I've been trying to get a hold of her all morning.' Wainwright made a face. 'She's maybe been held up at some fancy house party. Too hung over to let us mere mortals know when she'll grace us with her presence,' he said with a twist to his mouth.

'No email then?' Lorimer asked.

'Naw.' Wainwright hesitated. 'D'you want to have a look at her inbox, though, Sir? See if there's anything urgent that needs doing? That's her code up there.' The DS nodded, pointing to a list of figures pinned above the DI's desk.

Lorimer stared at the detective sergeant's back. Wainwright was involved in a case with three murdered old ladies and yet was behaving as if he didn't give a toss. Would the DS have been so cavalier if it had been three younger women? Lorimer asked himself, cynically. Maybe the man was just an example of a police officer who was inured against any sort of tragedy, he thought, giving the man the benefit of the doubt.

At least Dodgson had slipped back to his own desk at the other side of the room, intent on some work, leaving the Superintendent to boot up DI Martin's computer.

It didn't take Lorimer long to scroll down the messages in Martin's inbox and find the email from Callum Uprichard. All thoughts of why the officer might not have made it into work disappeared as he printed off the report. This was more like it! he thought. A bit of superior forensic work might indeed help to nail the bastard who had murdered these three old women.

'Want to read this, young Dodgson?'

The lad was out of his chair and beside Lorimer's outstretched hand in a shot.

'Good grief, Sir!' he said at last. 'This could . . .'

'Bring us a lot closer to finding out who killed them,' Lorimer finished for him. 'How far have you got with the investigation into local cycle clubs?'

'Well, we've been concentrating on the two main ones, Inverclyde Velo and Johnstone Wheelers. The Wheelers tend to go out for practice rides with other club members and so although it's got a huge membership, they all seem to know one another quite well. Davie McGroary didn't belong to either club,' he added.

'Didn't think he would. Not the type,' Lorimer said.

'But we do have some familiar names, sir. Mr Tannock is a member and so are the two Jackson children.'

'Anybody else from the Kilmacolm area?'

'Aye, quite a few. But most of the members are from the Paisley, Johnstone and Elderslie areas.'

'Names? Addresses?'

'We've got a whole list of them compiled, sir, but there hasn't been any authorisation of a home visit to them. We just haven't the time to do that sort of thing – unless it's justified,' he added, glancing at the paper in his hand.

'We want to know the whereabouts of all these cyclists on the nights the three women died. And,' he added with a sudden stern look that made Dodgson take a step back, 'I want the date of the Jackson fire included as well.'

The young officer stood speechless for a moment, taking in the enormity of Lorimer's words.

'You don't think it was the same person, sir?' he asked at last. 'I mean, oh, dear Lord . . .' Dodgson's eyes widened in astonishment.

Lorimer did not answer but his mouth became a hard, thin line.

Dr Solomon Brightman had suggested this to him only yesterday. And, although the theory had chimed with Lorimer's own thoughts, the psychologist's words had had a converse effect on him, making him question it all the more.

The police constable nodded as their eyes met. It was a long shot. A hunch, maybe. He'd heard of senior officers acting on such things before. Police lore was full of stories like that. Up until now the young man had only experienced the hard graft that police work demanded and he felt a sudden thrill as he stood beside this tall man whose very presence spelled out authority.

'I'll have a word with DS Wainwright,' Lorimer murmured, 'but expect me to take over as SIO on this one. At least until DI Martin turns up,' he added with a twinkle in those piercing blue eyes.

As the morning wore on, it became evident that Rhoda Martin was not going to come in to Greenock for work on time. Wainwright had chuckled that she'd be roasted for her absence when she finally did appear. It was clear from his attitude, thought Lorimer, that there was no love lost between the older man and his senior officer. For the hundredth time he found himself wishing to be back in his own division in Glasgow where the officers around him were more than mere colleagues. With Kate now out of the team Lorimer felt that sense of loneliness he had experienced on his arrival in Greenock. Or was it simply a Monday-morning feeling after an enjoyable weekend with his wife and mother-in-law at home?

Alice's arrival had made the house feel more alive, somehow. They'd watched television together on Saturday evening like a normal family and he'd even played a couple of games of Scrabble after one of Maggie's Sunday roasts.

With a frown he suddenly recalled where Rhoda Martin had been going at the weekend: Serena Jackson's house-warming party. Searching through another buff-coloured file, Lorimer picked up Serena's home details and dialled her number. He let it ring out until the answering machine clicked on, giving a female voice that to his ears always sounded like an automated Barbie doll. He waited impatiently until the sing-song message had finished.

'Detective Superintendent Lorimer for Miss Jackson. I'd be obliged if you might call me at Police Headquarters, Miss Jackson,' he said, giving the Greenock number before ringing off. He looked at the telephone thoughtfully. If Rhoda Martin had spent her weekend down in Serena Jackson's flat then where were they both now?

The black car drove slowly along the cul de sac then turned, stopping right outside the house with the white painted door. For a moment the driver sat still, hand on the steering wheel. A blackbird pecked at some unseen prey below the surface of the grass, worrying it in a series of jabs. The sound of a lawn mower could be heard round the back of the houses, its drone competing with an airplane overhead. But the street itself was deserted, just as she had expected; not one single person strolled along the pavement to witness her arrival. Slipping a black leather bag over one shoulder, she left the car.

At the back of the house Flynn walked up and down, the din of his mower a vague noise behind the sounds from his iPod. His head moved in time to the beat as the grass was swallowed up by the blades of the machine. This was a satisfying sort of job, he thought, watching the stripe of bright green appearing in the overgrown lawn. The Lorimers wouldn't know the place by the time he'd finished.

Flynn had been glad when the other gardener had agreed to drop him off with the mower for a half-day. Jimmy had owed him, he chuckled to himself, thinking of the man driving the pick-up truck back to the park. He had still looked a wee bit worse for wear after the weekend when he had been through to Edinburgh for the rugby and Flynn had covered his Saturday shift.

Flynn would be able to cut and strim the grass and still have time for a wee blether with Maggie's mum before Jimmy picked him up later. He began to sing tunelessly to the words of a song as he turned at the end of the lawn, whisking the machine in an expert arc and beginning a new strip. He didn't glance towards the kitchen window where the orange cat sat, washing its paws. Nor did he hear the metallic thud of a car door closing or the sound of the bell shrilling through the house.

Alice rose slowly from her chair. This recliner was going to make her so lazy, she thought, feeling the stiffness in her back as she tried to straighten up. This must be the nurse coming in to visit. 'Hope you're as nice as the ones in the Southern,' she muttered under her breath, edging towards the far side of the room, grasping at the backs of Maggie's dining room chairs to steady herself. They hadn't given her an exact time so she had been slightly agitated all morning, waiting for the sound of the doorbell. She shoved the door open wider with her stick and shuffled out into the hallway.

Chancer gave a purr and slithered down from his patch of sunlight on the windowsill as soon as he heard the front door being opened.

'Oh, hello, I've been expecting you. Come away in,' Alice

292

began, looking up at the blonde woman on the doorstep. But the figure standing there made no move to enter the house. Instead she held up a plastic card for a moment then pocketed it again.

'Detective Inspector Martin,' the woman told her, unsmiling. 'I'm afraid there's been an incident. It's Detective Superintendent Lorimer,' she added gravely. 'Can you come right away, please?'

Alice tightened her grip on the walking stick, one hand thrust out against the wall for support. She was aware of her heart hammering uncomfortably in her chest. When she tried to speak, to utter some sort of words, her lips simply parted in a silent 'O' of shock.

Just behind her the orange cat arched his back and hissed, tawny eyes glaring balefully at the stranger. The blackbird flew up and away, its alarm cry shattering the cold morning air.

Then the woman's hand was outstretched, offering assistance. Alice felt the strong grip under her elbow as she was ushered out of the house and into the waiting car. Detective Inspector Martin. She remembered hearing the name. She was from Bill's job down in Greenock.

'What's happened?' she whispered as she was helped into the passenger seat. 'Does Maggie know?'

But all she received was a sombre look and a shake of the head as a seat belt was fastened across her lap. Then they were off down the road and Alice had the strange sensation that everything was being put into reverse. She had scarcely arrived and now she was being taken away again, she thought wistfully, gazing as they left the house behind them and a disgruntled cat on the doorstep.

Half an hour later Joseph Alexander Flynn came whistling into the kitchen. 'Mrs Fin? Do you fancy a cuppa? Mrs Fin?'

*

293

'Lorimer,' he said, as the call came through.

'God, at last!' Flynn gave a huge exhalation of relief. 'D'ye know if Mrs Finlay was supposed to be going out anywhere? She's not in the hoose and I've been doon the road looking for her. Yer cat's goin' mental an' all,' he told Lorimer.

The sound of Flynn's voice, high with stress, made Lorimer straighten up. 'What do you mean she's not in the house? Have you looked upstairs?' he demanded, then realised how stupid the question was: Alice Finlay was not yet able to manage the stairs, was she?

'Aye, she's no onywhere in the hoose. I've looked everywhere. There wasnae anybody fae the hospital comin tae take her for physio or that, was there?' Flynn asked anxiously.

Lorimer sat silently for a moment, his mind whirling with possibilities before replying, 'I don't think so. Maggie would know, though. I'll call Muirpark. Hold on and I'll get back to you. But,' he added, 'ring the station here if she turns up, okay?'

His fingers were trembling as he dialled the number of Maggie's school and asked to be put through to his wife. What the hell was he going to tell her? Visions of his mother-in-law wandering off on her own came to his mind. But that was absurd! Alice had had a stroke. She wasn't suffering from the sort of awful dementia that made old folk wander out of their homes and into the unknown.

As he waited those interminable minutes for Maggie to come to the phone, Lorimer recalled his mother-in-law's ability at yesterday's games of Scrabble. Nothing wrong with her wits, he told himself. So why would she suddenly take off like that?

'Maggie,' he said, relief flooding him at the sound of her voice. 'It's your mum.'

*

The police station on the south side of the city took the Superintendent's call and within minutes patrol cars were scouring the streets around Lorimer's home on the lookout for an elderly lady fitting Alice Finlay's description. Flynn had made two pots of tea so far; one for the officers who had arrived then another for Maggie, her car screeching into the drive.

'When did you last see her?' Maggie asked, her mug of tea barely touched.

Flynn shook his head. It was a question he hadn't been able to answer when the police officers had asked him earlier.

'I honestly don't know. You'd been gone a wee bit afore I began the grass. Your maw,' he broke off, his voice choking back sudden tears, 'she wis here sitting on the recliner when I went outside.' He scratched his head as if the gesture would restore some absent memory. 'I havenae a clue whit time it wis. Or whit she wis doin when I wis out there.'

'It's okay, Flynn.' Maggie squeezed his hands gently. 'No one's blaming you. Maybe she just went for a wee walk,' she suggested, though her strained tone gave the lie to the words themselves.

'Huv they heard frae the hospital yet?' Flynn looked over Maggie's shoulder at the female officer standing in the kitchen, mobile phone to her ear.

The woman's nod and look of apology made the young man groan.

'She's not there, I'm afraid. There was no out-patient appointment for Mrs Finlay at all. The nurse is actually on her way now. What do you want me to tell them?' the uniformed officer asked Maggie.

'Better let her come,' she replied with a tremulous sigh. 'Maybe she'll have some idea what to do.' She shrugged, attempting a smile. 'Perhaps it's not so uncommon a situation for them.'

Maggie felt something soft against her leg. Chancer looked up, his eyes wide with expectation. She patted her lap and the cat jumped up lightly, butting her hand with his head until she began to stroke his fur.

'Ah, if only you could talk, Chancer,' she told the cat. 'Maybe you could tell us where Mum has gone.' As if in answer the orange cat gave a loud purr then sat absolutely still, staring ahead as if he was looking at something none of them could see.

CHAPTER 32

Alice was tired. The journey through the city was taking such a long time. Surely they should be on the motorway and heading towards the airport and Greenock by now? She'd been in such a hurry to leave that her spectacles were still on the side table where she had left them, so each road sign was a mere blur of letters and symbols. She hadn't even thought to lift her handbag. Or tell anyone. Biting her lip anxiously, she thought of Flynn out the back, cutting the grass. This woman officer hadn't known about him, had she? What would the poor lad think when he found she had gone?

'There's a young man . . . in the gar-den,' she said breathlessly. 'He'll . . . be worried about me.'

Was it her imagination, or had the policewoman touched the brake, slowing the car down as she gave Alice a sharp look?

'It's all right. My colleague will deal with him,' she told Alice, turning her gaze back to the road.

Alice sighed and tried to relax, remembering the exercises the speech therapist had taught her. Shoulders down, clench and unclench fists, same with the teeth, loosen the jaw. As she forced herself to go through these little motions, Alice tried not to think about Bill. But it had to be pretty bad. After all, why wasn't the tall young woman telling her any details? She thought of Maggie, imagining her daughter's reaction to the worst sort of news. Being a policeman was a hazardous profession. And hadn't Bill been in situations of extreme danger before now?

Alice watched as the streets became less and less familiar, dark tenements looming on either side as the car left the main road and headed uphill, away from the city centre. They passed a couple of rough-looking men with a long-haired Alsatian dog loping beside them and Alice stared at them from the passenger window as the car swept past.

'We're not going down to Greenock?' she asked at last, bewildered by this unknown area.

The woman beside her shook her head, her expression unfathomable as she drove the car in and out of a series of narrow streets, flinging the vehicle around corners.

Alice clutched the edge of the car seat, a sensation of dread sweeping over her. Something bad was happening, all right. But suddenly it felt as though it were happening to her.

'There's no sign of her,' the police officer at the other end of the line told Lorimer. 'The nearest CCTV cameras haven't picked up anyone answering to her description, I'm afraid.'

'Then, if she hasn't wandered off anywhere in the immediate vicinity of our house she must have gone off in a car,' Lorimer said. 'There really isn't any other explanation.'

'Does she have any other friends or family who might have taken her out for a jaunt?' It was a reasonable sort of question for the officer to ask. Yet Lorimer could detect a hint of scepticism in his tone. The choice of the word *jaunt* seemed to suggest that this whole exercise was risible. Eyebrows were obviously being raised about the haste with which Alice Finlay had been posted as a missing person. By a senior officer who was pulling rank. Was he making a nuisance of himself? Had Alice simply wandered off?

'No,' he replied at last. 'We're all the family she has. And she would have let us know if anyone had wanted to take her out. Besides,' he added sternly, 'she was expecting the health visitor this morning. She wouldn't go off when someone was due to see her. That's just not possible.'

'The stroke you mentioned,' the officer coughed delicately, 'it hasn't left her . . . you know . . . *impaired* in any way?'

'No,' Lorimer told him firmly. 'She's as sane as you or I. Maybe not quite as articulate as she used to be but there's nothing wrong with her mind.'

There was a silence at the other end of the line as the Glasgow officer thought about this.

'So, no admissions to any of the local hospitals and no trace of her on the CCTV cameras.' He paused again before continuing and this time his tone was brisk. 'It's a little bit of a mystery, Superintendent, but I'm sure our officers will find her before much longer. Don't worry.'

Lorimer replaced the phone, resisting the urge to slam it back on to its cradle. The infuriating thing was that he'd have dealt with someone else exactly as that officer had dealt with him. They were doing everything just as they should. But it was frustrating not to be a part of it.

There was a knock at his door and he whirled around, a deep frown furrowing his brow.

'Superintendent.' It was PC Dodgson edging around the doorway, an expression of anxiety on his young face. 'D'you think I should go round to DI Martin's place? Just to see if she's all right?'

Lorimer's answering scowl did not deter the officer who came further into the room.

'We've been calling her house all morning but there's still no answer.'

Lorimer gave a sigh that seemed to come from his boots. A missing mother-in-law was much higher up in his scale of concern right now; Dodgson was surely over-reacting.

'What do you want me to do? Suggest that you take one of the duty constables along with you?' He shook his head, exasperated by the very idea. 'Don't be so daft, lad. She'll kill you if she's in bed with the 'flu and doesn't want to be disturbed.'

Dodgson bit his lip and a wash of red coloured his cheeks. Lorimer immediately wished he'd been a bit more tactful. After all, this officer had been spurned once too often by his superiors and what little confidence he'd shown recently had come from Lorimer's own support. He gave a weak grin, holding one hand to his mouth. 'DS Wainwright thinks it might be more than the 'flu she's in bed with,' he said in a conspiratorial whisper.

Shaking his head, Lorimer gave a derisory laugh. 'And she'll welcome you even less if that's the case.'

He was rewarded by an embarrassed giggle from Dodgson who backed out of the door and closed it gently behind him.

The woman on the bed struggled against the metal biting into her wrists. It was no use. They were designed to confine and control after all, weren't they? If it had been under any other circumstances she might even have found that amusing. But the smell of her own vomit and the wetness below her made the woman weep with frustration.

What on earth had happened? Why was she here? And when had she dressed in this ridiculous, skimpy outfit?

She didn't need her hands to feel down there. That greasy dampness between her legs could only mean one thing: she'd had sex with somebody. But, try as she might, no vision of a man came into her mind, just a blur of loud music and that kaleidoscope of coloured lights before she awoke to this cold room and the awful realisation of her predicament.

She shivered, wondering how she was ever going to escape. And, worse, who would come to free her from these bonds.

It was the stairs that had done it, Alice knew, feeling that constriction in her chest. She just wasn't able to climb up one flight, never mind however many it had taken to reach the top floor. The woman had half-pushed, half-heaved her upwards, muttering imprecations at her back, cursing her whenever Alice had protested that she couldn't go on any more.

It should have been a relief to sink into a chair, but Alice Finlay only felt fear. The young woman had bundled her into this room, making her sit down before fastening her hands behind her back. Even now the tightness in her chest was worse than the feeling of that twine biting into her thin wrists. She'd tried to speak, to plead with her, but the woman had refused to meet her eyes and without a single word had left her there, closing the door behind her.

It was useless to scream, Alice knew. The flats on each level up this dingy, sour-smelling place had all looked abandoned so nobody would be nearby to hear her, even if she could utter a cry. She looked around the empty room, wondering how she might find a means of escape. The bay window was boarded up with brown plywood, one sheet covering each of the four long panes. Fragments of glass around the skirting told of vandals having thrown stones up high, wrecking the place just because they could.

Alice thought of the two men with their Alsatian dog and trembled. This was a part of the city she'd never been in before. She'd seen Glasgow Cathedral as they'd driven past and guessed that she was now in a derelict area in the East End that was probably due to be demolished before all that regeneration that was being talked about.

But why she was here and what was going to become of her was something she simply couldn't fathom.

It had to be something to do with Bill. That policewoman (if she *was* a policewoman) knew his name, knew whereabouts he lived. She had known the connection between them.

Alice continued to study the room. The floor was only bare boards, and some crumpled newspapers lay in a corner – abandoned by workmen, perhaps? She glanced upwards. The electric cable suspended from the ceiling held no bulb; the ends of the wire were frayed. No light, then, Alice thought, shivering. And no warmth.

Something scurried over her feet and Alice gave a scream, raising her shoes from the floor. If it was a rat, her panicked cry must have frightened it away for she saw nothing and heard no tiny scuffling noises. But perhaps it would return when darkness fell?

Alice gave a shudder, suddenly wishing she had put on a coat before leaving Maggie's. Her lamb's wool cardigan was unfastened and the thin polyester blouse that she'd chosen specially for the nurse's visit had come untucked from the waistband of her slacks.

She wanted so much to go to the toilet, but that was out of the question. She'd just have to hold on until someone came. Alice gave a moan of anguish, putting her feet close together. She wouldn't wet herself, wouldn't give in to that final indignity.

Her mouth closed in a firm line of resolve.

Bill would come and find her. She was sure of that. This was all a terrible mistake, surely. And Bill would sort it out.

Alice yawned suddenly, unable to resist the terrible lethargy that was overcoming her limbs.

Closing her eyes, she tried to blot out her surroundings. Sleep, she told herself. Sleep and perhaps when you wake this nightmare might be over.

CHAPTER 33

I wouldn't see her die, but that didn't matter now. The cold would probably finish her off tomorrow: if she survived the night. Nobody could
possibly find her and in several months these buildings would be reduced
by the wrecking ball to a heap of rubble and dust. Any human remains
would be impossible to find and the mystery of where Lorimer's relation
had gone would never be solved.

It gave me no little satisfaction to imagine the rest of his life spent wondering about that. Blaming himself, perhaps, and having to answer the
inevitable questions his wife would ask.

It was another sort of death, wasn't it? A different way to kill a man.
This might even finish his police career. Or destroy his marriage.

Smiling to myself, I stripped off the leather gloves then the layer of latex
below, feeling the sweat lingering on my fingers. It didn't pay to be care-
less, even though nobody would ever suspect someone like me.

As I opened the car door I felt a rush of cool air. I would have to leave
the Golf parked down in this concrete basement at least until nightfall.
Then what? A sudden memory came to me of laughter and faces illumi-
nated by firelight, the rush of excitement as the petrol tank had roared and
the flames had soared into the darkened sky. Yes, I decided. That's how I
would do it; only I would be by myself this time.

With nobody to see me.

CHAPTER 34

'Hello? Mr Lorimer? It's Serena Jackson here. You asked me to call you.'

Lorimer's voicemail recorded the woman's husky tones then there was a pause before a click sounded, cutting the connection to the line in the detective's empty room.

Lorimer was on his way home. Greenock could bloody well wait for his services for the rest of today. Being with Maggie was far more important than tyre treads or exploring some tenuous links between two different murder cases. The Lexus sped along the outside lane, the river to the left sparkling in the midday sunlight. But for once the detective was oblivious to the landscape around him, focusing only on the road ahead and what was waiting for him at home. There was only so much he could achieve from a distance. The south side force had put everything they could into motion and he'd been relieved to hear the report of what was happening. He glanced at his mobile phone slotted into its cradle. At the first ring he'd be able to click it into life and listen. Okay, so he could have done just that from K Division but right now he needed to be with Maggie.

DS Wainwright was officially in charge of things down in Greenock today. At least until Martin deigned to turn up for duty. He'd not shown much sympathy when Lorimer had decided to cut and run. *Wish I could make my mother-in-law disappear*, he'd said. But the joke had fallen flat and he didn't want to think about what the officer had made of his responding scowl. He thought instead of the blonde woman, her moods vaccilating between over-friendliness and cool disdain. She was an odd one, right enough. With her privileged background and expensive education, she was not the average sort of entrant to the police force. But, he reasoned, such a person was surely all the more welcome into the Force. They needed a police service that reflected a good social mix. His thoughts drifted to the Chief Constable. He'd become a resident of Kilmacolm, too. And was highly regarded amongst his very wealthy neighbours. Isherwood had been quite defensive about his home village, hadn't he? Warning off DCI Ray in the way he had and giving Lorimer that flea in his ear as well.

As the road took him towards Glasgow, Lorimer realised that he had absolutely no qualms about walking out on the situation in Greenock. They could demote him for all he cared. Everything else about this peculiar Monday was put to the back of his mind as he concentrated on what was happening in his own house in that quiet little residential street.

'Solly? Have you time to talk right now?'

The psychologist heard the catch in Maggie Lorimer's voice and listened as his friend poured out her story. She could not see the grave expression on his face or the way he nodded as she related the events of the morning.

'Solly, I think someone's taken her,' Maggie was sobbing now and he felt an overwhelming pity for the woman. 'I think she's been abducted.'

Even as he tried to calm her down with soothing platitudes, Solly's thoughts were racing.

Was this related to Lorimer's involvement in one of those cases down in Inverclyde? As he took in all that Maggie was telling him about Mrs Finlay's disappearance and what the police had already carried out in the hours since she had left the house, Solly began to wonder. Was this directed at William Lorimer, the senior investigating officer? Could it be a diversionary tactic to keep him from penetrating deeper into the murders? Or was it something more personal?

There was something wrong here, he told himself, something very wrong. And with a deep sense of foreboding, Dr Brightman realised that if Maggie's mother had indeed been abducted then it was very much in keeping with the sort of person whose profile was emerging in his own mind.

As he put down the phone, the psychologist stroked his beard thoughtfully. Should he doubt his instincts? Or was he so currently obsessed by his research into female serial killers that his feelings were being warped? Poison was a woman's weapon of choice, so said the old adage, but that was simply a way of expressing a deeper truth. Women were less inclined to be hands-on killers, preferring their victims to die off-scene, as it were. Like burning people to death in a fire. Or pushing old women down a flight of stone stairs.

Try as he might, Solly Brightman was more than ever convinced that there was a woman behind those killings in Kilmacolm and Port Glasgow. And that this same person might have inveigled their way into the Lorimers' home. After all, Mrs Finlay might be far less suspicious of a woman coming to the door. Hadn't she been expecting a health professional, most probably a female? It would be too easy, Solly thought to himself. Too easy by far.

Lifting the telephone again, he dialled Lorimer's mobile number.

He was almost at Eastwood roundabout when the phone rang.

'Lorimer.' Surely it would be news of Alice?

But it was Solly's English tones that came over the airwaves, not an officer from Glasgow, not Maggie with the words he was longing to hear.

'I heard about your mother-in-law,' Solly told him. 'It's a terrible thing to have happened.'

'Christ knows what's going on,' Lorimer told him. 'It's been a hell of a morning as well. My DC gave birth this morning, earlier than she expected, poor girl. And DI Martin's not turned up for her shift. Nobody seems to know where the hell she is,' he added, venting his pent-up anger at the psychologist. 'Goes out to a posh party at the Jackson woman's house and then doesn't show her face come Monday morning.'

There was the customary pause in the conversation that Lorimer was well used to and he had almost forgotten that Solly was on the line when the question was asked.

'Is your DI Martin a cyclist by any chance?'

'Yes, she is. Training for that charity race next weekend. The whole bloody world seems to be on their bikes right now. Hugh Tannock's a member of a cycle club and so are the Jacksons; Serena and Daniel. Too many of them. It's muddying the waters, if you want to know the truth.'

Solly felt a sudden chill that was nothing to do with Lorimer's obvious anxiety. All his fears seem to have become crystallised into one dreadful pattern.

Even as he asked Lorimer to keep him informed about Alice

Finlay, he was recalling his wife's descriptions of the two young women, the police officer and the girl whose parents had perished so horribly in that fire.

And he knew now which one he would identify as a killer.

Strathclyde traffic police had their work cut out for them this Monday. CCTV footage from the area nearest the Lorimers' residence showed the times of hundreds of vehicles passing each way along the main road and it was a task that took the utmost concentration to log them all, identify their registration numbers and look up the vehicles' owners on the computer. Names were now emerging from all of that data, and one in particular made an officer lift the telephone to call his superior.

'Bit odd, don't you think?' he asked. 'Should we make anything of it?'

There was a short silence before the reply came. 'Lorimer will want to know. And, yes, check it out. Have a look to see if there was a passenger visible on the footage, will you?'

The senior officer frowned, puzzled by the message. The black Golf GTI was registered in the name of Rhoda Martin, an officer from K Division who was on Lorimer's team. But the Detective Superintendent had let it slip that DI Martin hadn't turned up for duty this morning. Something very odd was going on. And Lorimer ought to be told right away.

Chancer sprang to the floor and trotted over to Lorimer giving a small miaow of welcome. For once the orange cat was ignored as Maggie hurled herself into her husband's arms and began to sob.

'It's all right,' he soothed, stroking her long dark hair. 'It's all right. We'll find her. I know we will.'

Behind them the family liaison officer lifted a two-way radio to her lips, affirming the message she had just scribbled down in her notebook.

'Superintendent, that was traffic. They've spotted something,' the woman began.

'Mum? Have they found my mum?' Maggie broke away from her husband, hope filling her pale face. Flynn emerged from the kitchen, his expression equally anxious.

'I'm sorry, Mrs Lorimer. There's no definite sighting of her yet,' the woman replied. 'But there was a vehicle seen in the vicinity that belongs to one of your officers, sir,' the policewoman continued. 'At approximately nine-thirty-five a black Golf GTI entered the main road from the junction along from here and headed towards town. It's registered to . . .' she squinted at her own handwriting, 'a Miss Rhoda Jane Martin. One of yours,' she added.

'Was she alone?'

'Traffic's still trying to confirm that, sir. The footage might not be adequate to tell us if there was a passenger beside her.'

Lorimer nodded, his mind in a whirl. The car would have to make a right-hand turn against the flow of traffic at that particular junction and the camera might not see anyone but the driver. But Rhoda Martin? What the hell had she been doing at his house?

Suddenly all the thoughts about the case down in Inverclyde became sickeningly clear. Colin Ray's case had been stymied from the outset and he'd always had a feeling that DI Martin had been instrumental in that. Add that to the fact that Rhoda Martin was a cyclist. Who lived near Kilmacolm. And hadn't she'd been going to and from the police station on those practice runs? Easy enough to take little trips up to Port Glasgow, follow vulnerable old ladies. But this was madness! Why on earth would a police officer turn killer?

But even as he tried to dismiss the thought, Lorimer felt a cold hand on his heart. Rhoda Martin was a tall, strong young woman but was she capable of such acts of violence? And she had known the Jackson family for years. Was there something in her background that might give a clue to a motive for murder? Or was she one of those women Solly had been describing to them: a person who could change from being a seemingly upright citizen to one who had no qualms about killing in cold blood? Lorimer bit his knuckled fist. Surely the psychologist couldn't have profiled someone like that?

Yet, hadn't he been considering the woman's strange mood swings only this morning?

'Get on to Greenock,' he told the woman. 'Tell them to head for Martin's home. Now!'

Maggie looked from the grim-faced policewoman to her husband, her mouth parted in a moment of incomprehension. Something was happening, something only the police could control. Maggie wanted to weep anew; it was *her* mother who was missing but she felt like an outsider, trapped within a dark and fearful place.

Lorimer's BlackBerry gave the tone that told him a message was waiting. He flicked the button to hear it and Serena Jackson's voice came through. For a moment he wondered what to do, torn between a desire to rush off down to wherever Rhoda Martin lived or to stay here with Maggie and wait. And yet ... the Jackson woman might be able to tell him where Martin had gone after that party. Pressing the reply button, Lorimer waited until he heard the same recorded message for a second time that day. He cursed under his breath. Still, it wasn't Serena Jackson's fault that she was out more than once in a day. She'd have no earthly idea that they were desperately trying to track down her old school friend, after all.

'Don't go,' Maggie pleaded, sensing her husband's sudden restlessness. 'Please stay with me.'

Across the room, Lorimer caught Flynn's eye; the young man's eyebrows were raised in a question. If he did have to go, then the lad would stay on here, his expression seemed to be saying. Lorimer nodded at him briefly before gathering Maggie into his arms once more.

CHAPTER 35

Rhoda Martin lived in a maisonette on the outskirts of Kilmacolm not far from Port Glasgow Road. It had been built in the nineties on farmland sold for development and now the entire area had pockets of residential housing. These were far from the elegant mansions within the nearby village; the housing estate contained the sorts of properties more suited to the average family whose aspirations had taken them to a home in the countryside within a desirable school catchment area.

Number Twelve, The Steadings, backed on to a row of lock ups, their metal doors painted in a bright shade of turquoise blue, a colour, DS Wainwright thought, more suited to a continental residence than to this wee estate in Scotland's west coast.

He'd taken young Dodgson with him; more because he wanted to show the lad just how things should be done than from any desire to curry favour with Lorimer. The Super had shown a distinct favouritism towards the police constable that rankled with the older detective.

'Ach, this is a' a waste of time,' he said, heaving his massive frame out of the patrol car. 'Rhoda'll go ballistic when she sees us here. If she's even at home.'

It seemed the DS was spot on. 'Naebody at home,' he concluded once they had stood at the door, his fat finger pressed on the bell for more than a minute.

PC Dodgson lifted the letterbox and peered inside.

'Nothin doin, laddie. Just whit ah said. Waste o' bloody time,' Wainwright snorted, taking his finger off the bell.

'Wait a minute, Sir,' Dodgson replied. 'Shush,' he said, lifting a finger as Wainwright began to protest. 'I think I can hear something inside. Listen!'

Sure enough a muffled sort of cry could be heard by both men; a cry that was certainly human.

'What the . . .?' Wainwright looked at his colleague in amazement. Then, taking a few paces back, the detective sergeant hurled himself at the door. It took only two more heaves till the wood splintered with a deafening crack, leaving the door sagging off its hinges.

The sound was coming from a room at the back of the house. Two pairs of boots thundered up the stairs, the detective sergeant puffing heavily as he followed the younger man.

'Oh my God!' Dodgson threw open the door of the room then reeled backwards, one arm protecting his face. Wainwright thrust past him. There on a single bed was a woman, her semi-naked body displayed in a red-and-black tart's outfit, blonde head lolling to one side. Vomit had dried into her hair and streaks of putrid yellow had run down arms that were pinioned by the handcuffs. Her bare legs were criss-crossed in purple welts from some sort of sado-masochistic whipping.

'Christ almighty!' Wainwright stepped forward and knelt by the woman's side, feeling for a pulse.

Then her eyes flickered and she groaned as she saw the policeman's face.

'Don't worry, hen. We'll get you out of here,' the big man

whispered. 'Dodgson. Ambulance. Quick as you can, lad.'

'There's no sign of Rhoda Martin's car. No. The lock up at the back was empty. What? A bike? Aye, there is. A silver colour. No, nothing else that we could see,' Wainwright told Lorimer.

The Detective Superintendent stood in the middle of his kitchen, thinking hard. Wainwright and Dodgson had done well to find the poor girl. The DS had not spared him any details about her predicament, even managing to make some lewd suggestions as to what had taken place over the weekend.

Who had taken Rhoda Martin's car? And who had abused the detective inspector leaving her imprisoned by police issue handcuffs?

The DI had seemed so full of vitality on Friday, anticipating a good time at the Jackson woman's party. Was there some man behind this? Someone she had wanted to play games with? Games that had led to sexual abuse, it seemed. Lorimer ran a hand through his thick, dark hair. It was more important than ever that he speak to Serena Jackson and find out exactly who had been at her party. Was the same man who had assaulted Rhoda the person who had taken his mother-in-law from the safety of their home?

Just as he was about to try her number again, the front doorbell rang.

'Mum!' Maggie leapt to her feet and was yanking open the door in feverish expectation.

But it was no old lady who stood there, but a bearded man, a long striped scarf wound several times around his neck.

'Oh, Solly, it's you.' Maggie stood back, allowing him to enter the hallway, disappointment clearly etched on her face.

'I'm so sorry, Maggie,' the psychologist had taken her hands in his own and was gazing into her eyes with concern. 'You must be feeling dreadful. The waiting . . .' he tailed off, nodding as she began to weep again.

'Here.' Lorimer took her shoulders and turned her round, sheltering her within the protection of his arms. 'It's all right. It's all right, darling,' he soothed as though calming a distraught child. 'We'll find her, I promise.'

Solly caught his friend's eyes and motioned with a finger towards the garden. 'We need to talk,' he whispered.

Lorimer shook his head but the expression on the psychologist's face made him pause.

'Is there something we really need to know?'

Solly nodded.

'Right now?'

The psychologist gave another nod and headed towards the back door.

'Darling, why don't you make Solly a cup of tea? Something herbal,' Lorimer suggested, steering his wife away from the room with its sofa bed and all her mother's bits and pieces that were such a constant reminder of the older lady's absence.

Maggie let herself be guided to the kitchen where she lifted the kettle jug to fill it again. Glancing at her as he followed Solly into the garden, Lorimer saw her going through the motions, exhausted but still trying to hold it all together.

'This better be quick,' he said. 'Maggie's in a terrible state. As you can imagine.'

'Have you found Serena Jackson yet?'

Lorimer frowned. 'What do you mean, *found*? She's not gone AWOL. I've had a couple of missed calls from her already today.'

Solly shook his head. 'That's not what I meant to say. We need to see her. Speak to her. She'll know where Alice is.'

Lorimer stared at the psychologist for a long moment.

'Drive me down to her home, will you? I have a lot of questions I would like to ask Serena Jackson,' Solly told him. 'And I think you will have, too.'

The trip back down the coast took less time than Lorimer had anticipated. It was well after the rush hour and the light was beginning to fade. Solomon had not spoken since giving Lorimer that brief outline of his thoughts. The Detective Superintendent had not responded then and now he was silently wondering just what sort of welcome they might receive on arrival at Greenock. If Solly was right . . . he gave a huge sigh. The traffic round by the Oak Mall held them up for a few moments as a large articulated delivery truck backed into the small car park to one side of the shopping centre, making Lorimer seethe with impatience, then they were off again. But every set of traffic lights seemed to turn red on their approach and Solly noted the detective's increased frustration as he glanced at his glowering profile.

'Not far now,' he muttered.

'I just hope she'll be in,' Lorimer snapped in response. 'Surely we should have checked?'

'No!' Solly shook his head firmly. 'We need to have the element of surprise if I'm going to assess her correctly.'

At last the Lexus was turning into Campbell Street and the block of luxury flats that overlooked the river.

'Park where she can't see us,' Solomon whispered. 'And buzz someone else's number to let us in,' he suggested eagerly.

Lorimer raised his eyebrows: Solly almost sounded as though he were enjoying this moment of high drama.

'Hello,' Serena Jackson's expression was one of curiosity as she opened the door to the two men. 'Mr Lorimer. This is an unexpected pleasure. Do come in.' She held open the door, a half-smile upon her face.

'Doctor Brightman,' Lorimer indicated his companion as they entered the flat. 'We wanted to ask you some things, Miss Jackson.'

Serena gave another smile over her shoulder as she regarded the men following her through to the main room. And once more Lorimer was struck by the woman's ethereal beauty. Taller and thinner than most women he knew, she moved with a sort of cat-like grace. Today her hair was falling smooth, sleek and glossy as though it had just been given a salon treatment. Was that where she had been when he had called: somewhere as ordinary as a hairdresser's? And she was dressed as though she had recently been out, a neat black skirt showing off those long legs, a matching cashmere jersey slung artfully across a white silk shirt.

'Do sit down, gentlemen,' she offered, her upper-class drawl the epitome of elegance and good breeding. It was a voice devoid of any sort of anxiety, Lorimer noticed. If she were agitated by their sudden arrival then Serena Jackson was hiding it well. Choosing to take her place in the middle of one of the sofas and casually curling her legs beneath her, she looked more like some contented, aristocratic feline than the suspect for a series of murders.

Lorimer took a deep breath.

'I wanted to ask you about the party you had here on Saturday evening,' he began.

Serena Jackson gave a frown. 'What do you mean? What party?'

Lorimer looked at Solly for support but the psychologist seemed to be fascinated by the woman before him, staring at her intently.

'Detective Inspector Martin told me that you were having a house-warming party at the weekend,' Lorimer explained.

Serena raised one shapely eyebrow. 'Did she, now? How

strange. There was no party here, Superintendent. Why on earth would Rhoda tell you that?' She looked around the room as though bemused by the notion and Lorimer followed her gaze. The lounge was in the same pristine condition that he had seen on his first visit here. There was absolutely no trace of anything that looked like the aftermath of a wild rave-up.

'Are you telling me that Rhoda Martin wasn't at a party here, then?'

Serena nodded. Then she looked thoughtful. 'Hmm, wonder if she's up to her old tricks again,' she mused. 'Oh, dear, what's she done this time?'

Lorimer frowned. 'Could you explain what you mean, please?'

Serena uncurled her legs and sat up a little straighter. 'Rhoda's always been a bit of a fantasist. Trying to emulate the people she would *like* to hang about with,' she said, tossing her head.

'You mean she copied things she might have admired about you?' Solly asked.

'Why, yes, as a matter of fact she did. Silly girl! It was the same at school. Always hanging around our little group. Trying to be best friends with me.'

'And buying the same sort of clothes?' Solly's question seemed to be a little absurd to Lorimer. Where on earth was he going with all of this?

'Oh, I doubt if she could have afforded something like this,' Serena said lightly, touching the charcoal pullover.

'But she did buy a car the same make and model as yours, didn't she?' the psychologist asked casually.

Lorimer saw the change in the woman's demeanour instantly. She seemed to freeze, the faint smile wiped off a face that had become suddenly pale.

Then she licked her lips, eyes darting from one man to the

other. 'My car's down there,' she said, standing up and pointing towards the window. 'See?'

Lorimer and Solly rose from the sofa and walked towards the pair of French windows as the woman twisted the blind rod, raising the slats apart. Then, pulling at a cord, the blinds slid upwards. Serena twisted the brass handles and opened the glass doors wide and stepped on to the tiny Parisian balcony.

There was still enough light to make out the red sports car below in the parking area, its shiny roof gleaming under an adjacent street lamp.

'A Spider. Nice, isn't it?' she purred at Solly as she leaned over the railings. 'Do you like fast cars, Dr Brightman?'

Solly smiled politely. 'That's my wife's department,' he said. 'I don't even drive.'

'Good Lord,' she murmured, regarding the psychologist from her amber-coloured eyes as though he were some strange species of human that she had never encountered before.

'But perhaps you might take us down to the garage in the basement and let us see your other car?' Solly insisted. 'A black Volkswagon Golf, isn't it?'

'Same as the car you used to take Alice Finlay from my home this morning,' Lorimer said, taking a step closer to her.

Serena Jackson shot a sudden look of hatred at them both.

'Don't let her . . .!' Solly yelled.

But Lorimer had sensed the woman's intention already and sprang forwards, pushing Solly out of the way as Serena Jackson made a desperate attempt to fling herself off the balcony.

One leg was already across the metal railing, impeded by the narrow skirt, when he seized her.

'Oh, no you don't!' he said, hauling her away from the balcony and back into the room.

Behind him Solly looked down at the concrete paving several floors below and shuddered. Was it more than mere irony that Serena Jackson had attempted to end her life the way she had ended the lives of those three old ladies?

Lorimer had already called for support from K Division but for now he held on to Serena Jackson securely as they entered the basement garage.

Solly threw a switch on the wall. There, side by side, were the two matching black cars.

'Where's Alice?' Lorimer demanded, digging his fingers deeper into the woman's arms. 'Where's my mother-in-law?'

For an answer, Serena Jackson gave him a distant smile and shook her head.

'Tell me, you bitch! Or I'll . . .'

'Lorimer!' Solly was stepping towards them now, a warning in his tone.

As the sound of blues and twos came whining ever closer, Serena slumped limply in his grasp as if acknowledging defeat. Her perfect face was devoid of any sort of expression now as she looked down at the ground, refusing to meet his eyes.

'Wait till we get you back to the station. And bring your precious brother in as well. Maybe you'll talk then,' Lorimer growled, shoving her in front of him.

Lorimer stood in the dim light of the basement, regarding the frames of racing cycles suspended from hooks on the wall. Only one of them still had its wheels attached. The others were stacked neatly against the brickwork. Putting out a gloved hand, he made the front wheel spin slowly till he saw it. There, almost invisible to the naked eye, was a V-shaped nick. Lorimer heaved a sigh.

Callum Uprichard would be able to fit this to the tyre impression back at the labs. Evidence of this sort was crucial. But he still had to prise a confession out of the woman as to why she had murdered her own parents. And find out where she had taken Alice.

CHAPTER 36

Daniel Jackson sat, head bowed into his well-manicured hands. 'I still can't believe it, Superintendent,' he said again, then looked up at the man beside him. 'Why would Serena do something so terrible to Mum and Dad? And all these other things . . .' he broke off, his voice ending in a choking sob.

'We were very much hoping that you could offer some sort of an explanation, sir,' Lorimer told him, trying to contain his rising anxiety.

It was after midnight now and Serena Jackson had not offered up a single word since her arrest. Neither cajoling nor threatening had made a bit of difference to the woman who had sat impassively staring into space as though her mind was miles away. And maybe it was, Lorimer realised. Maybe she was as mentally deranged as DS Wainwright had suggested when they had brought her in. In the previous hours several wheels had been put into motion throughout Strathclyde Police and beyond: the on-call senior forensic scientist was possibly even now making a match between the tread that Uprichard had examined and the tyre from Serena Jackson's racing cycle.

'I need to find out where your sister has taken Alice Finlay,' Lorimer said.

'Your mother-in-law?' Daniel Jackson said.

Lorimer nodded, running a weary hand through his unkempt hair. Time was running out for Alice, wherever she was. If she was even still alive.

'Why would she take an old lady away—'

'Look,' Lorimer snapped. 'Why she does things is probably a case for a psychiatrist. But right now it's our priority to find a sick old lady, do you understand!' he thundered.

'I'm sorry,' Jackson's eyes were full of tears, 'really I am. What do you want me to say?'

Lorimer gave a sigh that seemed to come from his soul. 'Can you think of *anywhere* your sister might have taken her? Somewhere secluded, perhaps? In the city?'

Jackson shook his head. 'We haven't any other properties in Glasgow . . .' His face changed suddenly. 'Oh, my God! Yes we have,' he gabbled. 'My father bought up these old derelict tenements. In the East End. Wanted to make a killing from them with the injection of finance from the Commonwealth Games fund.'

'Where? Tell me exactly whereabouts this is,' Lorimer demanded.

Daniel Jackson suddenly looked stricken. 'Oh, Lord,' he said softly, 'Dad owned several streets worth of these places. It's not going to be that simple to find her. If she did take her to that part of the city,' he added with a groan.

The whole area was crawling with uniformed officers by the time Lorimer's Lexus came to a halt.

'This is the last close, sir,' a middle-aged officer told him after glancing at the name on Lorimer's warrant card. 'No sign of her yet,' he added, a look of sympathy in his face.

Lorimer looked up at the building, its windows all boarded with sheets of wood and shuttered with metal from the outside. It was like looking up at a nightmarish version of Colditz. Rags and tatters of cloud raced across the night sky, revealing the ghostly outline of the moon, then it was gone again as the wind whipped scraps of litter around his feet.

'Okay. Last try, then,' Lorimer said, pushing aside the sheet of metal that served as a security entrance.

Inside, the close was in darkness, only a thin light from a window on the half-landing showed the steps before them.

'Here, take this, sir.' The police officer handed Lorimer his torch and he scanned the doors to their left and right. They lay open, testament to the depredations of the local youth, no doubt. The next two floors were much the same and Lorimer's hopes that they would find Alice here were rapidly fading.

When they reached the top floor, Lorimer and the police officer exchanged glances. One door was wide open but the other was secured with a bolt and padlock.

'Has to be,' the officer whispered. 'Why else would it be locked?'

Taking a bolt cutter from his pocket, the policeman worried away at the metal hasp until it fell with a clink upon the concrete floor.

'Alice!' Lorimer called out, rushing along the narrow hallway, holding the torch aloft.

When he opened the door, he stopped short, unable to believe what he was seeing. Her head had slumped to one side, the torch-light making a halo of her white hair. Everything about her seemed bleached of life: the pallid face, the arms pinioned behind her.

Lorimer was at her side in a few swift strides, untying the bonds, one knee supporting the old woman's body from falling off the chair. Gently, he lifted Alice in his arms, marvelling at how light she was. Then as he bent to feel her cheek, he winced. She was so cold. So deathly cold.

'Is she . . .?' the officer stood in the doorway, his face grim.

Lorimer nodded. 'We're too late,' he said, hearing the catch in his own voice and holding the old lady closer to his own body as though he could transfer some of his own warmth to her.

Then he heard it. A tiny sigh, but it was enough to make him hope.

'Here!' he said, carrying his mother-in-law towards the policeman. 'Feel her pulse for me.'

The police officer took Alice's thin wrist in his hand, his thumb searching for any vital signs.

Then he nodded, relief transforming his face. 'She's alive,' he said. 'But we better get her to a hospital. Quick as we can.'

Maggie wondered if the nightmare that had begun this morning (was it only this morning?) was ever going to come to an end. She'd hoped and prayed that Mum would be brought back home safe and sound but now she was being driven by a police car across the city to the Royal Infirmary. The High Dependency Unit, Bill had said, not telling her much more than that. But she could sense from his voice that it was not hopeful news. Yes, they had found Alice after an extensive police search of some derelict buildings in Glasgow's East End. That it had been her husband who had eventually found her was some small comfort.

As the car raced through the streets, its blue lights flashing, siren shutting out any other sound, Maggie felt as though she were floating above it all, a disembodied soul observing this chaotic dash to the hospital.

Inside the hospital she was met by a nursing officer and another policeman who whisked her away in a lift, then she was out in a daze of greenish light, being guided along a maze of corridors.

At last she was in the doorway, looking at the familiar figure of her husband sitting by a high bed where a patient was lying under a white sheet, tubes and wires leading to a variety of monitors that bleeped their rhythmic sound into the softness of the night. Maggie's sigh became a stifled sob as she tried to move forward to the bed and the still figure.

Lorimer stood up, moving slightly to one side allowing Maggie access to her mother. She felt his touch on her arm as she passed him, heard his low voice murmuring words of comfort, but she only had eyes for the woman who lay so quietly upon that white bed.

Alice was asleep, her eyes closed on wrinkled lids. There was no expression of pain on her face, just a slight downturn to her mouth as though she were cross about something. It was a look that Maggie knew well. But she could remember her smiles and her laughter too, she thought, as the tears began to slide down her cheeks. She could remember the good times they had spent together. Taking her mother's hand in hers, she stroked it softly, bending forwards so that Alice might hear her.

'Do you remember the time we went to Skye, Mum? The mist was all down when we arrived and you said we'd have been better off staying at home. Then the next day everything was so clear we could see the whole of the Cuillins. And that sunset? D'you remember the sunset? Dad and you made me stay up to see it until the sun had gone right down, even though it was past my bedtime. You were always so good to me, Mum, always. The best Mum in the world.' Maggie stopped then, unable to speak for the tears pouring down, clasping Alice's hand as though she would never let it go.

Even when the sounds changed and the thin green line upon the monitor brought nurses into the room, Maggie refused to let go of her mother's hand. Squeezing it gently in a gesture of farewell, she bent over and kissed the still-warm cheeks.

'Goodnight, Mum,' she whispered.

Then Maggie felt her husband's hands upon her shoulders and she leaned against him, taking her hands away from the bed at last.

CHAPTER 37

Five Months Later

Detective Inspector Rhoda Martin waited until she was sure that the courtroom had finally emptied. An usher looked her way, a frown of enquiry on his face so she rose from her seat and made her way out. She turned up the collar of her jacket. If she kept her head down, looked down at the floor, maybe nobody would see her, or try to engage her in conversation.

Ever since that dreadful night, Rhoda had been unable to face her colleagues. The extended leave of absence was coming to an end and she would be moving on. A desk job, the psychologist had suggested, but Rhoda had demurred.

Stumbling through the wide hall, the policewoman pushed open the door to the ladies' toilet and stood, gasping for breath. She would not let it happen. She would conquer the sudden trembling that threatened to overwhelm her whole body. Breathe. Breathe, she told herself, willing the shudders to subside.

Blowing out one long exhalation, Rhoda opened her eyes. Her hands still grasped the edge of the basin, the cool porcelain a relief after the stuffiness of that witness room. Above the basin the mirror showed a thin, unsmiling face, green eyes regarding her image critically. Yesterday she had gone to see James who had cut her hair. With every snip of his clever scissors, the hair stylist had shorn more than her blonde locks. Rhoda remembered how she had felt, gasping at her reflection in the salon mirror. James had handed her a tissue and she had blown her nose noisily, trying not to weep. 'It's wonderful,' she had assured him, smiling tremulously through her tears.

And now that elfin shape hugging the line of her jaw belonged to the person she had needed to become. The foolishness of trying to emulate another person was over. But the shame of it still lingered.

And when had it all started? Her mind had played over so many scenes from school during the last months, wondering how the girl that had fascinated her for so long could possibly have become a killer. Had there ever been any manifestation of evil in the slight, blonde child who had beguiled her? It was hard to remember Serena as anything other than the perfect girl. Yet hadn't she been the one to suggest the malicious little pranks that other kids carried out? Serena Jackson might have been on the edge of the action, but never at its heart. It was strange how she had such clear recall of events from her schooldays. The psychologist had given that some name or other, explaining how the trauma had triggered all these snippets of their shared past.

One memory stood out from all the rest. They had been in English class the period before lunch for a poetry lesson. Miss Michael had been in an inspirational mood, waxing lyrical about one of the best poems from a twentieth-century poet, as she had put it: Edwin Brock's 'Five Ways to Kill a Man'. They'd been issued with handouts of it and had stuffed them into their satchels, making a bee-line for the girls' cloakroom to eat their packed lunches. She couldn't recall who had asked the question first. 'How would you kill a man?' They'd giggled over their sandwiches, suggesting daft and even lewd ideas until Serena had spoken. 'I'd burn him alive,' she had said. The conversation had effectively stopped then and Rhoda could still remember the shiver that she had felt as the girl had uttered these words. Yet, until the night when her school friend had robbed her of every shred of dignity, leaving her drugged and trussed in the back bedroom, these words had been completely forgotten.

Rhoda took another deep breath. It was becoming harder to find the same inner strength that had made her become a police officer in the first place. Okay, so that little voice kept telling her worse things happened to other people. And hadn't she seen so many of them already in her young life? But she was ready to begin again. The memory of Serena disappearing down into the cells below the courtroom would fade in time. Like everything else. The transfer to Kilmarnock had been approved and next week a new chapter would begin for DI Martin. She could never pretend that these terrible things had not happened and she knew that police gossip would continue to follow her wherever she went. But she had to go on, as the psychologist had gently advised; there were people out there who needed her to be a good police officer.

Slipping her bag across her shoulder, Rhoda left the coolness of the ladies' room and walked past the people milling about in the foyer of the High Court. Men and women in black robes, bewigged and talking closely together; neds dressed up in their best gear for the occasion; officers like herself, coming and going for reasons of their own.

Out in the warm summer air, Rhoda stood for a moment looking around her. Over there was the back door of the mortuary: there were other deaths and other trials still to come. And perhaps, one day soon, she would play her part in bringing a culprit to justice. Straightening her collar, Rhoda Martin lifted her head and walked smartly into the afternoon sunshine.

*

Doctor Solomon Brightman winced as the blinds were opened, letting in the glare of light. Harsh shadows sliced across the room, making dust motes whirl in lozenges of sunshine. The click of the door made him look up and he stood politely as the woman was ushered in. The duty nurse who had opened the blinds gave the patient a cursory glance.

'I'll leave you all to it, then, shall I?' he said, nodding at the patient and her female companion. Serena Jackson sat down at the table, her head turning towards the window as if she wanted to bask in the warmth of the sunshine streaming in. It was a gesture guaranteed to remind Solly that she was a prisoner here. He leaned forwards and held out his hand. 'Good to see you again, Jacqueline,' he told the psychologist. They met from time to time for seminars and discussions but Jacqueline's time was mostly spent here as a full-time employee of Carstairs Mental Hospital. The woman smiled and nodded, her eyes always on the slim blonde woman sitting at the table, even as she retreated to the back of the room where she could quietly hear and observe.

Solly stared at Serena Jackson, marvelling at her perfect profile and translucent skin. The blonde hair was like spun silk in the sunlight. Her hands, he noted, were on her lap beneath the table where he could not see them. Clasped loosely together? Or twisting and turning in nervous agitation like a swan who seemed serene yet whose feet paddled furiously below the surface of the water. It was not the first time that Solly had thought the woman's name so appropriate; she did have a serenity about her but it was no more than a mask to hide that twisted personality.

That Serena Jackson had agreed to take part in Solly Brightman's research did not surprise him. He didn't flatter himself that she was greedy for the sort of fame that came with notoriety. No. Solly knew that the woman was only here to relieve

334

the boredom of this place. It was a diversion for her, no more. He doubted if she would ever bother to read the book once it was published, even though an entire chapter would be devoted to her killing spree.

'Why did she do it?' Rosie had asked him. He had shrugged, only half-knowing. But their conversations had provided more of an answer to that question.

'Good morning, Serena,' he said at last. 'How are you today?'

The woman turned to him, squinting her topaz eyes a little against the dazzling brightness. Then she gave him one of her rare smiles.

'Daniel's gone abroad,' she told him. 'The States.' She gave an insouciant shrug. 'Don't think he's going to come back.'

'Won't you miss him?'

She shrugged again in answer as if it was no big deal to her but Solly detected a small shift in her expression and knew that the loss of her brother was a real blow to the woman.

'Don't you miss your mother and father?'

Serena looked down at the table and traced a pattern on its plastic surface with her index finger. 'Sometimes,' she replied at last.

'What sorts of things make you miss them?'

She heaved a sigh then her mouth twisted as if the exhalation had come unbidden. This was a person, Solly knew, who liked to be totally in control of her own emotions.

'I never wanted to have my own place. I told you that already, didn't I?' she began. 'They wanted me out, especially *her*.' The pretty mouth made a moue of distaste. 'Thought we didn't know what was going on under our noses, filthy bitch!' She shook her head as if to rid herself of the memory. 'But I do miss Dad sometimes. He used to come and say goodnight. Nothing to titillate your nasty little mind,' she added with a sneer. 'He'd call out from the top of the stairs, that's all,' she said.

335

Solly nodded as though he believed what she told him. Perhaps it was true but it was more likely that she was feeling lonely and panicked at night times here in this place when she was so completely alone. The father figure that she had destroyed haunted her with good memories, even if they might be false ones.

Serena looked at Solly suddenly. 'I suppose you want to find out why I killed them.'

There was a long moment between them when the psychologist was acutely aware of normal sounds like that of a plane overhead and the metallic growl of a mowing machine in the grounds. Of course he wanted to hear that. But, he wondered, noting a sly smile cutting the edges of that pretty mouth, would she ever tell him the whole truth?

'They wouldn't let me be what I wanted, would they?' she told him, enjoying his discomfiture at her deliberately enigmatic remark.

'When did you first enjoy making fires?' Solly asked, changing the subject. He had asked this question in various ways before and was not really expecting an answer today, just the usual cold silence. So he was surprised when Serena leaned forwards and told him in a whisper, so that the other psychologist could not hear. He listened to the story of over-privileged teenagers bored with all the things that their parents' wealth could buy, joy riding and wrecking a car. Her face became more animated as she described the fire and the tree.

'I was alone with the sound of crackling wood and that moaning voice. It was easy to think of the tree as a living thing in its death throes,' she told him.

Solly locked eyes with the woman, 'And . . .?' he prompted her.

'And I liked what I saw,' she said, a gleam of triumph shining from those tawny eyes.

'You always wanted to find out what it would be like? To kill?' he asked.

Serena nodded then turned away with a yawn. It was a signal Solly recognised as the end of this current session. Her boredom assuaged, she would return to the hospital's routine until his next visit. Then perhaps he would ask her other questions. About the vulnerable old ladies who had died at her hand.

There was still a lot to learn about this woman whose strange beauty was so at odds with a nature that one journalist had described as pure evil.

It was quiet here and I liked it after that funny little man and his prob-ing questions. He amused me and I enjoyed trying to fool him. Sometimes I think I did outwit him, though today I had let rather too much slip, hadn't I? There were things that he would never hear from me, though. I hugged them to myself gleefully; that laughing child whirling through the air and the old vagrant, his face contorted with the poison choking him to death. These were my secrets and no clever bearded psychologist would ever find them out. And there were other secrets too, desires that might never be fulfilled – different ways to kill. I considered them in the long hours within this place, wondering if I would ever be given the chance to carry them out.

Maggie bent down by the flowerbed and pulled out a weed, adding it to the little pile in the plastic bucket. The rose garden had been Flynn's idea and Maggie badly wanted to keep it neat and tidy. The late July sun beat down on her head as she stood up, her eyes on one particular rose. Several buds had opened up now and the blooms were a shade of deep amber. She didn't need to examine the plastic tag to know the flower's name: *Remember Me*. Flynn had brought it the day after Mum's funeral, planting the rose where he knew Maggie would see it from the kitchen window. It had been a gracious gesture and she had hugged him silently, both of them weeping in that shared moment of grief. So Maggie had determined to keep this plot weed-free. Her mother's remains were scattered elsewhere and now she only had her memories of Alice Finlay to console her.

Sometimes the night of her mother's death would come back to her, a jumble of images and impressions like a bad dream that makes no sense on awakening. She felt the cat at her side, rubbing himself against her and automatically she put out a hand, stroking his fur. Chancer had howled like a banshee that night, prowling around the house looking for Alice. His eldritch screeching had unnerved them both. Yet once the sofa bed had been tidied away and all her things had gone he had settled down again. Had he sensed her death? Or was it simply that he could feel the tension created by all the hours of anxiety and sorrow? Maggie cuddled the cat at her side and sighed.

What should she do next? Perhaps she could cut one of the roses and bring it into the house? No, she decided, better to let it flourish out here, a constant reminder of Alice as she had been, vibrant and bright. She glanced across at the sunbed by the lawn. Bill was in Glasgow today and she had plenty of time to prepare work for her Advanced Higher class next session. Maggie rose to her feet, brushing the bits of grass from her bare legs.

There had been some altercation between the Chief Constable and her husband in the wake of their own personal tragedy. She was not quite sure what it was all about and Bill had been reticent on the subject. Still he seemed happy to be back in his own division even though Superintendent Mitchison had returned from the Met releasing Lorimer from his temporary designation. Now he was Detective Chief Inspector once more and he gave no sign that it bothered him in the slightest.

The books and papers were scattered on the grass beside her

sunbed waiting for her attention. Maggie smiled as she picked up one of the books. It was an old friend, from her undergraduate days, this book with its blue cover. Lying back, Maggie thought of the writer. Hadn't he spun tales that were woven around the changing seasons, giving a pattern to life? There was some comfort in such notions, she thought.

Come the winter there would be the time for Rosie and Solly's baby to be born. *A Valentine's child*, Rosie had told her dreamily, after calculating when she had conceived. The year would turn and death would give way to new life, just as the Orcadian poet had observed. Maggie smiled, browsing through the familiar stories. Her kids at school would love some of these.

Then she stopped, finding a page where her younger self had underlined an entire paragraph. Maggie gave a little sigh, feeling something heavy slip away from her as she read the words that told of this dance through the everlasting cycle of life.

> *'And then suddenly everything was in its place.*
> *The tinkers would move for ever through the hills.*
> *Men would plough their fields. Men would bait*
> *their lines. Comedy had its place in the dance too –*
> *the drinking, the quarrelling, the expulsion, the*
> *return in the morning. And forever the world*
> *would be full of youth and beauty, birth and death,*
> *labour and suffering.'*

Acknowledgements

I would like to thank the following people for their help. DC Mairi Milne for her constant patience in answering all my queries and also DI John Dearie, both of Greenock Police HQ; Detective Inspector Bob Frew; Elizabeth and Tom Clark for their expert knowledge of cycling; Andy Sweeney and the team of forensic scientists at Pitt Street, especially David Robertson; Sheila Campbell for afternoon tea and blethers at Kilmacolm Golf Club; Dr John Clark for advice regarding poisons; Cathy MacPhail for that fantastic view from her Greenock flat; John McGruther for a good translation; Alanna Knight for writerly advice; my wonderful agent Jenny Brown for support and encouragement; David Shelley, who is a prince amongst editors; Caroline Hogg, a huge thank you for keeping me right; Kirsteen Astor and Moira MacMillan whose friendship and PR efforts mean so much to me; all the other lovely staff at Little, Brown; last, but never least, my dear Donnie for keeping step with me in this crazy dance.